LOVE'S OLD STORY

"Aaron, we can't go on this way," Renee said. "Pretending to be just friends."

"Of course we can't," Aaron Lewis answered.

Suddenly his arms were around her and there was no resistance in her, no thought of anything but him. They were back on the strand at Coney Island and she was sixteen and he was twenty-two. But this time she did not try to break away, only held him tighter, as he brought her closer and closer to ecstasy. . . .

Renee knew how much she owed her husband. His kindness had rescued her from the abyss. His tenderness had melted her fear. His money had started her on the road to success. She owed him everything. But now in the arms of true love, could she deny what she owed herself. . . ?

THE GLORY YEARS

Joyce Carlow

AN ONYX BOOK

ONYX
Published by the Penguin Group
Penguin Books USA Inc., 375 Hudson Street,
New York, New York 10014, U.S.A.
Penguin Books Ltd, 27 Wrights Lane,
London W8 5TZ, England
Penguin Books Australia Ltd, Ringwood,
Victoria, Australia
Penguin Books Canada Ltd, 2801 John Street,
Markham, Ontario, Canada L3R 1B4
Penguin Books (N.Z.) Ltd, 182-190 Wairau Road,
Auckland 10, New Zealand

Penguin Books Ltd, Registered Offices:
Harmondsworth, Middlesex, England

First published by Onyx, an imprint of Penguin Books USA Inc.

First Printing, May, 1990
10 9 8 7 6 5 4 3 2 1

Printed in the United States of America

I

The Szilards 1901–1912

One

1

August 1901

*I*n her mind Margaret Szilard could see her grandmama's room as clearly as if she were still in it. It was a large room with a huge Persian rug and long heavy blue velvet draperies that framed the floor-to-ceiling windows. One set of draperies was pulled closed to keep out the light of the bright early-afternoon sun, while the other set was parted and the window was opened slightly to let what cool breeze there was into the room. Grandmama's room was furnished with a bed, two chests, and a large dressing table. All the furniture was made of dark wood and was intricately carved with swirls and flowers. Made in what her mother called "The Spanish design," it was heavy and massive.

Margaret was always fascinated with her grandmama's dressing table, which was covered with wonderful perfume bottles, little jars of creams, powders, and nests of hand-painted porcelain containers. There was also a beautiful jewelry box that made music when wound. Two lovers on its top waltzed in endless circles until the music got slower and slower and finally came to an end.

Once her grandmama's dressing table had been the focal point of her room, but now it was her high-canopied bed that commanded attention. Grandmama sat in it day after day, talking, then sleeping, then awakening to talk again:

" 'The Baroness Vetsera was such an exquisite creature! And only seventeen! Such a tragedy! And he, he was quite the most handsome of all the Habsburgs! I can see him now—so tall and trim and dashing in his uniform. He had a good face, you know. It was a narrow face with a long patrician nose and kind eyes. Yes, a good kind face, not at all like his father, the emperor. Franz Jósef has a hard face. You can tell he's very strict. One can only imagine the strain he put on his son. Poor Prince Rudolf.

" 'Still, I can't imagine what made Crown Prince Rudolf do it! I really can't. They say there was blood everywhere . . . that he shot the baroness and then himself.

" 'There were vicious rumors—all Vienna was talking. Yes, vicious, mean rumors. Some said Prince Rudolf had a touch of Wittelsbach madness, some said he had syphilis . . . some said he found out the Baroness Vetsera was really his illegitimate sister! Of course, if she was his sister that would have meant their affair was incestuous. Poor, poor Rudolf.'

"Grandmama paused then and wiped her eyes. She always cries when she talks about the suicide," Margaret said as she recounted the details of what had happened. "But she went on, she always went on.

" 'Of course, I suppose it was the most romantic way out. His father wouldn't let him divorce, and he and the baroness were lovers, you know. Yes, they made love at Mayerling and they died there in one another's arms. Tragic, but so romantic, so beautiful. . . .

" 'Mayerling was the emperor's favorite hunting lodge. I don't suppose he ever really wanted to return there, I suppose the memories were too painful . . . as they were for all of us. But there were other reasons for not going there. . . . They say it's haunted. They say at night you can hear the the star-crossed lovers dancing through the halls, they say her laughter is like the tinkling of fine crystal, but that his footsteps are heavy, restless. . . .' "

Margaret tried to imitate her grandmama's voice, but she could not. Her grandmother's voice was rather low and sometimes a bit rasping.

Margaret stood next to her fine Arabian horse, Prince Stanislaus. She brushed his blond mane as she recited her grandmother's words and the incident that had so recently driven her from the house. "Yes, Grandmama was going on. . . . In a few minutes she would have come to the part where she went to spend a few weeks at the imperial villa at Bad Ischl, and she would have said, 'It was a social "must" to have been at Bad Ischl at the right time.' Then she would have thrown her head back—in that way that she does—and she'd have started talking about her clothes, about her brocades and laces.

"Did I tell you I found a great trunk full of her hats? Oh, they *are* magnificent. Mama said I could try them on and model them if I made sure to put them all back in the right boxes. I'll bring one to show you when I can.

"Anyway, Grandmama was going on and Papa came in with Béla. I tell you, when Béla's home from the university he doesn't let Papa out of his sight. Whatever Papa does, Béla does too. If Papa is angry, Béla acts angry as well.

"So Papa came in and slammed the door and shouted, 'Now what's she going on about?' And Mama shushed him and answered, 'Just the usual, remembering her life. Right now she's talking about the suicide of Prince Rudolf and his mistress.'

"Papa shouted, 'That was twelve years ago!' Papa seemed angry and he took Mama's arm and pulled her out of Grandmama's room. Then Béla pulled my hair and pinched me and I screamed and Papa came back and smacked me for screaming and said, 'Haven't you got any respect for your grandmother? She's ill, you know.' I ran away then. I came here, straight to you.

"I hate Béla. He's always hurting me and Papa never sees him. Papa always believes Béla when he says he isn't hurting me. Béla lies all the time." Margaret's words trailed off and her thoughts drifted. There were other things about Béla, dark things she hardly admitted to herself and couldn't even describe to Prince Stanislaus. There was the night two months ago . . . But surely that was a nightmare. She pushed all thoughts of it away and continued talking, "And you know, I think Béla steals. I think he stole some money from Papa."

Margaret sighed and put down the brush. She lowered herself to the floor and leaned back against the stack of hay in the far corner of the stall. She inhaled deeply and sighed. She loved the smell of the barn, she adored the aroma of the hay and even the pungent smell of the fresh manure.

"The Baroness Vetsera was seventeen when she died for love. In two months I'll be fifteen and I don't even know someone I could love. I don't even know anyone I might love. But you know, love isn't always happy. Lately Mama cries all the time and Papa always seems vexed. And poor Grandmama. She just keeps saying the same things over and over and over."

Restlessly Margaret struggled to her feet once again and stroked Prince Stanislaus' long nose, and then, holding the bridle, leaned against the animal's warm face. Prince Stanislaus was her friend and her only confidant. He was three years old and she had owned him since he was a tiny foal. Probably, she thought, Papa wouldn't have given him to her if he'd realized the awkward little creature was going to grow into such an elegant animal. He had such understanding eyes, and the way he twitched his ears, she was quite certain he understood everything she said. At the very least she knew with certainty that he understood her moods.

"I love you," she said to the horse, which, in return, nuzzled her neck affectionately. "But sometimes I do wish I had a sister. Then we could go riding together and I'd have someone to play dress-up with. We'd even be able to study together. The trouble with having three brothers is that boys are allowed to do just what they want and girls have all these horrible rules. Even when they do the same things, boys do them separately. György,

Béla, and Konrad can ride alone wherever they wish, but I can't. And they can race. I'm not allowed to race. Papa even says I have to learn to ride sidesaddle. It's not fair. I don't even get to study the same subjects. I think boys have a secret world. . . ." Margaret patted her horse, and laid her head against his side.

"But boys aren't all alike. Konnie and György are different from Béla. György and Konnie are always good to me. Konnie daydreams a lot, but he's still kind. Béla is mean . . . not just mean . . . Oh, I have to tell someone, but whom can I tell? Mama doesn't talk to me anymore and Papa wouldn't believe me. He might even get angry and punish me. I don't even know if I should tell you . . ." Margaret bit her lip and shook her head. "I can't," she said aloud. "I can't tell anyone."

"Margaret! Are you in the stable?"

"Here, György—I'm just brushing Prince Stanislaus." György was her eldest brother; he was twenty-three and had just received his commission in the army.

"Mama wants you now. She said to hurry."

Margaret kissed Prince Stanislaus on the nose and gathered her skirts up so she could run. "I'm coming!"

György was waiting at the barn door. He was over six feet tall, and had flaxen blond hair and blue eyes like her own. But he was slightly tanned from the summer sun, which she was not. "Ladies," her mother and grandmother preached, "never allow their skin to be darkened by the sun."

György was also very muscular as a result of his army training and his participation in sports. He was a renowned soccer player and had been the star forward on the regional team before he became a forward on the army team.

György smiled at her and Margaret thought how very handsome her older brother really was. But, she reflected, what made him seem even more handsome was the fact that he was genuinely nice. She supposed Béla was handsome too, but somehow his meanness showed through, and when he smiled it was more like the snarl of a dog. Béla's was not a real smile, but merely a parting of the lips and a showing of the teeth.

"I'll race you home," Margaret said to György.

"I'll give you a head start. I'll count to five: one . . ."

Margaret darted forward, but in a few seconds her long-legged brother had caught up to her and together they raced across the field toward the big house. "What does she want?" Margaret asked breathlessly while György ran along effortlessly.

"She didn't say, but she was crying again."

Margaret frowned. Poor Mama. She was so beautiful—well, she had been beautiful before she began crying all the time. Now her blue eyes were red and swollen and she had dark lines under them. And her face was all puffy and she didn't take the proper time to fix her long hair. Every morning she used to brush her golden hair one hundred and ten strokes exactly; then she would bend over, grab it and twist it, and then, standing straight, would wrap it all into a huge bun, which she then pinned into place. When she took care, her hair glistened and there was never a hair out of place. But now her hair seemed lackluster and wisps of it fell down over her forehead and down her neck in the back. Mama looked tired, but above all she looked sad.

Margaret and György reached the wide portico that surrounded the house. For a moment they collapsed panting, and again Margaret thought of Béla. She could win any race with him. Béla was only twenty-one, but he was soft. He spent too many nights in the cafés and bars of Budapest, and he smoked long dark cigars that smelled to her like burning cow dung. "Is Béla with Mama?" she suddenly asked.

György shook his head. "She's alone."

"Are you coming?" Margaret asked.

"You better go alone," he replied. "She only wants you."

Margaret nodded and climbed the steps, entering the house through the double glass doors that opened into the solarium. It was quite a wonderful room filled with blossoming tropical plants that Mama called "exotics."

Margaret left the solarium and entered the hallway. Its floor was tiled in black and white and it seemed cold and empty in spite of the paintings on either wall. But then, the paintings were of her dead ancestors and the hallway was like a picture-book crypt. She always thought of it as the place of the dead, and although the priest said you went to heaven when you died, Margaret suspected most people never went farther than their own hallways. All the grand homes she had ever been in had a hallway like this, and she remembered when her Aunt Karla died, the painting of her in the living room was immediately removed to the hallway.

"Mama!" Margaret called out.

"Up here, in Grandmama's room. Hurry!"

Margaret hesitated for a moment in front of the door, which had been left ajar. Then she opened it a bit wider and tiptoed in. Grandmama was perched in her high bed, leaning against the neat stack of white pillows that Irina, the upstairs maid, came and puffed hourly, usually at the same time she came to empty the chamber pot.

"Yes, Mama."

"Is that my beautiful grandchild? Is that Margaret?" her grandmother called out.

"Yes, Mother. It's Margaret," Margaret's mother replied.

"Margaret, come here. Come here where I can see you. Ah, there you are. Yes, yes, you're just as beautiful as I remembered. Oh, my dear, you will be popular! When you're presented at the grand ball, heads will turn. Everyone will say it—everyone will say, 'Margaret Szilard is the most beautiful woman in the empire, perhaps she is the most beautiful in all of Europe!' Margaret, how old are you?"

"Fourteen," Margaret answered softly. "I'll be fifteen in October." She studied her grandmama's face. Her skin was gray, but it was flawless. Once it had glowed with good health. And once Grandmama's snow-white hair had been coiffed and perfumed. But now it hung down thin and limp and gray. It was as if Grandmama had once been a bright painting that had been bleached until the former colors were hardly discernible. There was a dullness in the eyes too. Once they had danced just as Grandmama had danced when she relived for Margaret the days of her youth, the days when all Vienna and Budapest waltzed. "Our glory years," her grandmama used to say as she spun about and demonstrated the proper steps.

Margaret felt tears filling her eyes. Her grandmama's legs were covered with sores and they were swollen and numb; her eyes were clouded with cataracts. No more handsome men would whisper, "Sophie, I love you," in her ear, and none would duel with pistols over her honor. The beautiful Sophie would dance no more in the palaces of Budapest and Vienna. Instead, Sophie would become Sophia Gyula Endes, a name that would be inscribed in the great family Bible, etched on a brass plaque placed on the bottom of her portrait, and finally carved on a tombstone.

Then the voice from the high bed spoke and Margaret was startled at its seeming strength.

"Fourteen," Grandmama repeated. "Are you really fourteen? Where have the years gone? Where?" Painfully her grandmama leaned over. "Here, Margaret, I have something for you."

Margaret watched as her grandmama removed her engagement ring. It was a stunning ring—a huge blue-white diamond surrounded by little sapphires, which in turn were surrounded by tiny diamonds.

"I don't want to take it to my grave. Such things are for the living. Here, here, put it on your finger and wear it always."

"Oh, Grandmama . . ." Margaret slipped the ring on her finger and wiped the tears from her cheeks. She sniffed and tried to hold back more tears, but she couldn't stop them. Her grandmama had lived with them for the last seven years, and Margaret adored her. It was her grandmama who told her stories, who described the great cities of Europe, and who took her on wonderful romantic imaginary voyages. Her grandmama had been everywhere, known everyone, and seemingly done everything.

"That's the last thing I had to do," her grandmama said, touching Margaret's blond hair lightly. "I was a great beauty in my day, but I think you will be even more lovely. I think all the men will want to dance with you. I think you will enjoy the grand balls even more than I. Have I told you about the Countess Zichy?"

Margaret nodded.

"I suppose I've told you everything, perhaps more than once. Ah, if only my head would clear, if only the pounding would stop. It is like a hundred hoofbeats of the emperor's horse guard in my skull." Her grandmama tried to smile.

Margaret watched as her grandmama touched the delicate cameo broach at her throat, then leaned back and closed her eyes. She turned toward her mother, who was once again crying. "I think she wants to sleep now," Margaret suggested.

Her mother nodded and sat down.

"Can I go back to my horse now?"

"Yes, yes, go. I only called you because she asked for you. And be careful of the ring. It's not loose is it?"

"No, Mama. It fits just fine."

Her mother grasped her shoulder. "Hide it, Margaret. Your father might try to take it away," she whispered urgently.

"But it's mine, she gave it to me."

"Do as I tell you and don't ask questions."

Margaret looked into her mother's eyes. They commanded her, then flashed toward the door as if she expected her husband to storm into the room again as he had earlier.

"And don't tell anyone you have it, do you understand? Not anyone," her mother reiterated.

Still crying, Margaret nodded, not understanding her mother's command. She slipped the ring off her finger and into her pocket, then turned and ran out of the room. She stopped in her own room and hid the ring among the scented hand-embroidered linens in the chest where the items she would take into marriage were kept.

Then Margaret walked slowly down the spiral staircase, and when she got to the bottom, she heard her mother scream. It was not the scream of one who is frightened; it was instead a sort of long wail filled with pain.

She herself fought back more tears as she hurried through the hallway. No one had to tell her what had happened. Soon—as soon as she was buried—Grandmama's picture would be taken from the living room and hung in the hall. There was, in fact, an empty space just between her maternal grandfather, Tibor Endes, and her great-grandmother, Christina Maria Endes.

2

The hot August sun hung like a fireball just above the dry hills. It was late afternoon, and from the balcony outside her bedroom, which went all the way around the top floor of the house, Margaret could look out over the immaculately kept lawn to the formal gardens beyond, and the distant rolling hills. Late afternoon was a quiet time when members of the family retired to their rooms to rest before dressing for dinner. At this time of day Margaret sometimes napped, but at other times she walked around and around the balcony, pausing to watch the hills as they seemingly changed color in the growing twilight. Sandy brown when she began her circumnavigation of the house, they were reddish brown within the hour, and then they turned blue, and after that a deep indigo. When all light from the sun disappeared and the moon and the stars came out, the hills were rolling black cutouts against a jewel-filled sky.

For four days now her grandmother's body had lain in state in a great dark coffin. Day after day visitors came to pay their respects, and day after day Mama, dressed in black, greeted the visitors with tearstained cheeks. But tomorrow was the last day Grandmama was to spend on the estate. The next morning, Papa and Mama would accompany the coffin by rail to Budapest and Grandmama would be buried next to Grandpapa in the cemetery near the church where they had been married half a century before.

It would take Mama, Papa, and the coffin over an hour to reach Kassa by carriage. Then they would take the train, which took five or six hours, depending on how many stops it made, to reach the capital of Budapest.

Kassa, the nearest town, was some thirty kilometers from the estate at the other end of the Hernad Valley. It was the capital of Abauj-Torna county and a town of some thirty-five thousand, the majority of whom were Slavic rather than Magyar. But even though the Magyars were fewer in number, they were greater in power. The machinery, iron, furniture, textile, and milling factories of Kassa were all owned by prominent Magyar families and the large vineyards and tobacco farms in the rich Hernad Valley were also Magyar-owned, while the vast peasant population were Slavic or, as they preferred to be called in many cases, Galician.

Even though their journey to Budapest to bury her grandmother was a sad occasion, Margaret envied her parents' journey. She went to Kassa at least once a month, but she had never been to Budapest or Vienna, both of which were the locale of a thousand oft-repeated tales. In her mind they were both magical places, destinations she dreamed of, with stores and shops that sold everything the imagination could conjure up. They were fairy-tale cities populated with handsome kind men and beautiful women perfectly and fashionably dressed. There was music night and day, theater, and the symphony. She imagined bookstores on every corner and wonderful cafés where artists and writers gathered to discuss their latest works and everyone was invited to join the conversation.

Margaret was daydreaming about Budapest when she turned the corner of the balcony and walked toward her own room, which was adjacent to her parents'. Both rooms had wide French doors that opened onto the balcony. She stopped short just a few steps from her parents' door because she heard their voices raised in argument. Crouching down behind one of the potted shrubs, she peered in through the glass.

Mama was wearing a pale blue diaphanous nightgown trimmed with lace. One of its narrow blue ribbon straps had slipped off her left shoulder, revealing the curve of her full white breast. She clutched her beautiful sheer blue negligee in the fingers of her left hand while her right hand firmly held the high bedpost as if for balance. Mama's long flaxen hair was loose and tangled, and tears streamed down her face as they had for many days now.

Papa was fully dressed and he held Mama's jewelry box upside down. "Where is it, Anna? Where is your mother's ring?" His voice was loud and firm. He spoke in a tone Margaret knew and dreaded.

"I don't know, Ferenc." Mama's voice was small and seemed to come from far away, as if she had removed herself to some netherworld.

"You must, you were with her all the time! Tell me that a sick, paralyzed woman got up out of bed to hide her ring! You have it, Anna. And I want it now."

Margaret crouched frozen, listening in fearful fascination. They were talking about *her* ring.

"Well, I don't!" her mother protested. "Maybe she swallowed it."

"Don't lie to me, Anna. I know you too well."

Margaret hesitated. For a moment she thought she should come forward, but then she remembered what her mother had said. Her mother didn't want Papa to have the ring.

"You have everything else, Ferenc. You took her pearls, you took all her jewelry just as you've taken mine. You've even sold her furs—and of course the land near Budapest is yours now, isn't it? And whatever gold she left. What more do you want?"

Her mother wasn't shouting. Her mother's tone was a mixture of fear, bewilderment, and pleading.

"I want the ring!"

"I don't have it, I don't know where it is. I really don't."

Her mother's voice trailed into sobs and her father crossed the room and seized her mother by the shoulders, wrenching her loose from the bedpost. He shook her. "Anna, I won't soon forgive you if you're lying to me!"

Margaret stared. Was Papa going to hit Mama? His face was set and hard; she could see it in the mirror behind Mama's dresser even though he now had his back to the balcony. For a moment he looked the way Béla so often looked—cruel and mean. But Mama only shook her head, and Margaret saw her mouth the words, "I'm not lying." And of course she wasn't. She has no idea where I put the ring, Margaret thought.

Papa dropped his hands then and released her. They stood for a long moment looking at one another; then Papa roughly pulled down Mama's slip so that her pink-tipped breast was bare. He covered it with his hand, roughly at first; then his expression changed and he seemed to be smiling. Mama's eyes were closed and she was shaking her head slowly and whispering, "No."

As suddenly as his mood had seemed to change, Papa turned and walked across the room toward the window. Margaret moved quickly when he turned, and flattened herself against the wall, terror-stricken, holding her breath. She heard the heavy drapery being pulled closed, and with great relief she heard her father walk back across the room. It was a miracle that he hadn't seen her.

She waited for what seemed forever, then tiptoed back to the French doors that led to her own room. Mercifully she had left one ajar, and she hurried in and silently closed it and pulled her own drapery shut. Margaret sat down on her bed and listened intently. If she held her ear to the wall, she could hear the rhythmic squeak of the great mahogany bedstead and her mother's muffled moans.

What were they doing? What was happening, and why had her father taken her mother's jewelry? Of all the questions that filled her head, the squeaking bedstead and her mother's muffled sounds made her the most curious, because she had heard them many times. She decided to ask György. He was older and he was in the army. Surely he knew about such things; he seemed to know everything else.

Then Margaret sat straight up. György had taken extra

leave only because of Grandmama's illness. He was leaving tomorrow to rejoin his unit. "I must ask him," she said aloud. Slipping on her shoes, Margaret hurried out of her room, down the staircase, through the hall of the dead, and out onto the wide lawn that surrounded the house.

In the formal garden, Starogan, the Slavic gardener, bent over the wild-rose beds, gently removing weeds that had become interlocked with the prickly bushes. Near him, carefully raking the ground, were his two daughters, Kristina and Ilona. Margaret had known the two girls all their lives, since both had been born on the estate. Kristina was twelve and Ilona ten. But no matter how well she knew them or how often she saw them, she was always struck by how different they looked from Magyar girls. She, of course, was a Magyar and she reveled in her proud Hungarian heritage. The Magyars ruled Hungary and, for the most part, the Slavs were peasants. Like her mother and grandmother before her, Margaret Szilard was a tall girl, her skin was milk white, her eyes stone blue, her cheekbones high and sculptured, her neck long and patrician. But Kristina and Ilona were short and heavy-boned. They had round, platelike faces and seemingly no necks at all. Their skin was swarthy and their eyes narrow and brown. Their bodies, like their noses and lips, were wide and thick. Waistless and neckless, the Slavs were in Margaret's mind, a race apart—indeed, far apart—from the Magyars. Not that she had anything against the peasants, and certainly she did not treat them badly as Béla did. It was simply that she didn't think the women attractive, but she supposed peasant men found them attractive enough. There seemed to be lots of marriages in any case.

"*Kde jé* György?" Margaret asked in Slovak. Few of the Slavic peasants spoke Hungarian, though she suspected more of them understood than ever let on.

Old Starogan looked up, and without seeking her eyes, answered, "By the stream, fishing." He grinned as if he were thinking of a joke.

Margaret ran off toward the stream, waving at him as she went.

She made her way through the trees and headed for the river. There, leaning against a rock in the warm sun, György relaxed, his fishing line in the tranquil water.

"György!" she whispered. He'd always told her not to speak loudly, lest she frighten the fish.

He opened his eyes and motioned her to sit down. "What brings my favorite sister here?"

"I'm your *only* sister," she said with mock irritation.

"Stay awhile. We haven't fished for a long while, have we?"

"Papa says ladies don't fish. I miss you," Margaret said, sitting close to her brother. "Béla is always mean to me, and Konnie is always writing when he's not at school. 'Sh, sh,' is all he ever says to me anymore."

"I know it must be lonesome for you."

"György, I need to know something."

"Ask. If I know the answer, I'll tell you." He smiled warmly.

"What do married people do that makes the bed squeak?" She decided against mentioning the strange noises she heard, or the fact that she had seen her father seize her mother's bare breast and noted an almost evil look on his face. Still, the sight had made her feel very strange indeed. It had sent a chill through her, and she had felt an unusual dampness between her legs, as if she were perspiring. Her cheeks had flushed too. For a second she thought of her own breasts. They had been small—dots on her chest, really—but for the past year they had hurt on and off and sometimes had seemed unbearably tender. They had grown, too, and she was surprised, because she thought she was through growing. She had noted that Kristina and Ilona already had big breasts, which she supposed they had had all along.

To her surprise, György sat suddenly stiff and upright. His face was flushed, as if he was embarrassed.

"Margaret! That is not a question for a young lady to ask a man, even her brother."

"Whom else can I ask?"

"Mama."

"Oh, I couldn't ask her. It is her bed that squeaks."

György's face seemed even more red now, and uncharacteristically, he avoided her eyes. "Then ask her what a man and woman do on their wedding night," he finally suggested.

"Mama and Papa have been married for a long time, and they do it, so I don't think it is something done just on the wedding night, György."

"They did it for the first time on their wedding night," he insisted. "So ask Mama that."

Margaret inhaled and leaned back against the tree, watching him relax slightly. "All right," she allowed. "I'll ask Mama."

And after a long moment she tugged on his sleeve. "If Mama won't answer me, I'll ask you again when you come home for the holidays."

"*No, baszd meg!*" György said under his breath.

Margaret ignored him. She didn't know what the phrase meant, but she had heard boys use it before.

3

The early-morning sun shone on the gilt trim of Count Horvath's largest carriage, a magnificent red coach used primarily to transport members of the royal family when they visited Kassa. Count Horvath was not only their nearest neighbor but also the wealthiest of all the estate owners in the area. He insisted that Mama and Papa borrow his coach to travel to the train in style with Grandmama's coffin. "It is the very least," he announced, "that can be done for a woman who was once the toast of Vienna."

Margaret stood on the wide stone steps of their home and watched silently as twelve men dressed in dark suits—her brothers and Count Horvath's youngest son, András, among them—carried the large coffin to the coach and fastened it with wide strong leather straps where the trunk, had there been one, would have gone.

When the coffin was firmly in place, Mama descended the steps with Papa at her side. Margaret's heart swelled with pride as she looked at her mother, who seemed to have made a remarkable recovery from the day before. She was stunningly dressed in a three-part traveling dress made up of a bodice, an overbodice, and a bell-shaped skirt that was longer in the back than in the front and thus trailed on the ground. The skirt fit smoothly over Mama's hips, but the bodice was very pronounced, with undersleeves that gathered at the cuff. The overbodice met at the front, and it too was bell-shaped, with set-in sleeves gathered into a cuff. The underbodice had a high, high neck, and Mama wore a cameo choker over a frilly lace jabot. Her dress was made of a subdued powder-blue crepe that made her eyes seem even more beautiful than they were. Her long flaxen hair was woven into a nest of braids and covered with a small curved hat lavishly trimmed with summer flowers and blue ribbons. Her parasol matched her dress perfectly, and her little white gloves matched her tiny tight white shoes.

Her mother, Margaret observed, looked more like a princess going to the palace than a dutiful daughter on the way to bury her mother. To be sure, Mama would wear her mourning outfit at the interment ceremony. Margaret felt greatly relieved that her mother looked so fine, and she was even more pleased that Mama was no longer crying.

Mama paused, looked at Margaret, and then smiled indulgently. She slipped her gloved hand around Margaret's shoulders and kissed her on the cheek. "We shall be gone a week," her mother whispered, "perhaps two weeks."

Two weeks! It was an eternity. Mama and Papa were going to Budapest and Béla and Konrad were returning to school there. György had already returned to his army unit, and Grandmama was dead. She would be alone with the household staff and would see only her tutors, who would come three days a week to give her lessons. Her eyes sought her mother's pleadingly. She did not want to be alone, nor did she want them to know how much she disliked being alone.

"I knew you'd be my grown-up girl," her mother murmured as she stroked Margaret's hair fondly. With those words, Mama turned and walked toward the ornate coach. The formally attired coachman in his bright red jacket with the gold epaulets on its shoulders helped her up the tiny little metal steps, and Papa followed. Then Béla and Konrad climbed in and sat opposite their parents.

Margaret watched dejectedly as the coach pulled away and turned down the winding dirt lane that led to the main road. There was no one with whom she could talk now. Count Horvath's wife was dead and he had no daughters. András, his younger son, was twenty and dashingly handsome, but like György, he was in the army and would leave today to rejoin his unit. Count Horvath's other son, Janos, was thirty, and had been born with one leg shorter than the other. But it was not his physical condition that caused Margaret to avoid Janos Horvath. It was his temperament. He was bitter and bad-mannered, as if he thought his affliction gave him the right to be nasty to others. Moreover, Janos was a good friend of Béla's. Indeed, he was Béla's mentor in all things, and when Janos went to Budapest, it was Béla with whom he stayed. Margaret knew these things only because she had overheard them making arrangements to meet at this hotel or that restaurant. She was unsure of what they did in Budapest together, but she was quite certain the two of them were up to no good, as her grandmama might have put it. That, Margaret remembered fondly, had been one of Grandmama's favorite phrases. She would often shake her ringed finger and pronounce her verdict on this person or that by muttering, "That one is up to no good."

Béla, Margaret decided, was seldom up to any good, and Janos was probably worse. Once Béla had been picking on her, chasing her and threatening to throw her clothes into the river. She remembered seeing Janos by the side of a tree laughing. Yes, they cooked things up together, but Margaret never told anyone because there was no one to tell. Mama would simply pat her head and say, "It's hard being the only girl with three brothers," and Papa would not believe her because there was no doubt in her mind that Béla was Papa's favorite. Well, he was going back to school now and Margaret was not sorry to see him leave. But she would miss the others, especially György.

Feeling very much alone, she climbed the stone steps of the house and went directly to her room. However unhappy she was at being alone, she was happy for her mother. When Papa had suggested they spend more time than necessary for the burial in Budapest, her mother had stopped crying and, indeed, had seemingly returned to her normal self, caring once again for her appearance and taking great care in the selection of her clothes. And last night at dinner Mama had even laughed when György told a joke.

No doubt Grandmama's long illness had been responsible for her mother's misery, and now that Grandmama had finally died, relieved of her pain, Mama was once again herself. And when she returns, Margaret thought, things will be as they once were. Her mother would spend much time with her and would take her visiting and shopping.

Lying on her bed and staring at the light blue ceiling high above, Margaret contemplated entertaining herself for the next few weeks. Perhaps while her parents were gone she could read some of the books in the library. Her ability to read was a great secret, one she shared only with György, who had taught her, and with Konnie, who bought her books.

Papa had ordained that only boys needed a "real" education, and thus her tutoring consisted only of learning to speak various languages—German of course, Slavic, and French. But mostly she concentrated on music and painting. In addition to these subjects, she also studied what Papa called "the womanly arts." These included sewing, knitting, cooking, intricate embroidery, and tapestry hooking. She also learned how to run a household, manage servants, plan menus, and such.

Margaret tired of the subjects she was taught, and the books in the library beckoned because she knew they held secrets about the world, not only beyond the estate but also beyond the great Austro-Hungarian Empire. Still, she had to be careful not to be found out. Whenever she borrowed a book, she loosened the books around it so as not to leave an empty space where the book she had taken stood. She read by the light of an oil lamp in bed, or sometimes in the afternoon by her window when Papa was away on trips, as he so often seemed to be these days. And she read quickly so as to return a book to the shelf before he discovered it missing. Not that he had forbidden her to read the books in the library, but Margaret was certain he would, had he realized she could read. In fact, once György had asked why she couldn't learn to read and Papa had replied that since she would marry like other girls, there was no use cluttering her mind with tales of adventure and faraway places. Papa held that for women, knowledge was synonymous with discontent. But, much to her happiness, György had taught her to read, and read she did. Now, she thought, with everyone gone, she could truly explore the books. And perhaps even use the ladder that slid around the room to climb to the highest shelves and read some of the books she had never seen before. Maybe she would find the answer to the question she had not yet asked her mother . . . maybe one of the books held the answer to why the bed squeaked and why her mother moaned so throatily in the dead of night.

And of course there was Prince Stanislaus. She could ride him every day, and she would, as always, confide her secrets to him. For a moment she thought of riding him now, but in truth, she did not feel at all well. Since early this morning she had felt slightly nauseated, and now she had slight cramps in her stomach. At first she had thought it simply the excitement of her parents' departure, but now she considered it might well be something else.

Margaret pulled herself up from the bed and went down the hall to the large bathroom. It had a huge marble tub and a pedestal sink with tiny painted flowers in the bowl. Beneath the sink were buckets of water brought by the servants, and there was a small gas heater on which to heat the water. If she were to take a bath, the servants would be required to bring additional buckets of hot water from the kitchen. Her mother had told her that in Budapest the water ran from the taps through pipes, and hot water was heated in large tanks. But here in the countryside water still came from the well and was still heated over the fire.

Margaret lifted her long skirts and pulled down her underwear to sit on the toilet under which was the chamber pot. But as her underwear dropped to the floor, she gasped slightly—it was red with blood! That accounted for the dampness she had felt. She shuddered slightly and wiped herself with a cool damp cloth. It was bright red! She was bleeding from between her legs! Suddenly she felt quite weak and terribly frightened. What would she do? Everyone was gone.

"Irina!" She called for the upstairs maid frantically. "Irina! Irina!"

Almost shyly Irina opened the door and poked her head in.

"I'm ill! I'm bleeding! You must summon the doctor!"

Irina pushed herself into the bathroom and looked at Margaret, then at her stained undergarments. A smile crossed her full lips and she began to laugh.

Hot tears filled Margaret's eyes. Frightened and embarrassed, she screamed at Irina, "Stop it! Summon the doctor!"

Irina stopped laughing immediately and shook her head. "You are not sick," she said slowly, "or hurt. All girls bleed when they pass into womanhood. Didn't your mama tell you? Don't you know anything?"

How could Irina, the Slavic upstairs maid, a peasant, know something she did not? In spite of her fear, Margaret tried to think clearly. She did not really hurt, nor did she feel faint. Perhaps this bleeding *was* entirely normal, and she allowed that while Irina was not the brightest person in the whole world, she was twenty-four. If this was something that happened to all women, then it happened to Irina too.

"Do you bleed?" Margaret asked bluntly.

Irina half-smiled and nodded.

As Slavs went, Irina was better-looking than most, and generally it was assumed she had mixed ancestry. Her face was angular rather than round like the gardener's daughters, and her body was shapely and reasonably trim, Margaret thought.

"I really don't understand. Irina, you must tell me everything."

"Well, when you become a woman—that is, when you are old enough to have babies—you begin bleeding from between your legs. You bleed every month, unless you are with child, and it lasts three, sometimes five days."

"But how do you keep your clothes clean?"

"Oh, we make pads to wear. I will get you some and show you how to make more."

"Thank you . . . but wait, don't go just yet. I need to know about being with child."

"That only happens when a man takes you. Men have a breeding bone, here . . ." Irina pointed to an area below the stomach in the middle of the body, between the legs. "They put it into women and the liquid that comes out of it makes a baby grow in the stomach."

Margaret winced at the thought. But she was puzzled too. "I have seen no such bone on men," she insisted.

Irina sighed, "It's a magic bone," she revealed authoritatively. "It is not always a bone. Most of the time it is soft, limp, and rather silly-looking. It is the thing they pee from, but then it changes like magic. All male animals have such an instrument—a man's is no different than a horse's or a goat's, except that it is smaller. Have you not seen one dog mount another? Or horses mating? It is only when a man takes a woman that it becomes a bone."

Margaret was shocked. Of course she had seen animals, but she hadn't thought that people did the same things. "Does it hurt?"

"A little the first time. It can be terrible if you don't want it and don't like the man. But sometimes it feels good, very good. Especially if you like the man." Irina smiled mysteriously.

"This has happened to you?" Margaret asked in awe.

"Yes, but I've never been with child. You don't always get with child . . . a man and a woman have to do it often for there to be a child."

Margaret took in all of this information and tried to understand it. "One other thing, Irina. When a man takes a woman, does it make the bed squeak?" she suddenly asked.

Irina did not just smile this time. She giggled and nodded. "Sometimes, I think," she replied.

Margaret pulled herself up to her full height. How she hated admitting such ignorance to Irina. "You are sure about all of this, aren't you?"

Again Irina nodded.

"Well, don't just stand there. Go and get whatever it is I need."

Irina bowed her head and hurried downstairs. Margaret was a good girl, not like her brother Béla at all, Irina thought. But Margaret was also a puzzle. She was, Irina knew, smart. But she was also very dumb about some matters, and she was alone far too much. Irina shook her head. In spite of the difference in their positions, Irina felt sorry for Margaret.

Margaret gathered up her clothing and went back to her room to lie down and await Irina's return. Oh, how could her mother have left her alone? How could she not have told her these things? But as she concentrated, she remembered little things—things long forgotten. She recalled days when Mama seemed upset, times when she wasn't as lovely and vivacious as she might have been. And she remembered one day Mama told one of her friends that she did not feel well because she had the monthly "curse."

"Well, now I am a woman," Margaret announced aloud to no one. "And I guess I too have the curse."

4

September 1901

When her parents and brothers had left the last week in August, summer was still very much in the air. But now it was the fifth of September and the prevailing winds had changed, bringing the cold, crisp days of an early fall.

Margaret could not remember when she had ever seen her mother look so beautiful. Her blond hair was intricately coiffed—braids intertwined with full rounded swirls piled high on her head. And a quite wonderful hat! It was a soft felt with a narrow brim and top like an inverted water bucket. It had a fine wide ribbon around it and a small feather in the center, pointing straight upward. Mama had new shoes too. They were shiny and black with little heels, and they laced right up to the knee. Her skirt was full and hung in high folds, and her jacket matched it. There was even a little bow on the peplum just below the waist, velvet trim around the sleeves, and a long wide collar with a great velvet bow right in the front center.

"Do you like it, Margaret?"

Mama twirled around like a model in a couturier's salon and Margaret nodded enthusiastically.

"I have a few more dresses in the carriage—one for you, of course. Oh, you can't imagine, my dear. The stores are full of wonderful new things direct from Vienna! This is from the couture House of Floge and designed by Kolo Moser himself. Oh, and I saw the most divine clothes! The fabrics are breathtaking! Embroidered prints and sequined brocades and velvets with laces overlaid! Oh, Margaret, I had a wonderful time trying on clothes, and in spite of everything, your father allowed me to buy a few."

Margaret did not ask what "in spite of everything" meant. Papa spoke of money a great deal and so she assumed they were not quite as rich as their neighbors the Horvaths. Still, they hardly seemed poor, and Mama did look ravishing. Margaret sat on the edge of her bed and watched as Mama opened her boxes one by one. She too loved clothes, but there *was* the matter of her womanhood.

"Margaret, you look distracted. Even sad. You must have been lonesome, and you missed your mama. Is that it?"

Margaret nodded and bit her lip, unsure of quite what to say.

"Oh, I know. While I was gone you began your cycles."

Margaret opened her mouth in surprise. Her mother's face was turned away, but Margaret could see that she was blushing.

"I call it the curse. When you're having it, you can stay in bed if you wish and you don't have to come down to dinner. And certainly you must be careful not to do anything physical. If you feel like it, you can stay in bed the whole time. I do sometimes."

"But how did you know?" Margaret blurted out.

"Oh, Irina told me as soon as we arrived. I suppose I should have warned you. I'm sorry you were frightened."

Margaret suddenly felt like crying. Her mother had discussed her cycles with Irina! "Mama! You should have talked to me! I need to know about being a woman!" She could hear the anger in her own voice and she saw the startled look on her mother's face.

Suddenly her mother stamped her booted foot. "No!" she shouted. "No. Ladies never discuss such things. And there is nothing further you need to know until it is time for you to marry."

"And then you will talk to me, tell me everything?"

"No. You will learn from your husband. Men understand these things."

Margaret scowled. "What things?"

Her mother pressed her lips together. "Their needs," she answered in a near-whisper. "It all has to do with their needs."

"Mama . . ." Margaret felt the anger drain from her. She was pleading now. "Mama, tell me . . ."

Her mother shook her head and continued pressing her lips together nervously. Then, still whispering, "Men . . . they need women in a way women don't need them . . . it's difficult . . . of course you must do it to have babies, but men want more . . . it's degrading."

Margaret studied her mother carefully. Irina had said it sometimes felt good. And she herself had heard Mama moan with what seemed like pleasure. And György had said Mama would talk to her, but now Mama wouldn't. "I don't understand," she murmured.

"You know enough for now. Go to your room, Margaret."

Margaret nodded. She wanted to leave anyway. She felt somehow betrayed. There was no one to talk with, no one to whom she could explain her feelings.

György would say she was a question box. He'd told her that years ago, but at least he tried to answer her questions. Men had everything, she decided. At least they seemed to know everything. Except, of course, for Mr. Flaubert. In her parents' absence she had found a French novel on the very top of the bookcase and had read it, hoping to learn something. But in the end, the French novel had not been much help. In fact, it raised more questions than it answered. What exactly was "adultery"? She did not know what it meant for a married woman to "be" with another man. Was just being there enough? Or did they have to be making babies for it to be adultery? Margaret mulled it over. If she was clever, perhaps she could get her father to answer the question.

At dinner they sat in the formal dining room. Her

father sat at the head of the table, her mother at the foot. Margaret sat in the middle on the left side. She waited patiently till the servants had cleared the table. "I have a question, Papa."

Her father tweaked his long dark mustache and leaned toward her. "Yes?"

"Papa, if Mary, the Mother of Jesus, was married to Joseph, and it was the angel Gabriel who made her with child, was that adultery?"

Her mother's crystal wineglass hit the tile floor and broke into a thousand tiny splinters. Her father's face clouded over and he stood up. "What blasphemy!" he said loudly. "Margaret, go to your room at once!"

Two

1

October 1, 1902

The winter was often cold and damp, the spring short and rainy, and the summer hot and humid. But fall was perfect. The days were warm and sunny and the nights cool and crisp. The blue sky turned the rivers into satin-smooth azure ribbons that cut through lush green valleys and meandered through the acres of tall evergreens. It seemed to Margaret that Mother Nature put on her finest show in those months before she slept—a kind of magnificent last waltz made vivid by turning leaves and summer's late-blooming flowers.

In two weeks, on the fifteenth of October, she would be sixteen, and once again Mama and Papa had gone off to Budapest. Margaret hoped they would bring her a new wardrobe from the fine shops in the capital city, but she knew they would bring one dress at least. This year she would be sixteen and her birthday coincided with Count Horvath's annual harvest ball. Her mother had promised her a ball gown for this annual event, which she would be attending for the first time. For once, she thought eagerly, Irina would have to help *her* dress, because a proper gown would require her to wear a heavily boned and laced corset, and over that she would wear several lacy petticoats.

On this particular morning Margaret wore her long blond hair in a single thick braid that hung loose and fell nearly to her waist in the back. Her plain tan skirt reached below the tops of her leather riding boots. Her sunny yellow blouse was partially covered by the three-quarter-length jacket that matched her skirt, and her hands were protected by leather gloves. She was perched sidesaddle on Prince Stanislaus, though, truth be known, she preferred to remove his English saddle, hitch up her skirts, and ride him with only a blanket between them. When she had been younger she'd been allowed to ride that way nearly all the time, but now Papa said such riding was unladylike and insisted she ride sidesaddle.

Of course Papa and Mama were still away. But she could not trust Ivan, the stablehand. If she rode as she wished, he would tell her father. Ivan was Irina's brother, and although he was not unattractive, Margaret disliked him. Ivan and Irina were too much a part of the fabric of the cocoon her parents wrapped her in for her to like either of them. Indeed, it was this cocoon from which she longed to escape.

"Where are you riding?" Ivan asked as he led Prince Stanislaus out of the stall with Margaret already mounted.

"Oh, just to our neighbors'," she lied.

"Count Horvath?" Ivan asked.

Sometimes he seemed dim-witted. "What other neighbors are there?" she asked with irritation.

He avoided her eyes. "How long will you be gone?"

It was Papa who insisted he ask all these questions. Still, it annoyed her that a peasant should be left to keep track of her comings and goings.

"Not more than two hours," she answered carefully.

He nodded and gave Prince Stanislaus a gentle pat on the rump. The horse trotted away and Margaret lifted her head high and did not look back at Ivan.

At least this time she had slipped away without anyone reminding her to wear a bonnet. But then, she reasoned, the September sun was not strong in any case, so there was no need to protect what Mama called her "delicate skin." "Only peasants have sun-hardened skin," her mother maintained. "It would be terrible for a lady to have skin darkened by the sun!" Mama was quite strict about skin care. Creams were used to lubricate it at night, hats were always worn to keep the sun away, and at the slightest sign of any disorders, a small amount of arsenic was taken to clear them up. "A woman's class is evident in her skin," Mama proclaimed.

Margaret waited till she was far from Ivan's prying dark eyes. Then she turned her horse away from Count Horvath's estate and headed toward her secret place, located in a fairly dense thicket near the stream that fed into the Tarcza River. Once a small chapel had been built there, a place for the peasants to worship. But now the old wooden structure was weakened and it leaned to one side precariously. Its windows, pews, and kneeling benches had been stolen long ago. But in one corner, the most sheltered spot behind where the alter had once stood, Margaret had created a space for herself. She had dragged logs to sit on from outside, brought several old blankets from the house, and recently added a lamp.

On occasion Margaret smuggled a book out of the house and brought it here to read. If the weather was warm she would tie Prince Stanislaus to a tree, spread out her blanket on the grass near the stream, and lie down and read in the sunlight that filtered through the trees. If it was rainy or too cool, she went inside to her little corner. There, too, beneath the loose boards that once supported the altar, she had hidden a number of books brought to her by her brother. This was her own little secret library; it was a place far from the prying eyes that always seemed to be watching her.

Margaret reached the thicket, dismounted, and led Prince Stanislaus to a tree around which the grass was tall and green. She slipped the blanket from beneath the saddle and spread it out on the ground. Then she removed from the waistband of her skirt the book she'd brought from the library. She hadn't been so careful today because there was no one to notice such a thing as a missing book, nor would any of the peasants have thought it unusual to see her with a book. Even if he had seen it, Ivan would not have thought to report such a thing to her father.

Margaret carefully opened the book. She had found it on the very top shelf in the corner, almost as if it were intentionally hidden. It was an American novel by one Henry James, entitled *The Bostonians*.

The dust jacket explained that it was the first Hungarian edition of the famous satire about "women's emancipation." Margaret shivered slightly, wondering what forbidden fruit she would find within its pages. The dictionary had revealed the meaning of "emancipation," and, satire or not, she was now anxiously looking forward to reading it. Did women have rights? Until she had glanced at this book the whole question of women's rights had never occurred to her, except in the most personal of terms. What had occurred to her, and it had occurred often, was her resentment that men had everything and could do anything they wanted.

Margaret settled down and opened the first page. She was about to begin reading when she heard heavy footsteps in the woods. Had Ivan followed her? She quickly hid the book in the grass and leaned back against the tree and closed her eyes as if napping. To have a book was one matter, but to be found in hiding reading it would surely arouse even Ivan's suspicions.

"Oh," she heard a male voice say in surprise. She knew instantly that the deep clear voice did not belong to Ivan.

Margaret opened her wide blue eyes to see a total stranger. He was tall and slim, with thick curly black hair, dark eyes, heavy brows, and fair skin. He was quite the most handsome man she had ever seen. In fact he looked like a painting of young King David she had once seen in an art book. He held up his hands as if to surrender to her, then smiled. It was a wonderful warm smile, a beautiful smile.

"Don't be afraid," he said slowly and in a fine cultured accent.

"I'm not," she answered. Then, cocking her head slightly, "Where do you live? I've not seen you before."

"I've just come to live on the estate of Count Horvath. I'm to work keeping his books and collecting the rents."

She smiled. "I'm Margaret Szilard—we're the count's nearest neighbors. And may I ask your name?"

He blushed, "Miklós Lazar."

"I suppose we shall have to wait till the count gives his annual harvest ball to be officially introduced, Mr. Lazar. But in the meantime, I'm pleased to make your acquaintance."

He frowned slightly and looked at the ground. "I doubt we'll be formally introduced at the ball. In fact, I doubt I shall be invited. I'm merely in the count's employ, and I'm a Jew."

A Jew! Margaret was truly shocked. Of course she had heard her father speak of Jews, but from what he had said, she had expected something quite different. She had expected an evil dark person with shifty eyes and an unclean body. But this man was very clean and neat. Moreover, his skin was fair. In fact, to her eyes he was actually beautiful. She controlled her facial expression well, she thought. He had surely not seen the surprise in her eyes. "I cannot speak for the other members of my family," she said, trying to sound older, "but I personally have nothing against Jews."

He looked slightly bemused. "I really have nothing against beautiful young women, either."

Margaret felt her face flush crimson. How old was he? Twenty perhaps, perhaps a little older. Well, in two weeks she would be sixteen. And as Irina was always pointing out, she was a woman now.

"Will you be staying with the count long?"

"For three years. Then I shall take the money I've saved and go to the United States."

"To America! Oh, that is exciting! I've never been beyond Kassa. I've not even been to Budapest." Margaret reached over into the grass and retrieved her book. "I dropped it," she said by way of explanation.

He glanced at the book and smiled broadly. "Do you read, then?"

"Oh, yes. This one is in fact an American novel. A satire about women's rights."

He glanced at the title. "Ah, yes. This is an interesting book. Mr. James is an interesting writer. There is, I should warn you, some debate about just how much of a satire it is. In fact, this book is quite controversial."

"You've read it?"

"A few years ago."

"Oh, it would be wonderful for me if when I've finished, you would meet me here to discuss it. It's lonesome here, you know. Almost no one reads."

"It's unusual to find a woman who reads," he said.

"My father doesn't know I read. My brother taught me secretly, and I have to spirit books away," she said somewhat too dramatically.

He smiled. "I don't imagine your father would be at all pleased to know that you were here now talking to a Jew, either. I'm afraid I couldn't meet you. Jews get in trouble easily, even when they've done nothing."

"No one knows I come here. It's my secret place."

"Perhaps we will meet accidentally," he allowed. "I have to go now—I'm expected back by noon hour."

He turned and walked through the thicket and back out into the open field, where she saw he had left a small buggy to which a tired black mare was attached. She sighed deeply. What an adventure! And what a handsome, intelligent man! His dark eyes remained the outstanding thing she remembered, and even as she stood in the wood and watched his buggy disappear across the field, she knew she would dream of him and plot to see him again.

A week passed, but Miklós did not return to the thicket, though Margaret looked for him each and every day. Still, at night her dreams were filled with him, and when she was alone where they had met, she engaged in imaginary conversations with him.

Margaret guided Prince Stanislaus through the tangle of trees. Last night there had been a sudden cold snap and the ground was covered with fallen leaves and the wildflowers were wilted and dying in the cool fall air. Prince Stanislaus' breath was white, as was hers, and they mingled in the frosty stillness as the ruins of the old church came into view. The nearby brook raced along, but where it had spilled over its banks earlier, the excess water had formed shallow still pools, and they were now covered with a layer of thin ice. The sun reflected off the ice like light in a cloudy mirror.

Margaret dismounted and loosely tied Prince Stanislaus to a gnarled tree. She gingerly lifted her skirts and walked toward the brook. She sensed the presence of another person even before he spoke, and she turned quickly to face the voice. It was Miklós and he stood by the corner of the old church holding his pipe in his mouth with one hand. It sent billows of white smoke to mingle with the low fog.

"Good morning."

He smiled warmly and she walked over to him, trying not to hurry or look as excited as she was. She'd come here every day and had not seen him. She had come early in the morning, as she came today, in the afternoon following the noonday meal, and at night, just before supper, when the sun was falling behind the rolling hills. But he was never about and she feared he would never return. Now, like one of her dreams of him, he stood there watching her with his beautiful dark eyes.

"Good morning," she answered, then added, "I've looked for you here, but you didn't return."

"I did, once or twice. I haven't had much time, though. The count keeps me busy."

She smiled at him. "Come in the church with me. I'll show you where we can sit down."

He followed her into the ramshackle old building past the empty spaces where the pews had been. They passed through an archway to what had been a small room behind and to one side of the altar. In it were several logs. She patted one with her hand and sat on the other herself.

"I really can't stay," he said even as he perched on the edge of the log.

"Oh, but we must talk, Miklós. There is so much I have to know . . . so much I cannot ask anyone about."

"And what makes you think I can help you?"

She searched his face with her wide blue eyes. He seemed a trifle nervous. "No one will find us here," she assured him. "As for my questions . . . well, I know you can help."

He half-smiled, and it gave her the courage to continue. She had to find a way to meet him on a regular basis. If they saw each other every few days, she decided, he would soon love her as she loved him. It was also imperative that he think of her as a woman, not as a girl.

Miklós shifted about and finally stretched his long legs in front of him. "Just what precisely do you want to know?" he ventured.

"First I want to know about Jews. You told me you are one, so you must know all about them. And second, I want you to tell me about America—why you want to go there and what it is like."

"Both subjects are complicated, especially the first."

"I'll be patient."

"Why do you want to know these things?"

"I'm curious. My father says the Jews killed Christ, and the peasants all believe that on Jewish holidays—well, one holiday—Jews kidnap Christian children and sacrifice them."

"Christ was a Jew, and the Romans killed him. And we never kidnap Christian children for any reason. The holiday you speak of is Passover, and sometimes a lamb is sacrificed for the feast."

"Why do the peasants believe these things?"

"They're ignorant."

"I never believed that story anyway. But the other . . . well, even the priest says it is so."

"We do not accept Jesus as the son of God. Some Jews believe he was another in a long line of prophets—like John the Baptist. Most Jews just don't think about him at all. We refused to believe in Christianity and we've kept to our own traditions. For that we have been endlessly persecuted."

"But Jews in Hungary can vote. I read that."

He smiled, "Ah, yes. But only since 1895, seven short years ago. Besides, you can make laws, but you can't so easily change opinions. We have some rights here, more than in Russia. Still, vile stories linger on."

"Is that why you want to go to America?"

"Yes, one reason. I believe I'll have more opportunity there."

"But you will have to learn English . . . I've heard it is a very difficult language."

"Not so difficult if you speak German. I've already studied English. In fact, I read that book, the one by Henry James, in English."

A small sound of surprise and admiration escaped her lips, and immediately she pounced upon an idea. "Oh, you must teach me, you must! I too want to go to America!"

"Why?" he asked.

"To be emancipated," she answered, thrusting her chin slightly forward. "You want rights. Well, so do I."

"Women can't yet vote, even in America."

"I'm sure they'll be able to vote sooner there than here," she replied quickly, though unsure of what voting meant.

He studied her carefully for a moment. She was truly the most beautiful woman he had ever seen. And in spite of her childlike quality—he assumed she was terribly sheltered—he knew she had a good mind or she couldn't have learned to read so well. And curious! She was most curious. But being with her alone was dangerous. He could be accused of anything—he could lose his position, or worse. Vaguely he wondered how old she was. He took her for seventeen or eighteen at least. Her body was that of a woman, and he was not unaware of her flirtatious manner with him. Still, there was something wonderful about her, and he wanted to see her again. "Learning English is an arduous task. I really don't have time to play teacher."

"Oh, please. I learn quickly, you'll see. If you could

just meet me for half an hour a day . . . or perhaps several times a week for longer."

He felt himself being drawn in by her. "I do have some books you could start on," he said hesitantly.

"Oh, you *will* teach me!"

She squeezed his arm gently and her sky-blue eyes caressed him affectionately.

"I will bring you a book and you can do the first exercise. We'll see how you do."

"Oh, thank you, thank you . . . When? When can I begin?"

He stood up and stretched. "I'll meet you here the day after tomorrow at this time."

"Do you have to go now?"

"Yes."

He turned his back and did not again turn around as he left her sitting there. This was not the right thing to do. He should never have agreed . . . Well, perhaps he would not come . . . perhaps if he didn't see her he would forget her.

"Good-bye," Margaret called after him. She waited awhile and then returned to Prince Stanislaus. Her heart was dancing with joy because, she thought, he would see her now quite often. Moreover, he would discover she was intelligent. As she remounted her horse and led him back toward the house, she realized that having Miklós respect her was almost as important to her as his presence. This was one man who must become convinced that she was bright, he must learn to see her as more than just a woman who had "womanly talents."

2

On the first of every month, Count Horvath's eldest son, Janos, traveled to Budapest to deposit funds, settle accounts, and purchase both luxuries and necessities. He also came to have a good time and enjoy activities that would have been frowned on in the smaller town of Kassa, where he would have been recognized immediately. But in Budapest he enjoyed both the liberalism of the capital and a certain anonymity. It was during these monthly visits that Béla Szilard left his Spartan student digs to join Janos. At such times the two of them spent an evening—and usually part of the next day—partying and engaging in acts of debauchery.

Those who saw Béla and Janos going about together in Budapest thought them unlikely but clearly dedicated friends. In truth, their seeming friendship was completely symbiotic. Like aphid and ant, they each benefited from their unusual relationship. Perhaps, Béla contemplated, what made it so unusual was that without a word ever having been spoken on the matter, each knew his own role perfectly—knew exactly what the other expected, and provided it without complaint.

Béla Szilard was tall, dark, good-looking, well-built, well-mannered, and well-dressed. He was twenty-two, but could pass for an older and more distinguished man. Youth was not valued in this society where age alone resulted in respect. The only exceptions were women who tired of older partners and longed for the eager enthusiasm of younger men. Thus Béla had two advantages. Men could not easily tell his age, but women quickly recognized his youth, his spirit, and, indeed, his intent.

Nor was Béla unaware of his prowess with women. How could he be? Conquests came easily to him, women adored him, indeed many invited him out and he was forever turning down invitations to attend this or that salon. His problem was money. His father was exceedingly strict with his son's student allowance, and his father also made it obvious that there was *no* money for any increase. Béla therefore could not entertain the ladies of his choice—he could not even entertain himself. In fact, the most Béla could afford was one night a month in the beer hall with his fellow students.

Béla's younger brother, Konrad, was not bothered by his lack of funds. Konrad was a serious student, and when he was not studying engineering—as his father dictated—he was studying writing plays, which was his own choice. And what spare time Konrad had went to the theater. There he built sets, took minor acting roles, and generally imposed himself upon the actors, actresses, directors, and producers to read his plays.

Béla regarded Konnie as being too ambitious and too dedicated. He himself slipped by, always engaged in some scheme to make or acquire more money, preferably without undue physical or mental strain.

Janos Horvath's effect on women was quite the opposite of that experienced by Béla. Women avoided him. They were put off not only by his crippled leg but also by his ill temper and his heavy drinking. Béla knew there was something else as well. Janos was given to certain sexual perversities—he enjoyed the "French" position because it hurt and humiliated the women with whom he copulated, and he often demanded oral stimulation before he was ready for any form of the act. On the plus side, Janos had plenty of money, and in exchange for Béla's finding him women, Janos paid all the bills up to and including the price of endless bottles of champagne and the best wines, dinner, and the theater. Janos also rented a lush hotel suite, where fine food and liquors were delivered to the room on elegant serving carts by silent and circumspect waiters. When Janos came to town for recreation, he forwarded money to Béla, who handled all the arrangements and details for Janos, managing along the way to siphon off some of the money for himself and easily rationalizing his act by telling himself that it was a "fee" for his services.

The Korzó was a wide avenue that stretched along the Pest side of the Danube. It was lined with fine hotels and apartments that overlooked the river and Margaret Island, a pleasure park in the river's center. The Hotel Bristol, the Carlton, the Hungaria, and the most famous, the Ritz, all faced the Korzó, even though their entrances were on Maria Valeria Street. Tonight Béla had selected the Bristol. The management was discreet in the extreme. Knowing full well that its rooms were sometimes reserved for the illicit assignations of the wealthy, the concierge turned a blind eye to all those registering for a few hours or for a night. What tales the walls of this elegant hotel could tell if they could speak, tales that might well cause a thousand divorces—or at the very least feed the gossips for a lifetime. Such was life in the empire, Béla thought. Hypocrisy was surely the most outstanding feature of everyday life. Women were attired from neck to ankle in the most restricting of clothes, their waists made tiny by heavy boned corsets that when properly laced pushed their breasts to exaggerated heights and added fullness, while at the same time giving additional emphasis to their bottoms. To create even further interest in this part of the anatomy, they wore bustles. And no one spoke of sex, yet Béla couldn't even imagine how many prostitutes there were in Budapest or in Vienna or how many "respectable" women were having dalliances with men other than their husbands. But there was also fear. The nineteenth century had been ushered in by a skull and crossbones in the form of cholera—it was ushered out by an equally deadly disease, syphilis. In Vienna and in Budapest the name of the disease was only whispered; to acquire it was to be branded a libertine. Yet all, and he was no exception, ran eagerly toward their fate, refusing to give up sexual variety and eagerly seeking new encounters. When the heroine of a melodramatic play threw open her arms onstage revealing her heaving bosom and spoke the words, "We are dying for love," more than a whisper and a giggle rippled through the audience. Perhaps, Béla thought, it was the risk; perhaps, like moths to a flame, the empire was drawn to satin sheets and feather mattresses, there to meet the grim reaper. No matter, he had no intention of giving up sex, and even if he had, he was not going to start tonight.

It was in one of the Bristol's finest suites that Béla now waited for Janos Horvath. Béla had engaged a three-room suite with a large sumptuous bath and a long balcony. The first room, which was reached only after passing down a tiled hallway, was decorated with red-and-gold velvet wallpaper. On a heavy mahogany marble-topped table there was a huge brass vase filled with fuchsia, black, and gold plumes. This bouquet had as its centerpiece a single peacock feather, whose brilliant-colored eye seemed to lean forward, taking in the splendors of the extravagant room. The furniture consisted of two long lounges upholstered in plush red velvet and one covered with soft black fur. A long plant-filled balcony overlooked the sinuous Danube as it wound downstream toward Margaret Island.

On the other side of the main room was a long hall off which were two large bedrooms and a bath. Each bedroom featured a wall of mirrors opposite a huge four-poster bed topped by a canopy.

Béla relished thoughts of the evening ahead. The women he had selected were a match for their surroundings in spite of their profession. The younger was seventeen and called Gizella. It was a common name, but there was nothing common about her extraordinary looks. She had auburn hair, large brown eyes, and ivory-white skin. Her young breasts were high and full, her waist tiny, and her hips rounded to near-perfection. But it was her shapely derriere that was most appealing, and given Janos' tastes, Béla was certain he had chosen wisely. At the moment she curled seductively on the fur lounge, its dark color making her appear even paler and more desirable. Like every other woman in Budapest, she was dressed modestly, though expensively. Her amber organdy gown had a high neck and long sleeves trimmed in Chantilly lace. It was gathered in back in a modified bustle and it hung to her ankles. If one did not know, one would never guess that she was a single woman whose favors were sold rather than won. She looked the perfect lady. He glanced up at her and felt almost sorry about the torments she would no doubt endure later in the evening. Still, she would be mollified in the morning. Janos could be most generous.

The woman he had chosen for himself was less attractive. He was always careful that Janos have the better one, lest jealousy develop. Then too, it was Janos who paid.

In spite of being less spectacular, Magdellena was a

good choice. She had rich brown hair and unusual green eyes. Her body was seductively plump—more mature, riper than Gizella's. Her breasts were heavier and her hips slightly fuller. And he liked the way she danced close so that he could feel the outlines of her body against his. She was a few years older and more experienced. She had humor, and he liked that as well. He had been with her many times before and knew from experience that she was full of surprises, a real whore who enjoyed her work and who would initiate sexual play as well as respond to it. The first time he had taken her out they had danced for over an hour. So exciting were her movements that he had grown ready on the dance floor and could wait no longer for her favors. She had taken him out of the ballroom and onto the winding steps that led to the back garden. There, midway down the steps, she had stopped and opened her dress in just the right place. Too stunned to move, he had watched with fascination as she opened his trousers and withdrew his anxious member. Standing higher than he on the steps, she had moved into the perfect position, and there, fully dressed while others passed by only yards away, he fully possessed her, unnoticed by those who went to stroll in the gardens. Later, of course, he had taken her again. But he remained in awe of her desire to satisfy his every need, and so he returned to her on a regular basis.

Both women sipped an aperitif and Béla walked to the liquor cart and poured himself a cognac. He carefully tilted the huge snifter and set it in a metal holder; then beneath it he lit a small flame. He turned the snifter slowly and carefully, heating the cognac. Then he extinguished the flame and removed the glass, carefully holding its stem, which had not gotten hot. For a moment he swirled the cognac, then took a long slow sip.

The door to the suite opened and Janos entered, followed by the overburdened peasant who carried his luggage. Janos' scowl changed immediately to a wide smile as his narrow eyes fell on Gizella. Béla lifted his glass toward Janos in a silent toast to the glorious evening ahead. "Was it a difficult journey?" Béla asked. Janos ignored him, fastening his eyes on the girl. His mouth twisted slightly, and his gaze narrowed. Béla could have predicted Janos' response. Janos wanted to sample the wares provided immediately, even if it meant they missed the theater and went out for a late dinner.

"A terrible journey," Janos muttered. "I need to clean up first—perhaps have a bath."

Béla smiled and tugged on the heavy gold cord that hung by the chair. In moments one of the staff appeared. "Run the bath," Béla requested. "My friend has had a long journey." The man disappeared into the bathroom and Béla poured Janos a cognac.

"This," Béla said with a certain pride, "is Gizella."

Janos went to her and stood over her, his eyes seemingly undressing her even now. Gizella stared down, unable, or perhaps, Béla thought, unwilling to look at Janos. Still, he had warned her what to expect, and of course he had made it clear that she would be paid far more than usual.

Janos lifted her ungloved white hand and kissed it. "Go," he said in a low voice, "and prepare to bathe with me."

Her large eyes seemed to grow even larger as she lifted them to look into his face.

"Take off everything but your corset and shoes," he instructed. Then, running his finger around her full lips, he whispered, "I will remove those myself."

"The bath is ready," the servant announced, and with that he disappeared, closing the door behind him.

Janos held out his hand and pulled Gizella from the sofa. "Go," he said, patting her behind. "Hurry."

As they disappeared into the bathroom, Béla felt himself excited by the mental picture of Janos and Gizella in the tub. He turned toward Magdellena and saw that she read his thoughts. She half-smiled and pulled him down next to her on the long lounge. "Don't pout because there is only one tub," she teased.

Béla smiled and slipped his hand under her skirt. "Enjoyment is enjoyment," he breathed as they toppled backward, embracing one another. And Béla thought to himself that it was indeed good to have a friend like Janos Horvath.

3

October 16, 1902

Miklós looked at Margaret in wonder. Each time he saw her, she seemed more beautiful than the time before. Today she wore a soft blue angora scarf around her neck. It caressed her cheek and its color matched her eyes perfectly.

"It's getting cooler every day," he said, not knowing what else to say. For the first time he felt awkward around a woman. Her appearance was distracting enough, but her personality was even more so. She seemed totally naive and innocent on one level, while on another she seemed both flirtatious and wanton. At the same time she was utterly straightforward. And curious! She had questions about everything, but, he admitted, none of her questions was stupid.

"No, I don't believe Mr. James intended to write a satire," she said seriously. "I believe he was indicating that while women are exploited by men, they can also be exploited by other women. Verena is most decidedly exploited by her mentor, another woman."

"Possibly," he said, listening carefully.

"Still, I see now that being able to vote—to help select the government—is a vital step for women. The first step, really."

"The first step toward what?" he questioned, wanting to know how much she really understood.

"Toward not being owned by men, toward being something more important than a piece of furniture or an acre of land."

"What's the second step?"

"To have money of our own. One day I'm going to

have money of my own. I'm going to own my very own business."

He smiled indulgently. "And what business are you intending to go into?"

"Fashion," Margaret answered without hesitation. "One day I am going to be a couturiere with my own shop."

"In America?"

"Yes, in America."

He rubbed his hands together. "To change the subject, it's getting cold. How are we going to study in the winter?"

"We'll have to build a fire," Margaret replied, acknowledging the growing cold.

"You seem a bit unhappy," he offered as they sat down on the logs within the confines of Margaret's secret place.

"I am. I wore a wonderful new gown to Count Horvath's ball last night. Mama brought it from Budapest. I wanted you to see it, but I couldn't find you anywhere."

Miklós closed his eyes. "Thank goodness. Margaret, Count Horvath must never know we meet like this. Or your father. Your father could have me jailed or even killed."

"I know, I know. I didn't tell anyone I was looking for you. I just pretended I was lost and looking for the powder room. But where were you, Miklós?"

"In Kassa. The count sent me into town on business—business intended to keep me away from the ball, I suspect. I didn't get back till this morning."

"How stupid," Margaret replied as she brought out her books and paper. "Here, Miklós, see? I've done all my homework."

Miklós took the neatly written papers and studied them. "Very good," he said. In truth, he was impressed. With almost no guidance she had managed her first English lesson with ease.

"This means so much to me. You will go on teaching me, won't you?"

"As I said before, it's going to get very cold here in the winter."

Margaret smiled. "I can stand it if you can. Look here, I've made you a scarf—that should help a little."

He smiled at her and took the hand-knit scarf. It was quite a handsome piece of handicraft. It was nearly three feet long and made of bright red wool with equally bright green trim.

"You're very talented."

"Everyone can knit, embroider, cook, and play the piano. Papa makes me study those things. But they're not at all interesting."

"I meant your ability with languages shows talent—this is all quite correct," he said, referring to the papers she had given him. Then he smiled and touched the scarf she had made, "I'm glad you can do this sort of thing too."

Margaret blushed and moved closer to him. "Have you brought a second lesson?"

"Yes. But you need to practice pronunciation too. Let's start with greetings. When you meet someone, you say, 'How do you do?' Try that."

"Who do u doo?" she repeated.

Miklós laughed in spite of himself. "No, no. I know that 'how' rhymes with 'cow' in English, but it doesn't rhyme with the German 'kuh' . . . it's 'how'—and don't emphasize the O in 'do' so much."

Margaret tried again and Miklós nodded, "Much better," he praised. "Now for the answer: 'I am fine, thank you.' Say that."

"I am fine, think you," Margaret repeated.

" 'Thank,' " he corrected.

Miklós continued for an hour, then withdrew his pocket watch and shook his head. "I have to go now. But I'll come on Wednesday."

Margaret nodded. "That's good, I'll be here."

"You're a good student . . . very good."

Margaret glowed with his words of praise. He was the nicest man—and so handsome, so very handsome.

"Miklós, there is another place. It's a bit farther, but it's much warmer in the winter. It's a sort of cave in the side of a hill. I think it used to be a rock quarry long ago. I can show you where it is next time."

"Is it safe? I mean, does anyone go there?"

"No. I've never seen anyone."

"We'll look at it."

Margaret nodded and watched as he left the glen and went to his little buggy. He was growing more fond of her, she could feel it. Soon, she thought, he would love her as she loved him. Then she imagined them running away to America together. Pictures of America filled all her thoughts, and in her mind she saw it all. She imagined her and Miklós sailing past the Statue of Liberty, walking down Fifth Avenue, or even summering in Martha's Vineyard. Pictures of such places were hers in three dimensions when she used her mother's stereoscope, and now, more and more often she sat for hours studying the streets of New York, pretending she and Miklós were the tiny characters behind the glass.

Three

1

February 1903

*A*nna Maria Szilard sat primly on the edge of her chair at the small round table in the corner of the Hotel Vadászkurt restaurant. The long jacket of her fox-trimmed suit was open in the front, revealing a light brown silk blouse with a large bow at the neck. As was the custom, her large broad-brimmed fox-trimmed hat was still atop her head.

Ferenc relaxed in his leather chair across from her. His suit jacket was also open, revealing a tightly buttoned vest. A heavy gold watch chain hung from the vest's tiny pocket, and he pulled on it, releasing his timepeace. For a moment he looked at it, turning it in his hand slowly so the light caught the gold and it glimmered. Then he replaced it and smiled across the table at his wife. He had finished his meal and there was still time to sit back and enjoy his strong black coffee and his traditional after-lunch cigar.

Anna Maria glanced at her husband, then looked into space somewhere beyond him as she always did when she was thinking about him. She supposed Ferenc Szilard was a handsome man. He was reasonably tall and well-built. His hair was graying now, of course, and certainly it was thinner than it had once been. Even his long well-groomed mustache had gray hairs, though, oddly, as the hair on his head thinned, his mustache seemed to grow thicker. But he was, she reminded herself, fifty-three years old.

They had been married twenty-five years ago today in 1878, when she had just turned seventeen and he was twenty-eight.

It was not a marriage she had wanted then and it was not one she relished now, even after four children. For one thing, Ferenc's ancestral estate was one hundred and seventy miles by train from the capital and she was obligated to live in wretched isolation far from her beloved Budapest. But of course that was not all of it. She had fancied herself in love with the dashing Count József Bodnar. Ah, the dreams of youth. She almost sighed aloud, but she caught herself just in time. Sadly, her József had been betrothed to another by his family, and her father and Ferenc's arranged her betrothal and subsequent marriage without so much as consulting her.

"You don't look as happy as you should, Anna."

Ferenc's voice drifted across the table and she broke her stare into space and looked at him. "I'm sorry. I suppose I'd hoped the weather would be better."

"In February? Come, come."

She forced a little smile. "Our fathers didn't pick the most temperate month for our wedding. Personally, I would have chosen spring."

"And another groom," he said coldly.

She dropped her eyes immediately. She supposed she'd made no secret of her unhappiness. He made no secret of knowing she was unhappy. In fact he seemed to take a certain joy in reminding her she was his whether she liked it or not.

"Well, Anna, I didn't come here to discuss your fantasies. I promised we'd come on our twenty-fifth anniversary, and here we are."

"You promised we'd go to Vienna. And besides, this trip is no different from any other we've been on the last few years. You came primarily to do business. This is no more special than when we came here in October."

His facial expression remained exactly the same, but

he kept his voice low. "Vienna was out of the question. Our finances, as I keep reminding you, are not what they once were. In any case, I must do some business. I shan't be gone long this afternoon. Surely, Anna, you can find something with which to amuse yourself."

"I might have gone to Margaret Island if it weren't so cold."

"Well, it is cold, and I imagine everything on the island is closed up tighter than a drum for the season. Except, of course, the Hotel Palatinus."

She looked at the windows. They were foggy from the steam inside, but she knew the sky was gray and that it was threatening to snow. "Perhaps I shall visit the museum," she finally said.

He ceremoniously reached in his pocket and withdrew his leather purse. He shook his change and handed her four silver florins. "Here, you'll need this for cab fare and perhaps for a cup of tea at the museum."

She quickly took the coins and put them into the tiny purse inside her fox muff. He would leave the pretty waitress more money than he gave her, she thought angrily. And at that it was her mother's money! The last of any money from her side of the family that had been brought into the marriage—not that she completely trusted Ferenc's word on that. He would lie to her about money. Not directly, of course, but simply by not telling her anything in the first place. He kept alluding to their financial condition, but what was their financial condition? She had no idea.

Ferenc drained the last of his coffee and butted out his cigar. Then he stood up and stretched. "I must go now, Anna. I'll meet you back at the hotel around five. Then we'll go to the theater and have a late dinner, perhaps even a bottle of champagne. What do you say to that?"

She nodded and her eyes followed him as he left the dining room. Dinner, theater, champagne. It all had a boring sameness to it.

"More tea?"

The little waitress hovered over her, and Anna shook her head. She wanted to give Ferenc time enough to catch a cab at the door and be off, but she didn't want to be sitting here all afternoon. She wanted to leave this place and to walk in the fresh air even if it was cold. She rose and walked slowly to the ladies' lounge. There she removed her hat and fixed her hair. She slowly repaired her makeup and then buttoned her coat against the cold and buried her hands in her large muff. She sailed through the front doors of the restaurant, turned down the doorman's offer to get a cab, and walked down Turr Istvan Street. Walk . . . walk. . . . Oh, how glad she was that Ferenc did have business. Oh, God, how she longed to be alone even if she could only window-shop. And of course she might go to the museum . . . at least she would go to the foyer to pick up a brochure, which would prove she'd been there.

She headed for Vaci Street with its elegant shops. She could try on shoes at Bencze and Brack, the famous shoemakers, or perhaps hats at Sopousek Karola, the well-known milliner's. All the clothing stores, without exception, were on the second floors of the shops, and she contemplated going to Salon Gergely on Andrassy Road nearby. Anne inhaled deeply. She felt like a prisoner set free.

How different this city was now, she thought as she walked along. Of course, it had begun to change in her childhood, but when one is in a place, one does not notice change so very much.

Indeed, she thought. She was an infant when the two cities, Buda and Pest, were united officially. Buda was a great fortress and had been for over a thousand years. Pest, called Ofen in German, was a sprawling market town on the opposite side of the beautiful Danube. In the 1870's, with Vienna as their inspiration, the Hungarians decided to celebrate the millennium of Magyar conquest by virtually rebuilding Pest. What had once been a dull landing spot on the Danube was transformed into Europe's largest Houses of Parliament outside of London. And across the river on Castle Hill, the fortifications were gradually replaced by the Fisher Bastion, a masterpiece of candy floss architecture. St. Matthew's, the church where Hungarian kings were crowned, was Gothicized, while the elegant exteriors in the center of Pest were faithful to the style popular at the turn of the nineteenth century. In 1892, fourteen years after her marriage, on the twenty-fifth anniversary of Franz József's coronation as King of Hungary, Budapest was endowed with the formal title "Capital and Residence." Yes, Budapest was her beloved city, the Paris of the East, and while Austrians would dispute it, to Anna it was the first city of the empire, not the second. She regarded it as the first because it was peopled by Hungarians rather than Austrians. Hungarians, she believed, knew how to truly enjoy life, while Austrians seemed to know only how to imitate it. Most Hungarians had a real flair for living, though she considered her husband an exception. Most had a fine sense of humor, and certainly they were noted for their intellectual bent. Austrians, by contrast, had a deep Germanic precision—a preoccupation with method rather than substance. Yes, in Austria everyone had a role to play—a part, as it were. But if the script were suddenly changed, they could not seem to improvise. Pleased with her little analysis, she stopped to look in some shop windows, then continued on.

Anna Maria came to Museum Boulevard, on which the State Museum was located. She turned the corner and hurried along. A chill wind began to blow and she tried in vain to bury her face in the collar of her coat jacket. Silently she cursed herself for not bringing her warmer coat. Hurriedly she climbed the steps of the museum, and when the doorman opened the door, she rushed gratefully into the sheltered foyer of the cavernous building. She looked about for the little stand that held the brochures announcing the latest paintings and showings. They always had them; indeed, they usually had stacks of them.

She finally saw a stand in the corner and walked over and perused its offerings. One advertised boat trips down the Danube, and another was a guide to Castle Hill. Behind them, to her relief, was a neat pile titled "State Museum."

She took one and opened it, studying for a moment the latest museum news. It was printed in Hungarian, German, French, and English. Then she put it in her purse.

"Anna?"

She turned, startled, to face the male voice that spoke her name. Oh, he was older, but he was to her eyes no less dashing. And he stood straight and tall in his military uniform, his kind brown eyes twinkling with merriment. "József . . . Count Bodnar." By force of girlhood habit she half curtsied, and he took her gloved hand and kissed it.

"Oh, Anna. Such silly formalities. Let's leave it at 'József,' shall we?"

Her face was flushed crimson, she could feel it. She was as embarrassed and as excited now as she had been twenty-six years ago when they had waltzed together endlessly at the grand ball in the palace. "Oh, József, I don't know what to say. You're the last person in the world I expected to meet here. I thought you were in Vienna."

He took her arm and began to guide her across the room. There were people milling everywhere, but she felt as if they were quite alone. "Come, Anna, there's a tea room downstairs. Come join me for a cup of hot tea."

"Of course," she replied, feeling in a total trance. *Lead and I will follow*—had she said that to him years ago, or only thought it? Memories converged with daydreams, fantasy with reality.

And in seconds they were sitting across from one another and he had ordered and she could not take her eyes off him. It was all illusion, it had to be. But no, he was really here, and so was she. His hair had gone gray too, but it was still thick and wavy. His wonderful large dark eyes flickered with merriment, and physically he was as trim and slim as a man ten or fifteen years younger. This man had a wonderful face! His jaw was square, which gave him a look of strength, his nose was very straight and well-shaped, and his mouth was wide. When he smiled, it was with true happiness rather than out of habit.

"I left Vienna some months ago. I live here now. And you, Anna? Where do you live? Here in Budapest, I hope."

She shook herself out of thought, "No. I live outside the capital . . . a day's journey in fact. We have an estate near Kassa."

He smiled warmly. "I've forgotten your husband's name."

"Ferenc Szilard."

"And are there little Szilards?"

"Not so little anymore. I have three sons and a daughter. My daughter is the youngest and she is sixteen."

"Oh, that can't be! Anna, you don't look a day older."

Again her face flushed. "I do, but you *are* kind."

"Well, I like you a little older. But you are no less beautiful. I wanted to marry you, you know. I thought you were the most beautiful woman in all Budapest."

Anna felt her heart skip a beat. Was he telling the truth? Had he really loved her? She looked at her steaming tea but was afraid if she picked up the cup her hand would shake and she would spill it. "I'm flattered," she murmured.

"I mean it. Of course, I had family obligations. We all did. I married the woman my father picked out, and it didn't work out so badly." He paused, then added, "My wife is dead now. I'm not as fortunate as you. I have no children."

Anna slowly lifted her eyes and looked into his. She felt suddenly like crying. She wanted to say, "I'd have given you children"—or did she want to shriek at the sins of their fathers . . . forced, *forced* . . . She felt a strange mixture of exuberance and joy at suddenly finding this man again . . . and she felt miserable too. Miserable for wasted years, empty years. "József . . ." She said his name softly.

"Yes?"

He leaned over the table toward her and suddenly covered her hand with his. "József, I think I wanted to marry you too." The words escaped her mouth like a confession . . . what was she saying? No woman should be so open with any man. He would probably laugh at her.

But he did not laugh. He only looked at her with sad eyes, as if he too felt the sting of the injustice done to them as young lovers. "Life is not always happy, Anna. Tell me, do you come to Budapest often?"

"When Ferenc has business, then we come. Sometimes once every two months."

He scribbled a number on the corner of his napkin. "This is my number. Anna, call me when you come to town. Call me and we can have lunch. I would spend this whole afternoon with you, but I have an important meeting. One I simply cannot cancel on such short notice. But please, please call me. I don't want to lose you again, you must believe that. Even if we are only friends, I must see you again."

She nodded and then pressed his hand. "I will, I promise."

She watched him as he left, and only after twenty minutes when her tea was quite cold was her hand steady enough to hold the fragile teacup. Her mind had been swept back across the years and she sat sipping the cold tea and remembering every second of the time she had known Count József Bodnar.

2

June 1903

Spring seemed to burst on Budapest. The hillsides were a new yellow-green and the early-blooming flowers—daffodils, tulips, and irises—filled the city's many parks with color. Everywhere there seemed to be young women pushing perambulators, and everywhere it seemed that immaculate children dressed in white chased hoops with sticks, jumped rope, or played other games while their nursemaids looked on indulgently or chattered among themselves.

It was an early spring, a welcome spring after a terribly long, dull winter. Ferenc Szilard walked briskly and inhaled deeply of the warm spring air, and mentally he assessed himself, taking stock after yet another difficult year.

I have too much pride, he thought silently. And certainly I have trouble expressing myself. If he were not a prideful man, he would not have spent so much on the education of his sons. But all his friends spent on their children—it was expected, and he had been able to do no less, even though it had meant more debt. And if he were not proud of his beautiful wife, he would stop her from spending so much on clothes. But he *was* prideful and he wanted her to be dressed as well as other women. Anna, he reflected, *was* beautiful and he did love her. Over and over he told himself that she had grown to love him too. Oh, she was not demonstrative, and he knew she harbored silly girlish daydreams of a count who had once courted her, but that, he supposed, was the way all women were. When he made love to her, he was capable of making her respond. And though she always resisted at first, she eventually allowed her sensations to rule her, and at such moments she became exciting, a wild lovely animal in the dark of night.

But how could he talk to her? How could he make her understand his distractions, his temper, his terrible, terrible worries? The answer was simple. He could not. He could only go on pretending. He pretended to Anna, to the children, to his servants—he pretended to everyone, and he covered his emotions with a kind of gruffness and a calculated coldness.

He shook his head wearily. He thought of all those old women who lived in rooms in the older hotels of the city. They were the destitute widows of penniless members of the aristocracy, or sometimes the daughters who had never married. They kept to themselves, living on meager amounts of money, on charity. But when they went shopping they hired some young girl to walk behind them with a basket so their peers would believe they still had enough to employ a maid. It was all a facade. And the way he lived was a facade too.

Inexplicably, on this lovely summer morning his eyes filled with tears as he crossed the park and walked toward Budapest's Tenth District. He should have taken a cab . . . but no, he actually felt like walking, as if by walking he could exorcise his devils and dispel them in the spring sunshine. But why, suddenly, did he feel his eyes grow moist and his heart full? Perhaps because it was spring and everything seemed so alive, so new, so innocent. "It is the season of new beginnings," he said aloud to himself. And he thought silently that it might really be a new beginning for him if only all the many pieces would fall into place and he could pull it all off. Then, God willing, he could pay all his debts and retain his honor. Then he could support his family without worry, and even, he contemplated, afford to take Anna on a trip. His mind jumped—not just a trip to Vienna, but one to Paris or even England. God, perhaps they could sail the Greek isles or sun themselves at a wonderful resort on the Black Sea. He turned the corner and was suddenly aware of a change of scene. The parks of Pest had been left behind and he had entered an industrialized area—streets of factories and warehouses, a slightly depressing street without children, nursemaids, grass, or flowers. Still, to Ferenc it was quite a beautiful neighborhood. It was a place that offered a new beginning.

He passed the Budai Goldberger Factory. It was world-famous as the inventor and manufacturer of a fabric best described as artificial silk and called Bemberg. The four-story building he approached looked like all the surrounding factories. Its architecture was drab, and inside, its walls were bare and unfinished. Beyond the wide front doors a large foyer was equipped with ten time clocks, and beneath each, in strict alphabetical order, were cards standing upright in long tall metal frames. He stared at the strange machines and saw on the bottom of one a small brass plate that gave the patent date as 1887. They were American machines, imported, no doubt, by the owner. He made a mental note to ask about them.

Ferenc pulled down his suit jacket and brushed himself off, then knocked on the door of Otto Fodor, the owner and manager.

Two hours later, Ferenc again found himself in the foyer among the clocks. Next to him Otto Fodor paused to light another fat cigar. He was a short man with a round belly, a fringe of white hair, and wire glasses.

"Yes, a quite wonderful invention," Otto proclaimed, waving his cigar at the clocks. "At seven o'clock each morning the foyer is filled with girls and women, each of whom inserts her card into the clock, which stamps it with the exact time. At seven each evening the process is repeated. In and out, in and out. We pay by the hour. No longer do we pay by the piece. But because of my fine clocks, there are no arguments. There is an exact record of how many hours and how many minutes are spent at work."

"The Americans think of everything," Ferenc said. The two men had just completed a tour of the factory, and the clocks all read ten o'clock. On the top floor Ferenc had seen the pattern and cutting rooms, on the third floor the sewing machines—rows and rows of them clacking in near-unison and operated by what appeared a hundred identical women in poor clothing with hair hidden beneath scarves. On the second floor there were finishing rooms, and on the ground floor the packing area. From the rear of the building large packs were allowed to slide down metal ramps under which large wagons were parked to receive the goods. The wagons then clattered off to have their contents loaded onto barges to be shipped on the river, or taken to the railway if they were going south.

"The work is endless and the profit sound," Otto Fodor informed him. "But don't take just my word. Come into my office and let's look at the figures. This is the largest uniform factory in the empire—we get all the best contracts." He turned to face Ferenc. "You know why? We get them because we are an honorable firm. We stand behind our work."

"Of course. Honor is the key to success," Ferenc said sincerely. "My family is known for its honor, its loyalty."

"That," said Otto Fodor, "is honor to God and country. It is good, very good. All you must do is transfer the feeling to product. Strict fulfillment of contracts, good materials, guarantees . . . and of course mass production—that, Mr. Szilard, is what makes profits."

They entered Otto Fodor's office. It was a large airy room, and unlike the others, it was quite finished, with dark paneled walls and comfortable upholstered furniture. Fodor settled behind a wide desk and withdrew a sheaf of paper. "I've had all the figures copied for you. Don't take my word for anything. Study them yourself, and study our future orders. Mind you, that is something that takes work. You have to give time to it, you have to entertain the right people, even get to know the quartermasters personally."

Ferenc smiled. "I have a son in the army and two at university. One, Béla, is quite an outgoing fellow. He's not so good at his studies, but I think he might do well with potential customers."

"Would that I had had sons. If I'd had sons, I would not be selling this business."

"And why *are* you selling it? You are not an old man."

"Not old, but quite rich enough. It's my wife. She's not a well woman. We're emigrating to the United States. I'm taking her west to a place called Arizona. It's supposed to be healthful there, very good for those with breathing difficulties. And who knows, I might even work. Two German Jews—perhaps you have heard of them—Levi and Strauss, have made a fortune in the West selling work pants that have the seams welded together instead of sewn . . . an ingenious idea, what? Something special for the cowboys."

Ferenc nodded even as he studied some of the papers. It all seemed in order, but he needed a bookkeeper. Perhaps the bookkeeper who worked for Count Horvath would have a look at them. He was a Jew, but Jews had a mind for such things. Yes, he would ask Count Horvath if he could borrow young Miklós for a few days. After all, the time was coming when he would have to confide his plans to Horvath in any case.

"Well, what do you think?"

"I think I should like to take these home and study them."

"Fine. I wouldn't expect you to make a snap decision. But I wouldn't wait too long."

Ferenc knew this game. He did not ask if there was another potential buyer, indeed he forced himself to look uninterested. "Only long enough to make a sound decision," he said firmly, then added, "and if another buyer appears, then that is my hard luck."

Otto Fodor smiled and patted his oversize stomach. "It would be, yes," he replied, "because my price is very fair indeed."

3

Even though Count Horvath's youngest son, András, was only twenty-two, Count Horvath himself was older than Ferenc Szilard by eighteen years.

The count had been married twice and widowed twice. His two sons, one by his first wife and one by his second, were separated in age by ten years.

The count, now over seventy, was well-settled into his country life and he gave every appearance of being in semi-retirement, away from, and uncaring about, matters of state or matters of money. But appearances were deceiving. Ferenc knew full well that beneath Count Horvath's relaxed demeanor there was a quite active, yea, shrewd mind at work. More than once since he had received his inheritance, Ferenc had wished his own father had been more like his neighbor the count. Many years ago the count had foreseen the changing times that lay ahead and had begun to diversify his family's financial interests. Some, but by no means all, of the family lands had been sold and the money invested in factories. Moreover, the count had had the foresight to provide his own packaging and distribution system for the major agricultural output of his lands. He owned acres of land near Budapest on which he grew the sweet peppers from which paprika was made. His fields of peppers were harvested and sent directly to the Bodnar plant in Budapest. There the peppers were ground and the resulting spice was dried, packaged, and sent all over the world. Count Horvath's interests were managed by others and overseen by his elder son, Janos. A gentleman of Count Horvath's generation did not dirty his hands too much with business.

Sitting now in the drawing room of the Horvath family home, Ferenc felt a mild wave of jealousy. If for nothing else, he was jealous of the count's peace of mind, a peace of mind that only financial security could bring.

Ferenc sat in a great blue velvet chair, a glass of sherry on the marble table beside him. The count, dressed in a rich brocade smoking jacket, leaned against the mantel of the oversize stone fireplace, his pipe clenched firmly between his teeth. In the hearth, a small fire crackled, taking the spring dampness out of the air. Summer might well appear during the day, but the nights were still cool and often damp if a fog embraced the rivers that watered the valley.

"It will be a difficult move," Ferenc allowed, "but in the end it will be for the best."

"Miklós has been over the books. He says the company is sound," Count Horvath revealed.

"Jews know about these things," Ferenc allowed.

"Oh, he is quite the best bookkeeper I've ever had. He collects the rents judiciously, pays the bills, and guards every cent as if it were his own." The count laughed under his breath. "And as he collects the rents, the peasants hate him instead of me. It is a good arrangement."

Ferenc laughed at the count's little joke. Then he frowned. "You didn't tell him too much, did you? I wouldn't want rumors started before I'm ready to make my move."

"I was the soul of discretion, my friend. I only told him

a friend was interested in the company and wanted to know if it was sound. He examined everything and told me it appeared to be a very good buy."

"If the firm is sound, there is nothing stopping me from making a down payment." Ferenc rubbed his chin thoughtfully.

"Have you a timetable?"

Ferenc nodded. "I will make all four payments over the course of this year and take over the factory completely one year hence."

"And is your financing arranged?"

Ferenc shook his head. "I have the money for the down payment, but it will be difficult indeed to find a buyer for the estate, or even for parts of it. I am land rich and cash poor."

The count smiled but did not comment.

Ferenc moved uneasily in his chair. The down payment was money originally put aside for Margaret's dowry, and he felt more than a little guilty about having appropriated it. Still, he intended to see his daughter married before he uprooted the rest of the family and moved them to Budapest.

"And when this is all arranged, you will move your family to the capital?" Count Horvath asked as if he had read Ferenc's thoughts.

"Yes. But I hope to see Margaret married first. She'll be seventeen this October. If she were married in November, she could remain with her husband rather than moving with the rest of us."

The count lifted his sherry off the mantel and sipped it. He could sense what was coming next. "And is there a husband on the horizon?" he asked carefully.

Ferenc smiled. "I've always thought that Margaret and András would make a stunning couple."

"Indeed," the count agreed. "But there is the question of a dowry. Ferenc, your financial condition is no secret to me. Besides what you have already told me, I know what debts your father left you with. And I know that when your mother-in-law died last year you even had to sell her jewelry. Now I suspect you intend to use your daughter's dowry to make a new start in life. God knows, I understand why."

"You would forgo a dowry?" Ferenc asked.

"I would consider it. And frankly, if we can come to the right agreement, I might even consider buying your estate, house and all."

"That would be most generous of you, most generous indeed. I'm certain Margaret would make András a good wife. She's most accomplished at the piano and she paints and sews as well."

"Not András," the count said, looking Ferenc in the eye. "András is a fine-looking man, he has a commission in the army, and the woman who comes to him must come with a dowry. But I would consider a wife for Janos without a dowry. He is, after all, a cripple."

Ferenc stared at the count for a long moment. The old man was as shrewd as ever, and still prepared to drive a hard bargain. He thought of Janos—certainly not the husband Margaret would want, and not even the husband he wanted for her. Janos was not only crippled, but older as well. Of course, the man was always older. Did his being crippled make that much difference? Janos was the elder son and would inherit the bulk of the estate. Janos was also the brighter of the two. Margaret would be upset at first, but in time, he thought, she would come to see the wisdom of his decision. "Then let us draw up a contract," Ferenc said slowly. "I accept Janos and you forfeit a dowry and agree to purchase the estate."

The count finished his sherry and nodded. "It is done," he said with finality.

Ferenc nodded and the two of them shook hands.

"When shall this be announced?" the count asked as he lifted the bottle of sherry and refilled their glasses.

"Not until her birthday in the fall," Ferenc replied.

The count lifted his glass. "To the betrothal of our children."

Ferenc repeated the words and tried to concentrate on what this arrangement really meant. His sons would have security, and Anna would be in her beloved Budapest at last. There would be money to pay off everyone, and money to travel with. . . . He loved Margaret, but he forced thoughts of her objections from his mind. She was a dutiful daughter, and after all, she too would be rich. Janos could buy her everything she wanted.

4

September 1903

Again the long summer days had begun to shorten, and now the gentle winds that began to blow out of the north were a harbinger of the winter to come. But for Anna, winter no longer held any meaning. Emotionally she was living an eternal spring.

Anna sat on the edge of Margaret's canopied bed and studied her own image in the full-length mirror across the room. Her ankles, she noted with relief, were still trim, and her hair, while streaked with gray, looked rather distinguished, especially as her complexion retained a youthful glow. It is because I'm happy, she thought. Sheer joy has restored me. Indeed, happiness was not the only emotion she felt. Her happiness was tempered by fear, and even, she was surprised to discover, a little guilt.

Since their chance meeting in the art museum, Anna had been seeing Count József Bodnar on a regular basis. Each time she and Ferenc went to Budapest, she and József met. Of late, she and Ferenc had been traveling monthly to the capital, and much to her joy, whatever business Ferenc had there kept him more occupied than ever. She was left alone for several days at a time, seeing him only for breakfast and dinner. On several occasions he had suggested she might want to remain home because she would be bored. But she had answered that she could never be bored in Budapest, and so he continued to take her on his increasingly frequent visits to the twin cities.

Bored! If only he knew. As soon as he was safely off for his day of mysterious business, she was off to József's.

Oh, at first it had been innocent enough. They had lunched and toured the city, they had talked and renewed their friendship, and they had gone to galleries, exhibits, and bookstores together. One warm summer day they had even gone to Margaret Island and taken a wonderful picnic to eat under the trees near where the water lapped against the grass-green shore and the ducks waddled about begging for crumbs. But gradually their relationship became more than two old friends enjoying one another's company. József was lonely and she was discontented, their old attraction grew into an intimacy neither could resist, and Anna and her long-lost count become lovers, stealing time but feeling that in truth it belonged to them. Oh, and their love was beautiful! She no longer thought of "men's needs," nor did she find it necessary to make love in the darkness. With József her inhibitions fled like ducks in the blind with the first shot of the hunter's rifle. And to József she confided everything, even her former inhibitions. There is an old saying, he told her: "One man's virgin is another man's whore." It was true. For Ferenc she was a virgin who shrank from his touch. But for József she was a whore—wild and young again, free with her kisses and her body, and adoring his touch.

But if Ferenc noticed anything, it was the fact that she now rarely shopped. He seemed puzzled that she was content to visit the fashion salons and not buy anything, but he could not complain, because he had formerly complained that she asked for too much money and that her wardrobe was already extensive. Of course, she did not really visit the salons. She visited the count instead.

Much to her surprise, on this trip Ferenc had given her money without even being asked. Indeed, he had told her to buy a dress for herself and one for Margaret. "To wear to Count Horvath's, Anna. And make certain that Margaret's dress is not childish. She is a woman now, a woman of marriageable age."

That was it, of course. Anna immediately saw through her husband's generosity. Ferenc was trying to arrange a marriage for Margaret to András, the count's younger son. Well, she did not object. András was good-looking, had a commission, and would certainly inherit something from his aging father. It was true that Margaret's dowry was not as large as it might have been, but it was still substantial, and given Margaret's good looks, it should be more than enough to placate the already wealthy Count Horvath.

Anna glanced toward the dressing room just off Margaret's bedroom. "Are you having difficulty with the gown?" Anna called out.

"No. I'll only be a minute more," Margaret answered.

Anna smiled at herself in the mirror once again. She was anxious to see the gown she had chosen modeled. It was, she knew, a far cry from the innocent dress she had bought her daughter last year. But then, Margaret was older now, and moreover, fashions had become somewhat bolder.

Margaret waltzed out of the dressing room and Anna sighed indulgently. In keeping with the latest vogue, she had chosen an embroidered brocade in the new bright emerald green. The back of the gown was open to the waist, and the skirt was split almost to the knee for dancing. It was the height of style, but it was also daring. "You look wonderful!" Anna exclaimed. "It will look better when you're wearing your satin slippers and the proper stockings."

Margaret lifted her hair. "What do you think?"

"In Budapest hair is being dressed higher on the crown, with soft curls falling around the face. I saw wonderful hair decorations, wired feathers fastened to velvet or jeweled bandeaux . . . I think I could make one, you know."

"Could you?"

"Yes, I'm certain I could."

"Did you bring me the fashion magazines I asked for?"

Anna smiled. "Oh, yes. I smuggled them into my luggage. I don't know why your father won't let you come to Budapest too. I suppose he thinks you would want to buy everything."

"He wouldn't let me."

"He doesn't understand. But it pleases me that you care so much for style."

Margaret gathered in her skirt and sat down on the edge of the bed next to her mother. Care for style, for fashion? Her mother didn't know her at all! If asked how she preferred to spend time, she would have answered that her first preference was to be with Miklós. Her second was riding her horse, but her third was to study fashions; to make clothes for her dolls, to draw, to design dresses. But she knew that even though she and Miklós had met secretly for a year, their friendship had to remain a secret. Her mother never understood about her horse, so she finally said, "I enjoy sketching clothes most." Then added, "I want to try to make a pattern and sew a gown. Mama, could I use some of the material from the dresses in Grandmama's trunk? If it's not used, the fabric will rot."

Anna reached across the distance between them and stroked her beautiful daughter's hair. "I can't see why not."

"I can hardly wait for the count's party." In her thoughts Margaret imagined Miklós. He might not be at the party, but he might be somewhere in the house. She remembered that last year he had been sent away. But if he was there she vowed to find him so he could see her in her gown. Perhaps, she fantasized, he would then make some move to carry their relationship beyond friendship.

But Anna could not read her daughter's mind and so she thought Margaret was looking forward to seeing András again. That was good. She hoped and prayed that Margaret's would not be a loveless marriage.

Four

1

October 10, 1903

Count Horvath's annual Harvest Ball was virtually the only real social event in the entire district, and owing to the count's personal charm and great wealth, it often drew guests from as far away as Vienna. In the past Anna had looked forward to it and relished making her preparations to attend. But this year neither the ball nor the rare opportunity to socialize interested her. All her enthusiasm was directed toward her trips to Budapest and to being with József.

Anna sat at the dressing table in her pink boudoir and brushed her long hair. Freed from its prison of combs and pins, it fell nearly to her waist. She wore a new nightdress, purchased with the money left from her ball gown. Not surprisingly, she had now developed an interest in the newest and most provocative undergarments: soft lacy camisoles with fine ribbon straps and French knickers with frilled legs. This nightdress was in the Empire style. It gathered directly beneath her full breasts and fell in soft transparent folds to the floor. It was a stark white, and where it was gathered, at the sleeves and around its neck, a thin blue ribbon was woven in and out of eyelet trim. She would take it to Budapest on her next trip, but tonight she wore it simply to see how it looked, and as she gazed at herself, she decided it looked delicious.

"Anna."

Anna jumped as Ferenc opened the door and strode toward her. She had not expected him, indeed she had left him locked in private conversation with Count Horvath downstairs.

"I didn't expect you," she said coldly, and she was aware of feeling suddenly angry. She had intended this nightdress for József's eyes only; now Ferenc was looking at her, and his eyes were filled with lust and anticipation.

"How lovely you look," he said, walking toward her.

She wanted to move, to put something between them, but she sat frozen. Even she had to admit that over the last year he had been less demanding of her favors, and this she attributed to his increased involvement with his mysterious business. Since he came to her so seldom, what excuse did she have for refusing? But she did not want his attentions tonight, and she especially didn't want them while she was wearing this special gown. He stood behind her now, his image filling her mirror. His large hand slithered round the back of her neck, and his blunt fingers played with her ear. She fought not to pull away, fought to keep her voice even. "How was the count?" she asked; then, "Is everything ready for next Saturday?" He had told her nothing yet, but he would not be surprised that she would guess he was arranging for Margaret's engagement to András.

"That's what I've come to talk to you about," he replied.

Somehow she had broken the spell and she felt relieved. He moved his hand off her neck, walked a few feet away, and then pulled up a straight-backed chair, straddling it so that he was facing her back and sitting only a few feet away.

"You look very serious," she observed, turning slightly on the bench before her vanity so their eyes could meet in reality rather than in the mirror.

"There are announcements to be made," he said evenly.

"Announcements?"

"On several matters. After some thought I've decided to speak with you now rather than shock or surprise you."

Yes, she was entirely right. Ferenc had arranged Margaret's engagement to András. He and the count were going to announce the betrothal at the ball. She smiled. "Go on."

"I'm selling the estate to Count Horvath. We'll be moving to Budapest."

His words so stunned her that she suddenly stood up, her fingers curled around her nightdress. Conflicting responses filled her mind, and for a long moment all she could do was stare at him in disbelief. Finally her only response was to repeat his words as if she were translating them from a foreign tongue. "Sell the estate?"

"Certainly you're not upset. You always hated the isolation and you always loved the city."

What he said was all true, and of course now she would be closer to her lover . . . but move? It seemed a tremendous step. Nearly everything about their lives would change. "Where will we live?" she blurted out.

"In a fine apartment I've rented. There won't be room for all the furniture, but we'll auction some of it off and put some things in storage. I've bought a business, Anna, a factory."

Her husband was going into business? An apartment? She felt as if she were caught in a maelstrom. "What about the children?"

He actually laughed, though she knew she must somehow have sounded stricken.

"Hardly children. Well, I've spoken with each of the boys. György will remain in the army. Béla and Konrad will go into business with me."

"But they're in university," she protested.

"Béla is a bad student and Konrad hates what he studies. I have given them an ultimatum, but frankly there's no more money to waste on their education. I've put everything into this—everything."

"And Margaret?"

"Will not be going with us. She'll be marrying Janos Horvath. It's all arranged."

Anna's mouth opened and closed in a silent scream. Janos! But what of András? "Ferenc, what have you done?" she whispered as she felt her whole body begin to shake.

"I needed the dowry, Anna. I needed it desperately. We were in debt, and then of course the new business was costly. Count Horvath would not have waived the dowry for András, but because of Janos' affliction he agreed."

Anna succeeded in finding her tongue. "He's years older than Margaret! He's bad-tempered and ugly! Ferenc, what have you done to our daughter!"

"It was our only chance, Anna. Margaret will have a good life, a protected life. Janos will inherit everything—she'll be rich. And in time she will learn to love him, as you learned to love me."

Anna wanted to shriek that she didn't love him and never had. But to do so would be to risk being found out. Her head pounded. Margaret would be devastated. God, she might even try to kill herself. "She won't accept this," Anna murmured.

Ferenc looked across at her steadily. "I am the head of this household. She has no choice, nor do you. Honor, Anna . . . honor is an important concept. Our entire way of life is based on honor and on loyalty. As I am loyal to the emperor, my family is loyal to me. You were given over to me by your father. You promised to love, honor, and obey. I realize that Margaret will be unhappy at first, but she will adjust. Indeed, must adjust. Right now her head is probably filled with the silly girlish thoughts women are so prone to have. That's why men must make these decisions."

Anna studied his expression and knew that all this must have been arranged for months. She cursed her own blindness. Perhaps she could have stopped it earlier had she not been so involved with József. But how could she stop it now? Ferenc had given his word, the agreement had been made. And his duplicity! He had used Margaret's dowry without even discussing it with her. She pounced on that—it was her only weapon. "How could you use her dowry? We set it aside for her when she was born . . . it was my mother's money. How could you? And *you* dare speak of honor? You've stolen from your own child!"

Ferenc forced a neutral expression even though her words cut deeply. Of course she was angry, he had expected it. But he had not expected her to attack his honor or question his motives. God, why couldn't she understand? He felt tired, but he also felt angry that whatever he did, barriers appeared. Did Anna think he hadn't agonized over this decision? Did she think he didn't care about Margaret's future? From his vantage point he had done what had to be done; indeed it seemed the only thing he could do. Still, he wanted her to understand.

"Anna, I had no choice. I've never burdened you with our finances—except to curb your spending. I shielded you from our reality. Perhaps I shouldn't have, perhaps had you known the truth, you would realize that I've taken the only logical course."

"Surely there would have been enough money from the sale of the estate to buy your little business, surely you didn't have to use the dowry."

He shook his head. "Horvath is buying the estate—he wouldn't buy it if Janos and Margaret were not to marry. Frankly, Anna, I doubt I could find another buyer."

"I don't understand."

"I'm sure you don't. You were reared to spend money, not to think about it. Anna, you were the only daughter in a family of four. I was the youngest of seven boys. Neither of us inherited much except a dying way of life we really could no longer afford."

She stared at him and tried to understand his words. "But to go into . . . into business. It sounds so . . . so crass."

"One day there will be no landed gentry. Anna, we're a dying breed. I've done what I thought best for my sons and for my whole family. It's not as though I've condemned Margaret to a life of spinsterhood. I've provided for her, made an arrangement. Anna, Margaret will have money."

"She hates him."

"It's a childish dislike. She really doesn't know him. He's well-educated and a brilliant financier."

"You can't just spring this on her, she must be told, Ferenc."

"Yes, and you will tell her."

"Me! Oh, no. No, Ferenc I will not tell her. This is one thing I will not do. You cannot make me, either. You must tell her."

"You can better deal with her."

Anna shook her head. "No."

Ferenc stood up straight. "Then there is no point putting it off. I shall tell her now."

Anna opened her mouth to say something, but he had turned and walked to the door. He paused for a moment and looked at her. "Get into bed, I'll be back," he said firmly.

Anna stood for a moment, then turned out the light and hurried to her bed. She got in and pulled the covers up even as she heard the door to her daughter's bedroom next door open. She lay in the darkness and strained her ears. She could not hear what he was saying, but she could hear her husband's voice speaking slowly, deliberately, unemotionally. Then she heard Margaret scream. It was a long wailing shriek followed by another and then another. Ferenc was shouting and Margaret was screaming. Anna covered her ears and shook as tears ran down her face. It was twenty-six years ago and her father was telling her she would marry Ferenc . . . it was monstrous! Suddenly she heard the sound of Ferenc stomping across Margaret's room and she thought she heard him strike his daughter. Margaret's screaming stopped in mid-shriek and then deteriorated into violent sobbing.

Anna tossed on her stomach and held her hands again over her ears. She began reciting her rosary and she spoke the words over and over to close out the sounds she heard. But fear of her husband's wrath kept her from interfering.

2

October 11, 1903

Margaret had lain in bed and silently sobbed, only vaguely aware of the pain from the long red welt on the back of her legs where her father had struck her with his leather belt. She had cursed her father and he had reacted immediately and with great pent-up anger. For a time she had held out, but his violence petrified her and so she had given in to his demands that she say she would marry Janos, promise to marry him even though the words choked in her mouth and she silently denied them. "Yes, I'll marry Janos!" she had choked. After her father left, she had remained crouched by the chair for a long while; then, still sobbing, she had dragged herself to bed, where she continued crying till she could cry no more.

As the first rays of light broke in the east, Margaret tossed restlessly. She watched as the blackness of her room turned to dim light, and as the light grew brighter, she began to think, to realize that something must be done.

A plan . . . Oh, she must see Miklós immediately! She lay and waited for the full light of the sun to fill the sky, and when it came, she got up and hurriedly dressed. The sun was still an orange line on the dark horizon when she reached the stables and nuzzled the comforting dampness of Prince Stanislaus' warm nose. Then, using the pencil and paper she had brought with her, she wrote Miklós a note: "You must come" was all it said. She gave explicit instructions to one of the peasant boys to deliver it to Miklós at Count Horvath's house. Never before had she tried to write to him, but what harm could there be? she rationalized. The peasant couldn't read, and the note was not signed. Further, it named no place. But Miklós would know it was from her and he would know that since the days were still warm, he should meet her at the old chapel.

Margaret mounted Prince Stanislaus and winced in pain. Her father's well-aimed blow had fallen on tender skin and now it was swollen slightly, leaving a bright red line across the back of her thighs. But by some miracle, or perhaps by her father's design, it had not broken the skin. Still, it hurt terribly, and she felt humiliated and shocked by what had happened. Still, her father's temper was nothing next to the fact that she was to marry Janos Horvath. Somehow she must escape, and somehow she knew Miklós would help her.

Margaret waited by the old church till the sun was high in the sky. And finally, to her great relief, she heard the hoofbeats of a horse and the clatter of Miklós' buggy. Miklós appeared, his face pale and filled with apprehension.

"I came as soon as I could. Margaret, you must never do this again. I could get into terrible trouble," he began to admonish her as soon as he had secured the horse and buggy. But then he looked at her and she burst into tears anew and silently turned around and raised her dress.

"My God. Who did this to you?" he asked, his voice grim and full of indignation.

"My father." She took his hand and led him inside the old chapel to the corner where they usually studied.

"But why?" In his wildest dreams he could not imagine anyone beating her. She was so innocent, so sweet, and so terribly naive. Her father must be a monster, Miklós concluded.

"He has betrothed me to Janos Horvath, and I refused. I finally said I would marry Janos just so he would go away, but I won't. I'll die first, I'll die!" Margaret did not wait, she flew into his arms and pressed herself against him. "Run away with me, Miklós! Take me to America! I beg of you, please."

Confusion and desire began to war inside Miklós. But he fought them both off and began to try to reason with her in order to find a sensible solution to her terrible dilemma. "It is not so simple," he started to say.

Margaret looked up at him and firmly grasped his wrist, moving his hand to her breast. "I love you, Miklós. I've loved you from the moment we met." Her eyes were large and she seemed to be commanding him, asking him to make love to her.

His hand automatically closed around her breast, and to her joy, his eyes seemed almost glazed over. He simply could not reject her and she felt her growing power in the face of his obvious desire. He was like clay in her hands, that he wanted her was completely obvious. "Miklós, make love to me!" She slipped downward onto the blanket she had spread out, and pulled him with her.

"Margaret, you don't know what you're saying," he weakly protested, but she was pressing against him and he could smell her perfume. It was like a bouquet of spring flowers to his nostrils. He half-closed his eyes. She was a dream, a soft vision luring him to respond.

"I do, I do." Deliberately she moved her hand down to the place Irina, the maid, had told her men hid their breeding bone. She felt it hard and seemingly at attention and rubbed it gently.

"Margaret . . ." His voice sounded as if he were pleading, and his skin was flushed as if he had a fever. Then he moved his hand and groped at her clothing clumsily. He was breathing hard, like a runner after a race, and she had to help him undo the unseemly number of buttons, hooks, eyes, and ribbons that were part of her clothing. "Get the blanket from behind the saddle," she told him. It was cold and she shivered till he threw it to her and she covered her bare shoulders. She was naked to the waist, but she didn't feel embarrassed even though he touched her and finally fastened on one of her breasts with his mouth. Like a hungry child he sucked, and she wriggled, because it made her feel good.

"Oh, God help me," he whispered just as he undid her skirts and pulled them away to reveal her white legs. Tenderly he touched the red mark on her thighs and whispered, "Monster." At the same time the sight of the belt mark on her legs heightened his own fears. What would such a man do to him if this act were discovered?

But she was touching him in a way that made it impossible for him to think of anything but possessing her.

His resolve had completely melted. She was the most beautiful of all women. He covered her breasts with his hands and gently nudged her legs apart with his own leg. Then, without further preparation, he entered her and she made a small noise.

"It hurts," Margaret whimpered.

"It won't . . . soon it will feel good," he assured her. But he was again confused. She had brazenly grabbed his member and touched him as if she were experienced. He now realized she was not. The realization made him feel even more terrible.

"Oh," she groaned beneath him, and he began to caress her even as he moved inside her. Then, unable to stand her sensuous sounds and movements for another second, he burst forth.

"Oh, God!" She gripped him fast and hard, as if she too were suddenly enjoying it, and in a moment they collapsed together and he pulled the coarse blanket around them.

For almost an hour they lay on the floor pressed together, wrapped tightly in the blanket like twin caterpillars in a single cocoon. They slept lightly, but when Miklós woke up, he was gripped with cold fear, and the moving of his body woke her too. She smiled at him innocently, trustingly. "Oh, Miklós, we'll be so happy in America!"

"We don't have enough money for the fares," he said, trying to reintroduce some reality into the situation.

"I'll sell my grandmother's ring . . . Miklós, we can be together always."

For a while she was absolutely silent, then asked, "When will we go to America?"

"I have to get things in order," he told her. "There are papers to get, and documents to file." Why was he talking this way? She had drawn him in, made it imperative that he consider leaving.

"Papa will want the wedding soon, Miklós. He won't waste a second marrying me off to Janos. We must hurry."

He nodded silently and tried desperately to think. But all he could think of was the retribution that would take place if it were discovered that he, a Jew, had deflowered his employer's fiancée after her betrothal. They would somehow get her to say it was rape and he could go to prison or perhaps be hanged. A thousand thoughts clung to the edges of his mind. Oh, she was beautiful and he did care, but how could he get her to America? How could he even get her to someplace where they would be safe? Wherever they went, they would be noticed because of her beauty and youth. And her father would look for her, just as her financé might. Janos Horvath was someone to be reckoned with—that he already knew. "I am mad," he said aloud, "mad to have done this with you."

"No. It's all right because we love each other." Margaret nestled in his arms and sniffed back more tears. Miklós would save her from Janos. Of that she was certain.

"I'll have to go back to the estate," Miklós said. "I must make some plans. Margaret, you must not write to me again—do you understand?"

"Yes, but it will be difficult."

"You'll have to go through with the engagement announcement. We can't possibly leave till afterward."

"When can we?"

"I'll take a few days off, perhaps even the day of the ball. I'll go to Budapest and see what I can find out."

"Do you want to sell my ring?"

"No, you keep it for now. I'll come back and then we'll make plans."

He forced a smile and then kissed her. "I'll be back before you have to marry Janos. I love you, Margaret. You are beautiful and I love you."

He kissed her tenderly and felt warm as she returned his kiss. "Remember, don't try to write to me."

She nodded and he edged away from the temptation of her body. "We must get dressed now," he stated.

Together they dressed and then he kissed her again

and watched as she rode across the plain toward her estate.

"Damn," he said under his breath. He hadn't intended to leave the count's employment quite so soon, but what choice did he have now?

3

October 15, 1903

My darling,

I have gone to Budapest to make arrangements and will return within two weeks. Don't worry, all will be well.

Margaret had found the note in the old chapel, and though Miklós had not signed it for reasons of safety, she knew full well it was for her. He did love her and he would come for her, and together they would run away to America! That knowledge filled her with joy and enabled her to playact her role as dutiful, if reluctant, daughter. In her parents' eyes she had solemnly accepted her fate, though she made no move to reconcile with them.

Indeed, since the night her father had beaten her she had said nothing to either of her parents save to answer their questions with either a cold yes or a cold no. Her mother seemed to beg forgiveness with her eyes, but Margaret showed her nothing but disdain. She had, after all, lain awake all night after her father had struck her. And much to her chagrin, she had heard her parents making love. Or, more to the point, she heard the bed squeaking and her mother moaning. Her mother could not have made love with her father unless they had agreed on her marriage contract, she decided. Thus, in her thoughts, Margaret blamed her mother as much as her father for what had happened. Her mother, she reasoned, must have approved of her father's action, and certainly her mother must have approved of Janos.

György and Konnie, the only ones in whom she might have confided, were in Budapest. Béla had returned home unexpectedly, but she would say nothing to him. In any case, he already knew about the betrothal from her father and had already begun taunting her. "Janos," he told her, "would teach her how to be a woman." Yes, Béla leered at her and made horrible comments. He was trying to frighten her, and had it not been for Miklós, she would truly have been frightened. As it was, she would get through dinner, through the ball that followed, and she would survive the announcement of her betrothal. Margaret was determined to pretend she accepted it all in order to fool Béla and her parents. Then, she reasoned, when she ran away, it would be a real shock.

Margaret's long blond hair was piled high on her head and she wore her new gown, her dancing slippers, and carried a brightly colored silk fan. Her mother had indeed managed to make a hair decoration and Margaret was pleased that the wired feather matched her silk fan. If only Miklós could see her in this dress, he would love her all the more!

"Ah, there you are, Margaret. I'd hoped to find you alone." Margaret was in the sitting room of their home, the house she had grown up in, the house that would soon be sold. Vaguely she wondered what would happen to the portraits of her dead ancestors that hung in the hall.

She looked up when her father came in. He was fashionably attired in black and wore a white silk neck scarf.

She looked up to acknowledge his presence, but she said nothing.

He shifted uneasily before her. "I want to say"—he paused and looked about, then carried on—"that I'm sorry for what happened the other night. But you defied me and angered me. I will not be defied, Margaret."

She narrowed her blue eyes and pressed her lips together. "If I am forced to marry Janos, I will be the most horrible wife imaginable. He will hate you every day of his life. As for me, I hate you now. Hate you, do you understand? You no longer exist for me." With that she turned to leave, and only stopped when her father spoke her name harshly.

"Margaret!"

Margaret turned and again faced him, though she averted her eyes and fastened them on the patterned Persian rug. How she wanted to spit in his face! How she wanted to leave this place and never see him again.

"You will not cause a scene tonight," he commanded.

"I will say only 'yes' or 'no,' " she responded. Then she added, "Don't worry, you will get your way." Mentally she added, "tonight only." She and Miklós could, she thought, be in Vienna in a matter of hours, probably before their disappearance was even discovered. Then they would leave immediately for a German port.

"I'm sorry you will hate me, Margaret. I did the best I could. It's not easy to know just what to do sometimes. I do, after all, have the whole family to consider."

She and Miklós would sail at dawn on a foggy November morning, and together they would stand on deck and watch as the German shore grew farther and farther away and America grew ever closer. Margaret closed her ears to her father, but he continued talking.

"After all, you are not the only one to be uprooted. Béla and Konrad will have to give up school and go into the business with me. Your mother will have to learn to live in an apartment."

She and Miklós would sleep in one another's arms till one morning when they would be summoned to deck. There, out of the fog and mist they would see the skyline of New York. What an adventure! If she had one regret, it was that Prince Stanislaus could not come.

"Giving up her house and living in an apartment, no matter how fine, will be difficult for her. Margaret, are you listening to me?" her father asked with irritation.

"No," she answered.

"You're childish and selfish."

Margaret lifted her skirt and walked from the room without a further word. She could endure anything as long as she knew Miklós was coming back for her. She surrounded herself with dreams and held them close like a blanket to keep her mind from the cold reality of her father's words and her mother's looks. Yes, she would miss Prince Stanislaus and she would miss György and Konnie. But she would not miss Béla or her parents one tiny bit. The three of them, she thought angrily, could go to hell.

4

Count Horvath's home was an expansive stone structure in the Gothic style so favored by the ruling classes. It had towers and turrets. Along its upper balconies grotesque gargoyles protruded outward, while inside, every fireplace featured plump carved cherubs on its heavy mantel. The floor-to-ceiling windows were heavily draped, and because this pseudo-castle was set among massive trees, it seemed the builders and decorators had conspired to keep out the sunlight, thus banishing all cheer from the interior.

The entranceway was a set of carved double doors that led into a wide dark hallway off which was a large and sparsely furnished reception room. The hallway was lined with busts of the count's illustrious ancestors, while the reception-room walls were covered with heavy tapestries. Other than a large credenza there were a few small marble-topped tables, two sofas, each covered in dark velvet, and a gentleman's chair standing alone in one corner. Still, the furniture was lost in the huge room, which had neither warmth nor charm.

To the other side of the hall there were a dressing room, a library, and a massive dining room. A great kitchen lay across the back of the house. To the sides and out back, beyond the kitchen, there were acres of formal gardens containing a huge gazebo, several smaller gazebos, and statuary from several periods.

It was in the reception room that the ball was held. And it was from a podium at the front of the room that Count Horvath announced Margaret's engagement to Janos. His words sent a gasp of seeming disbelief through the gathered guests, while Margaret herself stood stock-still, embarrassed by what seemed the sympathetic stares of the onlookers. At the same time, the count announced the purchase of the Szilard property and made reference to the fact that her family was moving to Budapest.

When Count Horvath stepped down and the orchestra again began to play, Janos made his way toward her.

"We'll walk in the garden," Janos said, taking her arm and forcing a smile to those who stood nearby.

"It's too cold," Margaret protested.

"We'll stop and get your wrap." He took her arm and propelled her around toward the door. His fingers dug into her flesh and she shook him loose. In the hall a servant held out her wrap and Janos put on his own jacket. They walked through the library and out onto the side terrace. Above in the night sky the stars were bright and the full moon illuminated the garden paths. But it was cold. Margaret breathed deeply of the night air, and her breath, white, floated in front of her. Miklós had been gone two days and she imagined him in Budapest, staying with relatives or perhaps dining with friends to whom he wanted to say good-bye.

"I admire your ability to look absolutely joyless," Janos said to her when they were well away from the building and headed down the path toward the formal gardens.

"I am joyless," she replied.

"At least you're not a hypocrite. I couldn't stand it if you tried to pretend you liked me, or even found me attractive."

"Why would I do that?" Margaret asked without emotion. She resented his intrusion on her thoughts of Miklós.

He laughed. "So that people would think you weren't prejudiced against cripples."

"I'm not. Your being a cripple has nothing to do with it."

He laughed again. It was not a real laugh, it was a caustic laugh. "Ah, but I am ugly. And you, my beauty, are afraid of ugliness."

Margaret glanced at him. He was ugly, but she didn't think she was afraid of that. "I just don't love you," she said flatly.

"And do you love someone else?"

She wanted to shout "yes!" but caution warned her not to be honest this time. "No."

"Well, Margaret, I don't really want your love. I do want children, however. I want male heirs."

They had come to the gazebo and she climbed the steps and sat down on one of the little benches inside. It wasn't really that cold out and the garden was lovely. She could have enjoyed it if she had been alone. But Janos came and sat next to her, laying the cane he always used across one of the lawn chairs.

"I suppose I shall also enjoy your body the first few times. You're young and firm and well-built. I shan't be loyal to you, of course, it's not in my nature. On the other hand, if you stray I will beat you. I believe in being the master of my house, Margaret. I want you to understand that from the beginning. As long as you are well-behaved, we'll get along."

He was terrible! She said nothing for fear of saying too much. Beat her! No, she certainly wouldn't put it past him.

"We're being married November 1 in the chapel next to the church in Kassa. Did your father tell you?"

A chill ran through her. She had known it would be soon, but November 1? Would Miklós be back so soon? She felt suddenly unnerved and once again frightened. "November 1?"

He leered at her. "Yes, no need to wait." He leaned across her and quite suddenly moved his hand beneath her wrap, running it down her bare back while he held her tightly with his other arm.

She tried to squirm loose, but he was much stronger than she had assumed. He laughed, dipping his hand below the waistline of her low-backed dress and pinching the flesh on her buttocks. His breathing grew heavier as his hand moved roughly over her, and the more she tried to wrench herself loose, the tighter he held her. "Ah, yes. You are quite intriguing, really. I intend to enjoy our wedding night."

Margaret's face had turned crimson, and her flesh crawled at his very touch. "I hate you, let me go!" she hissed.

"Struggle, you little bitch! When we're married I'll teach you how to behave."

With all her strength she pushed him away and stood up. She cursed her hobbled skirt, which in spite of the slit for dancing was far too narrow. Finally she picked it up above her knees and began to run. Certainly he couldn't catch her; she knew she ran fast. Hot tears fell down her face. Her father had all but sold her to a sadist, and her mother had said nothing. Her own brother Béla knew full well what Janos was like and he had only looked amused. Konrad was horribly upset about having to leave school and work in a factory, so he was no help, and György was still away. Miklós was her only hope.

She reached the steps of the house and stopped for an instant, panting. Behind her, far behind, Janos limped across the lawn, slowly, using his cane for balance. He was not even trying to pursue her. He had frightened her and that was what he intended. She did not go up the steps, but rather round the house and headed for the stables.

Under a dim lantern hung on the wall, the stableboy slept. She jostled him awake and ordered a horse saddled. Dumbly he followed her instructions, and in moments she was headed across the fields toward home. In the open country, under the bright stars, there was a sense of freedom and gradually she allowed her horse to slow to a canter so she could calm down.

Margaret forced all thoughts of Janos from her mind and thought only of Miklós. Tomorrow, no doubt, he would get their papers and book their passage. Yes,

Miklós loved her and she loved him. And soon they would both be free in America.

5

October 18, 1903

Miklós paused at the top of the steep iron steps, then carefully stepped down and off the train. He moved to one side and stood for a moment looking about. People of all descriptions bustled past him down the long concrete platform that led into the cavernous high-ceilinged Sudbahnhof—the south station—which was the terminus for trains coming from the south and southeastern part of Europe.

Miklós had been in the last carriage and found he had to walk a fair distance before he was even under the cover of the great yellow glass dome that protected most of the platform from the elements. He began walking, slowly at first and then more rapidly as the cold wind cut through his jacket and he felt the first drops of the thin drizzle as it fell from the storm-laden skies. It was raining in Vienna; it always rained in Vienna in the fall, and indeed for most of the winter. Clutching his small carpet bag, he followed the crowd, feeling somewhat bewildered, ashamed, and totally alone.

All the languages of Europe seemed to assault his ears as he walked. Here an old man asked directions in Yiddish, there a child nagged its mother in German. A group of Hungarian schoolgirls giggled and made some comment about his clothes as he passed them. Two Rumanians paused for a smoke and talked about the economy, and he picked up snatches of French, Italian, and Russian as he moved slowly toward the station and beyond into the city that was said to be the very center of Europe.

Miklós paused and discreetly watched as two lovers kissed good-bye on an adjacent platform. He felt almost like crying as the question "What kind of man am I?" popped into his head once again, and once again fear, guilt, and rationalizations flooded his thoughts.

Miklós closed his eyes and clutched his bag so hard his knuckles turned white. He had been on his way back to Margaret; he had summoned his courage and had fully intended to run away with her, when fate intervened.

He had actually been on the train headed for Kassa when it was stopped and boarded by the police in a small village. "They're looking for a Jew who stole a great sum of money," a woman revealed in a loud voice. "No, for a Jew who kidnapped a child!" another man announced with authority. Rumors spread through the carriages of the train faster than the investigation could be carried out, and Miklós had actually begun to shake, he was so certain the police were seeking him. But they were not looking for him. Before they reached his carriage they arrested a young man who was indeed Jewish, and he was dragged from the train shrieking protests of his innocence while being viciously manhandled by the authorities. Miklós had stared out the window and heard the young man's protestations that he had been framed. He had seen the police cuff their prisoner's ears, then kick him hard in the groin. Guilty or innocent, the incident with the young man served to remind Miklós of his own reality. Here, in the provinces of the empire, justice for Jews was hard to come by in spite of the emperor's proclamations granting equality. Even in the cities of the empire one's fate often depended on the attitudes of one's jailers if one were arrested, especially if one were a nobody. There were, Miklós knew, Jews who were rich, intellectually prominent, or famous in the arts. They were "somebodies" and they were treated as gentiles. But Jewish nobodies were still subject to the age-old prejudices—prejudices the emperor could not change by decree. And of course one of the most common anti-Semitic accusations was that Jewish men were sex maniacs, all desirous of raping gentile women and children. It was the sort of accusation that could quickly gather an angry mob in any small community or guarantee ill treatment in the jails of a larger one. Miklós shivered at the thought. If he and Margaret were caught running away, he would be accused of raping and kidnapping her and poor Margaret would be made to testify against him. Janos or Margaret's father would bring him back to Kassa for trial, but of course he would not live long enough to be tried. And they *would* be caught, because they did not have sufficient money to run far enough fast enough. Even if they sold Margaret's ring, it would take time, and surely they would be caught.

Miklós had gotten off the train and, ill with apprehension, had returned to Budapest, where for two agonizing days he had contemplated his situation. Or had he? Perhaps he had really made up his mind when the young man had been dragged from the train.

All the way back to Budapest, he vowed he would return for Margaret. Then he vowed to think about it, and the more he thought about it, the more impossible it all seemed and the more he wavered. Then, as if running from himself, he had left Budapest and come to Vienna.

Round his waist and hidden in his money belt was his year's salary, which Count Horvath had given him when he'd told the count his mother was ill and that he had to leave. It was a goodly sum, but it was not enough to get him started in America. It was the fact that he could not leave for America right away that had brought him to Vienna. He felt safer here. It was far from Kassa and it was a bigger city.

Miklós opened his eyes. The lovers had gone and he was nearly alone on the platform. He felt damned. If he had gone back for Margaret, they would be hunted down. But after all, when he did not return for her, who could guess what Margaret might do? She might tell them all that he had raped her. Then he would become a wanted man in any case. Yes, even without her he was in grave danger. Margaret's father was monster enough, but what if Janos Horvath found out he and Margaret had been lovers? Janos would have him murdered.

Another wave of guilt passed through him. But what was he to do? It was imperative he get away from the danger Margaret presented. He wanted her, but the obstacles were simply too great. He had reviewed every possibility in his mind, and in the end he took what seemed the only course of action. He had left by himself and, he reasoned, if he worked hard, he might have enough money to leave for America in the spring. Put her out of your mind, he commanded himself, knowing the command would not work, but wanting to be in charge of his feelings for at least a short time. Miklós moved down the platform, his eyes straight ahead. The future—he must concentrate on the future.

He paused for a moment in the station and looked around. He *was* in Vienna, he reminded himself. This was his third trip to the "Capital and Residence" of the empire, and regardless of the circumstances, he ought to try to enjoy it. It was, after all, the "Golden City," the "City of Dreams," allegedly the most beautiful city in a Europe he soon hoped to leave.

He stepped out onto the cobbled street and began walking in the rain toward what his map told him was the Jewish quarter. Apparently the Viennese paid no attention to the rain; the streets were a veritable patchwork of faces, nationalities, and tradesmen. There were Bohemian maidservants, musicians on every street corner, peasant Slovak peddlers, Bosnian infantry, and nannies with their small charges in tow. He felt bewildered and lost as he picked his way along, stopping now and again to check his map. Surely, he told himself again and again, no one could find him in a city of two million people. And just as surely, he could find work as a bookkeeper or a tutor.

Had he had money, he might have gone anywhere in this city, but since necessity dictated frugality, Miklós headed for Leopoldstadt in the second district, across the Danube Canal. This area housed large numbers of immigrant Orthodox "ostjuden" from Galicia. Here he could find a room to share for a pittance of what he knew accommodation of any kind to cost nearby or inside the

Ringstrasse, those avenues which formed a circle and marked the place where the walls of the old city had once stood. Moreover, in Leopoldstadt he would be almost invisible. Galicia was, in fact, his mother's home, and so he was not unfamiliar with the form of Yiddish spoken there, and although he was not Orthodox, he knew he would not feel ill-at-ease.

As he had expected, Leopoldstadt was filled with milling men wearing broad-brimmed hats and long dark coats. Their bearded faces and payess—the long unshorn ear ringlets and sideburns worn by many Orthodox Jewish males—clearly identified them. The coffeehouses too were filled with these men, who seemed to wander about doing their business and talking endlessly.

Miklós stopped and surveyed one coffeehouse. Assuming it was no better or worse than the others, he entered its smoky airless interior and slipped into a chair behind a small table. His stomach fairly ached with hunger; he had not eaten so much as a bite since leaving Budapest, and before that he had breakfasted only on tea and hot bread. Yes, he would eat first and then seek accommodation for the night. But he was aware that there was no time to waste. It was Friday, and at sundown the sabbath would begin, making it difficult indeed to find an open restaurant or accommodation in a strict Orthodox community.

When the waiter appeared, he ordered coffee and a kugel—a heavy pudding made of noodles.

When it arrived, steaming hot, he devoured it in silence, trying to decide how exactly to find accommodation.

"You eat like a hungry man," a deep male voice said.

Miklós crooked his neck to face the voice that came from the next small table. "I'm newly arrived, I've been traveling," he replied.

The man who had spoken scraped his chair across the floor and pulled up to Miklós' table. He appeared to be in his thirties, though his beard and untidy bulk made him appear older. Unlike most of the other men, he was not dressed in black, nor did he wear payess. Moreover, his accent was not Galician, but Polish.

"Shalom! Welcome to the city of dreams," the stranger said in a caustic tone. "Welcome to the city of waltzes and of whipped cream. Welcome to *our* poverty and to *their* dreams." He paused and ran his hand over his beard; then with equal sarcasm he asked, "Have you come to witness the gay apocalypse?"

"I don't know Vienna well," Miklós replied, not wanting to start negatively with anyone.

"To know it is to dislike it intensely, my friend. It is a city of hypocrites and of liars. Now, it is one matter to lie to others, but the Viennese lie to themselves. They attend the theater, the opera, and the symphony and consider themselves cultured when in fact most have understood nothing and have attended merely to be seen by their friends. And such events give them the opportunity to dress like peacocks and strut about. They live in their coffeehouses because in such places they are visible and not alone with their fears. Yes, a fine people! They attend literary salons by the hundreds, yet never read. But of course they waltz and soon they will dance themselves over the edge of a cliff." Again he stroked his beard, and this time he smiled, "Never mind. In Vienna you can always get the very best pastries, and our whipped cream is the finest in all of Europe."

Miklós frowned. The stranger's analysis was hardly the first negative appraisal of Vienna he had heard. Still, it seemed unusually harsh. "Are you a teacher?" he ventured.

"A philosopher," the man replied. "Yes, you will grow to understand and dislike Vienna. It's an absurd city. Every building looks like a palace and its claim to culture is as fake as the gold paint that is passed off as real gilt. But you will learn only from your bad experiences."

"My first experience here is going to be very bad if I don't find lodging for the night," Miklós said, putting his prediction into a more practical light. "Do you know of someplace where I might find accommodation, somewhere nearby?"

"Yes, best you see to that first, my friend. This city has the greatest housing shortage in all of Europe."

"Do you know where I might begin?"

"But of course. I live in a place which is a sort of dormitory for single men. It's not much, but it's clean and warm and you have your own cot. I spotted you when you came in. I knew you were from out of town."

Miklós nodded. He wasn't as invisible as he had thought. "I'm from Budapest."

"Budapest, Galicia, Krakow . . . we're all the same here. Come, finish your kugel and I'll take you to my place and get you settled."

Gratefully Miklós followed him. Tomorrow he would start looking for work, and even if he had to walk back and forth, he would save and save. Vienna was, after all, the first step on his journey to America. It was a journey he intended to continue soon.

Five

1

November 3, 1903

*I*t was early in the morning, perhaps only five o'clock, Margaret guessed. Outside the rush of cold air that always marked the dawn whipped through the forest in the form of a harsh north wind. It was this time of day that animals came out of their hiding places to drink at streams, it was at this hour that tiny rodents—shrews and the like—skittered across the roof, and it was at moments like this that deeply hidden thoughts and memories surfaced, crawling from the edges of the mind to the center of one's thoughts, to be discarded as mere nightmares, or sometimes, as was the case this morning, to be recognized as brutal reality.

For a long while Margaret had thought it a dream—a horrible nightmare. She had never spoken of it, not even to Prince Stanislaus. But this morning she knew it had not been a dream, and she now remembered it with a terrible reality. It had happened three years ago when she was only fourteen. She had awoken in the middle of the long winter night and felt hands on her nude body—hands roaming over her small breasts, hands slithering between her legs. She had turned frightened toward the panting, sweating body next to her in the bed, and in the dimmest of light provided by a sliver of moon outside her window, she had recognized Béla's twisted face. His dark hateful eyes threatened her to keep silent, but he leapt from her bed and disappeared, leaving her alone, afraid, and somehow ashamed, though she had done nothing. For hours she had lain awake unsure if it had been a dream or a reality; then she had drifted off into a troubled sleep, only to awaken in the morning with a high fever.

As close as she came to telling anyone was when she confided to her mother that she had had a horrible dream.

Her mother had only smiled. "One always has horrible dreams when one has a fever."

At the time, she had accepted that explanation, but this morning she knew it was not true. Béla had been in her bed and he had been trying to mate with her. But she had woken up and he had run away.

She knew all of this because of what had happened last night. She had felt Béla's touch in Janos' hands. She had seen his wild eyes in Janos' eyes, and she recognized them. Yet she had not even thought of Béla when she and Miklós had made love. That was because their love was real—it was because they had both desired it.

"You didn't come in time," Margaret said aloud to no one. And again she felt fear and emptiness, but more, she felt anger and betrayal.

Count Horvath's hunting lodge lay deep in the rolling mountains of Translyvania, an area of unique scenery where legend and reality mixed easily. Here were low-lying bogs half-obscured in fog which sprouted tall gaunt leafless trees dressed in dark hanging moss like giant cobwebs spun by some monstrous spider. Here were lakes so placid they looked like mirrors, and here too were hidden valleys, winding roads, and dense forests of coniferous trees. It was here, to this lonely, faraway place, that Janos had brought her after their wedding. It was here, in this very room, that he had raped her.

It had not yet snowed, but the rain fell in sheets of ice and covered the ground, making the surface slippery. All around the huge lodge a dense autumn fog hung like a curtain. The dampness was penetrating even inside and in spite of the fact that all four fireplaces blazed.

Margaret sat by the fire, a huge quilt wrapped around her, and still she shivered. Her face was deadly pale, her eyes ringed and puffy from crying. She was alone now in her bedroom. But her eyes watched the door warily, fearfully, afraid Janos would return to once again force himself on her.

For a moment she closed her eyes. Miklós had not come. Miklós had deserted her. She had waited with growing anxiety and had not given up hope till the wedding vows had been exchanged and until she found herself bundled into a carriage with Janos on the way to their honeymoon retreat.

At first she had cried because Miklós had deserted her. Now she cried because of Janos. Never in her wildest thoughts could she have imagined anything so horrible as her wedding night. Janos was uncaring and unfeeling. He sought only his pleasure, and he was cruel.

He had not kissed or caressed her. Not that she had wanted him to, but he had not even tried. He had merely had her undress and then he had felt her all over, pinching now and again and laughing if she complained that it hurt. When he had taken her, it had been as dogs take bitches. But that was not even the worst. When he had finished, he had hit her, not once but three times, with his cane. He had screamed that she was not a virgin, but a whore. He accused her father of deceit, and he had threatened her again and again, trying to make her confess the name of her previous lover.

"Have there been many?" he shouted.

"No, no . . ." She had sobbed and cried, but he did not care.

"I know you've been sheltered, but you found a way, didn't you! You whore! Perhaps the stableboys have had you, then?"

Again she had shaken her head.

"Well, you cannot fool me. I've had virgins and you are not a virgin. Young as you are, you've done it before! Tell me who it was! Tell me!"

She shivered even now at the thought of his temper. His face had grown red and he had seized her arm and with all his strength thrown her across the bed and hit her with his cane across the buttocks. Then, as if afraid of himself, he had stomped away, locking her in the room.

On and off all night and most of yesterday she had slept fitfully, crying when she was awake and suffering nightmares when she slept.

She looked up and cowered in her chair. The door handle was turning, and in a moment the door opened and Janos stood before her, his face still twisted with hatred.

"Are you rested?"

She shook her head.

"You look terrible. Why haven't you seen to yourself?"

"I'm ill." The words barely escaped her mouth.

"Soon some food will be brought for you. Some nourishing soup. You will eat it."

Food? She had not thought of food for days, and clearly all hunger had passed. "I'll try."

"You will eat it, all of it. I spent yesterday in thought and I've come to tell you how it will be for you."

She looked up at him, wanting but unable to avoid his dark eyes.

"I want children and you will have them for me. I will sleep with you until you are pregnant, then you will be left alone. I will come and go as I please. I will have other women when I desire. You will remain at home always. You will see to running the house and you will, at all times, keep yourself looking decent."

"How am I to do that if I cannot have my hair done or buy clothes?"

"A hairdresser will come, and clothes will be bought for you."

"And you will leave me alone when I'm pregnant?"

"Yes. Frankly, I don't find you that pleasurable."

Margaret stared into the fire, away from him. He was going to keep her a prisoner . . . but he would leave her alone when she got pregnant. She could only pray to get pregnant as soon as possible. His very presence nauseated her. And perhaps in time she would design her own escape.

"Considering your condition, I feel I am making you a generous offer. I could divorce you or have the marriage nullified. You were supposed to be a virgin and I have been grossly wronged. But I am doing this for your family. I am going to keep you without complaint. After all, it would kill your father if he knew."

His voice droned on. She wondered if he knew how she felt about her father, indeed about her whole family. How could they have done this to her? And why had Miklós run away and left her to this fate? Again tears began to form, and she shuddered as Janos' manservant came into the room wheeling a tray bearing the promised food.

Janos turned to him. "Tell the servants that Madam will be present at the breakfast table later this morning."

The servant bowed and left the darkened room. Janos returned his gaze to her. "I'm going now. Get up, Margaret, and eat, then fix your hair. I have a business associate coming and you must learn to play mistress of the house."

She looked at him for a long moment, when quite suddenly her means of revenge occurred to her. Janos and Béla were friends . . . good friends. "You're very kind," she said, trying to sound sincere. "So kind I have decided I must tell you the truth."

Janos looked at her steadily. His little dark pig eyes were narrow slits. But they flickered with interest.

"It was Béla," she said, looking down and away. "I've never been able to speak of it . . . until now."

"Béla?" Janos repeated his name in a low hateful tone. "Béla? Did your father know?"

"Yes," she replied.

Janos swore under his breath. Only after he had turned his back and was headed toward the door did she look up again. For the first time she almost smiled. Janos would find a way to take revenge on Béla and on her father, and in a way his revenge would be hers. It did not really matter that it was a lie. Béla had tried to take her virginity, but he had not succeeded. Never mind, she thought. They all deserve to be punished—Béla, Mama, and Papa, all three of them. Janos would certainly do something. And in time, she thought to herself, I will find a way to take revenge on you, Janos Horvath.

2

December 6, 1903

Anna Maria was dressed inappropriately in a white-fur-trimmed suit with a hobble skirt that fell just above her ankles. Ferenc, Konrad, and Béla walked through the dusty factory with ease, while she followed, taking tiny steps because of the constriction of her skirt, and watching constantly that she did not brush up against anything dirty. This, she thought with annoyance, was extremely difficult, because *everything* was dirty.

"Of course it's hard to understand the magnitude of the operation when the workers aren't here," Ferenc was saying. "But try to imagine these tables lined with cutters, just as on the floor above there will be fifty women at their sewing machines. We are the largest uniform factory in the empire, and we should do very well, very well indeed."

They had stopped and Anna caught up with them, wondering vaguely why she had said she was interested in coming on this little tour in the first place. "Is there much more?" she ventured.

"Only my office and the two offices I've had prepared for Konnie and Béla."

"Thank goodness," she murmured.

Ferenc placed one arm around Béla and the other around Konnie, who, Anna thought, looked as miserable as she felt.

"I know you both think you should have enjoyed the traditional education as György has—well, perhaps not you, Béla . . ." he winked at Béla knowingly. "But times are changing. To go to the university and then into the army is a dead end. Everyone, even the nobility, is going into business. I searched long and hard to find this opportunity, I made sacrifices to take advantage of it, and one day when you have learned the business and I get older, it will be yours."

Anna looked at him in disbelief. What sacrifices had he made? The only real sacrifice was made by Margaret. She shivered with anger, once again thinking of her beautiful daughter married to Janos Horvath, who, to make matters worse, had spirited her away to some god-awful hunting lodge in the wilderness of Transylvania.

"Come, come down to my office. I have some champagne there to celebrate our new enterprise, Szilard and Sons. What do you think?"

Ferenc turned before anyone could answer, and they continued down a long corridor and finally through double doors into what appeared to be an office. On a large desk sat a tray with silver goblets and two bottles of champagne chilled in ice buckets. Ferenc opened one and its cork popped and went spiraling through the air. He laughed when Anna jumped, and then he poured four goblets full, passing them out. "To Szilard and Sons," he repeated. Béla and Konrad lifted their goblets and muttered the toast after him. Anna simply raised her glass. Perhaps the champagne would at least kill the taste of dust in her throat, and God knew, if she drank enough she might even be able to stop worrying about Margaret.

"Well, you haven't told me, what do you think?"

Béla smiled broadly. "I like it. I think we will all be rich."

Konnie looked at the floor and Anna's heart ached for him almost as much as it ached for Margaret. Konnie loved the theater, he loved writing plays, and now the opportunity was being wrenched from him before he could even know if he would be a success.

"I haven't spoken to you about it yet, Béla, but I feel you would do well in sales. Oh, to be sure, it's not the ordinary kind of selling. More a question of knowing and getting to know the right people. You'll have to wine and dine them . . . it seems ideal for you." Ferenc grinned and Béla grinned back.

How, Anna wondered, could Ferenc understand Béla so well and not understand Margaret or Konnie at all?

"I thought you would begin as a floor manager," Ferenc said to Konnie. "The hours will be long, but you will learn all about the business."

Anna slid by the side of the desk and braced herself. Konnie's face had grown set, and she sensed his anger and hurt.

"I don't really want to go into business, Father. I want to write."

Ferenc's face clouded over. "I've told you that's nonsense. You must have something steady, something dependable. In any case, this will be a family enterprise."

Konnie was tall and slender. He had her blond hair and blue eyes, and a sensitive gentle face. But his face was red now and she could see a stubborn defiance taking hold. It wasn't easy for Konnie to stand up to his father; he'd never done it before, and anger came hard to him. Béla was different, of course, Béla was truly Ferenc's son. He would do whatever was necessary to maintain his position and to support his activities. He would also play Ferenc like a fine instrument, courting his father's affection and becoming closer at every opportunity.

"I don't think I can do this, Father," Konnie finally said.

Ferenc's eyes narrowed. "But you will do it."

"No."

"Konnie, be reasonable. Father is offering you a great opportunity," Béla put in.

Ferenc looked at him gratefully, then turned back to Konnie. "I will not countenance your insubordination. I shall end your theater days by ending your allowance and by restricting your activities. You are not yet of age."

"But he will be soon. Ferenc, you can't bend him to your will forever," Anna said softly.

"This conversation is for the men of the family, Anna. It will be continued when we are alone."

With something of a flourish to cover his feelings,

Ferenc stuffed papers into a briefcase and then straightened up. "Our driver is waiting. Let's go home and discuss this rationally."

Home, Anna thought. For all she had hated living on the estate so far from Budapest, she hated her new apartment more. It was large and well-furnished, but it was also cold and impersonal. There were no grounds to walk in and no gardens to tend. And then too, it wasn't really hers. She had come to it whole and had no part in even decorating it. They had been there a week now and she still felt as if she were staying in a large hotel.

As usual, Ferenc led the way to the car, which was parked at the curb. He nodded to the driver and in German directed him to drive them home. He held open the door for her and she climbed in the back. Konnie stepped in next to her, then Béla. Ferenc rode up front with the driver, who at the moment was cranking the engine.

In a moment it sputtered and then it jerked forward, giving the driver just enough time to leap out of the way and into his own seat before it began to roll off on its ungainly wheels. Doubtless it cost a fortune, but she detested this newfangled toy. To her way of thinking, their old carriage had been quite good enough. It was, in fact, more luxurious and more comfortable. The automobile, on the other hand, belched vapors of assorted varieties, and one felt each and every bump it crossed.

Anna closed her eyes against the wind and pulled her collar higher as the car clattered down the Andrassay-ut, Budapest's main shopping street. It was quiet today because it was Sunday and all that greeted them was the sight of rolled-up awnings and couples strolling down the sidewalk. Shortly they passed the telephone exchange, which had been built in 1897, and then they turned onto the Korzó where their apartment was located. Anna sighed inwardly. The best that could be said about Sunday was that Monday followed, and tomorrow she would see her beloved József. She yearned to talk to him and to tell him all that had happened. She wanted his counsel as well as his love. Time for her and Ferenc was running out. Anna was uncertain of what to do or even of how to go about doing it, but she knew she could not continue living with him much longer. And then too, there was Margaret. How, if at all, was she going to rescue her daughter?

3

January 5, 1904

Beyond the window a pale January sun fell on the hard crusty snow that covered the walkways and gardens surrounding the Horvath estate. In the distance the gazebo stood stark and empty, like a skeleton of summer as the wind rattled its delicate latticework as if it were dried bones.

Margaret stared through the frost on the window, and the light refraction created a distorted white winter world—it was like looking at the landscape in a distorted mirror.

In the hearth behind her a fire crackled, and on the table next to her chair there was a hot pot of tea and an unused cup. Instinctively she pulled her heavy robe around her tighter and then walked slowly to her chair, the image of the winter garden still vivid in her mind.

She poured some tea and was about to drink when her bedroom door opened and Janos entered. She hated the fact that he never knocked, and regretted that she could not hear him approaching because of the heavy carpet on the hall floor.

He was wearing tweed riding breeches and knee-high leather boots. As always, he walked with the assistance of his cane.

"I expected you at breakfast," he said, apparently without anger.

Margaret looked at him full and noted that he appeared to be in better humor than usual.

"I'm sorry, I didn't feel well when I first woke up."

He nodded. "And are you feeling better now?"

"Yes, much."

"I've come to tell you something."

She continued to stare at him. His voice was softer than it was normally and she felt he looked vaguely distressed. "Yes?" she inquired.

"My father died in the night—in his sleep."

Old Count Horvath had been neither her friend nor her enemy in the two months since her marriage to Janos. When her mother had written to him and asked to see her, the old count had urged her to come for a visit. But Margaret herself refused to see her mother or her father, and was adamant, insisting that they were both dead to her. Count Horvath pretended not to understand her reasons, but he respected them, and her parents did not come. In response to her mother's notes, Margaret wrote nothing. On several occasions the count had come to talk to her about her separation from her family, but she always rebuffed his arguments, and finally the old man came no more, but rather remained in his own apartment in the north wing of the house. That he had seemingly grown more frail in the past few months had eluded her. Now Janos stood before her, telling her his father was dead, and she was surprised. "I . . . I didn't know he was ill," Margaret confessed.

"It was his heart."

"I'm sorry."

Janos made a begrudging noise and nodded. "He'll lie in state here for a week—there will be a reception, of course—and then the funeral in Budapest. You will understand that I now have many things to do, I will be away more."

"Yes," she replied in a small voice. Frankly, the news that he would be gone more often pleased her. "Will I be going to Budapest for the funeral?"

"Of course, you are my wife."

"Janos . . ." She hardly ever called him by name, and the word sounded strange on her lips. "I should like to see the doctor."

His dark eyes flickered. "Are you ill?"

"I feel terrible in the morning and I have not bled now for two months. I feel as if it is all inside of me."

"Are you telling me I impregnated you in the first weeks of our marriage?"

She stared at the floor. "Impregnated? Am I pregnant?"

He walked around her in a wide circle. "You do look plumper. What on earth did you think the cessation of your blood meant, anyway?"

"No one ever told me it stopped when you became pregnant!" She stared at him and inwardly cursed. Did that mean she had endured him in her bed longer than necessary? Then she remembered that Irina had mentioned that you stopped when you were with child.

"This child *is* mine, isn't it?" he demanded.

"Of course. I told you it was long ago that Béla . . . that Béla came to me."

She once again stared at the rug, but was fully aware of his eyes on her. The child was not his—it must be Miklós' child! Her blood had been due at the time of her marriage and had not come. She felt suddenly elated, but she fought to control her expression as she thought it through. Since Janos believed that it was Béla who had deflowered her long ago, he would have no cause to suspect the child was not his, and thus the child would be protected.

"Then you will see a doctor in Budapest when we go for the funeral," Janos agreed.

Margaret again nodded, and abstractedly she placed her hand on her stomach.

To her surprise, Janos walked up to her and reached out with his hand. A thin smile crossed his lips as he too touched her stomach and then patted it almost affectionately. "He will be a strong baby," Janos said. "Yes, I shall have a strong son. Rest today," he said generously. "I'll see to the preparations for my father's funeral."

He turned and left her standing there still thinking about the life she carried. Yes, Janos would find a way to take revenge on her brother and father, because he believed they had knowingly fooled him by representing her as a virgin bride. "And now that I know how much you want a son," she whispered to herself, "I know how to take my revenge on you. In my own time I will take your sons . . ." Margaret whirled around and looked at herself in the mirror. There were new signs of life in her blue eyes. Her parents, her brother, and Janos had conspired to make her a slave, to take and keep everything away from her, to kill all her dreams. But they would not succeed. It was all quite vague in her mind now, but she knew she would find a way.

4

May 1, 1904

Janos' club in Budapest was modeled on a British men's club. Located on a quiet side street opposite a park and surrounded by a high iron fence, it offered comfortable lounges, a well-stocked bar, and it served individually prepared meals suitable for those with gourmet tastes. In addition, its cellars boasted racks of coveted wines from the better vineyards in France, Italy, Germany, and Hungary itself.

The main lounge on the first floor was a huge room with a domed ceiling. It had two fireplaces and a number of comfortable leather-upholstered chairs arranged around marble-topped tables. Off the main room there were billiard rooms, a massage room, and a library. A huge winding marble staircase led to the second floor, and a gilded rail ran all the way around the top. Off this circular hall were comfortable furnished rooms for those members who, for one reason or another, found it necessary to spend the night. From the top of the blue glass dome, an ornate, heavy chandelier hung from a thick gold chain. It cast a subtle light over everything on the main floor.

In one corner, near a fireplace, Janos relaxed in an oversize leather chair. Opposite him, on the other side of a table, Béla sat, awed by the opulence of his surroundings. He had never been to Janos' club because on all previous occasions he had been instructed to find hotel accommodation and women.

Outside, a cold early-spring rain saturated the ground and ran downhill toward the Danube, which was shrouded in a low-lying fog. Inside the posh club Janos Horvath stuffed the pungent Dutch tobacco into his pipe, lit it with a flourish, and then leaned back against the softness of his leather chair. He wore a dark gray three-piece worsted lounge suit with a red tie. Aware of his unappealing physical appearance, Janos always dressed expensively and well. Clothes, he had discovered, made all the difference in how he was treated. One never laughed at the rich; whatever their difficulty, a blind eye was turned. And where service was expected, it was delivered with efficiency only when it was apparent that the recipient could pay, and pay well.

Across the small round inlaid table, Béla sat sipping a brandy. "I was surprised to get your call, Janos. Usually you give me more notice," Béla said, lifting a heavy dark eyebrow. "But there is still time to find some companions . . ."

"Not this time," Janos answered. "I have pressing business, but on the other hand, we are good friends, yes? It didn't seem right to be here and not see you at all."

Béla masked his disappointment with a smile. "I'm glad you feel that way."

"How's business?" Janos asked with a wink.

Béla smiled. "Good. I'm going to Berlin day after tomorrow. If I can meet the right people, I'm certain of a lucrative order."

Janos half-smiled. "Tell me, Béla, just what are your aspirations?"

"To get the order, of course."

Janos waved his hand expressively to indicate his disdain. "No, no. Your long-term aspirations, your desires, one might say."

"To be wealthy." Béla smiled. "To be as wealthy as you."

"Then you will have to change your ways. You'll have to be willing to take chances, to gamble."

"I'm really not sure of what you mean."

"Well, tell me about your business enterprise—you've been in business for some months now. How is a profit made?"

Béla knew full well that Janos knew the answer to his own question, but Janos wanted to hear it from him. It was Janos' way of teaching. "Within the statement of the problem," Janos always said, "the solution is hidden." And so as concisely as possible, Béla began to explain. "We get so much for the order and we manufacture the goods and provide them. Profit is the difference between the actual cost of production and the amount we are to be paid according to the contract."

"Yes, and let us suppose you could provide the same uniforms for much less, would your profit not be higher in such a case?"

"Of course, but it would be most difficult to manufacture for less than we do now."

Janos shook his head in exasperation, wondering if he had to draw Béla some sort of picture. "Let us look at it this way. Suppose you tell your client that you will make a specific number of uniforms for a specific price. Suppose you use slightly less costly materials than you originally promised. Wouldn't you then make a better profit?"

"Definitely, but these people are not fools, Janos. They would know we didn't use the agreed-on material."

"Suppose you could not tell to look at the material. Suppose it only became obvious after a little wear and tear."

"Then I would say it would be worth a certain risk."

"Suppose it were worth thousands of florins—remember, there are others involved, and they would make a certain amount as well."

Béla studied Janos carefully. He knew Janos had made a great deal in business. He knew him to be ruthless. "Are you suggesting something specific? Bribery?"

"Yes, Béla, I am. You are quite right about a big order from the Germans. I know the man in charge personally, and he is willing to give you this order for a reasonable consideration."

"Explain," Béla asked.

"Yes. Hear me out. He will see to it that you receive the contract. You will then purchase the fabric from him. Naturally, this will all be a most quiet transaction—his superiors are to know nothing about his selling you the fabric. He makes his profit on the sale of the fabric to you. The fabric he will supply looks identical to that which you are supposed to buy, but is not as tough. It is, however, most reasonably priced and you will use it to make the uniforms, thus doubling your profit. There will be no problem with the finished product initially. As a result, you will make some twenty thousand. This you will share with me."

Béla thought for a long moment. "I will have to make all the book entries . . . I will have to have false receipts indicating that the fabric cost more than it did."

"These can be arranged. And if something happens, you need only claim that you were cheated by the supplier."

Béla sipped his drink and then set the glass down with some force as a smile covered his face. "I will do it," he told Janos. "I will do it and we will make some money of our own."

Janos lifted his glass to Béla. "I don't really need it, my friend. But you need an education if you are to achieve your goals. Besides, you have always been dependable. I mean, you've found me fine women with whom to take pleasure."

"I suppose our evenings of cavorting are over now," Béla said with some regret.

"I know she is your sister, but what if I said I found her to be somewhat inadequate?"

"I would hardly be surprised. She's a child. And she is like my mother."

"I'm afraid I will still require certain diversions."

Béla grinned. "It will be my pleasure to continue to provide them."

Janos raised his glass. "To variety," he toasted.

Béla raised his glass too in turn. "And to success in business," he added.

5

June 1904

Again the trees sported new leaves and the flowers were beginning to bloom. The rich earth still smelled of the rain they had had the night before, and Margaret inhaled deeply and wished she could ride her horse. But it was not possible, and so riding would have to wait till after she had the child.

Margaret walked slowly through the garden and finally mounted the steps to the gazebo. Carefully she sat down. Eight months with child, she found herself awkward and uncomfortable. Indeed, at night she wished her bed had a great hole in the middle into which she could thrust her swelling stomach. Unhappily there was no hole and she was forced to lie on her back or on her side. And active! The little creature inside her tossed and turned, it even hiccuped.

She leaned back and closed her eyes. She tried to conjure up a vision of what Miklós' child would look like. She frowned and hoped it did not look like him. She did not want Janos to be suspicious. No, it would be better if the child looked like her.

"Psst! Psst!"

Margaret's eyes snapped open and she listened.

"Psst! Psst!"

It was definitely a human sound, the kind made when someone tries to attract the attention of another without making too much noise. Margaret searched with her eyes, trying to determine from which direction the sound was coming.

"Psst!"

Margaret's eyes moved to the thicket beyond the far

side of the gazebo where she was sitting. There, partially hidden by the shrubbery, she saw Irina signaling her.

Margaret raised her hand in a signal, then groaned slightly and pulled her bulk out of the chair. She climbed down the steps and walked across the lawn toward the thicket. Irina! She hadn't seen Irina since her parents left and the house was closed. She had asked them what would become of the servants, and she had been told that Janos would keep them on. When they had returned from Transylvania, she had asked Janos about Irina specifically. She had been told that Irina and her brother had been invited to remain if they agreed to work in the fields.

Margaret reached the thicket. "Irina?"

Irina emerged from behind the bushes. "Come over here, where we can't be seen," she whispered.

Obediently Margaret went to her. "What are you doing here?" she questioned in a low voice.

Irina smiled. "I've been watching you. I waited till you were alone. I came to say good-bye."

Margaret frowned. "Good-bye? Are you leaving the estate?"

Irina nodded and pressed her lips together. "I must."

"Must? Is something wrong?" Margaret questioned.

"Forgive me, but we cannot stay here. Your husband is a monster. If we stay there will be nothing but trouble. Ivan wants to kill him now, but they would only kill Ivan."

Margaret frowned. Kill? What was all this talk of killing? "What has happened?" she asked directly.

"I cannot tell you."

"You must tell me, Irina. Please tell me. I won't be upset, and I certainly won't tell him."

"I can't."

Tears suddenly flooded Irina's eyes and she covered her face with her hands. Margaret felt utterly bewildered. She put her arm around Irina and patted her gently. "Please," she pressed. "Tell me."

"Your husband . . . I was in the barn alone. He grabbed

me and he made me lie with him. I didn't want to, he forced me."

Margaret enfolded Irina in her arms. "He's a horrible man," she said, "horrible."

Irina sniffed. "But you are married to him, you carry his child."

"I hate him," Margaret declared. "I hate him as much as you."

"I'm sorry for you, Miss Margaret, very sorry."

"I shall survive," Margaret said firmly.

"I just wanted to say good-bye to you," Irina reiterated.

"I know. Where will you go, Irina?"

"Ivan and I are going to Budapest. Your father said if I ever wanted to come to the city, he would give me a job in the factory."

Margaret nodded and then squeezed Irina. "I wish you well," she murmured. Irina in return kissed her on the cheek, then like a frightened rabbit picked up her skirts and disappeared into the woods. Margaret followed her with her eyes, then slowly turned and went back to her perch in the gazebo to sit in the warm sun.

She had resented Irina and Ivan, but they weren't so bad, she thought now. And poor Irina! Well she knew Janos had other women, and she had heard stories about him forcing his attentions on peasant girls before, so she was not surprised. "Bastard," she whispered to herself. "May you burn in hell!"

6

July 12, 1904

Janos sat in the large overstuffed chair in his study, inhaling the aroma of leather-bound books and surrounded by the clutter of his personal papers and materials related to his many business interests.

Upstairs Margaret screamed periodically as she endured her unseemly long labor. But, Janos rationalized, the two midwives would see to her needs. There was no reason for his presence till after the birth of his son.

A son! The very thought sent chills of anticipation through him. The boy would be strong and intelligent. He would have the physique that he himself did not have, he would be able to do all the things that Janos had always wanted to do but could not. No one, he vowed, would think this child ugly. He would be perfect, and more, he would inherit the vast holdings of the Horvath family. He was the heir apparent, the inheritor of a fortune built over generations and of a title hundreds of years old.

And Margaret would be a good mother, of that he was convinced. She was naive; there was no doubt of that in his mind. How could she not have realized that the cessation of her monthly blood meant that she was pregnant? But being ignorant was not the same as being stupid, and he had noted that Margaret seemed to have a good mind, certainly she had a better mind than Béla. No, in the matter of children, one could not leave things to chance. There was no question in his mind that, no matter what, Margaret, in spite of her shortcomings, was excellent breeding stock. For one thing, she was beautiful. For another, he suspected she could read. Too often he had noticed books out of place or out and out missing, and there was no one else about who could read. Well, he did not care if she amused herself with books, as long as she didn't use her knowledge in any way, and he regarded her ability to read as a sign of natural intelligence. It was, he had decided, unwise to have one's children reared by an idiot.

He returned his thoughts to Béla and again felt angry. He'd been cheated; there was no doubt about that. But he could not totally blame Margaret for her brother's unnatural act, although he could blame her for not telling him before the marriage. No, he was not fond of Margaret.

Not that he really liked any woman. Indeed, he disliked them all except for what pleasure they could give him, and that, he knew, was not given. Pleasure was always either paid for or forced. He half-smiled. Not even Margaret, who was his wife, would sleep with him if he did not bend her to his will.

Well, he *had* forced her, and now she was giving birth to a child. He felt proud in spite of everything. "And you, Béla, will pay," he said aloud. Indeed, the wheels of his revenge were in motion. Béla and his father were, Janos knew, as good as ruined already.

Janos glanced at his watch. Four hours had passed since Margaret had told him to summon the midwives. He was impatient, but he vowed he would wait another hour, and if nothing happened then, he would go and see what the problem was. At that moment he lifted his head. Again Margaret screamed. This time it was a long, wailing scream, a scream that echoed through the house and down the corridors.

Presently he heard footsteps and then a knock at the door. He opened it and the midwife beckoned him to follow her. He climbed the winding staircase behind the fat rear of the round-faced midwife, ignoring her endless chatter as she recounted nauseating details of the delivery in which he was not at all interested. At the top of the stairs, just outside Margaret's room, the other midwife stood holding a small bundle wrapped in a blanket. He silently peered inside and saw the flaxen-blond hair and the deep blue eyes. The child, he acknowledged, looked like Margaret.

Janos took the child and strode into the bedroom, where Margaret was sitting up, pillows propped behind her. She looked tired, but he supposed that was not unusual. "We shall have to name him," he said proudly.

"Her," the midwife corrected. She smiled. "You have a daughter."

"You had a daughter," he said with undisguised disgust.

"Yes, she's lovely," Margaret said in a faraway voice filled with weariness.

"Maybe, but I wanted a son."

"These things cannot be guaranteed, Janos."

"There will be a son next time," he said with conviction.

Margaret looked into Janos' hard eyes. She almost

shuddered because she knew her failure to produce a son would mean he was returning to her bed.

"I have no interest in daughters, Margaret. You name her."

Margaret lifted her arms to receive the child Janos offered her. "Verena," Margaret said. "I choose the name Verena."

"That's an English name," Janos complained.

"Many of the finer Hungarian families give their children English names these days. We can call her Renee for short."

"Very well," he said with a shrug.

Margaret nodded silently and watched as Janos turned away to leave her with the child. She felt a sudden wave of joy and happiness. She and Miklós had a daughter! And she had given the tiny baby its name. At last, at last, after all these years, Margaret felt she had something, someone, of her own.

Six

1

October 2, 1904

*I*t was twilight, an almost magical time in Budapest, Anna thought. From the long narrow windows in the living room of their apartment on the Korzó—part of the Danube embankment on the Pest side of the city, and a street largely given over to hotels, fine restaurants, and expensive apartments—Anna could see the Great Chain Bridge, the rising Buda Hills, and the cluster of famous buildings on Castle Hill. The sky above was purple with bright pink streaks, and the last rays of the setting sun caused ripples of light in the river and reflected off the many domes and steeples of Buda. So extravagant was this spectacular sunset that had it been a painting, critics would have said it was in bad taste.

Yes, it was a magical time. The cafés and pastry shops were filling with customers, and while the galleries and shops were closing, the scenery at the Opera House was being positioned, and at the concert hall the musicians were tuning their instruments. Budapest was physically two cities, Buda and Pest, but there were two cities in another sense as well. One was Budapest by day—bustling, sober, hardworking; the other was Budapest by night—musical, laughing, frivolous with its dance halls and cafés filled to overflowing with gaiety, with conversation, and with drama.

But for the moment, Anna knew only Budapest by day, when she was with József. At night she was with Ferenc, a man she deemed the only completely joyless Hungarian she had ever encountered outside of Janos Horvath. Ferenc was too tired to go dancing, too filled with the success of his business to converse in the restaurants and coffee shops, too busy to attend concerts or the theater. It was twilight now and it was magical. For most it was the beginning of their day; for her it was the end.

She stared out the window for a long while, and when the purple sky obliterated the last of the pink streaks of sunset, she walked across the spacious room and turned on a light. It was then that she noticed the envelope on the desk. It was addressed to both her and Ferenc. Carefully she slit the envelope and withdrew the folded piece of white paper. Her eyes scanned it quickly; then she reread it more slowly, gripping the side of the paper. Grasping it, she sank into a nearby chair and stared at it, the words dancing in front of her eyes:

Dear Mother and Father,

I have given great thought to my actions and I want you to know that the decision I have made is not taken lightly. I cannot work in business, Father. I have tried my best this last year, but it is not what I want and I do know what I want and will find a way to pursue it. This morning I left Hungary and I will continue to travel, perhaps to France or even America. I want to study theater, to write and to produce plays, but you already know this. I will find a way to do what I wish, Father. I knew I was not strong enough to defy you and remain in Budapest, so I have left, perhaps forever. I am most sorry, Mother, for I will miss you a great deal, just as I will miss Margaret, György, and Béla.

Your loving son,
Konnie

"Shall I begin to prepare dinner, madam?"

Anna looked up into the face of the cook whom Ferenc had engaged. "No," she answered. Then, her lips pressed together, "Tell the other servants they may have the night off."

The cook smiled, nodded, and hurried off with her good and unusual news.

With the night off, Anna thought, even her servants could enjoy Budapest's magical nighttime activities. But in truth she had not sent them away to enjoy themselves. She had sent them away so that she might be alone with Ferenc. She looked at the great grandfather clock. Where was Ferenc? He was usually home by now. Her first emotion on reading Konrad's note was one of immense loss followed by sadness. But as she had sat in the silence, her sadness fled, replaced by anger, an anger born of a thousand pent-up resentments. In her mind she began to list them, from the least to the most important, till she grew so angry she could not differentiate between them, and the smallest of Ferenc's crimes soon took on the same weight as the worst of his actions. And as the moments passed, her fury grew and she added to the list of his sins the fact that he was now late.

Ferenc rather relished his new life, even though he'd been living it for only a year. On the estate, he had seen to his horses personally, not because he had to, but because he loved horses and the rearing of fine animals gave him one of his few pleasures in life. But apart from that, he found the collecting of rents a bore, and agricultural management in general left him without satisfaction. It might have been different, he reflected, if there had always been enough money. But there hadn't, and thus he was always in the position of borrowing from Peter to pay Paul and of keeping the true state of the family's finances secret. When at last his financial problems became truly critical, he had set about making plans for change, and he was proud of what he had managed. He had taken the entire family into consideration and he had decided what sacrifices had to be made for the good of the whole as well as the individuals involved. His sons would give up their traditional education to help him run the business, but their eventual reward would be security and, without a doubt, a good inheritance. His daughter would have to give up romance for a solid marriage with a member of the nobility—but not just nobility, a family with business interests as well. He felt saddened by the fact that things between him and Margaret had gone so badly. He had intended to use reason rather than force to bring about her acquiescence, but at the time there were pressures from creditors on the one hand and pressures to close the deal for the factory on the other, so that her recalcitrance had simply caused him to lose his temper. Still, he could have wished that Count Horvath had been willing for Margaret to marry András rather than Janos. But, he reasoned, she would adjust to Janos. Doubtless he was lonely and would be good to her. In any case, she was secure, and he felt certain that one day she would forgive him.

And had he not sold his land to Count Horvath, to whom would he have sold it? The count had been quick and had not quibbled. The money had enabled Ferenc to settle his debts and buy the factory as well as set the family up in a lovely apartment in Pest, an apartment with which even Anna couldn't find fault.

Yes, his life had changed radically, but he liked his new life. He had kept several of his best horses and now boarded them at a stable in the park, where he could ride them on weekends. And unlike agricultural management, factory management suited him. Moreover, he liked his daily comings and goings best. To leave early in the morning and work all day gave him a real feeling of accomplishment. And when he finally arrived home, he could always smell dinner being prepared, and he relished the respect the maid showed him when she took his coat and hat. "Did you have a difficult day, sir?" she always asked. He answered that he had—and he felt rewarded, as if for the first time in life he had done something to deserve the way he lived.

He turned the long gold key in the latch and entered the darkened hallway. His face knit into a deep frown. The little maid was not there and no mouth-watering aroma greeted him.

Ferenc slipped off his coat and hat and draped them on a straight-backed chair near the door. He dropped his umbrella into the ebony stand and walked down the hallway, his shoes clicking on the tile floor. "Anna . . ." he called out tentatively. Where was everyone? And why wasn't dinner cooking?

"Anna?" He turned and went into the living room. In the dim light of one lone lamp he saw her sitting in the large chair. She was wearing her dressing gown, and her blond hair was loose and fell in a tangle to her shoulders. Her eyes settled silently on him and he felt suddenly uncomfortable.

"Where have you been?" she asked sharply.

He shrugged. "I was caught in traffic."

"Pig!" She hissed the name half under her breath, but he heard her.

"How dare you speak to me like—?"

She fairly leapt from the chair and caught him in mid-sentence. "I dare!" she shouted. "I finally dare to say exactly what I please!"

"What is it?" he demanded. Though he knew he didn't sound as strong as he should in the face of what appeared to be a colossal rage.

"What is it?" she mimicked his question, then turned on him, her blue eyes like stones, her lips tight. "It is the loss of my daughter, married to that ugly wretch Janos. Your doing Ferenc, your doing entirely! I should have stopped it. I loathe you for what you've done to Margaret. Do you understand? *Loathe.*"

"It had to be," he replied, retreating.

She shook her head. "No, no, it didn't have to be. And neither did this!" With a flourish she slapped Konrad's note into his hand. He unfolded it and read it by the light of the lamp. Under his breath, he swore.

"First you have driven a wedge between Margaret and

me, and now our son is gone . . . perhaps forever!" She didn't bother to hide her tears. "I have a grandchild I haven't even seen! Am not allowed to see! I hate you, Ferenc! I really hate you!"

"No . . ."

"Yes. Hate. I never loved you. I always hated you. My father forced me to marry you, as you forced Margaret to marry Janos. Oh, I suppose you thought I'd come to care for you, but no. The truth is, you're a pig. You were a pig then, you're one now, and I hate you, really despise you!" She turned on her heel and marched off into the bedroom without looking back. He heard the door slam and the lock click.

He stood for a long time looking out the window on the gaiety in the street below. Of course she was hurt and upset, but she would recover, he told himself. She had a good healthy temper; he had seen it before. But, he admitted, he had never seen her quite the way she had been tonight.

The door to the bedroom opened and Anna came out. To his surprise, she was dressed to go out. She was wearing her fur-trimmed blue suit and hat, and carried a smallish bag. "I'm leaving you, Ferenc. Forever."

Her words utterly stunned him. "What do you mean?" he finally managed to say.

"That I am leaving you," she repeated evenly.

"Anna, be reasonable. You have nowhere to go and no money."

"I have no money," she replied, going to the door. "I do have somewhere to go!"

The door closed with a resounding slam and he found himself standing in the empty apartment.

"Anna!" he called after her, and then opened the window and called her name out again. "Anna . . ." His voice sounded down the Korzó, and he called again and again, until he finally fell back against the window frame, large tears beginning to fall down his cheeks. He loved her. He really loved her. And how could she leave him? The thought that she might leave him had never even occurred to him, not once even in his worst nightmares.

2

October 9, 1904

Even though it was his only day off, Sunday in Vienna was not Miklós Lazar's favorite day. On Sunday most of the shops were closed and there was little to do but stroll in this "City of Dreams." So stroll he did. Stopping now and again to catch a free concert, he allowed himself the luxury of an ice cream around two in the afternoon, and at four he bought a paper and went to an outdoor café, weather permitting. There he ordered a coffee and sat and read till suppertime. When it was time to eat, he returned to the Jewish district and bought himself some food—usually a few knishes or a plate of goulash, and this he ate in the kitchen of the dormitory where he lived.

This Sunday, like all those that had come before, found Miklós discouraged. He was slow to save money in spite of his frugality and the low cost of his bed at the dormitory. The job he had found as a bookkeeper in a large factory paid less than his position with Count Horvath had, and furthermore, here his room and board were not free as they had been on the estate.

As if lack of money and friends were not enough, he was a man who lived in fear as well. Even after a year, Miklós still firmly believed that in her disappointment anger might cause Margaret to tell Janos about him and that when he found out, Janos would hire thugs to murder him.

On Sundays, because he had less on his mind, Miklós always reviewed his situation twice over. And even when he was reading his paper, imaginary little scenes crept into his mind. A strange voice would call his name and he would look up into the evil, angry face of a hired killer. There would be a knife or perhaps a gun. He would be killed. If he did not see himself as a murderer's victim, he saw himself arrested by the authorities for rape. As clearly as the paper in front of him he saw his own body lying in some alley in a pool of blood while others gathered round him and shook their heads; or, alternatively, he saw himself in prison, abused and beaten by the other prisoners.

Given his state of mind, it was only natural that when, some time after he had settled into reading his paper and was sipping on his strong Viennese coffee, he felt a wave of sudden panic as a voice floated across the late-afternoon air, pronouncing his name: "Miklós, Miklós Lazar! . . . Good heavens, you look like a rabbit," she exclaimed, placing a strong hand on his shoulder.

Miklós looked up into the ravishing and almost forgotten face of Leah Laszlo. Her rich brown hair fell to her shoulders in masses of curls, her skin was like ivory, and her expressive eyes were heavily lashed and a strange gray-green in color. He smiled broadly, half with relief, half with real happiness at seeing her. He stood up and quickly pulled out a chair for her. "Oh, please sit down."

"Thank you, Ah, Miklós, it's good to see you. How long has it been? Oh, at least four years. I was eighteen then. Now I'm twenty-two. Have I changed?"

She was dressed in a gray velveteen suit trimmed in black and red. It was styled in the S-shape of the Gibson-style silhouette, with a straight front, a full protruding bust, and a tiny cinched waist and pushed-back hips. She leaned toward him and he could smell her wonderful perfume. Changed! How could he tell her how she had changed without being quite rude? Once she had been a pretty plump child. Now she was a beautiful woman whose baby fat had disappeared, leaving her with curvaceous figure and full sensuous lips.

Ah, Leah! She was different. Even when younger she had been different. His family had lived next door to hers for five years, and though he was older, they had become friends because she followed him everywhere. Another girl might have followed him because she felt some kind of adoration, but not Leah. Leah followed because she wanted to do all the things he did and study all the books he studied. And she had had the nerve to argue with him over everything. He remembered her as delightfully willful, dangerously adventurous, and frighteningly directed. Leah always seemed to know exactly what she wanted, and she used all her wiles—her intellect, her talent, her humor, and even her looks—to get whatever she desired.

"Well, have I changed?" she asked again.

He smiled. "Yes and no. You're more beautiful, but I think you have the same will."

She laughed and touched his hand. "How's your family?"

Miklós pressed his lips together. "Mama died two years ago and my father shortly after."

Her face saddened and she shook her head. "As I recall, your parents were older than mine."

He nodded. "I had no brothers or sisters. And your family, how are they?"

"Angry, I imagine. I ran away, Miklós. My grandmother left me some money and I used it to free myself."

He looked at her long and hard. Yes, he had no trouble believing she would do such a thing. He was about to delve further, but she preempted him.

"What are you doing in Vienna?" she asked.

"Working, trying to save enough money to get to America."

"And escape whatever you're frightened of?" she asked boldly.

"How do you know I'm frightened?" he asked.

"Because I know you and I know I startled you. For a second I thought you were going to jump out of your skin."

He forced a smile. "Well, I've done nothing dishonest. Let me just say that there is someone who holds me responsible for something I did not do. And I don't want to meet him." It was vague enough, and he hoped it would satisfy her. "And what, I might ask, are you doing in Vienna?"

"Going to America. I will be here two days; then I'm traveling on to Germany, and from there to America. Would you like to come with me?"

"I don't have enough money," he replied. "If I had enough, I'd come with you in a minute."

"I'm alone, Miklós. I'm going to America alone to become an artist—a couturiere. If I stayed in Hungary I would be forced into becoming a mere dressmaker, but I can do better than that."

"Alone?" He was awestruck. "But it is very difficult for a woman to travel alone. I mean, I've heard these stories about New York . . ."

Leah smiled and touched his hand. He was as handsome as she remembered him. A bit naive, but nonetheless handsome. "When I began, I didn't place much faith in such stories; however, I must admit that I had trouble finding a hotel that would rent me a room in Vienna and that I am also bothered by stupid men who don't realize that I'm not a fallen woman. I was quite serious, Miklós. Come with me, pose as my husband until we get to America. I have enough money for both of us."

He looked at her for a moment and was stunned. Did she actually mean it? What would her reaction be if he jumped at such an opportunity? Well, he was tired of Vienna and tired of looking over his shoulder for Janos Horvath. He decided to test her. "I have some money, Leah. I wouldn't need the whole amount. And I would pay you back every cent with interest."

She smiled and again squeezed his hand. "Actually," she said, leaning close, "I really need you. I have learned that the American authorities sometimes turn away single women with no relatives."

"Is that true, or are you just trying to get me to accept your offer?"

"Oh, I suppose it is more likely if the woman is alone and has small children, but I'm told the authorities can be most arbitrary and that single women are sometimes suspected of being prostitutes and denied entry for that reason. And it *is* difficult to travel alone. Men can be such pests. If you don't come with me, I shall have to find someone else to play my husband. What do you say, Miklós?"

"I haven't really had time to think about it," he said, now beginning to be drawn back to reality.

"Miklós, there is no time. I am supposed to leave in a few days."

Never in his entire life had he made a decision so quickly. True, he had decided to leave Count Horvath's quickly enough, but even so, he had mulled over all the alternatives for several days. But as he now thought about it, meeting Leah might be a godsend. Her offer did, after all, solve his dilemma.

"I will do it," he suddenly said. Then, more enthusiastically, "Yes, yes, I will do it."

"And how wonderful that we met to solve one another's problems so quickly!" she exclaimed happily.

Miklós frowned slightly. "There is one thing, Leah. I think American Immigration will want documents."

"Then we shall get married, and when we get to America we'll get divorced. I know I will have difficulty if I'm not married."

He nodded. Leah was strong-willed and clearly had ambitions well beyond those of the average woman. But then, he again recalled their schooldays together, and he was not surprised. Her mind was quick and she had talent; he had seen some of her drawings. Even as a small child she had been the arranger, the one who selected teams for this game or that, the one who told everyone what to do. Well, he thought, he could do worse than to have Leah at his side. She would rekindle the fire of his own ambition, the ambition he felt he had lost since he had left Margaret and run away to avoid the wrath of Janos Horvath.

"We'll do it," he said, leaning toward her. "We'll go to America together."

3

April 1905

How beautiful the Austrian Alps were in the early spring! Anna thought as she stood on the balcony of the ski chalet in the little village near Innsbruck. The three-story chalet was perched on the side of a mountain, an idyllic location midway between high mountains and a lush valley below, complete with a tranquil blue lake all its own. The adjacent low hills were covered with greenery even though the higher slopes behind the chalet were still white with snow. It was eventide and it was still, so still she could hear the wailing of a dog clear across the valley below.

József stood beside her. He lit his pipe and watched as the white smoke curled upward in the evening breeze. "Have you regrets?" he asked, glancing at her profile.

"None. Except perhaps that I should have left sooner." In the six months since she had left her husband, Anna had never looked back. She was filled only with happiness and contentment.

"It's been wonderful having you all the time, Anna. I was weary of stolen afternoons and empty evenings."

"I suppose we'll have to return to Budapest sometime," she said softly.

"We don't have to do anything. We can go on traveling if you wish."

"You're good to me."

"I'd marry you in a minute if you were free. But since you aren't, I don't mind enduring the scandal our return will cause. Perhaps because I'm older and have nothing to lose, I might even enjoy it."

"We're hardly the first two people to live this way."

He smiled, and almost laughed. "Hardly."

"I do feel a bit of a burden on you, though. Oh,

József, I don't know what I would have done had you not been there when I needed you."

"A burden? You? Never, my darling. But I do admit I was surprised to see you with little but the clothes on your back."

"If I'd packed, he'd have stopped me."

"I know. If you wish, we certainly don't have to return. We could summer in the Nordic countries or even go to England."

"No. I feel we must go back. I'm worried about Margaret. I've written and written, and she's answered none of my letters. I haven't seen my granddaughter, and now Margaret is pregnant again. It makes me quite miserable. Think of it, I have a granddaughter nine months old and my own daughter has forbidden me to visit. I must keep trying, though Margaret may never forgive me for not doing something to help her—I haven't forgiven myself."

"And what could you have done?"

"Helped her run away like Konrad. I miss him, but I'm glad he's free."

"I know you are. Perhaps your daughter is not as unhappy as you think."

"I hope you're right." Anna turned toward him and he took her in his arms, running his hand through her hair, then moving his finger down her face and lightly over her throat. He bent and kissed her neck, slowly touching her ear with his tongue till he felt her press against him and heard her sigh in his arms. "I suppose I am used to possessing you in the afternoons now," he said, touching the small of her back and moving his other hand across her round buttocks.

"And do you think I mind?" She smiled at him and undid the front of her negligee, revealing her breasts as they pressed against the sheer pale blue material of her nightdress. She had only just awakened from her nap and had arisen to dress for dinner. His eyes caressed her as if for the first time, and she felt warm and excited by his intense gaze.

"God, you are a beautiful woman," he said, reaching

out for her. Her breasts were heavy but well-formed. Her skin was as white as snow and her stomach was flat and firm and her hips rounded. Even her hair was still magnificent. When it was loose it hung to her shoulders, and although gray was now mixed with the blond, it still looked healthy and youthful. He smiled, for the hair on her Mount of Venus was not gray at all. It was still flaxen, and beneath it her soft pliable flesh was pink and soft. Roses in a wheatfield, he thought as he touched her intimately and felt her react with all the passion he knew to be hers. Perhaps, he thought, it was better that they had not been young lovers. Young lovers had so little time for deliberate lovemaking—often passion and sheer energy overcame them and resulted in a less-than-satisfactory union. But when lovers were over forty, as he and Anna were, there was endless time, and love need not be a song, it could become a symphony with all the subtleties of the musical feast. First here and then there . . . fingers, hands, and lips in a fugue of sensations—nothing accidental, all movements calculated as the crescendo was finally reached.

"Will you tire of me?" she asked as he caressed her inner thighs and she moved to meet his hand.

"Never," he said, bending to kiss her. And he knew he meant it. Anna was the love for whom he had longed and waited. No matter what their situation, he would never let her go.

4

June 5, 1905

Ferenc leaned back in the plush leather chair and looked at the expanse of desk in front of him. It was neat and clean; even his ashtray had been newly washed and was as yet unused. He looked the proper manager and he felt comfortable and at ease as he prepared to meet Herr Schumacher and Herr Schmidt, two high-ranking German procurement officers for whom his firm had just filled a large and profitable contract. It was Béla who had obtained the contract, and his only regret was that Béla was not here to share this moment. It was quite obvious to him that since the order had been filled in double time they had come to thank him and possibly to place a new and even more lucrative contract with Szilard and Son. The company needed such an order, he admitted. Getting started was difficult. The last order had yielded a goodly profit, but they were still operating with a cash shortage, since some new machines had been needed, and the expanded payroll had to be met. But another order would settle everything—operating expenses for some months in advance would be in the bank, and for the first time he could truly breathe easily.

He checked his watch, and even as he did so, his male secretary knocked lightly on the door.

"Come in," Ferenc called out.

Young Stefan, his secretary, stepped into the office first. He was an inordinately pale young man with gold-rimmed glasses and thin blond hair. "Herr Schumacher and Herr Schmidt, allow me to present Herr Szilard."

Ferenc stood up and walked around his desk. The meeting would, of course, be conducted in German. Germans rarely spoke Hungarian. He held out his hand, and all around there were handshakes. Stefan bowed and left the office, closing the door behind him. Ferenc motioned to the two overstuffed chairs opposite his desk and the two Germans sat down. He returned to the chair behind his desk.

"I was most pleased when I received the message that you were coming," Ferenc said, withdrawing his own pipe as an invitation for them to smoke.

"These matters are best seen to in person," Herr Schmidt said, looking around the office slyly while Herr Schumacher lit his own pipe. Clouds of heavy German tobacco filled the room.

"Yes, I prefer doing business that way myself," Ferenc agreed. "Of course, you originally dealt with my son

Béla. He's away just now—he'll be sorry to have missed you."

"Perhaps not," Herr Schumacher said seriously.

Ferenc looked from one of them to the other and shifted in his chair. They didn't actually seem pleased; indeed he felt a wave of extreme discomfort pass over him. "Is something wrong?" he ventured.

"Everything is wrong," Herr Schmidt replied. "But then, you should not take us for fools."

Ferenc sat up straight in his chair. "Gentlemen, I would never take you for fools. I'm surprised; however, I didn't suspect anything was wrong."

"We placed a large order and we paid in advance. When the order was received, we found that most inferior materials had been used. We contracted for the use of specific materials—they were guaranteed."

Ferenc frowned. "Of course, I remember. Indeed, I remember quite well. Let me get out the contract." He stood up and turned to his filing cabinet. For a moment he shuffled, then withdrew a folder and opened it. "Yes, yes. It's right here. And if you will wait, I will get out the invoices to the fabric supplier. We ordered what you specified."

He looked for several minutes, a growing panic seizing him. He had never actually seen the orders to the fabric suppliers. "They don't seem to be here," he muttered. "Perhaps my son Béla has them."

The two Germans watched him suspiciously.

"Stefan!" Ferenc called out.

Stefan appeared at once. "Sir?"

"Go to Béla's office and find the invoices from the fabric supplier on Herr Schmidt's order."

Stefan nodded, though he was sure Béla would not like his going through his desk. In Stefan's eyes, Béla had already proved himself both strange and secretive. He insisted on doing the banking himself, and he kept many drawers in his office locked.

"Are you trying to tell us that you are not responsible, that you were duped by the fabric supplier?" Herr Schmidt surmised.

"I am trying to tell you that we used, or thought we used, exactly what was ordered."

Herr Schumacher sniffed. "I would expect someone who has been in business for as long as you to know one fabric from another."

Ferenc did not want to admit he was a novice. "I'm sure it will all be fine," he said, trying to soothe both them and himself. "Whatever the problem, we will stand by our obligations."

"That's good to hear. We came to present you with the alternatives," Herr Schmidt told him. "Either there will be full compensation or we will go to the authorities."

"I believe what you have done is called fraud," Herr Schumacher advised him.

Ferenc's face flushed. "I am a man of honor," he said defensively. "Assuredly, things will be made right." But even as he said it, questions filled his head. Where would the money come from? Only the profit was still in the bank. How could new uniforms be made without more cash? And most important at this moment, where was Béla?

Stefan hurried back into the room. His face was paler than usual, and when Ferenc saw his expression, he knew that whatever Stefan had found was bound to make matters worse rather than better.

"I had to break the lock on the desk, sir."

Ferenc nodded.

"I found this." Stefan extended a folder and Ferenc took it. He opened it and leafed through it. "This is not from the right supplier," he said slowly. Then he turned the page and saw that the original order had been canceled. And there were bills . . . "I do not understand," he said slowly. "This other fabric cost the same as what you wished . . ."

"You were billed the same," Herr Schmidt said. "I am quite certain an investigation will show that money was returned to you from the company—in short, you were billed ten thousand, but five thousand was returned."

"You are accusing me of theft, pure and simple," Ferenc said.

"We are accusing your firm. Can you make this good?"

Ferenc could feel his breath coming short. "Not right away, but certainly in time. I told you, I am a man of honor."

"The army cannot wait. I'm afraid we will have to go to the authorities," Herr Schmidt said carefully.

The two were standing, and Ferenc stood too, though his legs felt like rubber. "Are you going now?" he asked.

"I'm afraid we must."

"Then I shall go with you," Ferenc volunteered. Surely Béla could explain this. He turned to Stefan. "Find Béla and tell him what has happened. I believe he has gone to Count Horvath's estate near Kassa. Send him a message to return immediately."

Stefan nodded dumbly. "What shall I tell him?"

"What has happened, of course."

Again Stefan nodded. Vaguely he wondered if telling Béla everything was such a good idea.

5

June 5, 1905

Never had the importance of time been so evident to Béla Szilard as it was at this moment. People's lives crossed by seconds—you could miss knowing someone by not being at the right place at the right time, you could pause crossing the street and either be in, or avoid, a terrible accident. Being late for a train and missing it could save your life if the train were to be derailed. Life was a gamble, and time, Béla realized, was the currency.

Béla read the long message from Stefan in silence and thanked heaven that Janos had not yet returned from his hunting lodge with Margaret. They had agreed to meet here weeks ago. Béla had been early, his train arriving two hours before the train from Transylvania carrying his sister and brother-in-law.

Again Béla read the message. Between each line he read the outcome. Somehow they had discovered the shoddy goods, and somehow they had also discovered he had reordered from another supplier. The company would no doubt be ruined, and perhaps he and his father might be charged. At the very least, they would be held financially responsible.

He glanced at the small black satchel he had brought with him. He had intended to give Janos his share, and their German cohorts had not yet been paid either. He stood up and walked to the satchel, which contained the full amount in gold. There was absolutely no question about what to do. He was not going to jail, nor did he intend spending a lifetime working to pay the money back, as his father would surely demand. No, he could go a long way on this amount of money, and go was what he intended doing.

"Sergei!" He summoned Janos' manservant, and when he appeared, Béla conjured up a stricken expression. "I must return to Budapest immediately," he said. "Have the carriage sent to take me to the railway station."

"And when the count returns?" Sergei asked anxiously. "He should be here very soon, within the hour."

"Tell him an emergency sent me home and I will see him in a few days."

Sergei nodded and gathered up Béla's luggage, which consisted of only two bags, one quite small. He held out his hand for the satchel, but Béla shook his head. "I'll take this myself," he said.

Within a quarter of an hour Béla was in the carriage rumbling toward the railway station. He would have to find a way to hide the gold. He would have to get new clothes before crossing the border, and eventually he would require a new passport and a new name. The authorities would want him, Janos would want him, and the Germans would want him. But Béla was confident that he could outwit them all.

At the station he went directly to the ticket seller.

"Budapest?" the old man asked. He remembered Béla; he had sold him tickets before.

"No, Zagreb," Bela replied, and in his mind thought:

From there, Constantinople, where all things can be bought.

The old man nodded and filled out the ticket. He handed it to Béla. "You had better hurry, the train leaves in minutes."

Béla gathered his things and hurried off. The train passed through Budapest, but he would sit in the car that went on to Zagreb. Clearly no one was looking for him yet, and by the time someone was, he would be long gone.

Béla leaned back and closed his eyes. The train jolted forward, and as it gathered speed it passed a long train coming into the station—the train from Transylvania, with Janos and Margaret aboard.

Seven

1

June 15, 1905

*F*erenc Szilard sat in his darkened office. He had been released by the authorities, who assured the Germans he would not run away, but would remain for the investigation and would make the proper restitution. After all, he did have the reputation of a man of honor, a gentleman.

But Béla . . . Béla was his most trusted son, and it seemed that Béla had committed a terrible crime. How could he? Over and over the question ran through Ferenc's mind, as did all the events of the past two years. His youngest son, Konrad, was gone, his enemy forever. Margaret, whom he had forced into a loveless marriage, had had her child and was pregnant with another, but she would not speak to him or see him. Anna, his beloved wife, had left him, and indeed disgraced him by running away with Count Bodnar. And now Béla . . . Béla had committed the worst of all possible acts—he had betrayed a trust and tarnished the name of Szilard with the scandal of crime. Of all his children, only György still cared . . . but György was away serving in the provinces and had not yet returned.

Tears filled Ferenc Szilard's eyes. To him it seemed he had only tried to save his family. But to them he was a monster.

And where was he to turn? Money that should have been in the bank was not. The payroll could not be met, and he owed thousands in compensation to the Germans. His new business was destroyed, his children either hated him or had deserted him, his wife was gone forever, and his family's honor lay in ruins.

He thought for a few minutes of Anna, beautiful Anna. She hadn't loved him nor he her when they had married. But soon he did love her, and he had believed that she had come to love him. Their life together had been a lie. Each time he made love to her, he had felt her respond. Now he knew she responded only because she thought of someone else, dreamed of someone else, and succeeded somehow in pretending he was that someone.

If Anna's love for this Count Bodnar had begun in the last few years, when he had been alternately angry and despairing about their finances, he might have understood it. During those years he had given Anna less than she deserved. But no. She had always loved this stranger, and yet she had borne him four children and playacted from the day of their wedding till the day she ran from the apartment, angry because Konrad had run away.

Only György had been spared, he thought. But György didn't yet know about the disgrace that had been brought to the family name by Béla and inadvertently by himself. He prayed that György was strong enough to bear the chattering tongues and the accusations that would be spoken in whispers wherever he went. Ferenc clenched his fist and hit the table hard, as his tears continued to flow.

Then slowly he opened the third drawer of his magnificent oak desk and from it withdrew a small revolver. I will never hold my first grandchild, he thought morosely. I will never walk again with Anna in the purple sunset along the Korzó.

For a moment Ferenc stared at the note he had left. Honor was all a man had. When it was stripped away, there was nothing. He opened his mouth and pointed the gun upward. He closed his eyes and pulled the trigger.

The sound of the gun reverberated through the office

and Ferenc Szilard tumbled backward in his plush leather chair, his concerns and worries ended with his life.

2

June 30, 1905

György removed his white helmet and wiped the perspiration off his forehead. He was wearing his summer dress uniform, which consisted of a bright red jacket, white trousers, and knee-high black boots. It was, he noted, an exceptionally hot day even for the end of June, and today his uniform seemed heavier and warmer than it had ever seemed before.

He looked around uneasily and acknowledged the fact that he felt he was living someone else's life. He had been summoned from his unit because of "urgent family matters," and when he had returned, discovered that his world had turned not once, but many times. Why had no one written to him? His mother, he surmised, was ashamed. His father must have been too upset to put anything in a letter. And Margaret, he presumed, had not been entirely informed herself. He finally sat down on the edge of a large chair and ran his finger round his high collar. Damn wool in summer. Damn everything!

There was a story about a man imprisoned in a room in which all four walls move slowly inward, gradually reducing his space and threatening to crush him. György seemed to remember that particular horror story quite vividly, and now, as he sat in the library of the Horvath house, waiting for Janos, its details returned, sending a chill through him.

Neither the muted colors of the room nor the rich scent of leather-bound books soothed his inner turmoil. For over a year he had been in Serbia serving in the emperor's army. Now, on his return, he found that his entire life had changed without any participation from him whatsoever.

First, Konrad, his younger brother, had run away; then his mother had scandalized the capital by leaving his father and openly becoming the mistress of another man. Now his older brother, Béla, had disappeared with a great deal of money, and was wanted by the authorities, while his father, a hapless victim of Béla's duplicity, had killed himself. How these things had come to pass were still very much a mystery to György. He had not yet even spoken with his mother, who was still away and toward whom he felt a certain ill will. He admitted to himself that his feeling toward his mother was not entirely justified; even his father's suicide note made it clear that her escapades were not the reason for his action. Still, György did not look forward to their meeting—why she had done such a terrible thing tortured him, and he was certain it must have tortured his father as well.

And Béla! What could he even think about what Béla had done? His brother had tarnished the family name in a way far beyond what the actions of any woman could achieve. His brother had stolen from the empire and forever ruined any honor attached to the name of Szilard.

The door to the library opened and György's eyes met the cold eyes of Janos Horvath, his brother-in-law.

"Janos . . ." György held out his hand.

"I do not shake hands with a Szilard," Janos muttered. "It is a family entirely without honor."

György hadn't expected this rebuff. Though I should have, he thought belatedly. "Very well," he answered weakly.

"What brings you here?" Janos asked.

"Margaret. I've come to take her to our father's funeral in Budapest."

"Margaret is with child and should not travel so far."

György frowned. He had not known his sister was again pregnant. "We will go by train and return within a matter of days. I promise you nothing will happen to her."

"Is that the word of a man from an honorable family?"

Janos sneered. "Besides, you are not a doctor, you cannot promise such a thing."

György studied him for a moment. Janos seemed to take pleasure in reminding him at every opportunity of the depth of the dishonor he felt so strongly already.

Not that György had ever considered Janos a friend, but Janos' father had been his father's friend and he had supposed that the son of a friend, especially one married to the daughter of the man in question, might be more tolerant. "It is my word," György answered evenly.

"Well, no matter. She can't go. Pregnant women should not be seen in public."

"It's her father's funeral, and under the circumstances, it won't be a public affair."

"My answer is final. No."

György stared at him in near-disbelief. "I want to see Margaret," he said. "Or is she being held prisoner?"

"Hardly that!" Janos laughed and pulled the velvet cord that summoned the officious manservant who had shown György to the library in the first place. "Tell Madam Horvath that her brother is here," Janos instructed imperiously.

"I thought you might show a modicum of sympathy, Janos. After all, your father was my father's friend."

"It would appear that my late, great father did not exercise much taste in choosing his friends. In any case, even in negotiating my marriage to your sister, your family's honor was besmirched."

Was there more to this never-ending horror? "I don't understand," György admitted.

"I was to have a virgin bride, an honorable woman who would bear me sons. But your sister was no virgin."

"Of course she was," György replied defensively.

"I think I know this better than you. She was no virgin, and I happen to know that your brother Béla was responsible. I don't blame Margaret for this, but I'm certain your father knew—"

It was too much, and György's gesture was close to automatic. His hand gripped his glove and he swatted Janos across the face just as Margaret entered the room.

"I will act to defend my sister's honor," he said coldly. "And my family's as well."

Janos stared at him. "It takes courage to challenge a cripple," he retorted.

"György . . ."

Margaret's voice came from the doorway, and he turned to look at her. She was ghastly pale, and in spite of being pregnant, she appeared wan and as frail as a feather. "Don't interfere. This is something I must do."

Margaret stared at him questioningly. "What has happened?" she finally asked.

"Your brother has challenged me to a duel," Janos replied. "In spite of his obvious advantage, I must accept."

György turned to Janos. "I expect you to appoint a second if you are not up to it."

"Oh, I think I am up to it. Pistols, is it?"

György nodded. "If pistols are your choice of weapon, then pistols it shall be."

Duel? Margaret looked from one to the other of them. György was going to defend her honor? Of course, he had no way of knowing that what Janos said about her was true, nor did he know what she had told Janos. But what difference did it make? György was an officer and he had special training in dueling. Moreover, she knew him to be an excellent shot. It was a way out! György would kill Janos and she would be free.

"I want to speak with my sister alone."

Janos hesitated for a moment, then shrugged. "As you wish. We will duel at dawn."

Margaret's eyes followed Janos out the door, which he obligingly closed. Then, without hesitation, she threw herself into György's arms. "How did this happen?" she asked.

"He insulted you. I thought you heard."

"Only part of it. You are doing this for me. Oh, György, I love you, but you must be careful."

"Am I to be given no credit?" György smiled confidently.

She leaned against him. "I want so much to be free of him."

"Margaret, what's he done to you?"

She burst into tears anew. "Everything."

György sat down and pulled her to him. He put his arm around her in the way he once had when they were children, as if he were going to tell her a story. "You know about father and Béla?"

"Yes, Janos told me."

"And about Mother?"

Margaret nodded again. How could she make György understand how little she cared about the fate of her mother, father, and brother? He and Konrad were the only two of her family she cared for, and Konnie was gone. But György didn't understand, perhaps couldn't understand because he was a man and because he had been gone for so long.

"I don't understand it. I don't understand anything that has happened . . . Mother . . . any of it," György admitted.

"Nor do I." It was only a half-lie. She understood that Béla had stolen a great deal of money and her father felt responsible. She also strongly suspected that Janos had had something to do with it all . . . that somehow Janos had taken his revenge by arranging Béla's crime. Now, she thought, György would kill Janos and it would have come full circle, it would be over.

György again wiped his brow. "We need to talk more," he said seriously, "but I have to go into town and arrange for a second."

"Can you find someone?"

"Yes, I know just the person. But I don't have much time. Will you be all right?"

Margaret smiled weakly and nodded. "Now that you've come for me, I shall be fine."

3

"In our glory years, men were real men. If a man's family name or the woman he loved was insulted, he would not hesitate to offer the challenge and fight a duel—often to the death. Duels are not as common now because men are not as brave as they once were."

Margaret stood on the balcony in the early-morning mist, and her grandmother's words returned to her as she watched the faraway figures of Janos, his second, and two other men she didn't recognize stroll across the dew-bejeweled grass that led to the woods beyond the formal gardens.

She leaned over the balcony, trying to see better, before they disappeared. Were there not supposed to be only five men? The two participants, their seconds, and the man who judged such matters. Who was the extra person Janos had with him? And why indeed was the judge with Janos? A sudden cold chill gripped her, a terrible fearful premonition. Janos was going to cheat!

She ran quickly from where she stood to follow the grim parade, to warn György and to confess the truth to him so he would not have to fight.

She felt as if this were all a part of her recurring nightmares, or perhaps simply one of her many flights of imagination. She spent so much time alone that her world was peopled with fictional characters and her head filled with bits of made-up conversations.

And who could deny this was a dreamlike setting? For a moment her spirit seemed to leave her body and hover above, looking down on the totality of the scene. Her blond hair was loose and uncombed. Her robes were for nightwear and they were stark white and billowed ever so slightly in the early-morning breeze. She had hurried down the stairs and now she was barefoot on the downstairs terrace that overlooked the garden, and before her the carpet of green lawn sparkled with dew, while low-lying patches of mist floated in midair and bright-colored flowers began to open.

The men in their dark suits—even Janos—were mere cardboard figures as they trudged along, one carrying a large pistol case. She could not hear their conversation, but she knew as surely as she felt the cold of the terrazzo on her bare feet that Janos was plotting. Then Janos and his companions disappeared into the woods.

In a moment, from the far side of the garden, György appeared. He was accompanied only by his second.

"György!" She called his name and he turned toward her.

"You must stop! György, he will kill you!" she shrieked.

Across the distance between them, György shouted out to her, "Go back to the house, Margaret!"

"No! You must not fight him! I must talk to you!"

"It's too late! I must do this."

He turned away from her and he and his second continued walking. In a second they were in the woods. Janos was there—he wouldn't let them talk. Margaret felt paralyzed, as if she were made of stone or had been turned to a pillar of salt like Lot's wife.

She could see the sparse woods in her thoughts. The pine trees carpeted the forest floor with brown needles, and in the center there was a clearing. It was there that they would duel. She wrapped herself in her own arms and leaned against the wall, her own breathing the only sound she could hear till, after what seemed an endless length of time, shots rang out in the distance and from the silent woods giant birds, terrified by the sudden noise, took flight, their great wings casting shadows on the grass.

And Margaret knew. She moved forward on legs she could not feel. Then she ran down the stairs frantically and bolted across the wet lawn and through the garden. She was oblivious of the sharp pine needles on her bare feet, and she screamed when she saw György lying face-down. His second, a big boy named Stanz from the village, reached out and held her arm. With strength she didn't know she had, she shook him loose and bent over to her brother, sobbing. György . . . strong and so handsome in his uniform. György, who had taught her to read and who had always protected her from Béla. He lay in a pool of his own blood, his breath still.

Before she looked up again, Stanz was gone and Janos was standing over her, his face hard and set. "Murderer," she said in a low voice.

"Go back to the house," he ordered. "Immediately."

She looked up into his face and then averted her eyes. She stood up and started to stagger from light-headedness, but Janos steadied her. "Slowly," he said. "Walk slowly. You should not have come here in your condition. You're eight months with child."

She nodded dumbly and began walking toward the house, painfully aware now of the pine needles, of the cold, and of the wetness of the grass. How beautiful the early-morning dew had looked, and how terrible it felt. How wonderful her grandmother's stories of honor and glory . . . how wretched the reality!

"I killed him," she said aloud. And tears again began to flow down her cheeks. If only she had told him the truth about Miklós, he would not have fought for her honor and he would still be alive . . . but no, she had kept it to herself because he'd told her he was a good shot, and she had thought he would kill Janos.

Margaret made her way to her room and, once there, closed the door and lay down on the bed. Little Renee lay in her crib still sleeping, and in her womb Janos' child stirred and she patted her stomach with her hand, murmuring promises. But how could she run away now? To whom would she go? And there was Renee, and soon there would be another baby. "I have killed my brother and I am trapped," she murmured. And in her own mind Margaret felt she deserved to be trapped. Life with Janos was her punishment for the web of lies that had killed her beloved brother.

4

November 1, 1912

Margaret sat up in her bed with the pillows fluffed behind her head. She glanced at the clock and contemplated getting up. She had been up for several hours yesterday and not suffered. Yes, there was no doubt that her strength was returning.

She looked about her room. Its pale blue walls were all she had seen for many months, and she knew every crack, crevice, and imperfection in the plaster. How small her world had grown!

But something had kept her from dying, and she was quite certain that that something was her children. Renee was now a lovely, talkative, intelligent eight-year-old. Zoltan was seven, and looked exactly like György, much to Janos' unhappiness. And little Imre was four. He was the last of her children—she could have no more, thanks to Janos, who had given her syphilis, the most dreaded of diseases.

"Are you awake, Mama?"

Margaret opened her eyes and saw her blond, blue-eyed Renee standing in the doorway flanked by Zoltan and Imre.

"If I were not, I would wake up for you."

"I've made some new hand puppets and I have a show for you," Renee announced.

Margaret smiled indulgently. Renee was such a competent little girl, and she was far better with Imre than the nursemaid Janos had hired while she was ill. Imre was a wonderful child, but he was given to occasional tantrums, and he was a bit self-centered because he was the youngest. Then too, Zoltan and Renee were close in age. Imre was often left out, not by design, but because he could not do many of the things they did. But Renee could manage her little brother. She was like a second mother to him.

"You sit here, Imre," Renee instructed. "And you, Zoltan, sit there. Can you see, Mama?"

"Yes," Margaret answered.

Renee knelt behind the boudoir chair and slipped the puppets on her hand. She brought them around so that the seat of the chair was her stage. Then she began her play.

At eight, Margaret reflected, Renee had a wild, unbridled imagination, and certainly she had real talent. She had made and dressed all her puppets herself, and she used them to entertain her brothers.

"The end!" Renee proclaimed as she caused both puppets to take a deep bow.

Margaret clapped and felt a deep surge of pride. If Janos was the monster of her nightmares, her children were the joy of her life. Lovely little Renee looked like her, and in her heart, Margaret knew she was Miklós' child. Her two sons were handsome even though they were Janos' sons. All three children feared and disliked Janos, though perhaps Zoltan disliked him most. Janos had tried to train Zoltan to hunt with him, but Zoltan hated killing and refused to even try to shoot straight. Time after time Janos had tried to interest Zoltan in the things that interested him, but Zoltan would have none of it and instead preferred to study, play with his sister and brother, or simply walk or ride alone. Vaguely she wondered if it would be the same with Imre. As yet he was too young for Janos to bother with. Still, he was frightened of his father; there was no question about that. As for Renee, Janos simply ignored her because of her sex. But the thing the children most disliked about Janos was the way he treated her. She had their loyalty; he did not.

Margaret glanced down at her bony hands. She was so much thinner than she had been! She stared across the room into the mirror. Her face was still pale and her skin seemed stretched out on her body. Still, she was recovering. Daily she felt her strength returning, and daily she willed herself to live for her children—to live in order to escape Janos and take her children with her.

I'm not dead yet, she thought as she rubbed her fingers together. God knew Janos had tried to kill her, but she had survived. Yes, he had given her syphilis, and when she became ill, he accused her of giving it to him, even though he did not appear ill.

She shuddered at the thought of the disease and silently cursed it and him. But there was one advantage. Janos no longer came to her bed. Instead, he brought his whores home with him and openly flaunted them before her. Not that she cared. She was being treated with salvarsan, a new German drug developed by the famous

Dr. Paul Ehrlich. But the drug had made her almost as sick as the illness. Only now after many weeks could she say there was some improvement, and the doctor agreed.

The door to her bedroom was suddenly flung open and Margaret jumped, while the children looked up startled.

Janos looked from one to the other of them, then shouted at Renee, "Go take your brothers and prepare them for dinner!"

Renee nodded and in an instant they were gone.

"I see you are feeling better," Janos said as he turned to face her.

"A little."

"I think you are feeling a lot better and that you are hiding your condition."

"Why would I do that?"

"How should I know why you do anything? Frankly, I've come to give you good news. I'm divorcing you, Margaret, and judging from your progress, I would guess you would be able to leave within a few weeks."

"Leave?" Margaret spoke the word as if it were entirely foreign . . . and divorce? Was he actually setting her free? But where would she go, and how would she support her children? She stared back at him dumbly as questions filled her head and apprehension began to creep into her mind.

"I don't understand," she managed. She knew there was more. With Janos there was always more.

"And what is there to understand? I am divorcing you. You will leave here. It is quite simple. You can take your clothes, but everything else remains."

Her clothes? She hardly had any save those she had made herself. The sum total of her money amounted to some fifteen kronen, which she had found in the chair where Janos sat, and she did still have her grandmother's ring, which she had carefully hidden from Janos' acquisitive eyes.

"And what about the children? How will I support myself?" she blurted out, then added, "How will I support the children?"

Janos scowled. "The children are staying here, my

dear. As for yourself, well, I would suppose you could become a harlot in Budapest. Yes, that's it—you'll see, in the city men pay for it. It's much better than being taken by your brother. But you won't be able to tell anyone about your condition—if you did, no one would hire you."

Margaret felt her fists clench even though she had begun to shake violently. "You can't take my children! You can't! And you can't just throw me out! What will people say?"

"Your family is completely disgraced. Your father and brother were thieves, your mother is living with her count in Greece. And you are diseased!"

"You gave it to me!" Margaret shrieked back.

"That will be hard for you to prove. I have no symptoms. I also have several peasant men willing to testify that you slept with them."

"It's a lie!" Margaret retorted, but even as she said it, she knew Janos would win. Janos Horvath would bribe the judge and local officials. He owned everything in Kassa. He was a tyrant. And what did Janos care about people in the capital? Since his father had died he had grown ever richer and ever more separated from friends and acquaintances in Budapest. No, given her condition and her family, she had no weapons with which to fight. She had no money for lawyers, no friends; not even her mother was in the country. And even under the best of circumstances, what rights did women have? Good God, even the crown prince had sent his wife into wretched exile so he could live with his mistress. Janos could get away with anything he wished.

"I've already been to the lawyers. You will not be given the children. Indeed, I need give you nothing," he reiterated.

"You gave me this horrible illness!" Margaret sobbed as she stood up, holding the bed for balance, though the whole room seemed to be going in terrible circles.

"Rant all you want. You leave in three weeks. I'm a generous man—I'll pay your way to Budapest and give you a few kronen to get started."

Margaret turned away from his twisted, horrible face and simply wailed a long, frightening cry like an animal in the night.

In her room, Renee held her brothers, Imre and Zoltan, close. Her mother's crying was different than it had ever been. It was frightening and fearful.

When she heard her father's heavy limping footsteps leave her mother's room and disappear down the long corridor, Renee hurried into the bedroom. She helped her mother back into bed and held her tightly.

"It's all right, Mama. Don't cry. Please don't cry."

"He's sending me away from you forever . . . he's sending me away to Budapest," Margaret sobbed.

Renee shook her head and finally shook her mother's shoulders, forcing her attention. "We will run away and join you in Budapest, then we'll all go where he cannot find us."

"We'll never find each other . . . it's impossible."

Renee again shook her head. "We will meet at the church you showed me when we went to Budapest two years ago, the place where Great-grandmama is buried."

Margaret stared at her young daughter. "I'm surprised you remember, you were so young."

"I remember. Mama, go there and we will come. I will bring Imre and Zoltan."

Margaret brushed the tears off her cheek. Was it possible? Could Renee manage to bring Imre and Zoltan to Budapest? If she could, there was a chance . . . "We would have to plan carefully," Margaret said, allowing herself to feel a moment of hope. "You would have to wait till Janos was away on business so you would have a head start."

"We could disguise ourselves as peasant children," Renee suggested.

Margaret nodded. She would sell her ring and be waiting for them. When they arrived they would all leave at once for Germany and then for America. "There are documents you must bring, Renee. Important documents. Janos keeps them in his top desk drawer. It is not locked.

And the Bible where your births are recorded. We must have that too."

"I will bring the documents and the Bible."

"But what will you use for money? You will need money for the tickets."

"I know where Janos hangs his trousers. There's always money in his pockets. I'll take a little every day, not enough so that he'll notice."

Margaret bit her lip. "I want to believe it's possible."

"Promise me you will look for us at the church every day, promise."

Margaret nodded and fought back her tears and hysteria. Her child seemed more grown-up than she, and she took comfort from Renee's confidence, even though she felt little confidence in herself.

"Mama, be happy. Today is a new beginning for us."

Margaret pressed her lips together, praying silently that it did not mark the end instead.

5

Margaret stared out the window of the railway carriage all the way to Budapest. True to his threat, Janos had paid her fare, given her a few kronen, and allowed her to take only her clothes in her grandmother's trunk. Carefully hidden and sewn into the seam of her dress was the ring. But Margaret did not have the slightest idea how much it was worth, or even how she might go about selling it.

As the flat plains gave way to the rolling hills, the tears dried on Margaret's cheeks and she realized she was beyond more tears. She prayed that her intelligent daughter *would* be able to carry out their plan. She had to concentrate on that and think of nothing else save surviving in the meantime.

The ring, she vowed, would be kept to pay their fare to America. In order to survive, she would have to live on what few kronen she had and try to find some kind of work. But what work? She was totally untrained and unskilled. She had never worked a single day in her entire life. Then too, she was not entirely well. And where would she stay? She did not know how to look for a room. Even though she had never forgiven her mother, she would have gone to her for help had it been possible. But Janos had told her that her mother had left Budapest and was traveling in Europe with her husband.

It was five long hours before the train pulled into the station in Budapest. As she descended the iron steps onto the platform, Margaret shivered. For the first time in her life she was utterly alone in a city she hardly knew. She went through the first few motions of her new existence without confidence. She asked someone in the station if there was a place she could leave her trunk and was directed to a luggage check. For an hour she stood in line, and when she reached the counter they demanded three krona to fetch and keep her trunk. Reluctantly she paid.

Carrying only her large tapestry bag, which contained a change of clothing, Margaret simply began walking as if she might find the solutions to her problems as she walked. Map in hand, she decided to first seek out the church where she had promised Renee she would wait. It turned out to be much further from the station than Margaret had thought, and when she arrived, she sank onto a bench in a small park across the street and stared at it, weariness and fear overcoming her as a brisk wind began to rise in the north and the few leaves that still seemed to be clinging to the trees blew off and skittered along the sidewalk.

With her heavy coat wrapped tightly around her, her hat pulled over her ears and her hands buried in her muff, Margaret simply watched as peasants cleaned the streets, tended the gardens, and passed her talking and walking. How could she who played the piano, cooked, could read, and who spoke four languages be so desperate when the peasants who did none of these things seemed to have places to live and food to eat? None of it made sense to her and once again she began to cry with fright. Darkness crept up on her, and only when it started to rain did Margaret leave the bench and hurry into the church, seeking shelter. She looked around desperately. It was deserted, but if she tried to spend the night someone would come and tell her to leave. She looked about and noted the side altar with its long red skirt. She looked around again to make certain no one was watching, then she crawled under it, pulling her bag with her. She put the bag under her head and curled up into a tiny ball, making certain that none of her could be seen. There, in the cold darkness, she spent the night.

The next morning the sun came up like a great orange ball. In an autumn fog it seemed to hang over the Danube, as if refusing to rise further and give the city heat. On the green lawns and in some of the shrubs, diamonds of dewdrops sparkled like a king's ransom of jewels.

Margaret awoke stiff, cold, and hungry. She peeked out from under the altar skirt and saw the caretaker dusting and sweeping. She waited and after a long while he finished, and as he left, he opened the heavy doors of the church. Margaret crawled out, took her bag, and hurried back to her bench. She was cold to the bone and hungrier than she had ever been.

Jumbles of thoughts filled her head, but inaction gripped her. Then a voice spoke to her, a half-familiar voice, a voice that belonged to someone she known in what seemed another life.

"Miss Margaret? Miss Margaret, what's the matter with you?"

Margaret lifted her blue eyes and stared into Irina's face. "Irina . . . what are you doing here?"

"I live here. We moved to Budapest."

"You live with someone?"

"My brother Ivan."

Again tears began to run down Margaret's face. "Help me, Irina," she begged. Then, sobbing, "Oh, please help me."

Irina stared at her for what seemed like a long time, then nodded and helped Margaret to her feet. "Follow me," she said, and Margaret followed. As they walked along, and before Irina asked, Margaret began talking.

She told Irina everything without exception, though she wasn't at all sure Irina was even listening even though she nodded regularly. Oh, how wonderful Irina looked to Margaret! Of course she was older, but she was dressed quite well and had even had her hair fixed in a fashionable style.

Irina led Margaret up long flights of stairs and into a warm, stuffy row of little rooms off a central hall. There, with little said between them, she fed Margaret hot, rich soup and put her to bed while Margaret babbled on about her children and how she had to meet them.

Later, when Ivan came home, Margaret heard brother and sister discuss her in hushed tones.

"How can we feed another person and save enough money to go to America?" Ivan asked.

"I can't leave her. She's helpless like a child. She's a leaf in the wind."

"And was she so kind to you?"

"She was not mean. We talked sometimes. Anyway, her father made her marry Janos and he was a monster. That I know from personal experience. Yes, Margaret and I share one bond. We were both raped by that monster."

Margaret pulled herself from her bed at that point and staggered into the room where they were talking. She looked at Ivan. He seemed larger than she remembered him from the days when he used to tend her father's horses in the stables. Indeed, now he was heavyset and had a thick beard.

"I heard you talking," Margaret said. Listening to her own voice was almost strange. It sounded faraway to her.

"You should be sleeping," Irina insisted.

Margaret shook her head. "You must listen, please."

"Let her talk," Ivan said, leaning back in his chair and lighting his pipe.

"My children will come. You'll see they will. And when they come we too want to go to America."

"No doubt you plan to swim," Ivan said sarcastically.

Again Margaret shook her head. "I have a ring. It is worth a lot of money . . . if you could advise me, well, help me sell it, I suppose there would be enough for all our fares. Oh, please, please help me learn the things I need to know. I'm not afraid of work . . . I just don't know what to do."

Irina looked at Ivan steadily and Margaret looked pleadingly at both of them. Then Ivan's face broke into a wide grin and he shrugged and threw up his hands, "I see I shall become the guardian of two women and three children! If, of course, there is enough money."

How long it had been since she had felt happy, she did not remember, but that night Margaret too smiled and Ivan even opened a bottle of deep red wine and made her drink to their future.

6

Irina quickly got Margaret a job as a seamstress in the same factory where she worked, and to her delight, Margaret's sewing talents impressed the manager.

Margaret herself marveled at how little she knew of the world, and at how much she learned in those first few weeks of her freedom. Irina taught her to shop for food, and together they prepared dinner every night when Margaret returned from the church, where she went each day when work was over.

The days passed quickly—too quickly—and Margaret grew apprehensive. Perhaps Renee could not manage it as they had planned.

Then after six weeks they arrived—three little peasant children that Margaret herself hardly recognized.

Tears of joy almost consumed Margaret as she embraced her daughter and two sons, and when they joined Irina and Ivan, Renee told the story of their flight.

"I tried to prepare everything in advance," she said, sounding very adult. "As we planned, I had to wait for Papa to leave, to go on a trip. I thought he would never go, but finally he did.

"On the train I sat straight up, pretending to be asleep

so I would not look different. All the peasants seemed to sleep. One, in fact, snored loudly, her mouth open.

"I couldn't have slept, though. I don't know how the others did. Beneath our wooden seat in the third-class carriage we seemed to be sitting over a wheel, because we felt every bump and every vibration as the train clacked along. And it also smelled. It smelled like rotten fish."

Ivan laughed. "When I took the train, I think I sat in that same seat! It's as hard as a rock."

Renee smiled. "Yes, it was hard. Very hard. But one thing I learned, I learned that we wear absurdly uncomfortable clothes. These clothes are wonderful! I feel free in them! Look, Mama. Look at all my skirts." Renee whirled around to demonstrate her many skirts.

"I looked as round and as plump as the peasant girls sitting in the rear of the carriage. Tanya gave me five long skirts—I wear one on top of the other. The idea, Tanya told me, is that once a week you wash the outer skirt, and when it is dry, you move it closest to your skin. In five weeks you've rotated your skirts."

"You should have shown me that, Irina," Margaret good-naturedly admonished her former maid and now friend.

"So now you learn from your daughter," Irina returned.

"I braided my hair," Renee continued. "And like the others, I carried a bulky satchel which was made by simply tying the four corners of a large square of material. Inside it I packed one set of clothing and my coat. I also brought all the documents you mentioned, Mama. Our birth certificates and the Bible."

"You did very well," Margaret said in awe. "Better than I."

Renee smiled and again whirled around. "I brought some other things too. Little things we can sell, things I don't think Papa will miss too soon."

Renee went to her bundle and withdrew a smaller one. From it she produced a pair of solid silver jewelry boxes and a diamond-and-gold tie clip that had belonged to Janos. "These things and many others should be yours, Mama."

"All of it should be yours," Zoltan put in.

"Did you take food for the train?" Margaret asked.

"We ate only one meal. We had a breakfast of fruit, bread, and gruel in the station, and I paid for it with some change I took. Then I bought some bread, apples, and cheese. It was enough for the journey."

"I would have thought Janos would have missed the money," Margaret said.

Renee shook her head. "I planned for this journey. In fact, I began the very day he sent you away. First I assembled the clothing we'd need, and then each day I stole a small amount of money. I never took enough that he would notice. The night before he left for Vienna, I took a gold florin."

"I shall have to watch you," Ivan said, raising an eyebrow.

"I would never steal from anyone else," Renee said quickly, and her stricken look made Margaret realize how very much her daughter disliked Janos.

Ivan laughed. "I was teasing you."

Renee studied him for a moment before continuing with her tale, and Margaret could see that her daughter was beginning to like this bear of a man who suggested they all call him Uncle Ivan.

"Twelve hours after Papa left to catch the morning train for Vienna, we dressed as peasants and began the walk through the woods at night. We reached the deserted station at three in the morning and we slept beneath a huge blanket curled up on the platform like the other peasants waiting for the train. When it came, I bought the tickets and pointed to this tag I had printed and pinned to myself." It gave a false name and read, "Destination: Budapest." "I made identical tags for Zoltan and Imre."

"Very clever," Irina acknowledged. "How did you think of that?"

"I saw some children who arrived from Prague. They had such tags and I've seen the parish priest printing them for the peasants who can't write. Anyway, the stationmaster hardly blinked when I presented the florin, and in return he gave me considerable change and the three tickets."

"And here you are," Ivan summed up.

"And here we are," Zoltan agreed.

Margaret embraced them all again as Irina began putting soup on the table.

"We should all leave immediately," Margaret said when they were all crowded around the tiny table.

"To a bigger place," Ivan said, struggling for elbow room.

"No, to America," Margaret said seriously. "We should leave for Germany the day after tomorrow at the latest."

"The day after tomorrow? So soon?" Ivan asked.

"I know Janos Horvath," Margaret told them. "He will stop at nothing to find his children when he returns. We must go. I feel it."

"Mama is right," Renee agreed.

"Well, I have no real objections," Ivan said, again examining the items Renee had brought. "We should have plenty of money for all of us."

"I'm finally going to America," Margaret said slowly. "It seems impossible after all these years."

Irina touched her hand. "You're a young woman," she told Margaret. "Young enough to start over."

II

The Lazars
1919–1923

Eight

1

July 3, 1919

Seligman & Co. was located in an austere building nestled among other austere buildings in New York's cramped financial district. In the heat of summer, Wall Street lacked its usual hustle. Those who could afford to escape the city's heat fled to the seaside or the mountains. Those hundreds of minions who remained to toil in hot, airless buildings kept to their desks basking in what small relief was offered by whirring fans. Outside, the sun beat down on concrete sidewalks, and the heat, in turn, radiated upward. New York in summer, Miklós decided, was what he imagined it must be like being inside a giant beached whale suffering feverish death throes.

Miklós Lazar, whose fellow workers knew him as Michael, discreetly wiped the beads of sweat from his brow and glanced at the clock on the wall. It was ten minutes to closing, and as it was the Thursday before the three-day July Fourth weekend, he knew it would be the longest ten minutes of the day.

He had finished his work minutes before, and now he shuffled the papers on his desk, ostensibly checking over figures. In reality, his dark eyes darted about the familiar office, studying the faces of his coworkers while his imagination supplied the mysterious details of their lives. Sometimes he wondered if they thought about him the way he thought about them. Again he marveled at their similarity—all were in their late twenties and early thirties. They all wore highly conservative dark suits made of lightweight flannel, and in spite of their youth they all carried either a walking stick or an umbrella. The vast majority of them had mustaches, and he had noted that few dared to smile within the confines of the workplace, the most proper of all the proper investment houses in New York City. Whether or not they smiled outside their offices was one of the many things Miklós wondered about.

Miklós straightened his desk blotter, sharpened two pencils, and arranged the items on his desk. Then he gathered up a pile of file folders, perfunctorily glanced at them, and placed them carefully in the Out box for the file clerk to refile. Five more minutes had ticked by on the clock, and the July Fourth weekend was that much closer. Three days away from the office, three days to escape the unbearable atmosphere of the city, three days to evaluate his ongoing progress and his plans for the future, three days during which he would discuss everything with Leah and they would begin to plan their move.

Again he looked around. Of course he looked exactly like his coworkers; in fact he had made a point of it. And he had rigorously practiced and trained himself until he hardly had even a trace of a Hungarian accent. As for his work, he knew it to be exemplary. He had been promoted four times in three years—something of an office record. And he understood the business, really understood it. He had mastered every portfolio given him, and he carefully studied all the companies whose stocks he sold. He predicted market trends by using a rare combination of knowledge and intuition. To his credit, Miklós had seen the war coming and he had banked on the Americans becoming involved. As a result, he had advised his clients to buy certain stocks, and those stocks had doubled and even tripled in value. If he had had more money to invest himself, he lamented, he would be a rich man today. As it was, he had carefully invested his modest savings and had likewise profited. Miklós' skill had allowed him to save enough to go west and begin his own investment firm, and now that he felt prepared to make his move, he intended breaking the news to Leah. He would tell her while they were both enjoying a short holiday. Abstractedly he felt in his pocket for the little folder that held their tickets to Atlantic City, and he smiled when he thought how surprised and pleased Leah would be when he presented her with the prepaid reservations for one of the city's best hotels right on the famed boardwalk.

The clock rang, and as if each of them had been waiting as he had, the office suddenly broke into a scene of animation as the seemingly humorless men of Wall Street gathered up their belongings and headed for their own private worlds.

Miklós Lazar nodded pleasantly in return when he encountered his fellow workers, even though outside the office he had never socialized with any of them. He supposed he was what others referred to as a "loner." Not that he didn't enjoy the company of others; it was simply that his son, his work, and his studies took up all of his spare time.

Miklós gathered up papers to take home for the weekend, though this weekend he had no intention of even looking at them, and moved with the others toward the corridors and elevators that led to the street.

As he joined the throngs of workers on the hot pavement, he felt a new excitement, he felt that he was at last taking long overdue action. He admitted to himself that since the day he had left the estate of Count Horvath sixteen years ago, life simply seemed to have been a series of events to which he responded. "Today," he murmured under his breath, "I will take the first step toward making my own future."

Yes, looking back, it seemed to Miklós that he had made few if any real decisions about his life, that he was, rather, a victim of "cause and effect."

His involvement with Margaret had been almost accidental. His fears had resulted in his reunion with Leah, and Leah's actions had resulted in their remaining married and becoming parents.

He smiled to himself as he headed for the subway. He and Leah had been married in a civil ceremony in the German port of Hamburg hours before sailing for the United States, so that Leah would not be turned back as so many single women were. They had intended on living as brother and sister and on being divorced once they were in America. But that was not what had happened. Instead, when they arrived they repeated their marriage vows before a proper rabbi, and a short nine months later, on July 20, 1905, their son, Abraham, had been born.

It had begun innocently enough, Miklós reflected. But proximity had worked to bring about a new destiny for them both. He was young, and his experience with Margaret—beautiful Margaret, about whom he still dreamed—had awakened sexual desires, and Leah, though totally different from Margaret, was as beautiful, as daring, and as willing. They had been together for only a few weeks when their play became a reality. He remembered the night clearly, and even now his face flushed with excitement if he thought about it.

They had crossed the ocean as steerage passengers. They had two bunks—one atop the other—and around them they had draped blankets and sheets to ensure a modicum of privacy, though of course in such a situation privacy was truly impossible. But the other steerage passengers did the same, and in the end they all came to believe in the illusion of privacy within the confines of their tiny barricaded little oblong units, which consisted of no more than their bunks, the space under them, and two feet to the side of them.

Miklós had been ill the night before, and so at Leah's insistence he was sleeping in the lower bunk. It was warm belowdeck; he remembered that his body felt damp, bathed in sweat. All around were the noises of the others sleeping. Old Gregory, a bearded giant from Ruthenia, snored and snorted loudly, the ostensible conductor of the others, whose sniffs and whiffs and coughs and other night noises created a cacophony of sound.

Miklós had been lying awake, aware that it must be at least three in the morning. Vaguely he remembered wondering if any of the others were awake. He tried to sort out the sounds, to count and assign the individual noises, hoping the meaningless task would help him drop off into blessed sleep.

He felt Leah brush against him, and he assumed she was getting up to go to the bathroom, but instead she slithered into the narrow bunk beside him, their dampness instantly mingling beneath the single sheet that covered him. She was completely naked and he was silenced only by her fingers on his lips. He had wanted to object, he had wanted to tell her he couldn't possibly perform surrounded as they were by others, but nature quickly overcame his own protestations. Her hand had enclosed his organ and she rubbed him sensually till he thought he could stand silence no longer. His own hands eagerly explored her fine breasts and hips, but before he could even express his admiration for her, she had covered him with her body, guided her erect nipple into his willing mouth, and spread herself in such a way that he had only to move up to enter her. She took him inside her and held him till he could stand it no longer; then she had dictated his movements till she too was satisfied and collapsed beside him, breathing deeply but not loudly. It amazed him that their union had all been accomplished in utter silence, but on reflection he knew it had been all the more exciting because of its clandestine quality and his terrible fear that one of their supposedly sleeping neighbors would be watching or listening, or worse yet, vicariously joining them.

But in spite of all his misgivings, Leah had come to him every night for the rest of the voyage. He began to feel enslaved by her charms; waiting out the long days, he anticipated only the night. He was utterly captivated by Leah, and for a long while never thought of Margaret.

As soon as he and Leah arrived in New York, they were remarried in a synagogue. In spite of their marriage, he had paid her back the money for his fare. He insisted she keep it separate from "their" money, just as he set aside certain funds for himself—or more to the point, for the dream that he truly felt was for them all.

Within weeks of their arrival he had obtained a junior position with J. & W. Seligman. Leah, following her own desires, pursued jobs sketching fashions for various publications until Abraham was born.

Soon after Abraham's birth, Leah engaged a woman to look after him. She continued to pursue her career, working on and off when she could find employment.

Miklós descended the steps to the subway and waited on the crowded platform till the train rolled into the station. He rode standing up, grasping a leather strap for balance. He hated the subway because he hated crowds, and it was all the more unpleasant in summer, when everyone was hot and in ill humor.

After what seemed an unbearable length of time the train clattered to his stop and he pushed his way to the door, emerging onto yet another crowded platform. In moments he was out on the street and headed home.

Miklós walked briskly down Myrtle Avenue and soon crossed Fort Greene Park near Brooklyn Hospital. Catty-corner across the park on Cumberland, he, Leah, and Abraham shared a modest three-room flat. How much better the wide-open streets of the West would be, he thought. Abraham would be able to learn to ride a horse, and the air was fresh and the sun always warm without the blistering humidity of New York City. His dream was Los Angeles. He read about it constantly, and he planned as well. He would open the first indigenous brokerage firm there—it would grow with the city.

He reached the outside of his building and paused to empty his mailbox. It contained only the current *Saturday Evening Post.*

Wearily he climbed the stairs. Abraham was at a scout meeting tonight and Leah would not return from her temporary job until after seven.

He let himself into the neat apartment and stretched. Yes, this weekend the three of them were going to Atlantic City, and there he would discuss moving to the Coast with her. He hoped she would be surprised and happy.

He hoped she would cheer up and see it for the new beginning it was.

Miklós pulled off his shoes and stretched out on the couch. This move, he told himself, would make Leah happy. And, he thought, she's certainly not happy now. He shook his head. Truth be known, she hadn't been really happy since the day she'd discovered she was pregnant. Leah clearly hated motherhood, and she was equally frustrated in her work. She could not find a steady job that suited her, and she complained constantly that she was not allowed to be "creative." But Miklós knew the truth. What Leah longed for in a job was not creativity, but power. She wanted to be in charge; she didn't want to study with others, work as an apprentice, or be part of a cast of thousands. She longed for authority. He had often urged her to open her own shop, but she only scoffed at the idea, claiming she was not a mere dressmaker. "I want to sell fashion to millions of women, not sew one dress at a time!" she would rant. Miklós sighed. The world, he decided, was not yet ready for Leah.

2

Leah silently cursed her temporary position at the *Delineator*, which was devoted to "practical women's clothes." Time after time she had applied to *Vogue*, a fashion magazine devoted to the "ceremonial side of life," as they put it. The "ceremonial side of life" was a euphemism for a blatant appeal to the elite and it was well-known that one of *Vogue*'s most enthusiastic backers was none other than Cornelius Vanderbilt III, one of New York's wealthiest men and a brilliant financier. Leah had also tried to obtain a job with *Harper's Bazaar* without success. These magazines, and especially *Vogue*, featured fashions from Europe and the designs of a few well-known couturiers who submitted their "originals." Leah wanted to change things. She wanted to have the magazines present originals for the couturiers to copy.

The *Delineator*, on the other hand, did not cater to the

elite. It was the result of a merger of two other magazines, the *Ladies' Quarterly Review of Broadway Fashions* and *Metropolitan*. Both of the former magazines had been established by Ebenezer Butterick, who had devised the tissue-paper pattern used to make clothing, and both were originally intended to promote the use of Butterick patterns. Leah imagined that the clothes presented were good enough for the common woman, but to her way of thinking they were not fashion. They were simply practical, dull, and created for women who could not afford to have their clothes made for them.

Moreover, the art department of the *Delineator* was overcrowded and its illustrators overworked. Many of the drawing boards were without stools, so that the artist was required to stand, and some lacked the proper lighting. Leah's table was one without a stool, and because it was in the far corner of the room, away from the doors and windows, she found her work atmosphere stuffy and the hours on her feet tiring. But now she was done, and gratefully she stood up straight and stretched. Then she wiped a wisp of hair from her forehead and slipped her high-heeled shoes back on.

Leah Lazar held up her sketch critically. It would, she decided, serve its purpose.

Working on these illustrations was one of Leah's many temporary assignments, and it did not fill her with either enthusiasm or creative zeal. The models were plain, the clothes were middle-class, and she had had no role in their design. This was not the career she had dreamed of, and admittedly, she felt more frustrated than satisfied. At times she even felt angry.

She glanced at the clock. It was ten to six, and now that she had finished, she was free to leave. But Leah felt no urge to hurry. Instead, she began to gather up her belongings slowly, putting off the inevitable trip home to an evening of what had become boring domesticity. Why had she not succeeded? It plagued her, and it annoyed her even more that Miklós seemed to be making progress —at least he seemed untroubled and optimistic. He loved his work and he climbed the ladder steadily, advancing routinely from one position to another, while she still labored on doing little but copying the work of others.

And there was the child. She had not intended on becoming a mother—Abraham had been an accident, and one she still regretted. She had lost valuable time during her pregnancy and the child's infancy. And now, even though he was old enough to see to himself, there were still domestic demands on her time, time she might have spent developing her portfolio or meeting the right people.

Leah stuffed her shawl into her large linen bag and for a moment looked about, as if taking inventory of her surroundings. Then she went to the ladies' room, where she paused to look into the tin mirror that hung on the wall above the washbasin where she washed her hands.

Her large green eyes were clear and her skin unwrinkled. Her hair was still dark and thick, and, she thought with pride, the child had not changed her fine figure one bit. Her waist still measured twenty-two inches, her hips thirty-four, and her bust thirty-four. Below her emerald-green crepe-de-chine skirt, her black silk stockings covered shapely ankles and her high heels gave her added height. "I am still a beautiful woman," Leah whispered to her image. "Too beautiful to be trapped in such a dull and demanding marriage."

At the time of their marriage, she reflected, Miklós had seemed the most handsome man in the world. She had yearned to stroke his broad back and be held in his muscular arms. And sexually he seemed as hungry as she—they'd been like young animals, free and eager. When she had first discovered she was pregnant, she was furious, but after a time she tried to look on the bright side. Given the fact that it was difficult to find work in her field of interest, she reasoned that it would not be so bad to be married to a man with a steady job. Nonetheless, Leah hated motherhood; she hated it far more than Miklós realized. He, by contrast, doted on his son. He adored the child and she supposed this was a good thing, since it somewhat compensated for her own lack of loving emotion toward her offspring. Father and child could have one another, as far as Leah was concerned. She wanted more from life, and even though she had not yet achieved her goals, she felt somehow she would if she kept trying and could in some way free herself from wifely responsibilities.

Leah dried her hands and lifted her bag, taking one last long look at herself as she walked away and headed for the stairs. At the top of the stairs a group of well-dressed men who had been touring the magazine earlier were bidding each other good night, and she stepped around them and headed down the stairs, aware that one of the men was walking just behind her.

He was a tall, dark, handsome man and she was quick to realize that he was expensively dressed. She had seen him earlier, when he and one of the editors had come through her department.

She had noticed him then because he had paused and looked at her, and she was aware of him now as he reached around her and opened the heavy front door, stepping to one side and bowing slightly. She looked downward, her eyes fixed on his walking stick. It was made of fine black ebony and had a gold handle with a large diamond stud that sparkled when the light hit it.

"Thank you," she murmured

"My pleasure." He smiled at her and his dark eyes traveled slowly from her stylish feathered hat down to her gold-buckled black shoes. He was unhurried in his assessment of her, and his slightly twisted smile and dark eyes sent a chill of anticipation through her whole body—the kind of chill she had not felt since she first encountered Miklós in Vienna—and then it had been she who was the aggressor.

"I saw you earlier," the stranger said as they stood on the street in front of the door. "Allow me to introduce myself. I am Béla Szendi."

She smiled. "And you are Hungarian."

He returned her smile and bowed from the waist. Then, unexpectedly, he took her gloved hand and lifted it to his lips and kissed it. "What a pleasure to meet another . . . and will you tell me your name?"

"Leah—Leah Lazar." Again his eyes surveyed her slowly, and she brazenly returned his look.

"Are you a model?"

"No, an illustrator."

"Ah . . . I thought that was what you were doing. But has no one at the publication any sense? You are much more attractive than the models."

"Thank you," she replied, trying to sound as young and as innocent as possible. But her heart was beating wildly. Clearly he was rich and no doubt influential. Ever since she had been in New York she had been trying to meet someone with money . . . someone who could help her succeed.

"Ah, but then it wouldn't do to have you model the clothes, because no one would see the clothes, they would see only you."

She laughed lightly and pretended to move away, but he took her elbow gently. "I would like to talk with you," he said, then added, "professionally."

"I really should be going . . ."

"Surely you have time to join me for some tea or coffee?"

Leah again feigned resistance. She recalled her image in the mirror, for strength. She was wasting evening after evening with Miklós and Abraham. She was still young, still vital, still full of adventure. In any case, this man seemed important—he had been with one of the editors. Possibly he might want to offer her a job. "I suppose I could," she agreed.

He took her arm and led her down the street. Then he stopped by the side of a long sleek two-tone Packard Twin Six, one of the most expensive cars being built. Leah forced a neutral expression as Béla opened the door for her, and as if in a trance, she allowed him to help her inside. He then walked around the car and climbed into the driver's seat. "Your wish is my command. Where should we go?"

"I'm sure you know more places than I. You choose."

The car almost purred as Béla slipped it into gear, and unlike all other cars she had been in, this one was almost silent as it pulled into the dense traffic. They drove for a few minutes and came to a stop in front of the elegant

Algonquin Hotel. He turned the car over to the uniformed doorman and steered her inside to the lobby, where couples and groups gathered at small round tables and talked softly in the muted atmosphere provided by the high ceilings, the rich thick carpets, and the heavy brocade draperies.

He pulled out a velvet chair for her and sat opposite. He ordered two coffees and leaned toward her. "May I call you Leah?"

She nodded, overcome by the atmosphere, the suddenness of her being here, and by Béla's overpowering presence. Everything about him excited her. He was suave and commanding. He seemed to have a sense of his own power, and she considered this to be an indication of his ability to control circumstances and events, perhaps to guide destiny, her destiny. He was a big man, a man whose large physique seemed to offer unending energy and thus immense pleasure. Yes, he seemed capable of giving her considerable pleasure, but she in turn could well make him happy. She was, after all, quite inventive and in bed totally uninhibited. Not that Miklós appreciated that side of her at all; indeed he would have been shocked had he realized what she fantasized about in order to achieve any satisfaction from their now-infrequent couplings. But this man was different. She could tell by the way he looked at her. And in addition to the electricity she felt between them, he was obviously rich.

Béla leaned across the table now, demanding her attention. "I am looking for an illustrator—well, more than an illustrator, really. Have you had much experience?"

Again she nodded. "I have some drawings with me . . ."

"I doubt they will tell me what I want to know. Tell me, how long will you be working on this issue of the *Delineator*?"

"My work is actually finished."

"Then I want you to come and see me tomorrow, even though it's a holiday, and bring what you need to work. I will have some models for you to sketch . . . and then we will talk, perhaps over dinner if you're free."

"I can be."

"Here is my card. Come around four."

She took the gold-embossed card and read it. "Béla Szendi, Inc." was all it said.

"You have your own business?" She felt suddenly awestruck; it was as if her long-held dream were suddenly about to materialize. And so unexpectedly! She shivered with anticipation, but tried to hide it.

"I am just beginning," he told her. "But we can discuss business tomorrow. Tell me about Leah Lazar."

She smiled coquettishly and offered a carefully edited and abridged version of her life.

In return, he offered her an embellished and entirely untrue version of his. He wondered, as he talked, how long it would take to seduce this rather intriguing woman who had such hungry gray-green eyes and such a sensuous way of moving her well-shaped body. She was no child, Béla noted, but she was, nonetheless, extraordinary-looking. Everything about her breathed sexuality, raw, unbridled sexuality.

3

The Lazars' apartment in Brooklyn, located in one of many almost identical brownstones, was on the third floor, and consisted of two small bedrooms, a kitchen/living-room/dining-room combination, and a small bathroom. Since the building had once been a large private row home, it was joined to others on the street and thus had windows only in the front and in the rear. But it was a neat, clean little apartment in a good neighborhood, and its private bath was a luxury. Since coming to New York, they had lived in three different places. The first had been only a room with a shared bath and kitchen; the second had been slightly better, with only the bath shared. This apartment spoke of their progress, and Miklós was proud of it, though he expected that in California they would have even more room, and further, that there they would be able to acquire their own land.

Miklós' dreams of the future played vividly in his

thoughts while he waited for Leah. He had arrived home filled with enthusiasm, but forced to wait for her, he grew impatient. Then, as it grew later, he became worried as well. Abraham came home and went to bed. And still Miklós waited. It was not until after ten that the sound of Leah's steps on the stairs brought him to his feet.

He met her in the entranceway, his expression halfway between anger and relief. "Where have you been? It's past ten!"

"Is it really?" she asked airily. "It didn't seem so late."

"Stop it. You know perfectly well what time it is." He felt his face flush. "Abraham came home two hours ago. He's already gone to bed. At least you should have had the consideration to call."

"I'm sorry . . . but I got so busy, I really didn't realize it was as late as it is."

"Leah, I had wanted tonight to be special . . ."

She heard his voice trail off and she watched as he turned and walked into their living room. She followed, undoing the top buttons of her blouse and slipping out of her shoes. "Why tonight?" she asked. "What's special?"

"Because it is a long weekend and I arranged a surprise."

She smiled, dropping onto the overstuffed sofa. "I really am sorry, Miklós. But why does my being late spoil your surprise?"

He watched as she curled herself up. Her look at him was one of wide-eyed innocence. As always, he forgave her instantly. "It doesn't really—I just wanted time to talk with you."

She pulled the pins out of her hair and it fell loose, to well below her shoulders in a rich dark tangle. She shook it, ran her hand through it, and tossed her head back as if undoing her hair were a celebration of freedom. "Come, Miklós . . ." She patted the sofa with her hand and beckoned him as if he were a puppy. "We can talk now," she said as she twisted a curl around her finger.

He went and sat down on the sofa. "I've arranged for us to go away tomorrow morning—to the seaside for the weekend. I've rented a hotel room, Leah."

"Oh." She frowned and bit her bottom lip. "Oh, Miklós, I can't go—I have to stay here in New York."

"Even on the holiday? You can't. Leah, this is the first time in ages we've been able to get away." They had gone to Cape Cod two years ago, and before that, when Abraham was ten, they had gone to Boston. Miklós remembered the trip with great happiness. He had taken his son to Bunker Hill, the Paul Revere House, and to Faneuil Hall. He'd lectured him on American history and Abraham had memorized *The Ride of Paul Revere*, by Longfellow.

"I know we haven't been away for a long while . . ." She reached across the distance between them and touched his forehead with her fingers. "Miklós . . . I just can't. Not this weekend."

"I have the reservations, it's paid in advance. Leah, what could possibly keep you in New York on a holiday weekend?" He could hear the irritation in his own voice.

"A job offer, a wonderful job offer. I have to go there tomorrow . . . I must, darling, I really must."

His heart sank and he stared at her. A new job might mean she wouldn't want to leave New York. Secretly, he knew she had failed so far in her career, and in truth, her failure pleased him because it meant he could pursue his dream of taking them all west to California. But of course he couldn't tell her that; in fact, he deemed it best not to mention the trip west at all at this point. "I don't think I can get the money back," he protested.

"Then you take Abraham and go. I'll stay here."

"Leah, I can't. I had wanted us to be together. You don't understand."

He watched as her face clouded over and as tears suddenly filled her wonderful eyes. He braced himself even though he knew it was no use—he was impotent against her quick emotional reactions. He always gave in to her tears.

"It is always you," she sobbed. "You have a good job, a position. You are seeing your dream come true while I walk around New York begging for a chance to show my drawings—even to get horrible little jobs doing this and that! Miklós, this may be my chance. I must take it, no matter what. Why are you being so cruel? Why can't you understand?"

He drew her into his arms. "I do, Leah, I do. Please, don't cry. I'll take Abraham and we'll go alone . . . if you're certain."

She looked into his eyes and nodded. "I'm certain."

"We could stay here—the money doesn't matter."

"No . . . I mean, I have to prepare for this. Perhaps it would be better if you and Abraham were gone."

"I never like being away from you." He drew her closer and kissed her long white neck.

She did not answer him, but she lay back and allowed him to continue kissing her. He would then undress her and make love to her. She didn't entirely feel like it, and then too, her thoughts were still full of Béla Szendi. But she would allow it, she decided. It would make him feel better about leaving for the weekend, and she knew her weekend would be decidedly happier without him.

4

From the moment Leah walked into the offices of *Men's and Women's Fashion Catalog*, she was impressed. The corporate name this Béla Szendi had chosen left something to be desired, but his offices did not; they reflected a gentleman's taste for elegance, comfort, and utility.

The lighting was excellent in the large art department, and the drawing boards were new and each had a fine leather stool. A long elevated runway for models wound around the room so that the artists could sketch the models in front of them, and beyond the art department, Béla's private office offered genuine comfort.

He met her there in his office and then took her directly to the art department. In a nearby dressing room Leah could hear several girls talking, and these she assumed were the models he had spoken about. Apart from the girls, they were alone in the building because it was the Fourth of July and an official holiday.

Having situated her at one of the drawing boards, Béla brought on the models one by one, and when they had disappeared, he asked Leah to draw as quickly as possible from memory, and to include the maximum detail.

"That's enough," he ordered after four had appeared. He leaned over Leah's sketchpad. "Very good," he said, rubbing his chin, "but it solves only half the problem."

Leah looked up at him, puzzled. "Only half the problem?" she repeated. Her curiosity was truly aroused. Why these copies? Why was she asked to do it after the models had left the room?

"Ah, yes. Now what is needed is a pattern. One must transform what is seen on the model into a usable pattern so that the dress might be reproduced."

Leah studied him. "If one already has the dress, doesn't one already have the pattern?"

Béla smiled at her and leaned ever closer, "Not if what is sketched is the design of someone else, my dear."

"You mean you want to copy other people's creations and make patterns from them?"

"Yes, my clever lady, that is exactly right. Now, listen carefully. The greatest influence on America's women today is the fashions of the wealthy. The wealthy buy them in Europe, and when they are worn in public they are copied by a hundred little dressmakers for the upper middle class. All that is currently produced in our great garment district here on Seventh Avenue is clothes for commoners—shirts and skirts and blouses. Clothes without style or flair, Clothes for shop clerks and housewives."

"And what do you intend doing?"

He laughed. "What I want is to have fashions sketched directly in Paris, during showings. I want them then made into patterns quickly and produced here before even Mrs. Astor can wear her original to the opera. I want to produce a catalog that offers the average woman clothes that will turn her into Mrs. Astor."

"How can the average woman afford such clothes?"

"Because they will be styled like the clothes of the

wealthy, but made from far cheaper materials. I know about these matters."

"The sketches would have to be made very quickly—on the sly, really."

"No, not on the sly. From memory. And the best person for such a job is a very beautiful woman who looks like she might be a customer. Still, she must have the requisite artistic talent, and above all, she must want to become my partner and also become very rich."

"Partner?"

"Yes. I have money, but I will require an additional five thousand dollars as a kind of guarantee of good faith."

"Five thousand! That's a small fortune," Leah gasped.

"For the right person it is the opportunity of a lifetime. I have the experience in manufacturing and I am putting up all the rest of the money—over forty thousand. You, my dear, need only ambition. I know you can raise the money, I feel it."

Leah looked into his eyes. It was certainly an opportunity . . . heaven knew she couldn't keep on doing what she was doing. And it would mean travel! Fabulous, wonderful travel! She had a few hundred of her own money left and she knew full well that Miklós had been investing and saving. Vaguely she wondered if he had that much money. It seemed unlikely, but with his job he could probably borrow the rest of what she needed.

She eyed Béla and then said, trying to give nothing away, "If I were to enter into such an arrangement, I would have to have a lawyer check it over. You are, after all, really a stranger to me."

"I would expect nothing less, my dear." He touched her hair and looked deeply into her eyes. "Pardon my saying so, but I hope we are not to remain strangers."

Again Leah felt the pull of a powerful physical attraction. This man was devastating, and no doubt dangerous. But she was up to it. He looked and felt like true adventure, and she longed for adventure. As handsome as Miklós was, he seemed dull to her. He was concerned only with his work and with his son, and worse, he seemed determined to turn her into what she was not. He failed to understand that the child had been an accident, that she hadn't wanted to be a mother, and that even now she resented it. But that was only one of many things. "I shall have to make some inquiries," she murmured.

He waved his hand expansively. "Quite all right. I have to test two or three more artists. But do remember that catalogs are a growing business. Look how well Sears, Roebuck is doing. And there are others starting up. Of course, the catalog would not be our only outlet. We could sell to some of the big department stores as well."

She absolutely forced her expression not to change even as she determined that she *must* somehow raise the money. "I'll be in touch with you as soon as possible."

"I hope you aren't running off. I had hoped we might have dinner together."

Leah smiled her most charming smile. "Of course," she replied. "But I really must go home and change first."

"Where shall I call for you?"

Leah scribbled her address on a scrap of paper. "I stay with my brother," she lied. "Michael Lazar—the name is on the buzzer."

Béla folded it and put it into his vest pocket. "Until seven," he said, looking into her arresting eyes and imagining her naked in his bed. Yes. She would make an excellent partner in bed and out. She seemed to have ambition, a certain restlessness, and above all, she radiated desire. Her talent was limited, but she didn't need more, and what she did, she did well. The five thousand was more important—that and the fact that she could easily pass for a customer in Paris. She knew how to dress, and he would see to it that she looked the part. Yes, all in all, he felt he had made quite a discovery.

Nine

1

July 6, 1919

The July heat hung over the city even though the sun had set. With each mile the train traveled, Miklós Lazar had felt his discomfort increasing. Not that the weekend alone with his son had been unenjoyable. In fact, he and Abraham had enjoyed a restful two days in Atlantic City romping in the surf and playing volleyball on the hard-packed sand. At first Miklós had thought Leah's absence would ruin their time together, but he soon realized he felt more relaxed without her and that Abraham too seemed more at ease. Father and son had thoroughly enjoyed one another's company, and when they approached the brownstone where they lived and Abraham spied some of his friends and ran to join them, Miklós waved him off.

Now, poised on the threshold of their apartment, he paused to think through his presentation to Leah. In his mind he had delivered his little speech over and over and he felt ready for any reaction she might give. If she was negative, he had his arguments. If she was enthusiastic, no arguments would be needed, and so much the better.

Abraham agreed with him—that much he knew. Over the weekend he had taken the boy into his confidence, asking him again and again how he might feel about moving to the Coast. "It will mean giving up your friends," Miklós told him.

"I don't mind, I'll make new friends," Abraham had insisted.

No, Abraham had no reservations. He was adventurous and more than ready to try out something new. California held as much allure for the boy as it had for the gold miners seventy years ago.

With Abraham's support to bolster him, Miklós opened the door to the apartment. "Leah," he called softly, so as not to awaken her if she were asleep.

"I'm in here," she called from their bedroom.

Miklós made his way through the crowded hallway and paused for a moment at the bedroom door. On opening it, he found Leah sitting at her dressing table. She was brushing her hair and she was dressed in a pair of deep red silk Chinese pajamas. She looked beautiful. More beautiful than she had looked in years, and she glowed with the kind of raw nervous excitement he had almost forgotten she possessed.

"Oh, Miklós, I got the job," she gushed. And in a second she had run to his arms, pressing herself against him in a way that flustered him and melted his resolve.

"Where's Abraham?" she whispered.

"Outside, telling his friends about our little trip," Miklós replied.

"Good. I want us to be alone for a bit. Oh, Miklós, I have so much to tell you."

"Leah, I have wanted to talk to you too."

"I'm going to become a partner, the head designer for a new manufacturer with his own catalog. It's what I've dreamed of and worked for . . . Oh, I can hardly believe it!"

For a long moment he looked at her dumbfounded. It was worse than he had even imagined it might be; how could he now tell her they were leaving?

"There is one thing . . ." She was holding on to his lapels and her eyes were penetrating his. "Miklós, I need five thousand to get started. I have a few hundred of my own and I know you have some too . . . Miklós, I need to borrow your money."

"Leah, that's money I've put aside for my own business in California. I've dreamed and planned to open my own firm—I'm ready to make the move now, and you will have to come with me."

"I'll never come!" Her reaction was instant, cold and violent. "Never!" She had pulled away from him and jumped back. Her hands were on her hips, and her wonderful full lips were pressed tight.

He was still staggered by her news and by her request for so much money, and in the face of her temper he was bewildered. "Leah . . ." He tried to calm her, and hated the quality of pleading in his own voice.

"Don't Leah me! *Lofasz a seggedbe*!" she cursed in Hungarian. "You want to take me away, imprison me!"

Her voice was not high and hysterical; rather it was low and menacing. For a moment he was totally taken aback by her vile language and vehemence; then he managed to stutter an answer. "That's not what I want at all. I want my own business. I want a new chance for us. Leah, I have to make the move soon. I'm the right age and I have the money now."

"And I have the opportunity of a lifetime to travel all over the world, to design my own clothes, to own half a fine company." Leah ran her fingers through her hair and suddenly lowered her voice. She leaned toward him as seductively as possible and looked intently into his eyes. Then, after a long moment of silence, tears began to run down her cheeks. "God, I'm selfish. . . . Miklós, forgive me, I was just so excited."

He wrapped his arms around her and rocked her comfortingly. "Of course I forgive you. I know how much the offer must mean to you . . . and, God knows, Leah, you deserve success. It is I who am selfish . . . but in the end, we'll all be better off."

She sobbed against him, her whole body shaking, and he felt like a monster.

"I thought you would do this for me, Miklós. I thought you would lend me this money because when you needed money to come to America I lent it to you. I knew you wanted to go to California, but I thought it would be at least two years. I mean, by then I would be successful and could sell my partnership and move to the Coast with you. I could start my own catalog in California. But I understand. . . ."

She was leaning against him, whispering. It was true that she had lent him money when he needed it. He felt rotten and he held her away from him and looked into her deep green eyes and felt weak. He could not argue with her request when she put it this way, but at the same time he saw his own dream slipping away into oblivion. Tears filled his eyes as he looked back at her and nodded silently. But his emotion of the moment eluded Leah.

"Only two years?" He almost choked on the words, trying to sound normal.

Leah forced herself not to smile. She nodded solemnly and buried her face in his chest. He was going to do it! He was going to give her the money!

"Oh, Miklós! I knew I could count on you, I knew it!" Her arms were around him and her fingers moved across his back. He buried his face in her hair and fought back his own disappointment, trying desperately to feel some happiness for her. Still, he could not fully let go. The question "Why now?" kept popping into his head and he wondered about this mysterious investment she had to make.

He summoned himself and pulled back. "Leah, I won't let you be duped. I must know more about such a business arrangement."

"It's all right," she said, touching his cheek. "Our lawyer is looking at it now. Really, Miklós, do you think I am such a fool?"

He shook his head, feeling the flow of final defeat. If it were at the lawyer's, it was almost over and done with—he only had to empty his bank account and provide the money that would seal the deal. Leah, as so often before, had presented him with a fait accompli.

2

July 15, 1919

Béla Szilard, who since he had acquired a new identity in Turkey many years ago had called himself Béla Szendi, leaned back in the red leather chair in his wood-paneled den and congratulated himself once again. He had fled Hungary with all the profits from his ill-gotten uniform contracts and gone to Turkey. There he had obtained—for a price—new papers and a new name. He had emigrated next to England, where he doubled his money with a shrewd investment in a firm that manufactured patent medicines. Just before the outbreak of war, he reinvested in another uniform-manufacturing company. In a short time some of the profits of the Great War found their way to his accounts, then at war's end he had come to the United State, where, he discovered, the clever could achieve almost anything. Among other investments, he had just bought the factory and adjoining offices that had so impressed Leah.

And once again he had chosen wisely. A cursory investigation had proved Leah Lazar to be a semitalented artist, but more important, she was overanxious for success. He had discovered she was also married and the mother of a son. But none of these things alone was enough to make him select or reject Leah. The most important thing in her favor was, in fact, her husband. He was a respected broker who had managed to save cash and who had some stocks. Moreover, this husband's job would enable him to borrow money easily. "On such assets are successful businesses built," Béla said aloud to himself. Yes, he had chosen well. This business could be built with someone else's risk, and most of its profits would be his if things went right. Moreover, Leah Lazar was a most attractive woman in spite of being in her late thirties. It was equally obvious that she was attracted to him, like metal to a magnet. Yes, he reflected, he and Leah might just be two of a kind.

He glanced at his pocket watch, and even as he did so, the buzzer on his door rang. He hastened to answer it.

"I thought you might be late," Béla said as he admitted Leah, who looked utterly devastating. Her hair was pinned up, but a few select curls were left to caress her long neck and frame her face. Around her forehead she wore a headband with a delicate wired plume in the center. She carried a matching ostrich-feather fan, as was the latest vogue. She was wearing a flimsy black dress made from clinging crepe de chine, with a daring décolletage trimmed in black lace. It clung to her every delectable curve, Béla noticed. He moved his eyes slowly down from her deep cleavage to her trim ankles. She wore black silk stockings and black pointed shoes, and though she really didn't need it, her high cheekbones were lightly rouged, as were her inviting lips. Vaguely he wondered if she had also rouged the tips of her breasts, as was done by many European women.

"I always try to be punctual," she replied, casting her fan aside a bit too dramatically.

Béla looked sternly at her. "It must be difficult with a husband and son to care for."

Leah met his accusative eyes unblinkingly, almost boldly. She had intended to tell him in any case—life was too complicated to lie to everyone. "Not at all," she responded. "Abraham is a big boy and can take care of himself. Miklós understands."

Bela stepped closer to her. "Does he understand that you will be away a great deal? Does he understand that you will be traveling with me?"

"He understands I will be away. He doesn't need to know whom I travel with. In any case, he will give me the money."

"Were I your husband, I would not be so liberal."

She half-smiled. "Fortunately, you are not my husband, darling."

He returned her smile. She pronounced "darling" "dar . . . link," and her voice was throaty, which added to her sex appeal. But, he thought, clearly she assumed she would be master of this relationship. Well, Leah had a lot to learn. "So, you have come to accept my offer."

"Yes, and I've brought a contract and a check to seal the bargain."

"I like a woman with a head for business."

He took the contract from her and read it quickly. "I will give it to my lawyer tomorrow, and then tomorrow night we will sign it if everything is in order." He took the contract, to which the check was attached, and laid it on his desk.

"And?" Leah said, lifting her brow.

"And now you will step into my lair and we will share some fine wine."

Leah followed him into the living room of this spacious Park Avenue apartment. It was furnished with antiques and lit by small electric lights meant to look like the old gas lights. The colors were subdued and Leah knew she looked younger than her age in the soft light.

"Sit where you like." Béla's hand swept around the room.

Leah slipped onto the sofa and curled her long shapely legs up, after first discarding her shoes. She gazed at him and could almost feel Béla's admiration for her as his eyes fell on her feet and ankles. The electricity that was between them continued to draw her to him, and she knew the question was not if, but when. She also knew that with a man like Béla she ought to play hard-to-get. He must never be sure of me, she thought, even after we have been in one another's beds.

Béla turned away from her and poured the wine, handing her one large goblet. He poured himself another and lifted it in a toast. "To us," he said, smiling.

"To us," she rejoined. Then, looking at him steadily, "Why did you have me investigated?"

" 'Investigated' is rather a harsh word."

"Well, how else did you find out about my husband and child?"

"Why didn't you tell me you were married and had a child?"

"It was not important for you to know."

He laughed. "Nonsense. You wanted to be free to seduce me."

Leah felt her face flush a deep red and she started to protest, when he dropped to the floor in front of the sofa and seized her ankle with his hand. At once he began caressing her foot slowly.

"Lean back," he commanded, "and close your eyes. . . . That's a good girl," Béla said, smiling. "False protestations bore me. I feel what is between us, Leah. We deserve each other, you and I. We are two of a kind really." His hand and fingers moved from her ankle to her calf and then to her thigh, where her dark stockings attached to her frilly garter belt. His hand moved in slow semicircular motions and she moaned once, then twice as he adventured higher beneath her dress, using only his left hand, while his right held his wine goblet and he sipped now and again. As he continued, she gripped the back of the sofa with her long fingers, giving in to the rare sensations that his touch caused within her.

Miklós had never had such an effect! Not even the first time. She felt the dampness of anticipation between her legs as his hand reached ever higher.

He lingered where he was, and she heard him set his wine down. Then with his other hand she felt him push her dress down till he had exposed her breasts. He flicked his tongue over her hard nipple, then drew back to look at her. She could feel his eyes even through her closed lids.

"You are quite lovely that way," he said as once again his fingers began to move beneath her lacy undergarments. "You know, a half-dressed woman is more seductive than one fully undressed." He laughed throatily. "Then too, there is no need wasting time on that which is not desired."

Just as he began his almost magical movements on her most sensitive area, he again moved his tongue on her nipple. She twisted in his grip and moaned again and again, unable to control the desire that swept over her.

Béla smiled as he heard her gasp, and watched as she tried to pull him to her. Then she cried out and shook violently. He held her bare breast tightly and felt her as she shivered against him. "That's good," he whispered. "Very good."

Her eyes blinked open and she looked questioningly into his. "You, my dear, can experience multiple pleasures. A man must pace himself."

"I never . . ." she began.

"Came so intensely," he finished. "You see. Our partnership is truly sealed now." He toyed with her absently, and thought to himself that she was indeed torrid baggage.

Leah felt unable to move or even think. For once in her life she was at a true loss for words.

3

October 1919

Autumn had come to New York, but for Konrad Szilard it was truly spring, the springtime of his life.

At thirty-six, Konrad was lean and looked a bit like an actor playing the role of a true aesthete. When pensive, he tended to look off into space, but it was not a blank stare. He seemed to see something that others couldn't see, and at times he bent his head a little, as if, like his mysterious vision, he could also hear what others could not. But there were times when he was concentrating; at such times one could feel his intensity. When he spoke, Konnie's voice had a smooth, almost hypnotic quality. He was frighteningly intelligent, and with little effort he could make people listen. There was, in addition, another side to Konnie. On occasion he could be extremely funny, and his sense of humor was razor sharp. He was a man of moods, keenly aware of his own creative side, yet capable of a logical coolness. Konnie did not suffer from hero worship, but he enjoyed what might be described as "place" worship. There were locations where he "felt" strong connections with the past, places that had a certain ambience that spoke to his personal tastes, and places that seemed to be haunted by spirits with whom he communicated. Physically, he resembled his mother's family. He had blond hair and blue eyes, and beneath his patrician nose he sprouted a small blond mustache, which he fancied made him look more distinguished.

As he walked in New York's famed theater district, he "felt" the excitement of a hundred opening nights, and in his thoughts the actors and plays of the past paraded across his mind, in spite of his new and all-consuming interest in what the Europeans called "films" and the Americans called "movies."

Nonetheless, his first interest *had* been the theater, and certainly his current interests had grown out of the first. Indeed, it was as if the world had seen him coming and invented whole new toys for him to master.

In Paris, half-starved and desperately searching for a job, he had stumbled into the camera factory of Auguste and Louis Lumière. At first he had been employed as a sweeper; then he had learned about the moving pictures being made. How had he not heard of these before? How had he not heard of America's Mr. Edison? He continued working as a sweeper, but he also began to study. Konrad's imagination ran wild. It seemed that every day he lived and worked in Paris, some new development was made in the art and technology of film. And the potential! From the very first moment, he saw the potential. Plays would no longer have to be performed in theaters, to be seen by only the very few. One day they would be put on film—living film, in which the characters moved as they would onstage. Once on film, these "plays" could be sent from one place to another and could be seen by all. The theater would no longer be a place for only the elite. Now it would belong to the people. But the Lumière brothers were not interested in making fictional films. They were interested only in factual films.

From the Lumière factory Konnie went to Georges Melies, the famous magician who was then making films of short plays. He begged for a job. Melies himself was dedicated to the theater, and he spent hours talking to Konnie before hiring him. Clearly there was a meeting of minds. Konnie did not know if Georges had hired him because of his wild ideas or because of his knowledge of the theater, but it did not matter. Melies opened the entire world of French filmmaking to Konnie. He soon met Zecca, head of production at Pathé, and he witnessed the growth of the film as art with the formation of Film d'Art, a company that made films from the novels of Dumas and whose last film had featured the internationally known actress Sarah Bernhardt.

But in spite of wonderful actresses and splendid scripts, something was lacking in the finished film product, and Konnie soon realized what it was. It was reality and a sense of spontaneity. Most films were shot inside, and the sets were stiff, the lighting contrived, and the actors and actresses dressed and made-up incorrectly for the black-and-white camera. The films with the most life, he noted, were those shot outdoors, where the sets were real. All the potential for drama was available in the natural setting, and Konnie yearned to make a whole dramatic film without resorting to sets. He could feel the possibilities in the depth of his soul. Yes, the current product was flat; it lacked vitality and often it lacked intelligence. Konnie wanted to change the way in which films were made.

With his small savings, he soon left France and began to travel around Europe. He had spent considerable time in Germany as well as in London. But soon Europe was in turmoil and then at war. After the war the empire collapsed and Konnie, who had been an exile because of his father's demands, now found himself among thousands of Magyar exiles trying to escape the communist government that had come to power earlier this very year.

In Germany Konnie found his old friend Béla Lugosi, whom he had known at the Budapest Academy of Theater Arts, and the child star Pola Negri was there, as well as the Korda brothers, Alexander, Michael, and Zoltan.

In spite of the warmth and friendship he found in Germany with his fellow expatriates, Konnie wanted more. Then, through Pola Negri, Konnie learned the address of a young man he had once tutored, Joseph Somló. Joseph, eighteen years Konnie's junior, had gone to America in his early teens and now worked at one of the big studios. Joe had begun as a dishwasher in the cafeteria and was now working as an assistant to a director.

For some months Konnie corresponded with Joe. He heard about developments in America, and because he associated America with the best of everything and the newest of everything, he determined to leave Europe and travel to New York, and from there to Los Angeles, where D. W. Griffith, a filmmaker to whom he had also been writing, was currently making films.

But at this moment Konnie stood in the heart of New York's theater district in front of the Palace, a wonderful ornate theater in the Old World tradition. He walked around slowly and read the advertisements, then settled in a small coffee shop nearby to watch the fascinating parade of pedestrians as they trudged up Broadway in the October sunshine.

When his coffee had come, he reached into his pocket and removed the letter that had been waiting for him in care of general delivery when he arrived. He had already read it once, but now he unfolded it to read again:

My darling son Konnie,

You cannot imagine how wonderful it was to hear from you after all these years. Our lives have changed, Konnie, and I hardly know where to begin.

First, your father is dead. He killed himself after a terrible scandal caused by Béla, who committed fraud and ran away with a large sum of money. I have no idea where Béla is, and I do not care. He is responsible for much suffering and he is the only one of my children I never want to see again.

Your sister, Margaret, has also disappeared. She took her three children—a daughter and two sons—with her. The daughter is called Verena and is now fifteen. The two boys must be fourteen and eleven. Before she ran away I wrote letter after letter, but she did not and would not answer. She refused to see me and had held me responsible for her terrible marriage. I have begged her forgiveness, but to no avail.

György, our beloved György, is also dead. He was killed in a duel by Janos Horvath some years ago.

Finally, as you know, I have remarried. I am most happy with József, though I long to see Margaret again and hold my grandchildren in my arms. My new address is on the envelope and I hope you will use it to write to me often, since you are the only one I have left, Konnie.

If, my darling son, you hear from Margaret, please tell her I beg her forgiveness and that I never favored her marriage to Janos.

Enclosed, please find a check for two hundred American dollars. I hope this money will help you to travel to California, where I know you will be successful, no matter what you choose to do.

Your loving mother,
Anna Maria Bodnar

Konnie refolded the letter and stared for a moment into his coffee. His father had been a hard man to love, but his brother György was quite a different matter. And poor Margaret. Why had she never written to their mother? Certainly she was bitter, but he hadn't thought that she would remain bitter for so many years. And vaguely he wondered where she was. Poor girl, how could she care for herself and three children? What would she live on? Konnie shook his head sadly. Margaret's story, if he ever learned it, would be worth writing. Surely it was filled with the drama of self-sacrifice—and, he hoped, survival. At least, he reflected, his mother was happy. He had thought he would never find her, because although he had written, his letters were always returned "Addressee unknown." Then in Germany Alexander Korda had called to say he had met Konnie's mother while attending a party at a ski resort in Innsbruck. She had told him she had a son interested in theater and he had asked the son's name. When Korda had told her he knew her son, she had burst into tears and given him her mailing address, explaining that she and the count traveled a great deal. She begged Korda to ask him to write. Konnie smiled to himself and stirred his coffee. Hungarians were clannish—perhaps because of their language. Wherever they went, they congregated together; thus coincidental meeting upon coincidental meeting took place.

4

July 31, 1921

Margaret Szilard Horvath's appearance had changed radically. Not that she was unattractive. Miraculously, neither the ravages of illness nor the last eight years of poverty and hard work had destroyed her essential beauty. Her hair was now silver blond, her complexion still perfect, her eyes still compelling. But she was not the same. Over the years Margaret had grown extraordinarily thin, so that her once soft curves were now angular, thus giving her body more definition. Her face, which had been heart-shaped, was now characterized by magnificent high cheekbones, slightly arched brows, and a certain tightness around the lips, which seemed narrower than they once were. Her eyes, which had been round and innocent, were now slightly slanted, like those of her ancient Asian Magyar ancestors, and when her mind focused on something important, one could see a touch of the predator in their stone-blue gaze. It was as if her body had made itself over to better suit the personality that now inhabited it; a personality molded by hardship, deception, and fear. Margaret had simply been through too much, seen too much, and suffered too much. She was no longer the orphaned kitten who purred for the smallest drop of milk. She was the full-grown cat, poised and ready to pounce upon her prey. Not that Margaret desired anything for herself—except perhaps a modicum of comfort and peace of mind. But her children were a different matter. She hungered for them. They should have fine careers, make money, live in the luxury she felt they deserved. And Margaret hungered most of all for her daughter, Renee. Renee, she ordained, should have all the opportunities she herself had been denied, and toward that end, Margaret worked ceaselessly. Nonetheless, success had not yet come; though, she admitted, the key to the doors she had dreamed of was at hand. Now, today, it was up to her to make a bargain that would affect Renee's whole future. Margaret steeled herself to the task.

Dressed as fashionably as possible in remade used clothing, Margaret wore a straight tweed skirt, a silk blouse, and a flannel blazer jacket as she walked briskly along Park Avenue that morning toward a meeting that she knew would change her daughter's destiny.

She felt full of determination. Would that she could have had such determination years ago, but then, years ago, when she lived with Janos, she had known nothing of men and less of the world they inhabited.

Margaret passed a jewelry shop, and for a moment she paused to look into the window at the necklaces, bracelets, and rings that glittered in their display boxes. She thought of the ring her grandmother had given her and how Ivan had sold it in Germany to get the money for their fares to America.

Vaguely she wondered how Ivan and Irina were getting on. For a time after they had all arrived in New York they had lived together. Ivan had been a dockworker, Zoltan a sweeper in a factory, and she and Irina seamstresses. But Ivan was not meant for the docks. He yearned for farm life, and after a year he and Irina had moved to the Dakotas, where it was said that many Slavs had emigrated and where land grants were still available.

Margaret and her children had remained in New York. In order to survive, they all worked. But they also all attended night school in spite of the hardship. Renee, who had been promoted ahead of time, would graduate from night school in the spring, and Zoltan was two years behind her. Both Renee and Zoltan were fine students; only Imre lagged behind, often complaining, usually failing to study, and sometimes skipping work. Margaret worried about Imre, and she knew she was too indulgent with him. At the same time, she made excuses for him, saying he had been too young when their lives changed to understand what had happened.

Margaret turned away from the window and its jewels, simultaneously laying aside her problems with Imre and returning her thoughts to Renee. Something had happened to Renee, something quite important. That something was the cause of Margaret's optimism and the reason for her early-morning journey uptown on this quiet Sunday.

Margaret wasn't certain when her current plan had first occurred to her. Perhaps many months ago, when she had first seen young Aaron Lewis touring the factory where she and Renee worked. On that day Aaron Lewis had seen Renee for the first time, and for the first time, Renee saw him. When they had looked at each other—and indeed Aaron Lewis had stopped to speak with Renee briefly—Margaret could almost feel his beguilement. At that moment she could have predicted everything that would follow.

Over the last few months she had done nothing to discourage their relationship, in spite of her ambitions for her daughter to attend art school. Perhaps on her part it was intuition, perhaps more, but from the beginning Margaret realized that Aaron's attachment to Renee might well become the instrument of their successful escape from poverty.

From the outset, what Margaret had thought about most was how Aaron's father would react when he discovered that his only son was involved with a girl who worked in his factory—and not just any girl, but a gentile girl.

Miklós had told her long ago: "Some Jewish families consider their children dead if they marry non-Jews, and they don sackcloth and ashes and mourn them." He had added that this was not true of secular Jews or of Reform Jews, but was generally true of Orthodox Jews. Aaron Lewis was not Orthodox, but his father, David, was, and he had become obsessed with seeing Aaron's relationship with Renee end.

Still, for nearly a year David Lewis had played his cards carefully so as not to drive young Aaron into Renee's arms. In the meantime, Margaret tested the waters herself. She discovered that although Renee liked Aaron very much, she had no intention of giving up her dreams.

Once certain of how Renee would react, Margaret encouraged the relationship and waited for the inevitable. And yesterday the inevitable had arrived in the form of a gold-embossed envelope containing a polite summons to meet David Lewis at his town house for brunch.

David Lewis was in his mid-sixties. He was a stout, short man with a fringe of white hair and a shiny bald scalp. The son of a tailor, he had come to New York as a boy from Germany, eager to succeed. He had started out wheeling long steel racks filled with clothes from the warehouses on Seventh Avenue to waiting trucks. He adjusted quickly to the pace of the street, where everything seemed to happen twice as fast as elsewhere. In his thirties he had taken over a shirtwaist factory, and soon he bought others, including his most recent purchase, the factory where Margaret and Renee worked sewing.

David Lewis was well-known for his generosity in giving to charity, but in business he had not one sentimental bone in his body. If it turned a profit, you kept it; if it didn't, you threw it out, and that went for people as well as for the products they produced.

David Lewis was also a strict but loving father. He insisted his son learn the business from the bottom up, and he made Aaron work fifty hours a week as a floor manager in his factories. Secretly he was pleased that Aaron wanted to be a lawyer and indeed that his son had the brains to be accepted into law school. But he divined that a year in the business would give the boy grounding—a grounding he would need when he eventually took over the legal affairs of the business.

Margaret had observed her prey carefully. She knew that David Lewis sat behind his plush desk and chewed on the end of a fine Havana cigar. She knew he was strict but fair. She knew from what Aaron had told her that at home David Lewis would discuss almost anything but business with his son. "If I want to discuss business," Aaron told her, "I have to go to his office, and there he does not treat me like his son, he treats me as he would any other employee." She also knew that David Lewis and his son differed on the matter of religious traditions.

Margaret paused for a moment on the steps of the tasteful town house. It was surrounded by a black iron fence and its windows were heavily draped, preventing her from even glimpsing the inside. She adjusted her hat and climbed the steps and rang the bell.

David Lewis himself answered the door. He was wearing a dark blue smoking jacket trimmed in black velvet. His fringe of gray hair was carefully smoothed down, and he smiled and offered his hand as if she were a business acquaintance.

"Forgive me, it's the butler's day off."

"We don't have a butler," she replied a bit too sharply.

He did not respond, but simply ushered her inside, took her jacket, and then motioned toward one of the rooms beyond the tiled foyer.

It was a pleasant sunny room furnished with antiques and plants much like those her mother had raised in the solarium of the house in which she had grown up. "Exotics," she remembered. Yes, that was what Mama had called them.

"I hope you don't mind, but we will be dining alone," David Lewis was saying. "My wife has been dead for many years."

The table was set for two, and a gleaming silver coffee service dominated its center. The feast included hot bagels, cream cheese, smoked salmon, and a variety of rolls, jams, and jellies. He pulled out a chair for her and silently poured coffee, then expansively offered the rest with a simple, "Help yourself."

Margaret studied David Lewis. She wondered how long it would take him to get to the point of their meeting. She sipped some of the coffee he had poured and placed a bit of smoked salmon on the delicate Wedgwood plate in front of her.

"Your daughter looks a great deal like you," he commented. In David Lewis' eyes Margaret Horvath was a good-looking woman, but she did not look entirely well. Her skin was white, tissue-paper white, and he thought her too thin. But her eyes were certainly like Renee's. They were stone blue.

Margaret Horvath was also not dressed like a woman who worked as a sewing-machine operator dressed, and he noted the way in which she held her coffee cup. He knew that her hands had not always been the hands of a workingwoman. Everything about her suggested she came from a family of money and breeding—a family that had somehow fallen on hard times. He felt a wave of sympathy for her, but he reminded himself that he had a bargain to strike with this woman, and sympathy might well cost him a great deal of money.

"Yes," he said slowly, confirming his comment, "your daughter does resemble you."

"We have the same coloring," Margaret acknowledged. "But I suspect I'm not here to discuss family resemblances."

He noticed that her eyes narrowed slightly, but he appreciated the fact that she wanted to get on with it.

"Quite right. It's just that I'm unsure of how to begin."

Margaret spread some cream cheese on a bagel. "You don't strike me as a man who is unsure very often," she observed.

"No, not very often. Still, this particular subject is delicate."

"I assume it involves our children," Margaret ventured before biting into the bagel, which she held between thumb and forefinger.

David Lewis nodded and drank some coffee. "They've

been going out for many months now, and Aaron has told me they are in love and he wants to marry her."

"I imagine you object," Margaret surmised. Then, before he could answer, "I always vowed to allow my daughter to marry whom she pleased."

"They're too young," he said quickly. "Much too young."

"And Renee is not Jewish."

He looked at her for a long moment. "She's a beautiful girl—a very talented girl. Intelligent, I can tell. But my Aaron is special . . . yes, I want his wife to be Jewish. Is that so wrong? Surely you cannot be so excited about Aaron either . . ." His voice trailed off as he realized he had said too much. He cleared his throat and then tried to recoup. "Of course, Aaron does have money, and money is never unappealing."

"Renee is not interested in Aaron's money," Margaret replied. "My daughter is not a fortune hunter."

"I'm sorry, I didn't mean to imply she was."

"Of course you did. But Renee is young and idealistic. She and Aaron still believe that people can live on love. I've taught my daughter the importance of love. Now, Mr. Lewis, let me tell you this: I understand the importance of love, but I also understand the importance of money. Money is opportunity."

"I apologize," he said, looking her in the eye. In truth, he felt ill-at-ease with this woman; she seemed to anticipate him all too well. And the truth was, he himself did not believe Renee was interested in money alone, even though he knew the girl to be ambitious. "Well, for me the essential matter is the fact that Aaron is Jewish and your daughter is not."

Margaret did not tell him that Renee was in fact half-Jewish, though she wasn't at all sure it would have made a difference. As Miklós had told her, "For the Jews to consider you Jewish, it is your mother who must be Jewish." Instead Margaret smiled. "I'm not prejudiced."

"Nor am I," David Lewis said quickly.

"It is difficult to end a romance," Margaret said carefully. "Do you have something in mind?"

"There is only one thing to do, and that is to see to it that they are separated. But I know that Aaron won't go. He's too stubborn. It is your daughter who must end it."

"I'm not sure she will."

He shook his head. "There must be something she wants . . . something I can help her achieve."

Margaret forced herself not to smile, not to show any emotion whatsoever. "She wants to go to art school."

There was absolute silence, and Margaret bit into her bagel and stirred her coffee with a silver spoon. He was thinking about it, and from what she could see, he was rich enough to buy Renee an entire art school if he wanted. That, naturally, was not necessary, but his obvious wealth ended any qualms Margaret might have had. What she wanted from him would deprive him of nothing he really needed; it was probably no more than he might have given to charity. She had made all the estimates and she knew exactly how much the tuition was and how much it would take for her to open a couturiere's shop so that she could fully support her children and they would not, like her, be forced to work. She deemed their progress at night school too slow, and she had a strong desire to see them all living a better life. But essentially it was Renee who mattered, for it was Renee who had the greatest talent.

"Even if she were in art school, they'd go on seeing one another," David Lewis finally said.

Margaret looked directly into his eyes. "Not if the art school is in Boston," she said slowly.

"You'd have to move. She wouldn't be able to work . . ."

In his mind, David Lewis was working it all out.

"Two thousand dollars," Margaret said flatly. "That's what I need. Neither you nor Aaron will ever hear from us again. I'll see to any letters that might be sent, and I'll simply take her away."

"Two thousand . . ." He repeated her figure under his breath and stared at her.

"I like your son," she said almost coldly. "It will be difficult for me to discourage their love."

Lovely, blond, frail. The woman across from him was

made of steel. Two thousand was a small fortune. Still, the girl did have talent, and he would actually be helping her. No, he wasn't simply buying her off, he was actually providing a sort of scholarship to a young woman who probably had a future. He mentally shrugged—what "probably"? With a mother like the one he faced, there was no question in his mind about Renee's future success. "Two thousand," he repeated. "Very well, Mrs. Horvath. You can go home and start packing."

Ten

1

July 31, 1921

*M*argaret stood in front of the door behind which was the dismal room they had lived in for so long.

I have never denied Renee anything it was in my power to give, Margaret thought. I have done the right thing, the only thing, she told herself for the tenth time. Oh, there would no doubt be a tearful farewell, but Aaron's love for Renee and Renee's for Aaron was a young love, a first love—what the Americans called "puppy love."

She wondered if "puppy love" was what she had felt for Miklós. His memory had faded across the years, though she had forgiven him for not returning for her. Miklós *was* Renee's real father, and Margaret now judged her family to be strong enough to know the truth. Zoltan and Imre would love their sister no less when they learned she was only their half-sister. And then too, their lives were again about to change drastically. It was time they all learned about the past, about their relatives, about how things had come to be. Not to make them feel sorry for me, Margaret thought, but to make certain they understand who they are and what they are capable of becoming.

Margaret opened the door and found her family waiting curiously. She took off her jacket and hung it up, then sat down and motioned them to come and sit beside her. "I have something important to tell you."

They faced her expectantly, and for once she did not disappoint them. "We're going to Boston. Renee is going to art school there. She's going full-time, and both of you will go to school full-time too."

"Boston! Art school! But Mama, where did the money come from?" Renee looked at her mother wide-eyed, and Zoltan and Imre seemed equally taken aback.

"The money came from your grandmother in Paris. I wanted to surprise you, so I didn't tell you I'd found her. I wrote to her . . . and, well, she sent the money."

"Oh, Mama . . ." Renee couldn't stop the tears from running down her cheeks, and she threw herself into her mother's arms. "Art school . . . oh, Mama, it's like a dream come true. I can't believe it, I just can't believe it."

"Well, it is true." Margaret held her daughter close. Then she looked up at her two sons. "I have something important to discuss with Renee alone. Womanly matters. Could the two of you go out for a while?"

"Sure," Zoltan said happily. "C'mon, Imre, let's go to the bookstore and buy a map of Boston."

"What a good idea," Margaret said, waving them off.

But Imre didn't move. His face was twisted, and his lower lip thrust forward in defiance. "I don't want to go to Boston," he declared.

Margaret looked at him steadily, aware of the fact that at thirteen he was a big boy, a tall sturdy boy who was becoming increasingly hard to handle. "You must go. We are all going, and you are only thirteen."

"I don't like going to school, and anyway, I don't want to leave my friends."

"You are going to school because otherwise you will amount to nothing. As for your friends, well, you will make new ones."

"I don't want to go!"

He shouted loudly and Margaret scowled at him.

"I don't want to go! I won't go!"

In that instant Imre looked like Béla, and Margaret's blue eyes hardened as she stood up and in one motion lifted her hand and smacked him hard across the face. "Go with your brother! And don't talk back to me, Imre!"

Imre stood back, his hand on his face, and stared at her hatefully. Then he turned and ran out the door ahead of Zoltan.

"I'll find him and talk to him," Zoltan volunteered.

Margaret sat back down and nodded. It was an unpleasant beginning, she thought.

When the door had closed, she led Renee to the sofa. "I must talk with you," she said earnestly. "It's time you knew certain things, things I have kept secret all these years."

Renee nodded and sat down. "You sound so serious."

"They are serious matters. I have told you I was forced to marry Janos when I was only just seventeen, and that I loved someone else."

"Yes. You've told me that."

"The person I loved was a young Jewish man. He worked for Count Horvath. He was very good-looking and very intelligent. He taught me English, you know. If he hadn't, we might not be here now. His name was Miklós Lazar."

"Miklós Lazar." Renee repeated the name and looked steadily at her mother.

"We had planned to run away together so that I would not have to marry Janos. We . . . I . . . Renee, you are Miklós' daughter, not Janos'."

Renee's blue eyes seemed to grow larger as she listened. Miklós' daughter . . . "Oh, Mama, you should have told me sooner. Did Janos know?"

"No. He knew I was not a virgin, but he did not know about Miklós. I did a terrible thing. I did not tell György the truth, and György died defending my honor." Tears began to flow down Margaret's cheeks. She had forced all thoughts of György from her mind for years, but still the pain and guilt she felt lingered on.

"Oh, Mama, how awful."

"Yes, awful. I thought György would kill Janos and free me. It never occurred to me that Janos would cheat . . . he did cheat—I know that."

Renee leaned over and took her mother's hand. "Didn't Janos want to know who your previous lover was?"

Margaret nodded. "When I was younger—fourteen or so—Béla came to my bed and tried to possess me. I woke up and frightened him away. I hated Béla, and so I told Janos it was Béla who had taken my virginity."

"And that satisfied him?"

"He believed me, and he knew Béla was a liar and a cheat. He drew Béla into the scheme that caused my father's firm to go bankrupt, then I think he arranged for Béla to get caught. But Béla fooled even Janos. He ran away with all the money, even what was left in the company's bank accounts."

"Oh, Mama. And that's the reason your father committed suicide?"

"Yes, but I don't blame myself for that. Béla did that." Margaret leaned back against the sofa and closed her eyes. "I love you and your brothers very much, Renee. I've done terrible things, but you must try to understand how it was for me. My father practically sold me. He used my dowry and he deserted me. I did desperate things—but I was young and ignorant of the world and had no choices."

"Oh, Mama, I don't blame you."

"There is something I need to know. It is very important to me."

"Yes, Mama."

"Would you choose to go to art school if Aaron wanted to marry you?"

"Yes, Mama. I love Aaron, but I want to be someone."

Margaret smiled faintly. "You do realize that you and Aaron will grow apart since you will be separated?"

"I haven't had much time to think about that yet, but I suppose we will."

"And you still choose art school?"

"Yes."

Margaret sniffed and brushed a tear off her cheek. "I

hope you will forgive me for not telling you the truth sooner."

Renee nodded and took her mother in her arms. She held her for a long while. Then she said softly, "I wish you had told me sooner . . . but I'm not sorry. I didn't like Janos. I'm glad I'm not his daughter."

"Zoltan and Imre are nothing like him, Renee. They are good boys even though he fathered them. Imre is headstrong and he does have a volatile temper, but he will mature. I love them both."

"Of course. So do I, Mama. But what happened to my real father? Where is he?"

"I don't know. He was kind and intelligent, but he might not have been strong. He never came for me. Perhaps he came to America, I don't know. Lazar is such a common name. How would I ever find him?"

Renee frowned. "I must look."

"Look when you have the opportunity, but get on with your life. We will go to Boston and you will study."

Renee kissed her mother. "I will make you proud, Mama. And so will Zoltan and Imre. We will take care of you, and we'll make you proud."

Margaret smiled. "I'm proud now. Very proud."

2

August 29, 1921

"Look at the engine!" Zoltan said, poking his brother and trying to engender some enthusiasm from Imre, who remained sullen in the face of their move.

"I don't give a shit about the engine!" Imre retorted, shoving Zoltan away. "Leave me alone!"

The two boys walked ahead, and Zoltan, who was sixteen, carried the largest bag, while Imre reluctantly carried two smaller cardboard cases. Behind them Renee and Margaret both carried bags and boxes, and in Margaret's pocket was the baggage check for the cartons she had checked through.

The platform at Grand Central was filled with commuters traveling to Boston and other coastal cities. Redcaps hurriedly pushed dollies filled with suitcases up and down, while passengers lingered with friends and lovers saying good-bye.

"It's not a very long trip," Margaret said.

Renee held the tickets firmly in her hand and checked the car numbers. "There it is!" She pointed toward number twenty-two.

A steel stool was placed in front of the steep narrow metal steps that in turn led up and into the train. The porter glanced at their tickets and confirmed that they were entering the right car. Then he assisted the two women onto the metal platform, then up the steps one by one.

"So different from a European train," Margaret said as they entered the car. Each window had a little green shade, and the seats were upholstered in a matching dull green. And of course there were seats on both sides of a narrow aisle, whereas on European trains the seats were located in compartments off a narrow aisle on one side of each railway carriage.

"And a lot different from a third-class carriage," Renee added. Then, turning to her brothers, "Do you remember our trip to Budapest?"

Zoltan nodded, but he was clearly distracted by the wonderful brass rails and the reversible seats. "Here," he suggested as he scrambled into one of four empty seats that had already been turned to face one another. "Hey, look, that one over there has a table. Do you think if we ask, they'll bring us a table?"

"I'm sure," Renee answered. One by one she put their cases up on the racks provided. Then she slipped off her own jacket and carefully folded it before adding it to the pile.

"Do you want me to hang your jacket, Mama?" she asked.

"No, I'll wear it for a while," Margaret replied as she

leaned back against the little lace doily that covered the back of the seat.

Renee moved in beside her, and for a time they sat in silence, watching with interest as the car gradually filled with other travelers.

Then with a forward jolt and a jerking backward motion the train began its slow backward wind out of the station, snaking its way through tunnels and then into the daylight of the railroad yards, where dozens of tracks intersected and boxcars sat bereft of their engines. There were cars that read "Indiana Central," "Wabash Line," "Southern Pacific," "Union Pacific," "Pennsylvania Central," and even "Canadian National"—a thousand cars from hundreds of places. It was like the index to a geography book written on blocks and scattered around as if some child had forgotten to put away his toys. There were flatcars and open boxcars, tank cars and cars with ramps for automobiles. There were cattle cars and cars with unknown uses.

Zoltan got out a deck of cards and the porter brought them a table at their request. "Do you want to play cards, Imre?" Zoltan asked.

Imre shrugged and put his elbows on the table. "I guess," he finally answered.

Margaret studied the copy of *Vogue* she had just purchased, while Renee leaned back and considered her mixed emotions. A part of her was filled with excitement; a part of her was filled with a kind of sadness, a strong feeling of loss.

Today was Monday, and she thought: Monday is the day of the week that Aaron and I first met. Aaron. She wondered if he would write. A part of her wanted him to: a part of her didn't want to be reminded of what might have been. But it didn't matter—she would never forget Aaron because he had changed her life. Eight months ago . . . Was it only eight months? Aaron's father, David Lewis, who owned several factories already, had bought the factory where she and her mother worked as sewing-machine operators. David Lewis had personally taken over the factory for six months, and he installed his son, Aaron, as a floor manager to learn the business. Aaron had noticed her on the very first day, and soon after, their relationship had begun. As the long train passed through a series of tunnels, the lights flickered on and off and Renee closed her eyes. Yes, she could remember every minute, every detail. . . .

Aaron Lewis seemed to be about six feet tall, though Renee found it hard to judge height when she was sitting down. He had thick brown hair, brown eyes, and was solidly built, though not heavy in any way.

He wore a light tan suit, and by noon he had loosened his tie and undone the top button of his shirt. He walked about looking at what the fifty seamstresses were doing, though in fact he seemed bored and not at all interested until he approached her table. Then he would look at her till she felt his eyes on her and looked up. At that point he always grinned at her, then, afraid others were looking, quickly turned away. Renee always smiled back and was grateful that her mother worked on another aisle. It seemed like a game they were playing, and indeed had been playing for several days. But when at six o'clock on Friday he called her name and, trying to sound all business, asked if he might see her, she was not surprised. She sensed the game had entered an entirely new phase.

"Yes, Mr. Lewis." She stood before him and looked into his eyes. He seemed flustered, and then he looked around, checking to see if the others had all filed out the door. Several remained, fiddling with their bags, turning now and again to glance at them.

"Could you step into my office, Miss . . . Miss . . ."

"Horvath," Renee said. "Renee Horvath."

"Miss Horvath . . . yes. I wanted to speak to you about your work."

He spoke loudly, too loudly, and she realized it was not for her benefit, but rather so that the two lingering girls would hear.

"Of course," she replied softly while fighting to keep a smile from creeping round the corners of her lips. He was quite funny, embarrassed and awkward.

He cleared his throat and led the way to his office,

opened the door, and ushered her in ahead of him, closing the door after them.

Renee slipped into the chair opposite his desk and waited till he walked around to face her. But he did not go behind his desk; rather he stood in front of it.

"You wanted to speak to me about my work?" she reminded him.

"Yes . . . yes that was it."

"Well, what about it?"

Poor thing, he was out of his depth, and his embarrassment gave her a sudden feeling of power. "Isn't it satisfactory?" she asked.

"No, no. I mean, yes. Yes, it's excellent. In fact, I wanted to tell you how very excellent it is." He paused, and his face turned red. Then, almost stuttering, "In fact, I wanted to speak to you about something else."

Renee finally smiled—she could hold it back no longer. But she didn't press him to explain himself either. She thought of her brother Zoltan and the girls he stared at. It would be cruel to taunt a young man who was already so ill-at-ease, so she sat waiting, still smiling.

"You're laughing at me," he said, frowning.

She shook her head. "No. Really I'm not laughing at all."

"Are you sure?"

"Yes, I'm sure."

"I wanted to . . . I wanted to ask you out to dinner."

It was her turn now. Her cheeks burned red and she nodded. She was certain he had liked her from the beginning, but she had not expected him to ask her out. She was, after all, only a factory girl and his father owned the factory. But she liked him and she decided to accept.

He exhaled and suddenly seemed to relax. "Next Friday night? After work?"

"I'd like to go home and change first."

"Of course . . . I could pick you up at eight."

"That would be fine."

"I'll need your address."

Renee nodded and hurriedly wrote it down on a scrap

of paper. She handed it to him and he seemed to study it curiously.

"I'm sure it's not in one of the neighborhoods you frequent," she said pointedly.

The smile faded from his face as a more serious expression took over. "I don't care where you live," he said, staring into her blue eyes. "Is it eight o'clock, then?"

"Yes, eight o'clock."

3

When Renee had announced that Aaron Lewis was calling for her on Friday and taking her out for dinner, her mother had not seemed surprised—just nervous and worried about where and how they lived. She fussed every day until Friday, and she fussed then too.

"I feel like crying." Her mother had waved her hand to indicate their living quarters. Their fourth-floor room was one large square with a single window that faced the brick wall of the tenement opposite. Its walls were a gray-white except for one, which someone, sometime, had wallpapered with giant roses. No doubt when it was new the paper with the green vines and yellow roses cheered the interior, but now it was a faded, torn garden, and up near the ceiling there was a large hole that disappeared into the building's mysterious interior. Her mother had made Zoltan climb up and nail a board across it in order to keep both the cold air and wandering rodents out of their room. The bare scuffed floor was covered only with one small rug. It was tired and worn from too many footsteps. In one corner there was a large double bed where she and her mother slept, and on the far side of the room behind a curtain suspended from the ceiling there was another double bed where Zoltan and Imre slept. In the middle of the room a large wine-colored chesterfield and several wooden chairs were positioned around a crate that had been covered with chintz and now served as a coffee table. Behind it was a rickety wooden table and several more chairs. To one side there was another elongated table, and on it were a small gas burner, a dishpan, and some dishes neatly stacked next to a shoebox that contained knives, forks, and spoons. Next to that was the small icebox that Zoltan filled twice a week with a giant twenty-five-cent block of ice.

"This," her mother lamented, "is no place to invite friends. It's been dreadful just living here all these years. I'll never get used to the sounds and smells. What will your young man think? Especially that young man. His family is rich, Renee, very rich. He probably doesn't have the faintest idea how we live—I'm sure he's never been to a place like this."

Renee remembered standing in the middle of the room in her homemade but stylishly designed dress. She felt incongruous. Her mother was a genius when it came to the way they all dressed. She searched and searched through piles of used clothes and bought only those made of the best fabrics. Then she brought them home and ripped them up, cleaned the material, and remade them.

Across the room her mother cried. "You should not have had him come here," she lamented. "He'll never take you out again."

"I thought you didn't want me going out with him anyway?" Renee responded.

"Well, he is older than you . . . I certainly have my reservations. What does a young man so wealthy want with us?"

"He doesn't want us, he wants Renee," Zoltan had put in. He smiled as he looked at his sister. "And who could blame him? She's the prettiest girl in the factory."

Renee opened her eyes and glanced at her brother now. He and Imre were playing poker for matchsticks. The train was inching past factories that belched smoke into the clear blue sky. Then she closed her eyes again and went back to her memories. . . .

"He's going to own the factory one day, and he's the son of a rich man. A very rich man. He doesn't even know places like this exist. You should have had him meet you somewhere. But even so, I think it's a mistake. What kind of intentions does he have? Oh, if things don't go right, we could lose our jobs. Then where would we be?" her mother had fretted.

"Free," Renee replied. She turned then and looked at her mother. "We'd be free, Mama. I don't think you realize how much you've given that company—hours and hours of hard work for pennies. Mama, I'm not spending my life this way. If Aaron Lewis is interested in me and if I can use him to get a better job, I will. I swear I will."

"Renee!" Her mother had pretended to be shocked, but she wasn't really. And as it turned out, Renee thought, I didn't have to pretend with Aaron. I really liked him. Maybe I loved him.

Zoltan had answered the door that first night, and ushered Aaron Lewis into their room. Aaron handed Renee a bouquet of roses and he silently bowed and gave Margaret a large box of chocolates. If he was dismayed, surprised, or repulsed by their surroundings, his expression did not show it. He smiled and took Renee's arm. "Shall we?" he asked.

"I think I'll need my wrap," she remembered saying.

She looked behind the second curtain that was draped across a rod in the corner of the room and withdrew her coat. Aaron Lewis helped her slip into it, and then he bade her mother and brothers good night as he took her arm and led her down the dark stairs to the street and into another world.

Cinderella went to the grand ball in a glittering coach that turned into a pumpkin at midnight, Renee reflected, but she herself had gone out in a long white Lincoln that was still quite intact long after midnight when Aaron Lewis drove her home and escorted her to her door.

Aaron had said not one word about the poverty in which she and her family lived, and if he thought she was dressed oddly, he did not comment. Quite the opposite, in fact. He had complimented her on her dress, and she had explained that she had designed it and her mother had made it. He had taken her to a place in Harlem where a fourteen-year-old named Josephine Baker was performing. But the singer had seemed much older to her, and Aaron had explained that she'd been singing in Harlem clubs since she was eight.

They had then dined on wonderful food, danced to glorious music, and were entertained by two more singers and a comedian. But what was best of all was Aaron's ease with her and her ease with him. It was as if they had known each other forever. It was a night like no other she could remember.

"I don't really want to work in the factory," Aaron confided. "I want to go to law school, but my father says I have to work in the factory for at least a year. If I still want to go to law school, he will let me go then. I *will* still want to go." He paused and ran his hand through his hair. "And you, Renee . . . what do you dream of?"

"Of being a designer. I have a whole book of fashions I've drawn and made patterns for. At first I wanted to be a couturiere, but then I realized that if I were a couturiere, I would design and make one dress for one person. I want to create fashionable clothes for mass production. What they sell in the stores now is dreary. Why can't ordinary people have more choice in ready-to-wear clothes, Aaron? That's my first dream, but if I succeed, I could fulfill my second dream automatically. My second dream is to help my mother. She's had a terrible life, really terrible. She was once very wealthy, you know. She came from an aristocratic family."

He had not laughed. Instead he had leaned over and said earnestly, "She seems like a real lady, not like so many others at the factory."

"She is a real lady."

He had smiled then. "Can I see some of your designs, Renee? I don't know if it will help—my father seldom listens to what I say—but I will show him the designs."

"Would you? Oh, Aaron, I can't thank you enough."

"Don't thank me yet. My father is very stubborn."

"But you care about him, don't you?"

"Of course. Don't you care about your father?"

"He's dead," Renee said, lying without even blinking. She had wished Janos dead. At the very least she wished him to suffer as he had made her mother suffer.

"I'm sorry," Aaron whispered across the table.

"It's quite all right. It was a long, long time ago," she replied.

"Oh, not that long ago. You're young."

Renee smiled. "I'm eighteen," she lied. "Old enough."

He grinned boyishly. "It's still young."

And then they danced a dance called "the black bottom," and she had thought of stories her mother had told her about her great-grandmother, who loved to dance. After a long time he noticed the time and said, "I'd better get you home, it's nearly one-thirty."

"Oh," she had exclaimed, "where did the time go?"

"I want to see you again and again. And don't forget the sketches. Bring them Monday."

"Monday," she had repeated. At that moment Monday had seemed like a hundred years away.

True to his promise, Aaron had taken her drawings to his father, and the following week his father had called her into his office.

"Renee, how old are you?" he asked.

"Eighteen." She knew that she *looked* eighteen.

"So young. . . . Where have you learned to draw so well?"

"I could always draw. But my mother helps me make patterns and sew."

"I see. Well, it is clear to me that you are wasted where you are, and so I am moving you into the pattern department and giving you a raise. I will speak to the director there and you will follow his instruction completely, is that clear?"

"Yes. Oh, this is wonderful!"

"It is only a step in the right direction. Now, listen carefully, you have a great deal to learn, do you understand? For example, this is a scrapbook you have given me, not a proper portfolio . . . but I have some imagination so I can see your talent. Anyway, you go and work with Brockman for a while. He can give you some practical training."

Renee nodded. It was all like a dream and Aaron was like a knight in shining armor. She looked at Mr. Lewis' face and wondered if she dared . . . Then, thinking of her mother, she knew she did dare. "May I ask how much of a raise?"

David Lewis looked into her eyes. "Not as much as the others earn, because you are an apprentice. What do you make now? Four dollars a week? Well, let's make it six."

Six! It seemed like a small fortune. "Oh, thank you," she managed to say.

David Lewis avoided her eyes and only grunted. "I do not expect thanks, I expect results."

Renee remembered that she had fairly danced down the hall and away from David Lewis' office. She remembered to insert her time card in the slot and then she hurried away and headed toward home.

Awaiting her were her mother and brothers, anxious looks on their faces.

"It's wonderful!" she burst out. "I'm being put in the pattern department! Mama, I got a two-dollar-a-week raise!"

"Did Aaron Lewis arrange this?" Zoltan asked abruptly.

"He arranged for his father to look at my work, that's all."

Zoltan frowned. "Sometimes men want things in return for such favors, Renee."

Renee blushed, and she suddenly hugged her brother. "It's all right, there wasn't even a good-night kiss." Her eyes were damp when she looked her younger brother in the eye. "But thank you for being so protective and caring so much. I'm a lucky girl to have such a good brother."

"We'd better eat," Margaret suggested. "It's almost time to leave for school, and it wouldn't do for any of you to miss a night."

"I have a test," Imre had muttered.

"Then all the more reason to hurry," Margaret urged. She turned quickly to the small stove on which the stew simmered. Tonight Renee noticed that her mother ladled out their dinner with some enthusiasm. For the first time in years her mother seemed hopeful. They were going to escape poverty, they were going to have a future. Tonight, for the first time, she really felt it.

The cold winter melted into a rainy spring, and then April came to New York and the early-blooming flowers burst into bloom and the first warm clear days brought rare smiles to the inhabitants of the city, who now sat outside to eat their lunches.

Renee found each day an adventure, and in the evenings after night school, she pored over worn copies of *Vogue.* Of course, its fashions were too expensive for off-the-rack clothes. But it was filled with ideas. She became more interested in accessories, determining that even the simplest of dresses could look elegant if properly accessorized. Now, in addition to her designs, she began to take notes on what she thought of various fashion ideas.

On Saturday nights Aaron took her out, and sometimes they met on Sundays to walk in the park or even to go to Coney Island, where they would walk along the beach like lovers. But they were not lovers. She had allowed him kisses, but no more. Her mother urged propriety and Renee herself desired a future, and so she guarded the present in spite of her strong feelings toward Aaron.

One day stood out in her memory. It was Sunday and they had walked along looking in the windows of the closed storefronts of Seventh Avenue and down the side streets where small shops wholesaled a variety of fascinating products. One sold hat forms, another nothing but beads, and a third specialized in sequins and dyed feathers. A thousand dressmakers came here to buy the odds and ends that completed their little masterpieces, and the larger factories ordered such items as five thousand white pearl buttons at a time.

"I love this street," Renee said, pausing before a window that featured plumes of all lengths and colors.

"They're out of fashion now. You never see women with plumes in their hats anymore," Aaron remarked.

"They're coming back in headbands, Aaron. Fashion is cyclical, but individual style is something different. I think that every woman must have her very own style—it's a way she can express herself. It should say something about her. I think colors say a lot. Reds and golds for the brazen, greens and blues for the reserved."

"You're getting very theoretical. Where do you get all these ideas?"

"From reading, I guess. But I've been fascinated with fashion since I was a child. So was my mother."

"What a dilemma! You're fascinated with fashion, and I'm fascinated with you." He had suddenly taken her in his arms and nuzzled her neck with his cold nose.

"Aaron, we're in the middle of the street."

"Sunday in the garment district! There's not a soul around." He kissed her cheek, then her mouth. "Renee, I love you. Please marry me. . . . Think of your mother. She could stop work. I'd take care of her, and your brothers too. I swear I would."

Renee looked into his soft brown eyes. "You're such a good man," she said sincerely. Then she shook her head. "Aaron, I have dreams, and so do you. We can't marry."

"It's because I'm Jewish, isn't it?"

"Oh, no. Of course not. Aaron, I have to succeed. I owe it to my mother. I know I wouldn't or couldn't if we married."

"I'd let you. You could do whatever you want."

"No. There would be children, and then I would have to care for them because I wouldn't want anyone else to care for my children."

"Renee, I love you, I dream of you . . ."

"Dream of law school, Aaron. Maybe one day, but not now. I couldn't."

He had nodded silently and they had continued to walk slowly. "Care to go to a moving picture?" he finally asked.

"Yes," she had answered enthusiastically. "I'd love to go to the movies."

"Gloria Swanson is playing in *Why Change Your Wife?* How about that?

"That sounds good. I like Gloria Swanson."

Renee opened her eyes and shifted in her seat. Her

mother had drifted off to sleep and her copy of *Vogue* had slipped off her lap. Zoltan and Imre, long since tired of card games, had gone for a walk through the train. She looked out the window and saw only the dense woods they seemed to be passing through. It was such a large country, such a diverse country. And I've only seen one corner of it, she thought.

Renee turned from the window and looked around the railroad car at her fellow passengers. Four seats away and on the other side of the aisle two lovers had fallen asleep in one another's arms. She looked at them for a long while and was filled with a bittersweet sadness. Aaron's touch had excited her, and he was a fine man, an intelligent, sensitive man. He was also a man with humor. Vaguely she wondered if she were making a mistake leaving him. But what else could she do? This was her opportunity, her chance to escape the pattern. She glanced at her mother . . . No, she was doing the right thing. She felt certain in spite of the fact that she knew a part of her loved Aaron and would cherish his memory. Again she closed her eyes, but this time she told herself to float free of the past. Her life was in the hands of the Fates, but she would do her best to mold those Fates to her own ambitions.

4

December 15, 1923

Outside, a cold wind swept across the Common, shaking the bare trees and sending a shudder through the opaque glass windows of the subway entrance in front of the park on Tremont Street. In the spring and summer the shops and stores along Tremont sported red-and-white scalloped awnings with white fringes. But in winter the awnings were rolled and covered, giving the street a bleaker appearance and leaving only the gold dome of the State House on Beacon Hill to brighten the street and the park. In summer people poured onto Tremont to shop for imported foodstuffs from the carefully arranged shelves of S. S. Pierce or dry goods at the Stearns Company. In the heat of the sun old women sat on benches dressed in their faded finery and talked to the hundreds of pigeons that gathered to be fed. Old men with gold-tipped canes read newspapers, and there was always a speaker haranguing those who stopped long enough to listen and risk conversion to either a philosophy or a religion. The Common was also filled with children and their nannies. They flocked to the little lake and there rode the swan boats—little vessels built to look like swans—which to Margaret's eyes looked for all the world as if they'd been removed from the set of a Wagnerian opera. But in December the swan boats were covered with canvas and pulled to the tranquil shore of their ice-bound lake. Skaters in long scarves had replaced the wooden birds of summer, and along Tremont the shoppers did not linger because of the biting wind. Even the rosy-cheeked bearded Santa with his iron pot and clanging brass bell had sought refuge behind the wall and under the marquee of the Tremont Street Theater.

Margaret stood by the window of her shop and looked out on the Common. Heavy gray clouds were moving across the sky, threatening snow. But inside it was warm and cheery; there was even a small Christmas tree decorated with tinsel and homemade ornaments.

From the very first moment that Margaret Szilard Horvath had stepped off the train in Boston's South Station two years ago, she had been intensely aware of her new beginning.

First there was the matter of the money. Renee would have her tuition paid, and her sons would complete school during the daylight hours rather than working and going to night school. But she herself intended to work so that some, if not most, of the money she had received from Mr. Lewis would remain as a nest egg.

But gone were her days of slaving over a sewing machine in a dismal factory, or working at home and carrying in her little bits of piecework in a heavy sack. Money in the bank restored Margaret's sense of being and of worth, and Boston, as it turned out, was the city of her dreams.

For the first few days in Boston she and the children stayed in a spacious old rooming house on Salem Street near the Old North Church. Renee, Zoltan, and Imre began school immediately and Margaret walked the streets familiarizing herself with the shops and stores. Then with a surety she had never known, Margaret rented a small shop just off Tremont Street, a shop with a three-room apartment above it. They purchased a few pieces of used furniture and immediately moved in to save further expense. Next Margaret bought a good sewing machine, a cutting table, and all the accessories she would need. She decorated the shop lovingly and Zoltan even built a raised dais for display purposes. Next the sign painter came, and at the same time Margaret had a small tasteful brochure printed. At night Zoltan and Imre delivered it to all the houses on fashionable Beacon Hill, as well as to the large spacious homes in Back Bay. Simply, it announced the opening of "Madam Marguerite's" and advertised, "clothing created by one of Europe's fine couturieres." If lower-echelon Russian nobility—most of whom had never seen the inside of a kitchen—could open expensive restaurants and succeed, surely she who had had a lifetime interest in fashion could also succeed. What Margaret now perceived about Americans was that they were at heart snobs. And she quite rightly guessed that Boston was one of the most snobbish of cities.

In a matter of weeks Margaret also succeeded in becoming her own best advertisement. She wanted a rich clientele composed of women over thirty. She herself had been thirty-five when they arrived, and so she shopped for unique fabrics and created a wardrobe for herself. A stunning wardrobe quite unlike what was seen in ordinary stores. She wore a different outfit each day in her shop, and she took care to have lunch in a fashionable restaurant near the Common. People noticed her and soon a reporter from the Boston *Globe* came to interview her. Thin and angular, she posed for some pictures and stated her views on individual styles for individual women. Within six months Margaret had more work than she could handle and was obliged to hire two additional seamstresss. When she had time, and in the summers, Renee also worked in the shop. Using her own designs, she created clothing for younger women, and as was true of her mother, her own attractiveness helped to sell her line. It was Renee's idea that Madam Marguerite's should also begin to sell special accessories for their creations, thus becoming more than a simple dressmaking shop.

Not that Madam Marguerite's made them a great fortune; it did not. But it made them comfortable, and for the first time in her life Margaret was happy, and each day seemed to bring her more happiness.

Zoltan had graduated from high school the year after they arrived. To Margaret's joy, he went on to college, where he studied engineering. Imre was a bit more of a problem. He did not like school and resisted all Margaret's attempts to interest him in a college education. After numerous arguments, she relented. Imre, if he wished, could work when he finished high school.

Margaret drew the curtains slightly to keep in the heat. Then she returned to the back room, where a clutter of dressmaking materials testified to the amount of work they had to do over the holidays. In an adjacent room two seamstresses worked hard and fast. Christmas and New Year's demanded that ladies have new gowns, and Margaret had over twenty orders to be filled.

Margaret unrolled a bolt of green velvet and folded it neatly in half on the cutting table. She pinned the pattern she had made to the material, then turned to look for her pinking shears.

Renee came in from the back, her cheeks red as apples from the cold, her hair damp from falling snow.

"Oh, it's cold," she said. She rubbed her hands together and made no immediate attempt to remove her hat and gloves. "Where's Imre?"

"Not where he's supposed to be," Margaret said with a sharpness in her voice. "The school phoned to say he'd skipped classes again. He's not home yet, from wherever he is."

"He's probably gone to the movies. He says he wants to be an actor."

"I suppose I should rejoice that he wants to be anything. I won't force Imre to go to college," Margaret told her daughter. "But I hope he'll change his mind."

Renee watched as her mother carefully cut the deep green velvet material. "When I graduate I want to work with you," she said casually. "Right here in this shop."

"You'll do no such thing! This is my business."

Renee frowned. "You don't want me?"

Margaret smiled and laid down her scissors. "Of course, I want you, but this is not what I want for you. I want you to create dresses for one of the big stores or for a factory. Perhaps one day have charge of a whole catalog. I don't want you to be a mere dressmaker. You know more than that, Renee. You know about all the elements of design . . . you're an artist, not a dressmaker."

"I might have to leave Boston, you know. I might have to go back to New York."

"If that's where you have to go, that's where you have to go."

Renee smiled, then leaned over and kissed her mother on the cheek. "I'll try to find a job here first," she promised.

III

Renee
1924–1927

Eleven

1

June 1924

They weren't the Rothschilds, the Guggenheims, or the Astors, but they *were* rich and Leah Lazar occasionally reflected on how easy it was to adjust to the finer things in life. So easy that unless reminded, she could hardly remember living any other way. Did she ever once actually reside in a small crowded apartment with Miklós? Did she ever really pass her time feeding a squalling infant and washing his diapers? It was a world she had left behind without regret.

No, there was no question about it. She belonged here. Leah looked around their penthouse with enormous pleasure. It was her, it expressed her taste perfectly, and she had taken immense pleasure in decorating it. It consisted of nine large airy rooms and a roof garden. It was glass along one wall—the wall that gave way to French doors that led to the garden. All of its rooms were painted stark white and each featured furniture with rectilinear lines, covered in bright audacious fabrics of various textures.

There was a simply wonderful chaise longue covered with a throw of silk screened to look like tiger fur, there was an outrageous gilt clock on the mantel that featured stark naked little cupids that traveled once around the base on every hour, and there were plants potted in oversize planters and gay velvet ribbon, and print pillows everywhere. It was all very avant-garde and she had scoured the shops of Paris to find most of the objects she cherished, as well as the fabrics, which excited her because of their sensuous textures.

Leah sighed with contentment and threw herself carelessly on the chaise, arranging herself seductively and tossing her head back dramatically.

"Leah Laszlo, Leah Laszlo . . ." Leah repeated her maiden name and stared out onto her roof garden. "No . . . it has no class, it creates no mental images, and it's not memorable," she said aloud to no one. Nor did the name Lazar excite her, and for that matter Béla's last name of Szendi was impossible. What she wanted was a name with zing, a name to match the new person she felt she was rapidly becoming. This was the perfect time. Next week she would go to court and her divorce from Miklós would become final. At that time she could take back her maiden name, retain his, or, as she planned, choose a new one. "Leah," she determined, could stay. She liked it. But choosing a new last name was most difficult, and again she turned to her fashion magazines, hoping for some inspiration. Her new name should be something French—something the Americans associated with fashion. And then there was the label . . . she had to find a suitable name for her creations as well. "Fashions by Leah," she said aloud. No. She rejected it out of hand. She did not want her first name on five thousand identical garments. Of course, she could choose a label that expressed the reality, something like "Everywoman's" or perhaps "Saturday Night Attire." No, it would have to be the first if she went that route. Their new mail-order catalog was to offer competition to Sears, Roebuck as far as ladies' clothing was concerned, and they intended to offer a full line of clothing, not simply party dresses. Oh, God, why were these things so hard for her? Other people seemed to be born with the right names and she couldn't even select one when she had the opportunity. As for the label, well, that should be equally easy. Then, just when she had almost stopped trying to think, it hit her. Elégance . . . yes, that was it! "Elégance" was the perfect name for the label. In her mind she saw the swirling letters on the cover of the catalog. Elégance! It was so simple she couldn't think why it hadn't occurred to her before. As for her name, why not simply Leah? "Elégance by Leah." Yes, it was wonderful! Béla would be home soon and she would see if he approved. She arose and walked to the full-length mirror and smiled one last time at her own image. Free! Next week she would be free of Miklós at last, and then, she reasoned, Béla would no doubt marry her.

Poor Miklós. He was such a fool. How upset he had been when he'd come home that day and found her making love with Béla. And when she'd told him she was leaving him, he'd actually wept and begged her to stay. But she had not given in, and the truth was, she felt no remorse at all. Miklós could raise their son alone, not that Abraham was a child anymore. He would be nineteen next month and was already a university student. Besides, Abraham hated her. He felt strongly that his father had been wronged. Well, she thought, let them go their own way, I want nothing to do with either of them. Of course, she and Béla had not paid back the money either, even though Miklós had asked for it. In the end Miklós had been persuaded to accept stock instead of cash. But she knew the stock could not be sold. Béla would keep the company cash poor because he had plans to constantly expand. Soon Béla planned on opening retail outlets for their own imitation Paris fashions.

Every season Leah went to Paris to sketch the clothing modeled at the various salons. A small place in Paris prepared patterns from her sketches and then she hurried home on a fast ship. Within hours of her arrival the latest ideas from Paris were in full mass production, and now, she thought with glee, they could all bear the name Elégance and would soon be sold in stores that they would also own.

It was a wonderful, wonderful life. In Paris she could shop endlessly, and she stayed at the Ritz, one of the very best hotels. It was true that she worked hard there, but she also had time to walk in the parks, take in the galleries, and dine in the best restaurants. Sometimes Béla would join her for a few weeks of her usual month in the French capital. Then it was as if they were on their honeymoon. Yes, even after five years he was still the ardent lover and she was still very much his partner.

But she was her own person too. She had her own bank accounts, her own letters of credit, and above all her independence. To be sure, she intended keeping all of these things when she and Béla married. It was only right. It was her money—well Miklós' money really—that had made it all possible.

The door of their penthouse opened and Leah stood back from the mirror smiling. "You're home," she said, going to Béla and kissing him.

"This last trip to Paris was good for you," he said, looking at her admiringly. She was hardly showing her age at all, he thought as he looked her over. Leah, he contemplated, had many advantages. She cared so much for him that she never questioned where he might have been, even when he was very late. He enjoyed a freedom with her that he knew he could have with few women. Then too, what she didn't know wouldn't hurt her.

"My divorce from Miklós becomes final next week," Leah reminded him.

"So it does. He's leaving, you know, going to California."

"Really? Well, what difference does that make to me?"

"I'm sure it makes no difference. But he seemed to think it might. At least he seemed to think you might want the address so you could write to your son."

"Oh, you spoke to him, then?"

"He called while you were away. I wrote the address down."

"Good. I suppose I will have to write."

Béla eyed her and then sat down on the plush sofa. He withdrew his pipe and slowly lit it. "I've always known your personal ambition came before everything, darling.

But I had thought that you had some natural affection for your own child."

"I do. But I'm not going to play mother, and God knows it might be years before I see him again. Besides, he certainly isn't a child."

"Ah, Leah, what I like about you is your edge of sheer steel and your heart of iron."

"I rather thought you admired my talent."

Béla laughed. "Actually, my dear, your talent is very limited but you don't need more than you have. Otherwise you are perfect in all other ways—you carry your role off to perfection. That's what I admire."

Leah scowled at him. She was an artist whether or not he recognized it. She opened her mouth to say something more, but Béla seized her hand and pulled her down next to him.

"You've been away for a month. I don't feel like talking," he announced as he slipped his hand beneath her skirt and tugged at her silk panties. His dark eyes fastened on hers as his hand explored, and gradually a smile crossed his face as he watched her close her eyes and begin to breathe heavily, all other matters forgotten. He reveled in his absolute sexual power over her. "That's a good girl," he said, slipping her undergarments aside to feel her warm moist flesh. "That's a very good girl."

2

June 1924

"Mama?" Renee paused at her mother's door. It was slightly ajar, and though the light was still on, she thought her mother might have dozed off to sleep reading as she so often did.

"Renee? Is that you?"

"Yes, Mama. I just got home."

"Any luck?" Margaret asked.

Renee slipped into the room and closed the door. "No. There are so few places here in Boston. None of them are hiring original artists," she sighed. "They all say, 'Oh, you graduated from the Boston School of Fine Arts—that's the best school in the country. Oh, I couldn't afford to hire you.' I think I'll have to go back to New York, Mama."

"I'll stay here, Renee. I'm happy here and I'll have Zoltan and Imre. I don't like sending you off alone. You'll have to be careful."

"I won't like going, Mama."

"And I don't like having you go. But I'm used to the idea now because we've talked about it so much. I think it would be best if you stayed in one of those hotels for young women. Then I won't worry so much."

"Of course." Renee walked across the room and sat on the edge of her mother's bed. "What are you doing?"

"Remembering. I didn't bring many photos, only a few. Here, this one is of your great-grandmother."

Renee took the old tintype and held it to the light. She had seen it and the others before, but it had been a while and she always found them fascinating. "She's very beautiful. But I must say I'm glad all the whalebone has gone out of fashion. How uncomfortable it must have been!"

Margaret smiled. "Oh, you couldn't even dress by yourself. But I guess she didn't mind. She used to call those years—the last years of the empire—our 'glory years.' I don't think she could even imagine life without the steady ruling hand of Franz József, the old emperor. The poor woman must be turning over in her grave, seeing what a mess Austria and Hungary are . . . not to mention Germany."

Renee laughed softly. "I think she might have fitted in with some of the ladies of Beacon Hill."

"Maybe. She was certainly reared in a different time, and I suppose she accepted the idea of being owned by some man. I never did, you know. I always believed women should have rights. Renee, when I went to the polls last month and voted for the first time in my life, I was so proud. It's been a long, hard struggle—even here in America."

"I think there are more struggles to come."

"Oh, I know there are. But having the vote is so important. We can elect men who care about our rights now and reject those who don't. Yes, voting was one of the proudest moments of my life. Did I ever tell you the story of your name?"

"No. Does my name have a story?"

"Oh, yes. You're named for Verena, the character in Henry James's novel *The Bostonians*. She was a suffragette. It's a book your father and I spent a long while discussing. And even though I first read it in Hungarian, it was the first novel I read in English when I'd mastered the language."

"You never told me that before, Mama." Renee smiled and laughed lightly. "I think I shall have to keep one eye on the fashion pages and the other on the political pages now that I know whom I'm named after."

"Just promise me you'll always exercise your franchise."

"I promise."

Margaret patted her daughter's arm, then returned to her neat stack of photos. She lifted one and held it under the light. "These are my brothers. There's Béla, Konrad, and György. Ah, here is your grandmother."

"She's pretty too."

"Oh, I suppose we were all pretty. And you are the prettiest. But you are also the only one to graduate from school. Oh, Renee, I am so proud of you! I wanted to go to school. I had to learn to read from György and then pretend I didn't even know how. Then, when I learned English, I had to keep that a secret too. Yes, I always dreamed of graduating from school, and when you graduated . . . well, it was as if you did it for me, as if you were standing there for both of us."

Renee kissed her mother on the cheek. "I did," she whispered as she gathered up the photos. "You should get some sleep now."

"I suppose. But I like remembering."

"I know, but you must build up your strength."

"I'm not sure it is any use, my dear. You know, when you start remembering, you're close to the end."

"Oh, Mama! You're a young woman, for heaven's sake."

"And these last years have been the happiest of my life. Ah, I may be young in years, perhaps. But I've been ill. Very ill, and it all took its toll. Renee, be realistic. I haven't been well for the past two months. I may not get better. Sometimes I think I managed only by sheer will to last long enough to see you graduate from art school. Renee, I'm tired. So terribly, terribly tired. But you . . . you're going to have a very different life. No one is going to force you to do anything—"

"Mama, what do you mean you might not get better? I want you to go to Boston General tomorrow. I want you to see a doctor."

Margaret shook her head. "I've been to a doctor, Renee. A good doctor, the husband of one of my best customers. There's been liver damage—either from the disease or from the salvarsan.

"Mama, don't talk like this. You're frightening me." Tears filled Renee's eyes and she held her mother close, aware suddenly that it was like holding a feather. "Mama, you should go to the hospital tomorrow."

"What for? I don't want to be poked and prodded and given horrible injections and medicines. There is nothing that can repair the damage, Renee. There's no real treatment. Here I'm at peace. You're a woman now and you and Zoltan can look after Imre. You're free and I'm free, and that's all I ever wanted."

"Mama . . ."

"Hush, Renee. This is no surprise to me. Janos gave me his terrible illness, the medicine is toxic, and both the disease and the medicine can affect the organs. Still, the Lord has been merciful, he's allowed me long enough to see my wish come true." Margaret paused and then slowly began shaking her head. "There is one piece of unfinished business, though . . . one bit of my life that's been left hanging. Renee, I want you to try somehow to find your father. Promise me you'll look for him."

"I will, but please stop talking this way, please."

Margaret nodded and laid her head back on the pillow. "Did I ever tell you about the day the emperor came to visit Kassa? I was only eight, but I remember it quite well. And Grandmother was so excited. She wore the most elegant dress you can imagine. It was made of blue brocade and trimmed in gorgeous lace and velvet. She had a wonderful hat too. It had a brim so wide"—she made a motion with her hand—"and long, long feathers hung down the back. We had huge tents set up on the front lawn, in case it rained, and a whole pig was served, together with dumplings, apples, carrots, and a magnificent goose liver. Oh, I shall never forget that goose liver! I shall never forget any of it. Ah, we Hungarians are plagued by a good memory, a kind of collective memory of the way things were and should have remained. You know that after the assassination of poor Archduke Ferdinand, the very last of the Habsburgs was crowned in Budapest? That was after we left, of course . . . but I remember having Grandmother tell me about Franz József's coronation. I wonder if it was as grand? Remember . . . I love to remember . . ."

Margaret patted Renee's hand. "Most of all I love to remember your father. He was the most handsome man I ever saw—as a matter of fact, I never did see anyone half as handsome. And nice. Your father was a nice man, Renee, even if he didn't come back for me. I'm sure he wanted to. Maybe he did and Janos had already taken me away to that horrid place in Transylvania." Margaret paused and dabbed at her eyes. "Yes, Renee, your father was not only good-looking but also smart. Miklós was terribly smart. He taught me English and I know he knew many other languages. I wish I had a picture of him to show you, Renee. Anyway, you must promise me you will try to find him."

Renee watched as her mother closed her eyes and drifted into sleep. Could it be that she was really dying? A chill passed through her and more tears fell silently down her cheeks.

"*Lofasz a seggedbe*, Janos!" Renee muttered in Hungarian. It was the vilest of curses and she delivered it to Janos and his miserable disease. It was unfair that her mother should die just when she was happiest.

3

August 1924

Hot, humid summer air hung over the city, while in the eastern sky dark clouds billowed and moved into position with the prevailing winds.

Twenty-year-old Renee, nineteen-year-old Zoltan, and sixteen-year-old Imre stood in front of the small gravestone in the burial ground behind the Catholic church in Malden just outside of Boston. The names on the surrounding stones was nearly all Irish, so the name Margaret Szilard Horvath stood out.

"Poor Mama," Zoltan said in a near-whisper. His eyes were still moist with tears. "I knew she was sick, but I thought she'd get well."

Imre glanced up at his older brother and shifted his weight from one foot to the other impatiently.

"She lived to see us graduate," Renee said. "She wanted that more than anything."

Zoltan bent down and put a bouquet of purple violets on the green grass in front of the headstone. "Who knows when we'll get back here?" he said softly.

Renee bit her lip. Since last Christmas she had run her mother's shop, putting off her trip to New York because her mother was too ill to even consider leaving. Then, when her mother had died, her brothers had decided to go back to New York with her. Zoltan was going because he now considered himself the head of the family, and Imre was going because he'd never liked Boston in the first place.

Wordlessly they all three turned and began walking back toward the subway station. "Do you realize she died a month ago? It doesn't seem like a month," Zoltan finally said. Then added, "I guess that's because we had so much to do."

Renee nodded. They had cleaned out the shop and their apartment. They'd packed, and tonight the three of them were taking the train to New York.

"I should be able to get a good job even in New York," Zoltan said confidently. He'd taken a course in practical engineering and temporarily set aside the idea of finishing college as a full-time day student.

"You can work *even* in New York, and I can work *only* in New York," Renee sighed. "I'm so sorry we have to move back there."

"It has one advantage," Zoltan allowed. "I can go on and take my degree at Columbia in the evenings."

Renee nodded.

"Still, it means leaving Mama," Zoltan lamented. "We can't visit her grave."

"Her spirit will come with us," Renee whispered. Her mind was on her mother's legacy. It was mysterious. Mama's bank account had had five hundred dollars in it, and Renee assumed that was what was left from the money her grandmother had sent. But it was not the money that constituted the mystery. It was the absence of letters. Her mother had always announced when she had received a letter from her own mother and she told them what was in it. Moreover, she made them all write . . . yet Renee and Zoltan had found no letters, and they couldn't find their grandmother's address either. Nonetheless, Renee didn't mention it again now. The three of them had discussed it for days and come to the conclusion that they should simply accept the fact that they had five hundred dollars on which to move and get settled. Perhaps, they reasoned, more letters would arrive from their grandmother, and if so, they would be forwarded to general delivery in New York.

Renee leaned back and closed her eyes, listening to the subway wheels as they sped along in the eternal darkness of the tunnel. Then they were in the South Station, and outside the wind had changed directions and the threatened storm materialized. Boston's South Station was a huge triangular building with three entrances, five stories, and over the center entrance there was a huge clock with an American flag on either side. All along two sides of the triangle, the two on either side of the main entrance, there were faded red awnings that extended over the wide sidewalk. The elevated railway tracks ran right past the front of the station. As the rain poured down, the three of them ran for the cover of the awning. "I'm glad we left our luggage here in those lockers." Renee meant their personal luggage, which had been put in a day locker. Their heavy luggage had been sent ahead by train.

"Everything will be all right," Zoltan said again for the one hundredth time.

Renee patted his arm gently to make him feel better, but there was no use trying to distract him too much. The fact was that Zoltan, as he always had, felt a strong responsibility toward her and toward Imre.

"I could work too," Imre suggested.

Zoltan and Renee answered "No" together and then both smiled at each other.

"Do you think Mr. Lewis will hire you back?" Zoltan asked.

"I don't know. I don't know what to expect. All I know is that this time I have a proper portfolio." For a moment she thought about Aaron. But he wasn't in New York anymore. He'd gone away to school and he hadn't answered any of her letters. At first she had been hurt, but later she decided he must have wanted to make a clean break, or, she thought, perhaps he had found someone else.

"There's a New York paper," Imre said as they passed a newsstand.

Zoltan stopped and bought it and they opened it to the classified ads.

"Rooms for rent first," Renee suggested. "Here, I've got a pencil. Circle the ones we can afford."

Zoltan's eyes scanned the long page of ads and at intervals he marked a few.

Then the announcement for their train came over the

loudspeaker. They hurried down the track and boarded, finding empty seats in the third car. Then once again they opened the paper and continued to familiarize themselves with types of accommodation, prices, and locations.

When Zoltan had finished with the rooms-for-rent section, he divided the want ads in half. He handed Renee the page marked "Help Wanted—Female."

She read down the long list of jobs, most of which were for secretaries. Then her eye fell on one particular ad. It read, "Artist Wanted. Elégance—Béla Mail Order Fashions, 127 Seventh Avenue."

"Look!" she exclaimed. "Here's an ad for an artist! And look, it's called 'Elégance' and says 'Béla Fashions.' "

"What's important about that?" Imre questioned.

"Béla was Mama's brother's name. Perhaps it bodes well that a company with this name is looking for an artist. Sort of like a good omen."

Zoltan looked dubious. "From what Mama said, I don't think Béla was a very nice person."

"Well, that doesn't meant this Béla isn't a nice person. Anyway, it's a Hungarian name, so he must be Hungarian. Maybe that will help."

4

The offices of Elégance were ultramodern. The walls were white and the furniture was massive, curved, and covered with wildly colorful fabrics.

Renee, who had long ago decided to use her real father's name, sat in front of Leah Lazar's desk. Miss Lazar was Hungarian and worked for the person whose first name was Béla. Béla was a distinctly Hungarian name, so she might have guessed she'd find another Hungarian here.

Leah looked at the girl in front of her uneasily. She was well-dressed—even stylishly dressed. And she was pretty. Too pretty. And young. That was the worst part, she was young and beautiful and, yes, talented.

Leah had rapidly begun going through the drawings in the portfolio, then had slowed down. Deep inside she knew they were better than any she herself had ever done; outwardly she managed to look critical, even unimpressed.

Renee watched her carefully, then decided to take courage and ask the question that had plagued her since she'd come into the office.

"Your name is Lazar. I've been looking for a man with that last name."

Leah looked nonplussed and nodded. Her eyes had fallen on an exquisite design for an evening gown.

"I know it's a very common name. In fact I've called many in the phone book, and once placed an ad in the paper. I'm looking for a Miklós Lazar. You don't know him, or perhaps he is a relative? He is from Budapest."

Leah looked up in such a way that Renee actually felt both her recognition and suspicion. "Why do you want to know? I mean, what is your interest?"

"He is a relative," Renee said carefully.

Leah turned from her portfolio to her application form. "Oh, I see, Lazar is your last name too. I hadn't noticed before. And what do you want of this Miklós Lazar?"

"Only to get in touch with him." Clearly this woman did know someone of this name, and that someone was from Budapest. Just as clearly, she was for some reason hesitant. "I want to get in touch with him because of my mother," she lied. "My mother was his cousin and they were close friends too. My mother is dead, but she wanted me to find him. It was her last wish."

"Well, he may be the same one, and he may not. But if he is, let me tell you, he couldn't help you. He's a simple man who used to work for an investment house. Now I believe he is in Los Angeles trying to start his own business . . . though he's much too unimaginative to be a success. I should know. I was once married to him."

Renee stared at her and tried desperately to control her own expression. "Oh, I see," she replied softly.

Leah had returned to the drawings with a scowl. The girl was too good to hire. She was also too original. And in all truth, Leah did not really want original artists. She wanted someone like herself who could view something and then quickly reproduce it.

It was at that moment that the office door opened and a tall, dark, good-looking man in his forties entered. Renee looked up into his dark eyes. She felt stunned into utter silence and wondered how, if anyone spoke to her, she could possibly answer. In these few minutes two astounding things had happened: the woman interviewing her had been married to a man with her real father's name, and the man who had just come into the room was her mother's brother!

He was older, certainly. But the features were the same, and so was the thick dark hair. Yes, there was no question in her mind. This was the brother her mother had disliked and feared. He was the man who had committed fraud and who had stolen his own father's money and honor. He was the man who had caused his father to commit suicide. She knew him from the picture her mother had so often shown her.

Renee's first instinct was to blurt out who she was; her second, and the one she obeyed, urged caution and silence. He would not know who she was, after all; her last name was now Lazar.

For his part, Béla stared at her as boldly as she stared at him. The resemblance, he thought, was quite remarkable. This girl looked for all the world like his sister, Margaret. "What is your name?" he asked.

"Renee Lazar," she answered, half-wanting to run away from this man her mother always called "evil," but compelled to stay because he might lead her to other members of her family.

"She does original designs," Leah put in somewhat disparagingly.

Béla bent over and looked at a few of her drawings. "We have no rules against original designs," he said, giving Leah a menacing look. "Besides, the girl is Hungarian! We must all stick together. How about it, how about working here?"

"That depends on my salary," Renee said.

"Ten dollars a week."

"All right," she agreed. At least, she reasoned, it might give her the time to learn Miklós' address from Leah, or even her grandmother's or Konnie's address from Béla. Meanwhile a thousand questions plagued her. If Leah's ex-husband was the same Miklós Lazar, what was his wife doing with Béla, Mama's brother?

Béla's voice broke through her thoughts. He was looking at Leah, whose expression was tight. She looked as if she might spit like a cobra at any minute. "She can be your assistant. One of you will learn a great deal." He laughed.

"When do you want me to start?" Renee asked, trying to sound practical, even though she was in fact fascinated by the strange relationship these two seemed to have.

"Let's see, this is Wednesday . . . Monday. Be here Monday at eight."

Renee nodded and murmured a thank-you. Then she quickly retrieved her portfolio and hurried away, anxious to speak to Zoltan and tell him what had happened.

As soon as she heard the door close, Leah got up and went into her private office, slamming the door behind her. She was seething inside, and her hand trembled as she lit a cigarette and instantly exhaled smoke.

"*Bassza meg*!" she muttered under her breath. When she was angry she always reverted to Hungarian.

Leah tossed back her long dark hair and walked to the window. Below, the street was flooded with people leaving work. From her vantage point on the sixteenth floor they appeared as miniatures, little people running here and there. Little people leading little lives. "I'm a world apart from them," she said to herself. "I have this office and my own business. Tomorrow I'm leaving for Paris. . . . I have everything, everything," she thought silently. But saying it—even thinking it—did not make it true. She didn't have everything. She had lost something. Her youth. And now, for the first time, it troubled her. And her talent was limited. She was no better today than she had been years ago. She wasn't an original in any sense of the word. But she really couldn't think about that or about her youth. She shook her gold spangle bracelets nervously, taking small comfort in the fact that she had one thing and that thing was money. "So why do I feel so threatened by that wisp of a girl," she said aloud. And the answer was obvious. She was leaving tomorrow and she did not trust Béla one bit. She had seen the look in his eyes and she knew exactly what that look meant. He wanted that girl and he might do almost anything to get her. And just how ambitious was the girl? She seemed ambitious to Leah. She had seemed to bask in the warmth of Béla's attention; she seemed to know how to get ahead.

Leah turned abruptly as the door opened and Béla strode in.

"Don't you believe in knocking? This is my office," she said irritably.

"My, my. Aren't we possessive? Are you packed? Are you ready to leave tomorrow?"

"Of course I'm ready. You can hardly wait till I'm gone, I imagine."

Béla feigned innocence. He turned to her wide-eyed and his very expression annoyed her even further.

"Darling, how can you say such a thing?"

"It's quite easy. Do you think I'm blind? You're quite taken with that new girl. You want me out of the way. Well, I warn you, it's a bad idea to get involved with—"

"An employee," he finished brightly.

"Yes."

Béla eyed her up and down and rubbed his chin slowly, appraisingly, as he circled her. He took a step backward and locked the door. Then he moved again toward her. She felt suddenly like a trapped animal and she stood rigid because inside she knew she had gone too far. Never, ever, had she questioned him about another woman . . . never, ever, had she expressed jealousy. She supposed he strayed now and again, but he was a man, and that was to be expected. But those women, the kind one might spend a night with, were different. They were not a threat to her. But this new girl, she sensed it with all her being, this Renee was a threat. Still, she should have said nothing. She knew that as she looked into Béla's eyes. They had narrowed meanly.

"You're not as young as you used to be, Leah. Oh, you're not unattractive, but you're not fresh either. Perhaps our business needs a little new blood. Indeed, perhaps there is room for an American fashion house, one that has its own label. Perhaps it's time I hired a woman with real talent, and then we might be able to do away with our European designs. Then you could settle down, my dear, right here in New York."

"What are you talking about?" Leah asked, her voice almost cracking.

"Dear me, you're all upset now. The truth is painful, isn't it, Leah?"

It was, as if for the past few minutes he had been stretching and stretching a rubber band. Now it gave and she sprang at him like a tigress, her hands in tiny tight-clenched fists. "This is my company too! I won't allow you to give away what belongs to me! I won't allow you to become involved with that . . . that girl!" She blurted it out and instantly regretted it.

Béla roughly seized her wrists and pulled her toward him, shaking her like a small rag doll. She had long underestimated his raw strength and she was startled as he held her tightly and glowered at her.

"*Az anyad picsaja!*" he hissed. "You will never tell me what to do, how to do it, or whom to do it with. You overvalue yourself, Leah. You mean nothing to me. Creatively, you can easily be replaced, and sexually I am sure more than half the women in New York could please me as well as you do."

His dark eyes were narrow as he looked at her. She felt like shrieking, but instead she began to shake violently. "There, now," he said, still looking nasty, "I didn't mean you weren't good for occasional usage."

As he spoke, he forced her back on her own wide desk and her skirt rode up as well, revealing her upper thigh. Béla held her struggling with one hand while he felt up under her skirt and pulled down her panties.

"Oh, God," she muttered as he roughly touched her,

and then ran his hand up to undo her blouse. He tore off her lacy undergarments and stared at her in the bright sunlight that poured in the window.

"Your nipples are faded, Leah. Your skin is too soft, too supple."

She tossed and groaned, tears beginning to fill her eyes.

"Look at you. I'm insulting you and you can still hardly wait to be satisfied."

Béla unzipped his trousers and fell on her, holding her down while he quickly took his own pleasure with no concern for hers whatsoever. Beneath him he could feel the heat of her flesh as she struggled, cursing him because he shook her loose before she could come to her own pleasure.

Leah reached out for him, her hands like highly manicured claws, and tears ran down her face. Then, as if she had no bones, she slipped slowly off her desk to the floor and covered her face with her hands and sobbed violently. And just before he left, he turned on her, dark eyes cold and voice hard and set. "Don't ever tell me what to do again," he said. "Don't even make any suggestions."

Leah dropped her hands slightly and her eyes followed him. After a time she stood up weakly. Her face was still red with humiliation and she was still shaking with fury. "I'll get even with you!" she whispered, digging her long polished nails into the folds of her skirt. "*Le vagy szarva*! I shit on you!"

Twelve

1

June 7, 1926

*I*t was truly the land of dreams. Konrad Szilard loved Los Angeles; he loved it more than any place he had ever been or any place he had ever seen. It was sprawling and unlike European cities its architecture completely lacked any cohesion or discipline. On top of the indigenous Spanish architecture, which featured stark white adobe, red tile roofs, patios inside and out, high walls, and missionlike towers and entranceways, there were flat modern buildings with rounded corners, houses that might have been imported from New England, great Victorian gingerbread masterpieces, Gothic castles, and now, buildings designed by Wright—bold buildings that let the sunlight in. And there were other periods and styles. The city was a hodgepodge, a veritable carnival of styles where one could find Chinese pagodas overlooking a replica of the Temple of Isis. But there were also wonderful parks. One, Griffith Park, was a wilderness really, over four thousand acres of rugged mountain terrain virtually in the heart of the city. And right on the corner of Wilshire and La Brea, in the middle of a residential area, there was a great tar pond that bubbled out of the depths of the earth, tossing up the bones of long-extinct mammals that were studied and reconstructed by delighted university professors and their students.

Above all, Konnie loved the way people dressed. They dressed as they damn well pleased and lolled by swimming pools or ate elegant meals in the Brown Derby, a restaurant shaped like a man's hat. It was also a city of hard work and hard play, of stressful creative sessions and of all manner of excesses.

The studios had lots and sets, but many films were just shot on the streets, where one could find almost any kind of locale and where the willing populace stood in line for the opportunity to be an "extra." Or one could take the cameras to Griffith Park and shoot "wild woods" or "barren mountains," and to Santa Monica to film an exotic South Pacific isle. Within fifty miles one could have snow in Alpine Village, then roaring down out of the mountains onto the dry desert floor there were dunes, a collection of dunes just made for camels and ready to be the Arabian desert. Now as never before the kind of action films that Konnie had dreamed of were possible.

Then too, he was among friends. People joked, they called them the "Hungarian gang." Béla Lugosi had come from Germany just a few months ago. Pola Negri had come almost at the same time as Konnie to star in *Bella Donna, The Cheat,* and *Spanish Dancer.* Pasternak and Adolph Zukor had been here a long while, and Alexander Korda had written that he intended coming next year at the latest.

At first Konrad had stayed with his friend Joe Somló. Then, after he'd been given a job as an assistant to the assistant producer, he found himself a place in one of those little bungalow courts that sprouted on the streets around Hollywood and, indeed, all over Los Angeles. They were, he decided, a uniquely Californian solution to housing. Not apartments, and yet not exactly houses. They were one-story, all attached, and built around a courtyard. Each bungalow was self-contained, with a living room, kitchen/dining-room, bedroom, and bath. They were wonderfully private, yet communal in a sense because the courtyard was shared.

Konnie left his own little bungalow at exactly nine A.M., feeling an incredible mixture of excitement and anticipation. He was going to see Zukor this morning, and although he saw him often socially, this morning he was seeing him for the first time on business. What he had clutched under his arm was a script, one he had been working on for many months, one he was convinced would make a spectacular film. He checked his watch. Zukor was to meet him at nine-thirty sharp in his office.

Konnie walked briskly toward the office of Famous Players, and he thought about the man with whom he had made his appointment. Zukor was a kind of chameleon, a man who had had several varied careers. Adolph had been born in Risce and he'd come to America at the age of fifteen. He began as a sweeper in New York and then he had gone into the penny-arcade business. Two years after starting the business, he was joined by Marcus Loew, who'd been born in America but whose parents had originally come from Austria. Together they had gone from penny arcades to theaters and now owned over four hundred movie houses. Zukor had made a great deal of money on his own distributing the European production of Queen Elizabeth. With the proceeds, Zukor had opened his own American production company, Famous Players in Famous Plays. Then Zukor had merged with Lasky and now they had merged with a small firm, Paramount. Rumor had it that they were going to change the name of Famous Players-Lasky Productions to Paramount because it was shorter and had more strength.

Konnie reached the studio gates and showed the guard his pass. Then he ambled past the sets toward the main building, which housed Zukor's office. Movie sets, he reflected, looked bizarre at the best of times, but in the early-morning sunlight the make-believe world was ruthlessly exposed as little more than glue and cardboard. The impressive double doors of a false public library led to a mud puddle on the unpaved studio pathway, and the books on the library's shelves were revealed as painted blocks of wood.

Konnie entered the main building and went directly to Zukor's office, where the secretary, a young shapely blond in a tight skirt, ushered him to a seat. Konnie waited.

At twenty to ten he was ushered into Zukor's office. The diminutive Zukor ran out from behind his desk and shook Konnie's hand. "Come in, come in, my friend. Sorry to have kept you waiting. Here, sit down. I'll get us some coffee . . ." He opened the door and called out, "Rose, bring coffee!"

Adolph Zukor was slightly paunchy, and unruly graying hair encircled his head, forming a halo of white fuzz. He was an energetic man, high-strung, and volatile. He wore a slightly crumpled gray suit and an open-necked white shirt.

Konnie shifted in his chair. Then he decided to plunge right in. "Did you read the script I sent?"

"Yes. I liked it. It's a fine piece of work, a fine piece of work." Zukor rubbed his chin thoughtfully.

"Are you interested in doing it?" Konnie asked bluntly.

"You know I do Famous Plays . . . your play is very good, very good indeed. But it's not famous."

"But transferred to film, many famous plays are too static. My play is tailored to the medium. I even know where exactly all the locales can be found."

Rose, Zukor's secretary, came in with the coffee, poured it quickly, and discreetly left. She didn't look like a girl who should be named Rose to Konnie. She looked more like a Rita or even a Mae.

"I know they're static." Zukor laughed. "But look, I make millions." He shook his head. "The public is never wrong," he announced.

Konnie sat back. "I thought you might try something new."

"I will," Zukor agreed. "Look, you make the film. Raise the money and make the film. I'll distribute it."

Konnie frowned. It was far more of an offer than it would have sounded to a lay person. Distribution was the trickiest part of the business. A film that never got into distribution didn't make a cent, it simply rotted in its little tin box. "Will you put your intention to distribute it in writing?"

"If I wouldn't put it in writing, I wouldn't offer. Anyway, without distribution guaranteed, you couldn't possibly raise the money."

"I hardly know how to go about raising it now," Konnie admitted.

"Oh, you're not going to raise it. You let this man raise it." He had reached into his pocket and he proffered a card to Konnie. "He's Hungarian. Seems to have good connections to Eastern investors, works hard, is really very good."

Konnie stared at the card. It read simply "Michael Lazar Investments."

"Ahem!" Zukor cleared his throat.

Konnie looked up. "Thank you," he said.

"No thanks necessary. I've been thinking about some of your experience in Europe. I think you would be right for me. I think I want you to produce a little Shakespeare for me, *King Lear,* perhaps?"

"King Lear?" Konnie was taken aback. Still, his mind worked rapidly, and he could already imagine which shots could be done outside and how it could be made less static.

"It takes time to raise money. More time than to make a film. While you're getting your finances in order, you might just as well be working. How about it?"

"Yes . . . I can certainly try."

Zukor grinned and passed him a box of Havana cigars. "When you work for me, you try, and you always succeed."

2

Renee had left her drawings to go to the ladies' room. She came back into the main office just as the mailman entered. She smiled to herself. All the time she had worked at Elégance she had gotten up when the mail was due, but this was the first time she had timed it so exactly. Still, each day she did manage to see the mail and go through it on the excuse that she was expecting a letter from a friend who did not have her home address.

As casually as possible, she began leafing through the morning letters, aware that she was more relaxed because Leah was again gone to Paris. She stopped dead at the third letter and her fingers curled around it. It was what she had been waiting for and she had all but given up hope. Addressed in a neat hand, it was clearly a letter from Leah's son. Renee flipped it over and saw the return address: "Abraham Lazar, 11368 Sunset Boulevard., No. 5, Los Angeles, California."

She committed it to memory and hurried back to her desk. There she scribbled it down on a scrap of paper and put the paper in her purse.

Now what? she asked herself. Was she to write to this Abraham Lazar and ask him his father's address, or was she to write to Miklós Lazar in care of this address? And what was she going to write? Was she going to ask, "Are you my father?" Or, more accurately, was she to ask, "Were you ever the lover of Margaret Szilard?" and then perhaps add, "If you were, surprise! You have a daughter." No, she couldn't do it that way, and truth be known, she hadn't thought at all past learning his address, even though after Leah had told her she had a son who wrote, Renee knew it was only a matter of time. But now that she had it, she wasn't at all certain what to do with it.

Renee pushed it all from her thoughts temporarily and went back to her work. To her relief, Béla had not bothered her at all. In fact, he had been gone a great deal himself in the past year, and when he was about, he seemed immersed in business. Leah would be back tomorrow, and although Leah didn't seem to like her very much, Renee would be glad to have her return.

Then too, as soon as she arrived, the slack would pick up and the new catalog could go to press. And when finally it was printed and in the mail, perhaps, she thought, she could ask Béla for a few days off.

Renee and her brothers had rented a pleasant flat in

Brooklyn. Zoltan had a good job in construction and at night he continued his studies in engineering. But Imre was a growing problem. Not quite eighteen, he refused to return to school and announced he had a job and wanted to work. For some reason, Imre had grown secretive, and of late he had been gone a great deal. When questioned, he only replied that he had new friends.

"You should go back to school," she had urged. And Zoltan had sided with her, arguing, "You need an education. Mama wanted you to have one, and besides, you can earn more money with a college degree."

But Imre was unmoved. "Mama," he retorted, "didn't want us to be forced to be or do anything."

Renee had been unable to argue that point, and Zoltan, as good as he was, was not Imre's father and could not offer the kind of support needed.

For a time Renee had simply hoped Imre would grow out of his rebelliousness and see that he should return to school. But Imre's job seemed to pay well enough. He contributed his share to household expenses and had enough left over to go out. In fact, both she and Zoltan were puzzled by their brother's seeming affluence, puzzled and a little troubled.

"I'm going to find out more," Renee told Zoltan. "As soon as I can, I'll take some time off work."

"Perhaps he only has a girlfriend," Zoltan had suggested.

"I hope it's something like that," she had replied. Yes, she thought to herself, she would be pleased if it were a girl. But she was afraid. She and Zoltan had always done everything together, perhaps because they were little more than a year apart in age. But Imre was often left out because he was younger and his interests did not coincide with theirs. Perhaps, she reasoned, it had been better when their mother was alive. Then they had been four, but now they were three, and with three, one was always odd-man-out. No, she reflected, that was not it. It had begun long before their mother died. Imre had always been difficult and there was no point denying it.

Renee's eyes strayed toward the window, and while the view was only that of a brick wall, she recalled

Sundays in Central Park with her mother and brothers, Sundays when they had first come to New York, before they went to Boston, Sundays when they were dirt poor. She could see one day in particular with clarity—the day she had first begun to think of Zoltan as a man on whom she could depend.

"Once all of my days were like Sunday," her mother had said wistfully. "Once my hands were smooth and soft. Once I used to ride my horse from dawn until sunset. I'm sorry you don't remember those days . . . I'm sorry the only horse you've seen has been here in the park and is owned by others. Perhaps you'd have all been better off with Janos. At least you'd have had a proper education." Her mother had leaned back against the wooden bench, her eyes fastened on a small child nearby who was struggling with a large hoop, rolling it along, trying to keep it upright as it careened crazily down the rutted path. "Some days I can hardly remember who I am or how I came to be here," her mother added.

Renee, tall, slender, and blond like her mother, had smiled tenderly and patted her mother's arm. "No. We belong together, Mama. No matter what, we belong together."

Across the wide expanse of green lawn Renee's brothers, fifteen-year-old Zoltan and twelve-year-old Imre, were playing. Zoltan was playing kickball with some older boys; Imre was alone on the swings.

"Look at them," her mother said. "They're still children, and so are you. But this is the only day for childhood. The rest are spent working for a pittance to keep us all from starving."

"It's the same for all the newcomers," Renee said. "It will change. I know it will."

"Newcomers. We've been here for six years—six long years of working day in and day out. And look at us. We live in one tiny room and we all have to work just to pay the rent, put food on the table, and clothe ourselves."

"In another two years I graduate from night school. Then Zoltan and Imre will follow. I can get a better job then, Mama."

Her mother's fingers had squeezed the rough material of her skirt. "Always next year, or two years, or a month, a day. . . . Whatever is good is always for tomorrow. I'm tired, so tired I can feel every bone in my body."

"Mama, you could stay home now. We earn enough to—"

"No. I won't have you leaving the night school, and there wouldn't be enough money if I stopped working. No, I'm not that tired. You must forgive me, my darling. I just ramble on and on. I was spoiled as a girl . . . so very spoiled. Forgive me."

Renee had reached over and silently covered her mother's hand with hers. There was nothing to forgive. The four of them were trapped and would remain trapped until they had more education and could leave the clothing factory where they all worked. She and her mother worked at the sewing machines and Imre and Zoltan worked in the shipping department. The war had brought a little more money and prosperity to some, but now it seemed everything had come to a halt and there were no raises or promotions. "Perhaps," Renee said after a long silence, "the new owners will pay us a little more."

Her mother had shrugged. "I saw them touring the plant yesterday. I don't think they will pay more."

"The young one is good-looking," Renee said, smiling. "His name is Aaron and he's to be our floor manager. I heard he is the only son of David Lewis, who has bought the factory and who owns other factories."

Her mother had smiled indulgently. "You hear more than I do."

Renee laughed and leaned over, kissing her mother's cheek. "Be happy, Mama. It's spring and we can get out more. And I'm hungry—can we eat soon?"

"You can eat when you want. Call the boys and I'll spread it all out."

Renee had stood up and stretched. When the weather was good, this was their Sunday ritual. They always came to the park to eat a picnic and to get away from the overcrowded communal kitchen and small room they lived in. In spring and summer New York was a wonderland;

in winter it was drab and dull and cold, and the very best places were the library and the museums. Renee had spent every Sunday of the previous winter in the art department of the library reading about her passion and checking out book after book on sketching. At home her mother helped her, and together they had created scrapbook after scrapbook of drawings and designs. In the evenings when the stores were closed, they walked together and studied the clothes in the windows of the most expensive shops.

But in the summer other activities beckoned. There were Sundays picnicking in the park or at the beach, when once every few weeks they traveled out to Coney Island for a long day on the sand and in the surf.

But however much Renee enjoyed Sundays with her family, her favorite day was Saturday. After work, winter and summer, she and Zoltan always went to the movies. There in the darkness of the theater they escaped to other worlds. How she loved Theda Bara! Theda Bara was also known as "The Vamp" and Renee had seen all her films. She dressed outrageously and wore indigo makeup to make her look even paler than she was. Zoltan, who knew about such things, explained that indigo photographed dead-white. But as outrageous as her clothes were, they were a part of her; she wanted to be outrageous and her clothes matched her screen personality perfectly. And how Renee liked to imitate her. "Kiss me, my fool!" she used to say over and over while Zoltan laughed and often repeated the words of the hero.

But Sundays were for picnics, and Renee recalled her mother telling her to get the boys after she'd unpacked the food.

She'd gotten up off the blanket and called Imre first; then she had sidestepped a group of nursemaids and their small charges, who stared at one another from huge perambulators, and run across the lawn toward Zoltan, who, seeing her, stopped playing ball and walked toward her.

Zoltan was extremely good-looking and he seemed to grow in leaps; he was already nearly six feet tall.

"I am hungry," he announced.

Renee had looked up at her handsome brother and suddenly been aware of his maleness. "Zoltan, what does it mean when a man stares at a girl?" Aaron Lewis had stared at her.

Zoltan blushed slightly. "I guess it means he likes her and wants to get to know her."

"Do you stare at girls?"

"Sometimes. Renee, is someone staring at you?"

"Not here, not now. I just wondered."

Zoltan took her arm. "Tell me," he prodded.

"Not today, some other time."

"Hey, wait for me!" Imre tugged at her other arm and the three of them linked arms and walked toward their mother, who had finished spreading out the cloth and the lunch. In the distance, with the sun falling on her blond hair, Margaret looked young and healthy. She even seemed happy as she presided over her red checked cloth. But Renee knew she was none of those things. Her mother had suffered through too many years of deprivation, and her illness had taken its toll on her youth. But even so, Margaret Szilard Horvath had a kind of ethereal beauty, and one suspected that beneath her depression there was still a woman of will and creativity, a woman who could still laugh and perhaps even still love.

Later, when they had finished eating and Imre had again wandered away and their mother had gone for a walk, Zoltan returned to her question. "Who stares at you?" he asked.

"Just a man," she had answered.

"Do you want him to stare?"

"I think so."

Zoltan had nodded, then added, "Well, if anyone bothers you, let me know."

Renee now smiled to herself. Aaron Lewis had not bothered her. Quite the opposite. And, she could not help thinking, this was the first time she had thought of him in years. Well, in any case, beginning on that day in the park, Zoltan had become her confidant and protector.

Renee stood up and stretched. Two drawings were done, and it was almost time for lunch. Zoltan was working nearby, and they usually tried to meet for a hot dog. Aaron . . . It had been so long since she'd thought of him. After she'd come back from Boston, she had gone directly to the factory that had been owned by Aaron's father. She discovered that it had been sold, indeed that all the Lewis factories had been sold when old David Lewis died. Then she had looked in the phone book, but there was no Aaron Lewis listed. With that door closed, she had decided to answer the ad for an artist at Bela Fashions.

When Renee had told Zoltan who Béla really was, he had not wanted her to work there, but she convinced him it would be all right. And in fact it had been all right; she was making quite a good salary and she was learning and improving all the time.

3

Miklós Lazar, who used Michael on his business cards and on the door of his office, had rented offices in the center of Los Angeles in a five-story sand-colored building across from the *Times*. In the two years he had been in L.A. he'd acquired a secretary, his own teletype machine, and a large and prosperous clientele. But most of his clients were in the burgeoning film business, and he envisaged that one day soon he was going to have to uproot himself and open a new office in downtown Hollywood, somewhere near Hollywood Boulevard and Vine Street.

His entry into the film business had been largely accidental, but he found he enjoyed it, and certainly there were side benefits. For one thing, he found himself being invited to lavish pool parties and dances under the stars and indeed with the stars.

It had all started when one Joe Somló, a fellow Hungarian, had come to him to help arrange financing for a film he wanted to produce. He had arranged the financing and then Somló returned wanting to invest his profits safely. Miklós had found himself acting in two equally lucrative capacities, one as money man to those desiring to make films, and second as broker and financial adviser to those who had made money. Thus far he had not failed; far from it, he found himself earning a larger sum than he had ever earned before.

He sat behind his new desk and listened for his secretary, whom he had sent out for coffee. When he heard the door to the outer office open, he jumped up from his swivel chair and went outside to greet the individual who had come. Only moments before, Adolph Zukor had called and good-naturedly told him a prospective client was on the way over. Typically, Zukor had forgotten to tell him the young man's name, but he had told Miklós to treat him well—"as far as we're concerned, he's one of our bright production stars and I have guaranteed distribution for his film." It was the kind of information Miklós liked to hear. If Zukor guaranteed distribution, it was money in the bank and funding would be no problem.

Miklós peered into his outer office. The young man was tall, blond, and blue-eyed. He was dressed conservatively in a tan suit and he wore a white shirt and a yellow tie.

Their eyes locked onto one another's and both smiled. Konnie advanced, holding out his hand. "Konnie Szilard."

For a long moment Miklós stood stock-still and stared at him. Szilard was not a common name, and it seemed unlikely that there would be more than one Konrad Szilard. He knew full well, because she had talked about her family all the time, that Margaret's youngest brother had been called Konnie, and he also knew that Konnie's passion had been the theater. If he had even the slightest doubt, it was erased by his looks. There was a definite and undeniable family resemblance between Margaret and her brother.

Seeing his perspective client was Hungarian, Miklós retreated from his use of Michael. "Miklós Lazar," he said, extending his own hand and ushering Konnie toward his inner office with the other. "Well, come in. Come into my office and sit down. My secretary has stepped out for a few minutes and I'm afraid I've been left alone."

A thousand questions rushed through Miklós Lazar's thoughts: Did the whole family live here? Was Margaret here? No, it seemed most unlikely. She had no doubt been forced to marry Janos and she was probably still in Hungary. And judging from the way his visitor was looking at him, he too was in the absolute dark. Doubtless Margaret had never told him anything.

"I've brought a script," Konnie said first. "Zukor has a copy and has read it."

Miklós reached for it. "I'll read it tonight and let you know first thing in the morning."

"Of course." Konnie handed it across the table.

"We'll have to form a production company first . . . then there's the question of a prospectus to be sent to potential investors. I can do it for you, or you can do it."

"I think you should do it. Actually, I don't really know what one should look like."

"Why don't we do some of the initial work together. I'll have finished the script tomorrow—can you come to my house on the weekend?" Miklós asked.

Konnie nodded and watched as Miklós Lazar wrote down his address.

Miklós handed the paper to Konnie. "Around noon on Saturday?"

Konnie nodded.

"Tell me," Miklós asked, "is it funny?"

"A tragedy, in fact. It's about a young girl who is forced to marry a man she does not love."

Miklós felt his face redden slightly. "I see," he said, trying to sound normal. "It's all right, I like serious plays too."

Konnie grinned. "It's not really such a tragedy. In the end the lovers find each other. The public doesn't like unhappy endings."

Miklós Lazar picked up the script and nodded. Somehow, in spite of finding Margaret's brother, he didn't think their story would have a happy ending. "Till Saturday," he said, shaking hands with his new friend. And, he thought as Konnie left, they probably *would* become friends. Konnie seemed a very likable fellow.

4

December 31, 1926

Leah wore a knee-length tubular evening dress that was drawn in below the waist with a gathered band under the loose-fitting bodice with its fashionable scoop neckline. But what set this garment apart was its exquisite detail work. The gown was made of gold crepe de chine with a matching silk foundation revealed through glittering metallic lace inserts. One such insertion ran down the center front of the dress, while the others were at the back and sides. The hemline was made of scalloped lace.

Leah's shoes were gold glacé kid with little sharp-pointed toes, double T straps, and curved heels. Around her forehead she wore a gold bandeau, and her jewelry consisted of gold slave bangles, long drop earrings, a choker, and four rings.

Leah's magnificent hair had been cut into the boyish style that was now so popular, and she had her natural curls ironed straight.

She stood before the mirror in the hall and turned this way and that. It was a stunning outfit and it suited her perfectly. Reluctantly and begrudgingly she mentally gave Renee credit. For it was Renee who had made and designed this dress for her to wear this New Year's Eve to the home of Sandor Lipton, the wealthy owner of a growing Midwestern department-store chain.

As she examined herself, Béla watched. She was striking, and he had to admit that since that day two and a half years ago when he had disciplined her, she had behaved admirably. If she was jealous of Renee, she kept it to herself. He, of course, had made no move to seduce his young blond designer. Not because he did not desire her, but because her designs sold better than any others in the catalog. She was a huge money-maker and Béla deemed it wise not to do anything that might make her leave his employment. Indeed, he had even given her several raises.

Béla held out Leah's fur coat. "It's time we left," he suggested. "You can admire yourself more when we arrive. I imagine our host has mirrors."

"I still don't understand why I had to wear one of her dresses," Leah said, picking up her gold lamé evening bag.

"First of all, you should thank her. You haven't looked this alluring in years. Second, Mr. Lipton is interested in a very large bulk order of certain of our fashions to feature in his stores. He seems particularly interested in Renee's designs. Now, since we have yet to open stores of our own, I think it wise to let him see firsthand what we have to offer."

Leah said nothing in return. She slithered into the back seat of Béla's large black Lincoln and waited for him to sit beside her. When he was seated, the chauffeur started the car and it purred off into the snowy night.

"Yes, you look quite alluring, my dear."

Leah sat straight upright. Béla's hand slid up under her dress and for a moment he caressed her thighs. He knew she could say nothing without alerting the chauffeur—he did these things on purpose to torment her.

"Relax," he said without even turning toward her. "It's going to be a long evening."

She leaned back against the seat, but she could hardly ignore him. His fingers had slipped inside her panties and he toyed with her, waiting for her to make some sound. She bit her lip, closed her eyes, and shivered. How could he? He was outrageous, even cruel. She hated him and she loved him desperately.

Then, just as she thought that she might scream, the car slowed and stopped in front of a large brownstone town house. Béla smiled meanly at her and withdrew his hand. She glared at him because he had excited her and left her and now she felt flustered and frustrated.

The chauffeur helped her out of the car and soon they were inside the elegant, tasteful home Mr. Sandor Lipton rented for his visits to New York. Béla introduced Leah to their host, and then, not wanting to appear anxious, took a drink from a passing waiter and began to mingle with the crowd.

Leah made small talk and then excused herself, silently cursing Béla. After a time, when she had calmed down, she returned to the party. Béla, as always, was in the thick of it, so she once again sought out Sandor Lipton in order to study him. Men of such great wealth and power fascinated her.

Mr. Lipton was in his early fifties, but his face could have been the face of a thirty-year-old. It was unwrinkled and tanned. He had large green eyes and his hair was extraordinarily thick and snow white. He was a tall man, not quite as tall as Béla, but his physique was far better. Béla seldom exercised, while it was obvious this man did. His muscle tone was splendid.

"And how is it you have such a lovely tan in January?" Leah inquired.

Sandor smiled. "Oh, I'm thinking of opening a new store on the Coast. I go to California for most of the winter."

"So you lie about on the sandy beaches of the Pacific," she replied.

"No, I go to a place called Palm Springs, in the desert. The beach is a little cold this time of year in California. Now, if one goes south to Mexico, it is quite warm enough, but I cannot get away from my work for so long, which is to say Mexico has no adequate phone service."

Leah nodded.

"Your outfit is quite wonderful," he said with a twinkle in his eyes. "Did you design it?"

"No, one of my employees did. A Miss Lazar."

He touched the material with his fingers and walked around her in a wide circle. "Did Béla tell you that I am coming after the holiday to meet your Miss Lazar?"

It was at that moment that Leah had an idea. She smiled sweetly. "Are you going to try to hire her away from us?"

Sandor laughed. "That would be unethical."

Leah shrugged. "I'm a partner, you know, and I don't think it would be so unethical . . . after all, we simply can't afford to pay her what she's worth."

"Does Béla look on it that way?"

"I don't really know," Leah replied. Then, smiling her most devastating smile, she asked, "Why don't you find out?"

5

The Charda was not the largest or even the most elegant of New York's many restaurants. It was in fact quite small, relatively unknown, and catered to a quite average European clientele.

Down one flight of steps form the street, it was dark even before nightfall, but its colorful gypsy decor and large fireplace gave it a romantic warmth, Renee felt as she looked about, assessing her surroundings.

Sandor Lipton pulled out her chair and waited till she had seated herself at the small table with the flickering candle in its center.

"I own part of this restaurant," he confided after he had seated himself opposite her. "I invested in it so I would have a place to come and eat Hungarian cuisine. Mmmm"—he made an appreciative sound with his lips pressed together and rolled his eyes expressively—"and the chef is the very best. I'll tell you a secret: you can't get Hungarian food in Hungary that's this good. I recommend the chicken paprikash, or perhaps you would prefer the veal . . ."

Renee laughed lightly. "Whatever you suggest, I'll try. Now, are you certain this is the best Hungarian food in New York?"

He smiled back at her, a warm friendly smile. "It may be the only Hungarian food in New York apart from that cooked in private homes. But it is very good, and remember, I'm one of the owners so I would have to say that in any case."

"You're full of surprises. I thought you only had interests in department stores."

"Three department stores . . . soon to be four, I hope."

"Will you soon have one here in New York?"

He shook his head and leaned across the table toward her. "I think not. There's far too much competition here. I want to have a national department-store chain, but I plan to start it in medium-size cities, places like Toledo, Cincinnati, and Kansas City. I'd eventually like to expand to the West coast, but right now my largest store—my flagship, so to speak—is in Kansas City."

"Is there a large-enough market to open a store on the Coast?"

"It's growing every day. It's the land of the future and I'm betting that within the next fifty years there will be a huge population shift away from the eastern seaboard. Besides, as far as department stores are concerned, the big Eastern cities all have thriving stores that monopolize the market. No, I want to be on the ground floor west of the Mississippi. I want to go to Los Angeles, San Francisco, and perhaps Houston or Dallas. All of those places are going to have rapid growth, and the important thing is, land is cheap now. I've already bought land in all those areas, and as the market grows, I'll construct the stores."

Renee noted that Sandor's eyes flashed with life when he discussed his future plans. He was, she decided, quite an extraordinary man. He was older than she by over twenty-five years, but he was extremely handsome with his shock of white hair, his tanned skin, and his unusual sea-green eyes. He had an excellent physique too. He was tall and broad-shouldered, slim in the hips, and flat-bellied. He looked like a man who had been an athlete in his youth and who had worked to maintain his physical condition at top peak. In all ways, except for his iron-gray hair, he could have been fifteen years younger than she knew him to be, and certainly his enthusiasm for life was absolutely contagious. When she was with him, and this was the third time he had taken her out, she felt an incredible optimism come over her as she became caught up in his "anything-is-possible" philosophy of life. And she liked his attitude toward money. Sandor Lipton was wealthy and he didn't bother to hide it. He liked the best and he had confided that he intended to enjoy life rather than always seem to be postponing life for old age and retirement. Moreover, he was a genuinely nice man. He seemed to go out of his way to help people, and she had learned he was personally paying for the education of some fifteen young people who had excelled at school but those parents could not afford to educate them. She had also learned he was a widower whose wife and two sons had been killed in an accident six years ago. But in spite of the tragedy, which had left him depressed for many months, he had thrown himself back into life when he founded a trust fund to provide educational scholarships in the name of his deceased sons on the first anniversary of their deaths. "Yes," he had told her on the occasion of their first luncheon, "when my wife and sons were killed, I saw no point in living myself. I went on for a long while feeling sorry for myself; then I met this young man—a shipper in one of my stores. He'd been an excellent scholar in high school, but he hadn't been able to continue his education for lack of money. I saw I could help someone. He became like my own son and I sent him to Harvard. Today, he's one of the lawyers for my corporation. He was my first; now there are fourteen others. And gradually," he said, "my own sense of optimism returned.

"You're very quiet tonight," Sandor commented.

Renee jolted out of her thoughts and looked across the candlelight into his eyes. "Actually I was thinking about you."

"I'm flattered. Dare I ask what you were thinking?"

"I was thinking what a nice man you are."

He smiled mischievously. "Is it good that I'm, as you say, 'nice'? Don't young women prefer rogues?"

"Not this young woman."

"You are young, but I have trouble thinking of you as being only twenty-two. You're quite serious, you know. It worries me. You should be out with a younger man. You should be dancing and making love."

Renee blushed slightly. "Can't you dance?" she asked.

He looked at her steadily for a moment. "Yes, and I can make love too."

She felt her face flush even more deeply, but she only smiled. "One thing at a time," she said softly.

Sandor gazed at her as if trying to read her mind; then the waiter broke the spell. "What would you like?" Sandor asked.

"You order," she suggested. She listened as he ordered veal and chicken and little dumplings and a salad. He also ordered grape juice, which would in fact be wine disguised in a tall glass.

"Silly law, Prohibition," he said, closing the menu. "It ruins elegant dining not to be able to openly have good wine on the table."

"Fortunately, it's not too well-enforced," Renee replied.

"Fortunately," he agreed. Then, touching his chin with his hand, he looked at her thoughtfully. "I asked you out for two reasons tonight . . . well, three reasons really."

"Am I to guess?"

"No. First I asked you out because you are intriguing, beautiful, and entertaining. Second, I desperately wanted to be with you again . . ." He paused and studied her face for a long moment. "And third, I want to offer you a position with Lipton's."

Renee looked down and tried to think. She had known he was attracted to her, but she had not suspected he wanted to employ her. "Given your first two reasons," she said carefully, "what should I think of the third? Sandor, do you want to employ me so we can continue to see one another, or do you want to employ me because I have something to offer your company? If it's because you want to go on seeing me, I must tell you I would be willing to see you in any case. Perhaps I shouldn't be so honest, but I never want a position because of my appearance or because a man wants to be with me. I want a position only if my work is good enough to deserve it."

"Your honesty is utterly beguiling—of course I want to go on seeing you, if you don't mind going out with such an old man. And while on that subject, would you please call me Sandy and not Sandor, which makes me feel even older."

"Sandy . . ." she smiled. "I don't think of your age."

"I think of yours. I keep saying to myself, I shouldn't be taking out this beautiful wonderful woman who is young enough to be my daughter. I should leave her for some handsome young man to court."

"I'd appreciate it if you let me do my own choosing. There are no younger men in my life, and perhaps I would choose you even if there were."

"Not one?" he questioned.

"There was one once a long time ago when I was sixteen. It lasted less than a year and I thought I loved him. But time and circumstance separated us and I've not heard from him since. But I know now that at sixteen I wasn't really ready for real love."

"Could he find you if he wanted?"

"Oh, yes, I think so."

"Then I won't consider him competition. I do find it hard to believe that a woman of your beauty does not have a hundred suitors."

"Sandy, I haven't had that kind of life. My mother was married to a monster and we had to run away. We had no money and we all had to work hard to survive. Now that my mother is dead, I have to assume responsibility for myself. And I have two brothers. I want Zoltan to finish college, and Imre needs guidance . . ."

"Was your father really a monster?"

"He was not my real father. My real father was Jewish and I hope one day to find him, along with the survivors of my mother's family. But yes, Janos Horvath was a monster, even though he was also the father of my brothers. They are not like him, and when we ran away, we all left him willingly. He beat my mother, he gave her a terrible illness, and he kept her almost a prisoner. She lived in fear of him for years."

"Renee, I don't want to bribe you, but you know if you come to work for me I will pay you enough to send your brothers through college. In fact, I told you about my scholarships. If Zoltan qualifies, I would consider that too."

"That's very tempting, Sandy. Tell me why you want to hire me."

"Well, not because you are beautiful. I want to hire you because you have real talent. I want to have a line of clothes exclusive to my own stores. I want you to design those clothes and coordinate them with accessories, which we will also have manufactured and sell."

"There are hundreds of very good artists who could do that for you."

"Yes, there are. And although I am going to pay you very well, I am not going to have to pay you as much as someone who has more experience."

"Now it is my turn to appreciate your honesty."

"There is something else."

"Yes . . . tell me."

"I have learned that your present employer does not have a very good reputation either with young women or in business. Frankly, I would like to see you out of there, and it would be best for your career not to be associated with the name of Béla Szendi."

Renee inhaled deeply, bit her lip, and looked at him seriously. She had long suspected Béla of shoddy business practices, and certainly he always seemed threatening to her as well as to other young women. Of course, she knew a great deal about Béla from her mother, and she would not have trusted him in any case.

"I might add," Sandor said, "that I'm surprised you've stayed so long with him."

"I needed the money. I was totally inexperienced and he paid me a little more than I might have gotten elsewhere. But there is more . . ." She considered confiding in him, and then decided that she would.

"More?" Sandor questioned.

"It's a long story. Are you prepared to hear it?" she asked.

"Yes, of course. I want to know everything about you, and if there is something about you and Béla—"

"Oh, not about Béla and me . . . no, Sandy. Béla is my mother's brother. He's changed his name and he doesn't even know I'm his niece, though sometimes I think he sees the resemblance and suspects something. Béla is really a terrible person . . ."

Renee began to tell him the long story of Béla, and she stopped only when the waiter brought their dinner.

"Lord," Sandor said under his breath. "But why have you stayed so long? By this time you could have had a job elsewhere."

"I hoped that somehow through Béla I would find more of my mother's family. I hoped he knew where my grandmother was."

Sandor nodded silently and began to eat his veal.

Renee sipped some of her wine and then also began to eat. "It's very good," she said after a few minutes.

"As always," he agreed. Then, "Do you want some time to consider my offer?"

Renee shook her head. "No, Sandy. I've decided to accept. I'll tell Béla tomorrow."

"You will have to leave New York and come back to Kansas City with me, to the store headquarters."

"I assumed that," she replied as Sandy covered her hand with his. "And may I take you out on the weekend to celebrate?"

Renee nodded and squeezed his hand in return.

Thirteen

1

February 1927

I'm a coward, Renee thought as she glanced at the clock. She had let the morning go by without talking to Béla, and now he had gone to lunch. But perhaps, she rationalized, it would be better if she waited till after five, when the regular staff had gone home.

Do you just want to put it off or do you really think he's going to cause some kind of scene? she asked herself silently. It was a question she couldn't answer, and perhaps, she realized, she both wanted to put it off and feared a scene. Béla, as she well knew, had a totally unpredictable temper. But one thing she could be certain of, Leah would be happy to see her leave.

Zoltan was not only happy, he was enthusiastic. He had never really liked New York and he looked forward to moving westward, both to the adventure and to the prospect of attending a good school. Imre expressed his usual reluctance toward higher education, but he also wanted to move, and she found his attitude a relief, because for some months now she had been concerned about Imre's friends. So, she thought happily, they would remain together, they would still be a family.

Béla returned from lunch at two-thirty and ensconced himself in his office. Uneasily Renee went on with her work and waited. At three she took a short break. She left the office and walked two blocks to the mailbox. There she mailed her long-put-off letter to Miklós Lazar, addressed to him in care of his son, Abraham. It had been a difficult letter to compose, but she had finally thought of the right words and now she could only hope her letter would cause him no difficulty. Renee hurried back to the office. It was snowing now, and the February wind was bitter as it whipped around the corners of the buildings.

Then at ten after six, when nearly everyone had left, she walked down the long corridor from the art department to Béla's office. She knocked on the door and he called to her to come in.

For a moment Renee stood in the doorway looking about the office. Béla was on the phone and had his swivel chair turned toward the window and away from the door.

His office was spacious with wood paneling and heavily upholstered furniture. His desk was a massive oak piece, and in one corner there was a small cabinet where she knew he kept liquor and some glasses.

Béla turned then, wheeling about in one motion. His heavy eyebrows lifted when he saw her and he cupped his hand over the phone speaker and whispered, "Come in, come in."

Renee closed the door behind her and walked silently across his office. She sat down in an easy chair facing his desk. He went on for a few minutes talking, then hung up, folded his hands, and looked across at her.

"What a pleasant surprise, Renee. I could swear you spend most of your time avoiding me. I certainly didn't expect an after-hours visit."

The way he said "after-hours visit" seemed to imply something improper, and she quickly stiffened and replied coolly, "It's business."

He smiled wickedly. "Is it? What a pity."

A thousand thoughts ran through her mind. She was certainly resigning, but she toyed with telling him who she was and that she knew who he was.

"Are you going to come to the reason for this visit or, just look bewildered?" he asked, returning her own cool tone.

"I'm sorry. I was just thinking of how to put it. These things are difficult for me."

"I know. You're going to ask for a raise because of Sandor Lipton's order. I'm not blind, you know. I know you've been seeing him, and I suppose you're smart enough to see that your value has gone up."

Renee narrowed her eyes. This man had intimidated her mother, but she didn't feel intimidated, she felt angry that he would imply she was succeeding for reasons other than hard work and competence. "I assure you his order had nothing to do with his 'seeing me,' as you put it. It has only to do with his satisfaction with my work."

Béla stood up and walked around his desk to where she was sitting. He leaned over her and covered her hand with his. "You might get a raise quicker by seeing me. After all, I'm even younger than our Mr. Lipton."

Renee withdraw her hand quickly and stood up to face him. He was a large man, she thought. She came only to his shoulder. "I have no intention of seeing you except in this office, and I'm afraid that will not be for too long. I did not come here to discuss a raise, I came here to tell you I'm resigning."

"Resigning?" He repeated the word as if he hadn't understood.

"Yes, I've accepted a position with Lipton's."

Béla's face instantly clouded over, almost contorted with anger. "How dare you?" he hissed. "After all I've done for you."

Renee took a step backward, sidestepping the chair. "I appreciate what you've done," she returned confidently, and then added, "and I have given you quality work in return."

"You brazen little bitch. What did you do for old Sandor? You must have been good, eh? Well, I think that as you're leaving, I should have a sample."

Renee opened her mouth to scream and found she couldn't find her voice. His large hand gripped her wrist and he had pulled her close and whirled her around so that her back was to his desk. Whatever she had expected, she had not expected a physical attack.

"Let me go!" she said, finally able to say something. His fingers were digging into her flesh, hurting her, and she winced and tried to shake her arm loose. But he pushed her further back, and losing her balance, she fell on the desk, its edge cutting into her back, her feet slightly off the floor. She struggled, and he seized the neck of her blouse and with one hard pull ripped off its buttons, opening it to the waist.

"Let me go!" She had managed to be louder this time, but he paid no attention. He had twisted her wrist somehow, and she couldn't move without tremendous pain. To her horror, with his other hand he pulled away her slip and lifted her camisole. The smile that covered his face was filthy and his eyes blazed with the insanity of a crazed animal as with his free hand he touched her breasts, rolling one nipple between his thumb and forefinger.

"See, they're getting hard. You like this, don't you?"

At that moment she found her voice and screamed loudly. He was obliged to move his hand from her breast to her mouth.

"Shut up!" he commanded. "Everyone's gone. There's no one to hear you. *Bassza meg!*"

It was a vile Hungarian curse. He moved his hand slowly away and she didn't scream again right away because she suspected he was right.

"You can't do this . . . please," she said, trying not to sound as if she were begging. He was a sadist, and begging would make him more likely to carry out that which he had started. Like Janos, she thought. Mama had said they were two of a kind.

"I've been looking forward to you for a long time. I've exercised great restraint, but I'm not going to let you leave without a little farewell present."

"You can't do this, Béla Szilard. I'm your niece. I'm Margaret's daughter."

Clearly her words had some effect. He loosened his grip slightly and stared at her.

"Margaret's daughter. . . . I always thought you looked like her. You should have told me sooner, then Uncle Béla could have been more help. And where is dear Margaret?"

"She died," Renee replied. Then she tried to sit up, to break away from his grasp. But instantly he pushed her back down with greater violence and twisted her wrist even more painfully, till she cried out in agony.

"Dear Margaret," Béla said, looking at her. "Did she tell you I tried to have her when she was just a girl? Ah, yes, I remember the frustration of that night . . . such a lovely body. I'm sure yours is just as lovely. Certainly what I've seen so far is most promising."

"You're evil and perverted!" Renee screamed.

"Yes, struggle a little. It will hurt you more than me."

This time he pinched her breast very hard and she screamed again in anguish. Then he moved his hand and she could feel him pulling down her panties. His hand grabbed at her pubic hair and she heard him getting ready. Her whole body tensed and she let out a long loud scream as she felt his flesh pressing against her and his leg prying hers apart.

"*Lofasz a seggedbe!* I hate you! I hate you!"

Renee's eyes were closed against Béla's evil face; then through the fog of her own fear she heard another voice shrieking and screaming. Béla seemed to rear up like a horse, he let out a horrible cry, and Renee opened her eyes to see a contorted look of agony on his face. He tried to stand and to turn, he moved off her, then staggered and fell to the floor. Renee looked into the hate-filled face of Leah, who stared only at Béla's fallen body and the blood that spurted from one of two wounds in his back—the third did not bleed; from it the handle of the long, deadly sharp cutting scissors protruded like the wind-up key on a fallen mechanical toy.

Her back badly bruised and scratched from the sharp edge of the desk, Renee eased up and staggered as she tried to stand. She pulled her skirt down and held her torn blouse together as best she could. Leah had left the door open, and the janitor peered in; then there were voices in the hall, and shortly several men from another office appeared. They paled at the sight, and one dialed the telephone and asked for the police.

Leah had bent down and was sobbing violently and hitting Béla's lifeless form with doubled fists. Then there were sirens, and Renee sank into a chair and shivered as the conflicting emotions of anger and shame flooded over her. He hadn't actually raped her, but he'd touched her, felt her, lain on top of her. He had done everything but actually penetrate her, and she felt dirty and violated. He certainly would have raped her had Leah not stabbed him.

Questions. There were going to be so many questions. Renee closed her eyes and felt hot tears falling down her cheeks.

2

Outside, the sky was utterly cloudless and the sun shone brightly on the neat trimmed lawns and flowering bushes. The tall bearded palms that lined the street where Miklós Lazar lived swayed ever so slightly in the morning breeze. Miklós peered out through the edge of the curtain and saw the blue-uniformed mailman coming. Miklós waited by the door and presently his mail was pushed through the brass-plated slot and fell in front of his slipper-clad feet on the floor. Holding his bathrobe together with one hand, he bent down and picked up his mail. There were two bills, a bank statement, and one other letter. He looked at it curiously, turning the envelope in his hand. It was addressed to "Mr. Miklós Lazar" in care of Mr. Abraham Lazar. Miklós was puzzled; most people now called him Michael. This letter had to be from a fellow Hungarian, but what other Hungarians besides Leah and Béla did he know in New York?

Puzzled, he slit the envelope and withdrew its contents. He carefully unfolded the letter inside and read it slowly:

Dear Mr. Lazar,

This is a difficult letter for me to write, perhaps because I have been disappointed several times in my search for the "right" Miklós Lazar. If you are not the man I am looking for, I apologize in advance for any difficulty or personal embarrassment this letter might cause you. I also want to make it clear in advance that if you are the person I am trying to find, I do not want anything from you save friendship. I hasten to add that if you do not want to see or hear from me again, I will respect your wishes. If, on the other hand, you want to meet me, we can continue writing until such a meeting is possible.

The Miklós Lazar I am seeking worked for one Count Horvath on his estate near Kassa in the years 1903 and 1904. That Miklós Lazar had a liaison with my mother, Margaret Szilard (now deceased). She was forced to marry Count Horvath's son, Janos. But my mother told me she was pregnant before her marriage and that the Miklós Lazar I am looking for is, in fact, my true father. I am pursuing this because it was my mother's last wish that I find him. If you are the Miklós Lazar I am looking for, you may write to me at the address below. If not, I am sorry to have bothered you.

Yours sincerely,
Verena (Renee) Lazar

Miklós stared at the letter in disbelief. Then he walked slowly to the big blue chair in his living room and sat down to reread this unbelievable missive over again. After a time he leaned back in the chair and closed his eyes, thinking about the past and the woman he had deserted. Verena. A smile crossed his lips at the thought of Margaret naming her daughter—their daughter—Verena.

He shook his head slowly and tried to think. He found himself feeling sad and somehow elated at the same time. God, how he longed to see and talk with this long-lost daughter. Then he reflected: Perhaps I only want to be forgiven. But regardless of his reasons, he would answer the letter. And, he decided, he would arrange to meet her as soon as possible.

And what of Konrad Szilard, with whom he had become friendly? Did Verena know her uncle lived here in Los Angeles? Probably not. No, he decided, not probably, certainly not. If she had known, they would have been in touch, and if they'd been in touch, Konnie would have heard of him and would himself have made the inquiry that was in this letter. Well, it was a small world for Hungarian expatriates in America. They were few, and many seemed to be in the same business. After all, many of the Hollywood Hungarians he knew had known each other in the Budapest theater. Whenever they met they talked about evenings spent at the Royal Hotel at 45 Erzsebet Krt Boulevard, talking and partying together. They had certainly never dreamed they would all find each other again either, so why was he surprised that his own past had suddenly invaded his present? He smiled to himself, then asked silently: What shall I say to her, this daughter of mine? Then, rubbing his chin, he walked slowly toward the phone to call Konnie. It was time Konnie knew everything about the past, and certainly he had to be told about Verena.

3

March 1, 1927

A fire roared in the great stone fireplace of the den in the town house on Park Avenue that Sandy Lipton had rented during his stay in New York, the same elegant home in which he had hosted his New Year's Eve party two months ago.

Renee curled in a huge green velvet chair, a quilt wrapped around her. It was a lovely room, she thought. Its leather-bound books reminded her of the library at the Horvath mansion, one of the few rooms there she had ever enjoyed. But apart from the books there was little to remind her of Hungary in this room with its distinctly Early American furnishings. It was warm and cozy with its flickering make-believe oil lamps and its hand-hooked rug. It was a far cry from the cold Gothic rooms of the Horvath estate or the small tenement room they had all lived in for so long.

Sandy brought her a little tray and set it down on the table next to her chair. "A bit of brandy," he said. "Tell me, my darling, how are you feeling?"

"A bit better," she said, trying to smile for his sake. "I know it's been over a week . . . it's just that it keeps coming back. It was loathsome, and Leah . . . Oh, God, I shall never forget the look on her face. Then, when I found out she'd slit her wrists in jail . . ."

"I'm sure it will take much longer than a week for you to fully recover. Rape is a heinous crime. I know he didn't actually succeed, but he nearly succeeded, and such an experience is emotionally shattering."

He was right—she was emotionally shaken.

"Renee, you're a virgin, aren't you? I know you once loved someone else, but I suspect you weren't intimate with him."

She nodded, but said nothing. Still, inside she could not kill the hatred she felt for Béla, even though he was dead and even though he hadn't actually penetrated her. He hadn't stolen her virginity, but he'd stripped her and felt her. He'd touched her intimately. Technically, she had not been physically violated, but her soul had been violated.

"You're very angry inside, aren't you?" Sandy guessed.

"Yes, and I don't know how to get it out. I've spent the last week controlling myself so as to get through all the horrible questions. You know, I'm actually tired from controlling myself, physically tired. But I can't let go. I can't let go."

"Perhaps I should take you home to rest."

She shook her head. "Zoltan knows where I am. I don't sleep there either, I wander around all night."

"You can stay here . . . right here by the fire if you like. I can have the maid bring some pillows and blankets for the sofa, or there's a room upstairs."

"I'm burdening you with all this. I know you intended leaving two days ago. I'm sorry, Sandy. I'm sorry, but I don't know what would have happened if you hadn't been here."

"You'd have been all right, Renee. You're strong and intelligent and you would have been all right. But if I've made it a little easier for you, then that makes me very happy. As for my business, well, it will take care of itself a while longer. I'll stay until you're ready to leave, then we can all go to Kansas City together. That is, if you're still coming."

"Of course I'm coming. I shouldn't think it would take us more than a week to pack."

"The sooner you leave here, the better, you know. You don't need daily reminders of what's happened. You need a whole new life in a new place."

She tried to smile. "I think you're right."

"I have an idea. Are you too tired to listen?"

"No. Go ahead."

"Well, I thought we might send your brothers on ahead with your belongings. I can have one of my staff help them find a place and get settled. Why don't you come down to Cuba with me for a week or two? I think the sun, surf, and sand would do you a world of good."

Renee looked at him and couldn't help smiling. "I didn't know you were planning a trip to Cuba."

"I wasn't till just now. Come on, Renee. It's just what the doctor ordered."

"Actually, he ordered me to stay off my feet till the bruises on my back heal. But if you think I should go to Cuba with you, then I guess I shall go to Cuba."

"Oh, Renee, that is wonderful!"

At that moment he might have been twenty. He suddenly looked boyish. But he was a fine mature man. A kind man. She looked at him and felt warm and comfortable. And she knew she didn't have to say anything about their travel arrangements or worry about him trying to sleep with her. He wouldn't make the first approach, he would wait for her, and she knew it. "Sandy . . ." she said seriously, "will you kiss me and hold me?"

He closed his eyes and smiled. Then he lifted her out of the chair and set her down on the sofa. As if she were a china doll, he leaned over and kissed her cheek, then her forehead, then her lips. She put her arms around him and he held her close and stroked her long loose blond hair. She leaned on his broad shoulder and closed her eyes. She didn't need to see him. She knew he had tears in his eyes and that he was completely satisfied simply to comfort her. As satisfied as she was to be comforted.

4

Renee wiggled her toes in the warm white sand and looked contentedly at the azure water of Havana bay. Along the strand of beach in front of The Hotel Habana there were a hundred multicolored tents with their flaps waving like flags in the light breeze. These little tents were some four feet by four feet and served not only as shelters from the strong sun but also as changing houses so that the guests would not bring sand into the hotel lobby. In addition to the tents, there were some beached wooden boards that young men lay upon in the water, using them to ride the waves back to shore. "Here and in the Hawaiian Islands they've been used for centuries, but Americans only discovered surfing in 1917," Sandy had told her when she had inquired about them. Further along, a number of small craft were anchored; their sails rolled, they bobbed in the water together, their masts tilting this way and that like so many sticks.

Behind them was the Hotel Habana, built in a charming Spanish architecture to suit its surroundings. It was a small hotel of only five stories, with whitewashed walls, turrets, enclosed patios and balconies, and beautiful inlaid tile floors. There were plants inside and out, brilliant blooming flowers everywhere, and in the evening when they sat outside, even the graceful palms seemed to dance under the stars.

Sandy had rented a huge suite on the top floor of the hotel. It had a living room, a long terrace that overlooked the bay, three bedrooms, a dining room, and even a kitchen. When they did not want to eat in the dining room downstairs or go out to some restaurant, a cook came and made their meals, serving them on the terrace or in their own little dining room.

Renee sighed and stopped playing in the sand. She stretched out and turned on her side. She was wearing a long white sleeveless beach dress with a divided skirt, leather sandals, and a broad-brimmed white hat with a long scarf hanging from its crown. Her long blond hair was loose and she wore dark glasses to protect her eyes from the glare of the Cuban sun. Beside her, Sandor wore knee-length shorts and a striped sleeveless overshirt. His body had grown brown in the sun, and his clothing clearly revealed his muscular body.

"You look wonderful, Renee. You looked rested and relaxed."

She smiled warmly at him. He had been the perfect gentleman, had given her everything and demanded nothing in return save her company. "I feel wonderful. I feel like a new person."

"We don't have to leave tomorrow. We could stay as long as you like."

She laughed and playfully ruffled his hair. "Of course we could stay forever. I have no need to work and you can let your business run itself. No, I've kept you away long enough."

He nodded and she leaned closer. "Sandy, I want you to know how much this has meant to me. First, this is the most beautiful place I've ever been . . . and interesting too. I'd say historic, but having been founded in 1511 makes a place seem relatively new to a European. I laughed when the guide at El Morro talked about its age. I think there must be twenty churches in Budapest that are a century older."

"At least twenty. It means a lot to me that you've enjoyed yourself."

"Oh, more than enjoyed myself. I'm restored."

"And what would you like to do now?"

"I think go back to the room and rest a bit before

dinner. It certainly doesn't take long to get into the mood for daily siestas."

"Oh, good, you're sleepy too. I thought it was my age."

Renee leapt to her feet, poked at him, and laughed, "Your age indeed!"

Sandy stood up and stretched, then bent to pick up the bright red beach bag, and they walked slowly across the warm sand to the hotel. Once there, they took the little brass-cage elevator to the top floor. Only their keys brought the elevator to this floor, and it opened into their hallway.

Renee kissed Sandy's cheek and went to her own room. There she changed into a blue-green nightgown and donned a matching negligee. She brushed her hair and sprayed a little perfume on. Then she sat down before her mirror.

Rape—even attempted rape—was the worst conceivable introduction to physical intimacy. Her mother, even though married, had most certainly been raped by Janos. "But it can be wonderful when the man is gentle," her mother had told her with reference to her own father, Miklós Lazar. "It may have been only once, but how glad I am that we had each other . . . that I had him first."

Gentle. . . Sandy was gentle, and he was kind. The women in her family seemed to have difficulty finding such men, and she herself had concluded that they were rare. "I'm old enough to be a woman," she said, looking into her mirror. "I have to find out what it's really like, I have to experience gentleness and a good man." And he does love me, she thought. His love was evident in everything he did for her, in the way he treated her, and yes, even in his patience.

Renee stood up and left her room. She walked quietly down the hall to Sandy's room and quietly opened the door. He was lying on the bed in just his shorts. Tiny beads of perspiration covered his strong arms and glistened from the hair on his chest. Renee dropped her filmy negligee to the floor and climbed onto the large canopied bed beside him. His eyes flickered open and his face filled with a kind of delighted surprise.

"Renee . . . I'm dreaming."

She shook her head and kissed his lips, a long kiss, and in a second he had wrapped her in his arms and was returning her kiss, pressing harder, trembling as his hand ran across her back and down over her buttocks.

"You're so beautiful . . . too beautiful."

"I won't break."

He propped himself up on one elbow and looked into her eyes. "Are you certain?"

"Yes, I'm certain."

His eager fingers fumbled with the ribbons on her nightgown. "I feel like a young man . . . a teenage boy with his first woman."

He pulled away the top of her gown and looked for a moment at her breasts. "So perfect," he whispered as he kissed the tip, "like rosebuds." Gently, slowly, he touched her nipples, first caressing them between thumb and forefinger till she smiled and moved closer to him because the sensation was so very pleasant. Then he covered one with his mouth and played on it with his tongue, while still toying with the other.

"Oh, Sandy . . ." Renee moved in his arms and embraced him. She felt damp between the legs, her flesh felt warm, and her whole body tingled to his touch. He kissed her again on the neck, then on the ears, then again on the breasts, the tips of which were now hard and firm and had turned a deep rose in color. His hand slid down across her flat stomach and his fingers played in her blond hair, parting her, touching her in a place so sensitive she moaned and was aware only that her breath seemed to come in short gasps, and she felt an incredible desire. He moved away for a while and stroked the inside of her thighs, then lay on his back and pulled her on top of him.

For the first time Renee saw him. He was strong and hard and waiting for her. She straddled him as he seemed to desire. He took one of her nipples in his mouth and caressed the other. Then he gently eased upward, inside her.

Renee closed her eyes, but there was no pain. There was only the incredible sensation of his lips on her nipple and then his fingers playing where they had played before. He moved up and down now in a kind of rhythm, and she moved with him, moaning now and again and returning his kisses as she bent over his face. She could feel all her nerves on end . . . waiting, waiting. . . . Then, like rolling through snow down the side of a steep hill, she gasped and felt the strong throbbing of her own satisfaction. Sandy at that moment pushed upward hard and she felt him shake and then collapse backward. They lay flat together for a long time, breathing hard and holding on to one another tightly, each fearing the other might move.

Then Renee rolled off him and sleepily nestled in the curve of his arm. "You are a most exquisite gift," he said, turning to her. "A most precious gift."

Renee awoke and glanced at the clock. It was nearly five, and the whirring overhead fan was beginning to circulate cooler air as the sun moved off, dropping into the ocean like a ball of red-hot fire.

She went into the bathroom and washed, then brushed out her hair and went to stand on the terrace. The breeze coming up off the bay felt wonderful, and she folded her arms and leaned against the side of the building.

Now and again she glanced back into the bedroom, where Sandy's sleeping form was curled on the bed like a child. He was perfect, he was everything she could hope for in a man, and he was mature and caring.

"Renee!"

She turned to see him sitting up in bed, and she went to him. "I wanted to let you sleep."

"I didn't dream you, did I?"

She smiled and touched his cheek. "No. Nor did I dream you."

He wrapped her in his arms again and then kissed her. "I love you, Renee. God help me, I really love you."

She sought his eyes and then touched his cheek with her cool hand. "I love you."

"Renee, I have no right to ask, but will you marry me?"

She had known the question was coming long before . . . and had tried to sort it all through in her mind. What were the good points, what were the bad? But all her rationalizations and reasoning failed with her experience of the man himself, and her need for him seemed to have grown a hundredfold in the past several hours. The feel of his lips on her breasts had been indescribably delicious, the way he touched her was exciting, the feel of him inside her—the oneness of them—was more wonderful than she would have dreamt possible. He had aroused sensations she had not even known she could feel, and yet there was tenderness between them, and above all, kindness. She looked into his eyes and smiled. "You're the only one who does have a right to ask. And I shall have to marry you or face living in sin for a long while." She touched his hair with her fingers. "Yes, I'll marry you."

He hugged her so hard she almost lost her breath, and he devoured her with kisses. "Tonight . . . No, now. We'll find a minister or a priest or a rabbi or a something or someone! Is it all right? Do we have to wait?"

Renee burst into laughter. "Let's do it right away. No, we don't have to wait."

He picked her up off the bed and whirled around with her in his arms. "I want to make love to you all night. I want to feel you beneath me, on top of me, by my side . . . God, I love you. I can hardly believe you're real."

"Very real," she said, looking at him steadily even as she undid her negligee again and slipped her nightdress off to stand before him nude and thoroughly pleased with the lust she saw in his eyes. "But perhaps we could do it one more time before finding someone to marry us."

Like a man utterly starved, he reached for her and his hands fastened on her buttocks and lifted her closer to him. "We have time for everything," he said, kissing her.

5

April 15, 1927

The sky above Kansas City was a clear blue and the expanse of grass around the recently built War Memorial and the Union Station was a blanket of solid green from the almost torrential rains of the past few weeks. High on a lone flagpole, the American flag fluttered in the wind above the treeless landscape, and beyond, the low buildings of the city huddled together near their life blood, the wide, muddy Missouri River.

Kansas City, Renee decided, was totally unlike New York or Boston. New York was an island with a large immigrant population, a cosmopolitan city in which one could find almost anything and everything if one knew where to look. It was a little bit European and a little bit American, but it was really neither. In New York newcomers were allowed to keep their ethnicity and in time their groupings created "just another neighborhood." Boston, on the other hand, was historically American. It was rooted in its own history, and the newcomers who came there did not change the city, but rather it changed them into latter-day patriots who were fiercely independent like their newly adopted New England forefathers.

In Kansas City, Renee found yet another America and a slightly different kind of American. Here was an American molded by the frontier and tempered by the harshness of the prairie, which stretched for hundreds of miles in every direction. There were men in business suits and women who wore fashionable clothes, but there were also cowboys. Men in Levi's, decorative leather boots, and something called "ten-gallon hats." Like the landscape, these Americans seemed to have no boundaries. They were open and ambitious, given to impossible dreams, and sometimes outrageous schemes. To build the city they wanted, where they wanted it, they thought nothing of changing a river's path, and while they did not move mountains, they seriously discussed building some to relieve the flatness. Never in her entire life had Renee seen so much empty land—land devoid of buildings, almost devoid of human imprint. Away from the city, there was nothing but prairie as far as the eyes could see. And, she thought with a smile, it did not take much going to get away from the city.

Having been here only a month, she found it fascinating because it was so different from anything she had ever experienced. Bushes, shrubs, and willow trees had been transplanted from the river's edge to make a park. Low buildings lined wide avenues—there was no sense of crowding, it was an expansive and expanding city, a city that wasn't hemmed in by an ocean or by mountains. It was simply there, lying like a sprawling amoeba intersected by rivers and rail lines, a cluster of buildings on the flat landscape.

Renee, Zoltan, and Imre walked across the wide green lawn under the shadow of the War Memorial, a tall round 217-foot concrete tower that dwarfed everything around it, and headed for the pseudo-Greco-Roman splendor of Union Station.

"I'm so glad we're together," Renee said.

"It's good to be here," Zoltan answered.

Renee didn't mention to Zoltan how much she had missed him the past two months. He was attending the University of Missouri at Columbia full-time now. She glanced at Imre. Sandy had given him a job in the shipping department of one of his stores, and as always, Imre seemed satisfied, unwilling to work toward advancement. But she would say nothing to him, not today anyway. Today was going to be perfect. Absolutely perfect. Regardless of their differences, they were family, and today was a special day. Today at two P.M. the train from Los Angeles was arriving with the rest of their family—family none of them yet knew.

"You must be nervous," Zoltan said as they walked through the main entrance and into the station.

"My stomach is full of butterflies," Renee admitted. "Aren't you anxious to meet your uncle?"

Zoltan nodded and smiled. "Yes, but it's not the same as meeting one's father."

Imre thrust his hands in his pockets. He had taken to dressing like a true westerner. He wore Levi's and an open-necked shirt. He had yet to take up wearing a ten-gallon hat, but Renee felt it would be his next purchase. "How about you?" she asked.

"He's a producer. Frankly, I wouldn't mind being in the movies. Maybe he can help me."

Zoltan rolled his eyes heavenward but didn't say a word. Renee only smiled. "Maybe," she answered. She wasn't surprised. Imre had expressed this desire before. He loved movies. But of course, he knew nothing about acting and she wasn't sure he was willing to learn. Still, he was good-looking. The truth, she feared, was simply that he regarded acting as easy, and perhaps more important, as easy money. Then too, it was glamorous, and actors got a lot of attention. Money and fame without too much effort was how Imre saw it, and though Renee suspected it required work, she could see why he daydreamed about it. Unfortunately, her youngest brother wanted life on a silver platter. He didn't want to pay his dues.

"It's nearly two," Zoltan said, interrupting her thoughts.

Renee's eyes searched the large board on which departing and arriving trains were marked. "There it is . . . Track Seven."

Zoltan looked around. "It's over there," he announced. "How are we going to recognize each other?"

"I described us and told them what I'd be wearing," she answered.

"You'd be hard to miss," he agreed, "if someone were looking for a woman in a blue suit with an ermine collar."

"Do I look all right?" Renee asked anxiously.

"Better than all right," Zoltan told her.

"Looks like the train's already arrived," Imre said.

People milled about everywhere, and the train stood, its doors still closed, its engine still belching smoke as they pushed through the glass doors and out onto the platform.

Then, one by one the doors opened and black porters swung down, set down heavy metal step stools, and then pulled down the steep stairs. By each car's exit, a porter took up his position, ready to help the passengers down and onto the platform. Redcaps with luggage carriers lined up, ready to receive suitcases.

Renee watched as one by one the passengers began to alight. She trembled with anticipation, glad that Sandy had insisted she and her brothers come alone to meet her father and their uncle. "I'll meet them soon enough," Sandy had told her. "It's going to be an emotional moment for you, a moment you should share only with your brothers." So they had come to the station alone and left the car parked on the other side of the War Memorial.

Although Zoltan was taller, Renee saw them first. From the fifth car a tall blond man stepped down onto the platform. He looked like her mother and he looked like Zoltan. He was immediately followed by an extremely attractive man with thick dark graying hair. Renee pushed forward, followed by her brothers.

Miklós stopped short on the platform as the beautiful, arresting young woman in blue walked toward him confidently. He wanted to say, "Margaret . . ." but he knew it wasn't Margaret who remained frozen in his memory forever seventeen. He opened his mouth to say "Renee," but she spoke first, and suddenly her eyes were filled with tears.

"Papa . . . ?"

Miklós dropped his suitcase and held out his arms as he fought to hold back his own tears. Where had the years gone, that he should have a daughter so grown-up? How different it all might have been had he been a man with courage.

IV

Aaron
1930–1935

Fourteen

1

December 1, 1930

*R*enee handed her portfolio case to Elsa, the downstairs maid, then slipped out of her coat and boots, leaving her hat and scarf for last. Outside, dark clouds were being whipped by a vicious prairie wind, and there was no doubt in her mind that it would begin snowing before nightfall.

"Is Mr. Lipton home yet?" she asked. Sandy had gone to Cincinnati and was due back tonight. She hoped he'd come before the snow started; she worried when she knew he was traveling during a storm.

"No, ma'am. He hasn't called either."

"Well, if he does, I'll be in the study."

"Yes, ma'am. Will you want dinner at seven?"

"Yes, that will be fine."

Renee watched as Elsa padded down the long hall, her footsteps muted by the thick carpets. Then she followed, but turned off at the study. A fire burned in the fireplace, and she closed the door and stretched out on the sofa.

She looked around the room and her eyes fell on her mother's picture on the low table to her left. Abstractedly she picked it up. "Ah, Mama. My life has taken such twists and turns." Four years this coming March—it hardly seemed she and Sandy had been married that long. Four years since he had brought her home to Kansas city. It was still a prairie town really, trying to grow up, but it hadn't succeeded yet, and like everything and everybody, it had been hit hard by the stock-market crash. The lifeblood of Kansas City's economy was the farmers who came into the city to shop and to do business. But the farmers had been hit harder than most. Not only had they lost money; there was drought, and some said their soil was flying away on the wind.

Sometimes Renee thought she ought to feel guilty. She lived in one of the most beautiful homes in the city, and while Sandy had most certainly lost money, he had not lost much. The stores had had to lay off staff, but they continued to make a profit. And she even continued to work because those with money still wanted nice clothes and the sales of better-styled off-the-rack clothes were increasing daily. In any case, what would she do with her time if she didn't work? There were no children and that made her unhappy, so she kept working and driving herself even though she knew that after four years she needed new challenges. If there had been children she could have gone on working, but not the way she worked now. She'd have taken more time off and she'd have made Sandy take more time as well.

Renee set down her mother's picture and took a cigarette from the crystal container on the coffee table. She lit it and inhaled, expelling smoke into the still air.

I do love Sandy, she thought. But not the way a woman should love a man. Perhaps I once did, but now it's different. Sandy, she realized, had stayed the same. It was she who had changed. It was she who now realized that having been cheated of a father, she'd substituted Sandy. She had let him care for her, worship her, do everything for her. And indeed she had no complaints and had long ago vowed never to hurt him in any way. "I made my decision," she said aloud, "and I must live with it."

Again she thought how different it might have been with children. Then he would have been their father and she would have been forced from the role of child to mother.

Still, she had a world of things to be grateful for. She had opportunity and she had money. She could travel wherever she wanted, do whatever she wanted. And Zoltan was now a graduate engineer who had found an exciting job with the government. He had been hired to help engineer the world's biggest dam, the new one being built in Nevada near the California border. He was leaving next week, and he, she thought jealously, could see Konnie, Miklós, and Imre more often than she could. With Zoltan gone too, she would be alone with Sandy, who was himself often away. But she should be happy for them all. Konnie had his own film company, Miklós was a wealthy man, and indeed, he and Konnie owned a house together. Imre was living with them and going to acting school, and Abraham, her half-brother, was in San Francisco, where he taught at the university. Now Zoltan would be close to them, able to drive or take the train to Los Angeles for the weekend.

Renee closed her eyes and thought about that wonderful day nearly four years ago when Konnie and Miklós had come to Kansas City and they had all been reunited.

Miklós had spoken her name and stared at her, shaking his head as if he had seen a ghost.

"You're so like her. In my memory she'll always be a young girl, you know—I can't think of her as older, I can't think of her as gone."

Renee had walked up to him and he had opened his arms and enfolded her.

"I should have gone back for her. It could all have been so different."

"She always loved you."

"I would have gone back, I wanted to go back. But I was weak, afraid, and there was not enough money for us to get away from Janos Horvath."

Renee nodded. "I think Mama knew your fears were justified after Janos killed György. She knew that if you'd come back, he would have killed you too."

"But do you forgive me? Can you forgive me for not

being there? I didn't know, I swear I didn't know she was pregnant."

"I know that. As far as I'm concerned, there's nothing to forgive—you're my father and I'm only glad to have found you."

Miklós had kept his arm around her and all of them had walked back to the car talking.

Once at home, they had gone to the study and talked long into the night. "Tell me everything about yourself, Renee," Miklós had said.

Renee smiled and folded her hands in front of her. She had begun by telling him about their escape from Janos' grasp. And as she talked it had occurred to her that Janos Horvath was a kind of bogeyman, an almost mythic figure who had dominated their lives even from afar. Before they left Hungary, and even for years after they arrived in America, her mother had feared he would somehow find them and force them back under his control. For the first time she began to wonder what had happened to this man who had so haunted her early life and about whom she still had nightmares, even though he now had no face and was nothing save a name she associated with evil. And hadn't it been true that to her Béla had seemed a surrogate for Janos—taking from her what Janos had taken from her mother?

"It's odd," she had suddenly said, "that none of us knows what happened to Janos."

Konnie seemed to be looking elsewhere, though obviously listening intently—she felt that somehow his creative and imaginative mind had fastened onto the same thought that had just occurred to her.

"He's like the spirit of evil in our lives," Konnie said after a moment. "I remember when Béla first fell under Janos' influence. He changed, and tried to be just like Janos."

Renee looked at her uncle thoughtfully; then, deeply troubled by the opening of the old wound, she said softly, "He succeeded." And inside she wondered how to exorcise these twin devils form her memories. Then, as always, she pushed both of them out of her thoughts by turning her mind to the present. "I wrote to my grandmother last night," she announced. "I asked her to come for a visit."

"Did you tell her about me?" Miklós asked.

Renee nodded. "I think it will make her happier to know I am not Janos' daughter and that her daughter did at least know some happiness."

They had talked all that night and in the days that followed, and she had visited them in California for a few weeks when Imre decided to go there and live. Since then they had written and talked on the phone often.

Renee glanced at the clock and wished Sandy would call. I have nothing to complain about, she reminded herself. But she knew her mood was strange. She was neither happy nor unhappy, neither glad nor sad. She was contented and she wondered if that were altogether good. Dare I admit that I miss living on the edge? she thought. Dare I admit that I used to have an energy I don't have now? She didn't really believe that hungry artists were the best artists, but she thought she was beginning to understand the sentiment. Her life had lost a certain spontaneity, a spontaneity she had once had and remembered having with Aaron Lewis. Yes, that was part of the problem. With Sandy, events were planned long in advance, and with Aaron it had all been a spur-of-the-moment adventure. They had never thought about what they would do together until the very day they went out. But with Sandy she even knew what restaurant they would eat in on a given Saturday night a week in advance. Though, she thought with a smile, there weren't all that many restaurants in Kansas City, and more often than not they dined at the club if they didn't entertain at home. Still, with Aaron she had been more impetuous, and she felt it was a characteristic in her own personality that had somehow been suppressed by her current circumstances. Yes, that was it. The trouble was that she was forced into the role of matron, and it was a role she did not play well.

"What brought Aaron into my mind?" she asked herself sharply as she sat up listening. Yes, that was the front door. It must be Sandy, she guessed.

In a moment the door to the study opened and he strode in, rosy-cheeked from the wind.

He came right to her and kissed her on the cheek. "Sitting all alone in the dark?" he asked.

"I like to watch the fire."

"Mmm, so do I." He sat down on the hearth and stretched out his legs.

"How was Cincinnati?"

"Not much different from Kansas City—a little warmer, I suspect, but I think they'll get snow tonight too."

"I really meant how is the store?"

"It survives. Do we have any champagne?"

"Champagne?" She raised her eyebrow and studied him.

"Yes. I was going to tell you after dinner, but I can't wait. Besides, if I tell you now we can drink the champagne before dinner. Elsa!" he pulled the cord to summon the maid.

"Sir?"

"Bring us a bottle of champagne and two glasses. Big glasses."

"You're being too, too mysterious," Renee admonished.

"I like being mysterious. Care to guess what my surprise is while we wait for the champagne?"

Perhaps, she thought, he had read her mind and was now going to begin to cultivate a new impulsive personality. Renee leaned back and smiled. "A Christmas vacation?"

"Partly, but that hardly covers it."

"A Christmas vacation in a warm place?"

"You're no closer than you were before."

"Oh, you are teasing me."

The door opened and Elsa brought the champagne in a large silver bucket on a tray with two crystal champagne glasses. Renee watched as Sandy expertly began to open the bottle of Mumm's.

"Don't point that at me," she said, half-ducking.

He laughed and with a gentle pop the cork went flying

toward the door. He bent over and poured two glasses, handing her one.

"And now for my surprise. Renee, the time is right to open my new store in Los Angeles. We're going to the Coast next week to look around. I've decided that the West Coast store will replace the one here as our main headquarters, so we'll be moving to California and we'll have to find a house."

"I'll be with my family!" Renee clapped her hands together. "And moving!" Her face broke into a wide smile. She wasn't that fond of Kansas City, and she loved California.

"Good, you seem happy. Of course, this trip we'll only be out there for three weeks or so. But hopefully we can find a house in that length of time. Well, really, you can find a house. I'll be busy with the plans for the store."

Renee leaned over and kissed him. "Oh, I am happy."

"And one more surprise. My old friend and Konnie's as well, Adolph Zukor, has asked us to stay with him. He wants us to attend the premiere of Konnie's new film with him. I told him how excited you'd be because you're star-struck."

Renee looked thoughtful as she twisted a strand of her long blond hair. "I don't have much time to get my wardrobe together. And for a premiere I'll have to have a new dress." Then a smile crept over her face. "Star-struck? I am not."

"I'm certain you'll look more stunning than the star, and I promise you, we'll arrive in true Hollywood fashion to be the columnists' 'mysterious couple' for the evening—the devastating blond beauty with the older gentleman."

"I'm sure no one will pay the slightest bit of attention to us."

He laughed and squeezed her arm. "I wouldn't count on that. But see, you are star-struck. You're more interested in attending a Hollywood premiere than you are in the new store or in finding a house."

"No, I'm not. By the way, shouldn't I phone Miklós and Konnie and tell them we're coming?"

"The premiere's the first night we'll be there. Let's surprise them."

"Yes. Let me surprise them."

Renee sipped her champagne, feeling it going to her head immediately, since she'd left early and hadn't eaten since breakfast. "One store is much like another and one house is much like another. But I've never been to a Hollywood premiere before."

"Well, my darling, knowing you, I suspect this will not be your last. Frankly, I shouldn't be surprised if you ended up in the movies."

"Oh, really! You are flattering me tonight. You must want something."

He looked at her for a moment and then nodded seriously. "I want you to be happy."

2

Miklós Lazar stretched out contentedly on the chaise longue with his eyes closed. Through his light cotton shirt and trousers he could feel the hot sun, and he imagined himself a lizard lying on a warm rock. It was, by any standards, a quite wonderful day. It had rained lightly the night before, and the haze that often fell over Hollywood had evaporated so that it was clear enough that Santa Catalina Island could be seen from the top of Mulholland Drive. On days like this his swimming pool was a brilliant turquoise, and the hibiscus, trumpet vines, and bougainvillea in his garden were an even more intense red, orange, and purple than usual. Everything seemed heightened by the clarity of the air; it was, quite simply, an achingly beautiful day.

Somewhere, no doubt at the beach or driving along the top of the hills, Imre was out in his new cadillac V-16 with its top down and beside him was his latest young lady, probably yet another aspiring starlet. Imre seemed to have a preference for young starlets. Not that I blame him, Miklós thought with a smile.

"And just what are you grinning about?" Konnie asked

as he pulled up a chair, scraping its legs across the rough stones of the patio.

"I was thinking about Imre and his girlfriends. I was regretting the fact that, one, I'm too old, and, two, I'm too busy."

"More than half the women in this town are living with men three times their age, and those men are just as busy as you are. I might, in fact, remind you that you have a daughter married to a man older than you."

Miklós shrugged. "So I don't really want a starlet, I only want to think about it now and again."

"It's safer that way."

"Yes, safer," Miklós agreed thoughtfully. And mentally he thought that one experience with a Leah Laszlo was sufficient to last a lifetime. Fortune hunters he did not need.

"You're a lucky man," Konnie said as he watched Miklós pick up the financial section of the daily paper. "But for the grace of film, there goes you," he said, pointing to yet another horrid story of the depression.

Miklós could not have agreed more. His first year in Los Angeles, he'd worked almost exclusively with the stock market, and God knew, what money he had was all invested in stocks. Then he'd met Somló and Zukor and had begun raising money for films. Seeing that films were a gold mine, he invested his own money and he turned more and more to becoming one of the main money men in the business. By the time the crash came, he was totally out of the market, and indeed one of the films that had made him the richest was Konnie's first endeavor. They had been friends before he told Konnie about Renee's existence. But after their return from visiting her in Kansas City, they had grown together like brothers and eventually he had taken over all the financial aspects of running Konnie's company, Starlight Films. So close were they that the two devoted bachelors eventually bought a house and shared it. Of course, it was no ordinary house. It was a huge house with two wings. Konnie lived in one and Miklós in the other. When Imre came to live with them, he moved into one of the many bedrooms in Konnie's part of the mansion.

"It's good to see you relaxing," Konnie said, putting his feet up on another chair. "I can't relax, I'm on pins and needles."

"Because of the premiere?" Miklós ventured.

"Yes. I hate them."

"It's going to be a rip-roaring success. Stop worrying."

"Easy for you to say."

"Not so easy," Miklós corrected. "I do have a lot invested in it."

"Money you didn't even know you had," Konnie joked.

"Every time I think about it, I'm struck by the irony of it all . . . and why is it one always 'finds' money when one doesn't really need it, and when one is broke, well, there's no way to get lucky?"

"It's a basic rule of economics," Konnie said somewhat sarcastically. "Haven't you heard that blues tune, 'Them That Has Shall Get'?"

Miklós nodded. He'd just banked a huge profit on a film when he'd heard from two lawyers in New York. For two years they'd been sorting out the mess left by Béla's murder and Leah's suicide. Then they had found the stock Béla had forced him to take in lieu of repayment of the money he had lent Leah. It seemed he'd ended up with the catalog company, and as luck would have it, he'd sold it for a good price ten months before the crash.

"Yes," Miklós said philosophically, "films are a good investment. In fact, what is and what isn't a good investment these days fascinates me."

"What besides films?" Konnie asked.

"Well, books . . . I mean, publishing is pretty good now. Book sales have tripled since the market went through the floor. And magazines too. Look, *Vogue* and *Esquire* are both selling out every week, even at thirty-five cents a copy. It's amazing. It's like people still want to 'feel' rich even if they're not. And then there's dog food. That doesn't surprise me. I think a lot of people are eating it."

"Books, magazines, and dog food. Quite a list."

"And films. Everybody goes to the movies, everybody."

"Yes, everybody. And that reminds me, whom do you think I should escort to the premiere?"

Miklós laughed. Konnie, who was a very good-looking man, was considered one of the town's most eligible bachelors—he supposed he too was on the list, but of course the ladies preferred someone in Konnie's position, since he was able to get them onto the screen. "What are your choices?" he asked with a wink.

Konnie flushed slightly. "Well, there's that newly arrived star from Germany, Marlene Dietrich. Have you seen her? She's absolutely elegant, and a real sex goddess. The studio really wants me to take her because they want publicity before introducing her to the American public. And there's Connie Bennett, whom I like a lot, and the remarkable Tallulah, of course."

Miklós laughed. "Terrible, terrible decision, Konnie. I'd hate to have to make it myself."

"I come to you for genuine counseling and you make fun of me."

"I'm sorry, but I can't take your problems seriously."

Konnie laughed himself. "Neither can I. I think I'll go with the studio choice and keep my life uncomplicated."

Miklós stood up and stretched. "Time I got to work," he announced.

Konnie nodded. "Back to the typewriter. I've an Oriental mood coming on—going to call it *Last Train to Peking*."

Miklós waved Konnie good-bye and set out for his own office. Yes, he thought to himself, since the day he had left New York he'd made all the right decisions.

3

Renee examined herself in the mirror carefully. Her appearance, she decided, was nothing short of daring. But then, this was Hollywood and she was attending a film premiere with none other than Adolph Zukor himself. And the game here, she thought to herself, was to be noticed. Well, one could not be noticed if one ran with the crowd.

"Not the case tonight," she said, shaking her hair. "Tonight we'll give Hollywood a peek at a new look." For the last five years women's coiffures and clothes had been boyish. She herself had worn her hair up and flat to the head. And of course, all the dresses had waistlines that hit at about mid-hip. And the lines were straight, straight, straight!

"But not tonight!" Renee twirled around. Her long hair was loose and full. She'd washed and set it herself so that it fell in deep, deep waves and then curved slightly under at the ends. The dress she had designed and had made was light-years away from the fashion of the past few years. Far from making her figure appear flat and boyish, this dress clung to every curve. It was royal-blue silk and had slightly padded shoulders—very different from the usual slouch shoulders—and a deep neckline that fell in folds from the shoulders and revealed, ever so subtly, that the silk of the top half of the dress was lined with a glistening silver material.

The gown's waist was at her natural waist, emphasized by a narrow silver kid belt. The silk, cut on the bias, clung to her hips and then fell in deep folds to her ankles. She wore silver kid shoes with little straps and carried a silver kid envelope bag. She wore heavy diamond earrings set in platinum, and around her neck a matching platinum-and-diamond strand necklace.

"We will show them all," she said, turning again. For the entire time since she had graduated from art school and had been employed first by Béla and then by her husband, well-styled ready-to-wear had been in its infancy. But now she felt Paris designers and couturiers were losing their grip on the world of fashion. Department stores were making ever more stylish ready-to-wear available to more people, but what was really important was the popularity of the movies. She had sensed it from the beginning, but now, here in Hollywood, she knew she was right. Film stars were going to make or break any fashion trend, and in all likelihood they would begin their own fashion trends. Film and advertising were going to be the two biggest factors in fashion success, and a designer who created costumes for films was going to set the trends.

Suddenly Renee felt quite alive as idea after idea flooded her thoughts. A film or an actress could initiate a "look," and stores like Sandy's could carry a line that expressed that look—perhaps under the same name. Perhaps one could sell the Constance Bennett look, or maybe it would be better to use the film title. And wouldn't Mr. Zukor love it! The fashions would promote the film and the film the fashions!

"Renee, the limousine is here to pick us up. Are you ready?" Sandy's voice called from the bedroom, and she took one last look in the dressing-room mirror.

"I'm coming," she called as she sailed dramatically through the door.

Sandy was standing by the bedroom door and he stopped short and stared at her—first in awe, then, as she could plainly see, in pleasure. "I'm speechless. You look wonderful—no, that's not a good-enough word . . . there isn't one."

"It's going to be the latest fashion," she said confidently.

"I'm proud." He took her arm and together they walked out into the evening. Zukor had already gone on in another car, since he was going to escort the film's star, Lucinda Larmé.

The chauffeur opened the door and Renee and Sandy climbed inside. Then the car set off, winding its way down Sunset toward Hollywood Boulevard and Grauman's Chinese Theater, where the premiere was to be held.

When they turned onto Hollywood Boulevard they picked up a police escort that fell into a line with other sleek cars. Crowds lined the streets, and it seemed to Renee as if the whole world were made of neon and bright lights. Then, when at last their car pulled up in front of the theater, they were let out to walk across a long red carpet to the front doors. Huge crowds had gathered on each side of the roped-off walkway, and Renee felt as if they were running a gauntlet.

"Who's that?" she heard an awed male voice ask.

"Look at that dress!" a woman exclaimed in a most complimentary tone.

"They must be very important," another whispered.

Then, to Renee's amusement, she heard it murmured that she was a foreign starlet. That rumor seemed to run in advance of them as they approached the door, where Mr. Zukor greeted them and, smiling slyly, embraced Renee just in time for their picture to be snapped by a photographer from *Motion Picture.* Adolph whispered in her ear, "You're putting Lucinda in a vile mood!" and Renee smiled gently and whispered back, "Next time, perhaps I'll dress her."

"That," he said, arching a heavy brow, "would put Maybeth LaFarge in a murderous mood."

Renee laughed at his mention of the well-known costume designer.

Then, after being nearly blinded by flashbulbs, they were in the half-darkened theater and the great organ was playing. The music finished in a loud fanfare and the multicolored curtains parted with a swish and a swirl of color. The theater went totally dark and on the black screen the white credits began to roll. Renee stared at the words A KONRAD SZILARD FILM and felt a surge of pride. How she wished her mother and grandmother were here to see this and to share Konnie's success. But her mother was dead, and her grandmother, to whom she now wrote all the time, would not leave Europe and her ailing husband. Yes, Renee reflected, that was one mystery that had never been solved. Her grandmother had never sent money to her mother. Zoltan, Imre, Konnie —no one knew where the money that Margaret had used to take the family to Boston had come from.

The credits finished and the music began. Renee discarded all thoughts now and concentrated on the film.

When the last frame had flashed, there was loud applause and then a standing ovation. The stars went to the stage and bowed and accepted bouquets of flowers till the entire front of the stage was filled with a rage of colors. Then a tall blond man came to the stage and there was more applause. Renee leaned as far forward as she could, dying to let him know she was there.

When the applause died, Adolph took her arm and she walked toward the milling crowd at the bottom of the stage. The theater was emptying, and the crowd, as might be expected, had followed the stars.

"Konnie, over here, please!" Zukor shouted, and Konnie strode over. He stopped short when he saw Renee, and a wide grin covered his face. Miklós was there too, coming from the other side of the theater, and they all embraced.

"What a wonderful surprise!" Miklós kissed her on the cheek.

Holding her father's hand and looking into her uncle's eyes, Renee could hardly contain herself. "We're moving here," she said, smiling, "and I have the most wonderful idea!"

4

Renee climbed out of the chauffeur-driven black Rolls-Royce that Adolph Zukor had lent her for the day. She felt incredibly buoyant and happy, as if she might actually burst with enthusiasm.

"I won't be too long," she told the chauffeur as she walked up the flower-lined path toward the fourth house she had looked at in as many hours. Well, house hunting ought to be exciting, she told herself, but in truth she was already too excited to be excited further by the lavish interiors of the various Hollywood mansions she had thus far viewed.

Yesterday she had seriously talked with Konnie about the possibility of doing the costumes for one of the studio's forthcoming films and he had agreed quickly, knowing that she had both the talent and the zeal necessary. Yes, all traces of the depression she had felt in Kansas City were gone completely, and much of the credit had to go to Sandy. He must have realized that she was restless and in need of a real change. It was true that he had always planned to build a store here, but she doubted he had planned to move. Not that she had ever complained, and indeed, the first year in Kansas City she had been blissfully happy. But then he had begun traveling more and more and then both her brothers were gone too. Her work at the store grew routine; she even felt her creativity was lessened because in Kansas City there was little to inspire her. She carried on designing lines for the store, but it was all output with no input. It was certainly different here! This, she sensed, was the land of constant change. There was a craziness, a zaniness, and most certainly an openness to everything new.

Yes, I am up to working here, she thought. The morning after the premiere, her picture had appeared in no fewer than three publications. One paper asked, "Who is the mystery beauty in the daring dress?" Another columnist asked, "Is this woman's dress the next fashion craze?"

Renee knew she was a good advertisement for her own creations, and certainly Joan Crawford, Bette Davis, and Lylyan Tashman would be even better advertisements. Their pictures were everywhere and they could only serve to influence the nation's women. This was already evident in hairstyles. The boyish look was already being replaced by the longer, wavier styles worn by Joan Crawford and Constance Bennett—but in their cases the waves were tight and pressed close to the scalp. The new European stars were bringing with them an even freer, more feminine look—Anna Sten wore her wavy long hair as she herself had worn her hair to the premiere, long and loose, with deep waves caressing the sides of the face. Yes, in all matters related to fashion, the movies were going to set the style; she felt it, and now she was going to be part of it.

Renee shook her hair as if to clear her head. She had to concentrate on the house and stop thinking about the movies and her new job.

Having obtained the key from the estate agent, Renee turned it in the lock and began to wander through the empty rooms of this sprawling house just off Sunset Boulevard. After yesterday's hours of tedious looking, she had decided she hated being "shown" houses and that she preferred instead to examine them on her own.

Perhaps, she thought, she would be even happier when she and Sandy were settled in a place of their own, a place of her choosing and her taste. The house in Kansas City had, after all, been the choice of his first wife, and although Renee had redecorated it, she never felt it to be truly hers.

Why, she wondered, did two working people with no children need a house this huge? But Sandy insisted they did. He said that they would be entertaining more and that a large house was essential for that reason. "And besides," he had added, "one day real estate here will boom. It's always good to buy when prices are low."

Well, Renee thought as she walked down the wide center hall, this most certainly was a large house. And, she admitted happily, it was the first one that she felt had real possibilities. For one thing, it had an absolutely immense sunken living room. For another, it was not simply boxes on boxes, it had curves and corners, nooks and crannies. And the dining room, four steps up from the living room, would easily seat twenty-five to thirty guests. The kitchen was certainly adequate to the task, and there were five bathrooms in all, excluding a powder room off the hall.

All the bedrooms were light and airy, and one opened onto a delightful sun porch that overhung the patio below. One of the bedrooms had an almost castlelike square tower and a slanted ceiling that gave it a special character. How would one define the architecture of such a dwelling? Pseudo-Spanish medieval, she decided, and she also decided that it was a house that would actually be "fun," a house that seemed to fit into the atmosphere here in California, an atmosphere she had fallen in love with when she had visited Konnie and Miklós over a year ago. It was a clean town, but it was also a rude, brash, experimental place—a kind of pretend place where everyone seemed intent on acting out his own favorite fairy tale.

She stood in the window of the tower and looked down

on the manicured lawn and the circular drive lined with bushes lush with flaming flowers. And what was her favorite fairy tale? "Rapunzel, Rapunzel . . . let down your hair . . ." Yes, perhaps that was why she liked this absurd tower so much. This house, she said to herself, is the house we'll buy.

5

Konnie's spacious office had windows along one side, which looked out on the Hollywood Hills. It was an ever-changing landscape in the various lights of early morning, noon, afternoon, and evening. Sometimes the mountains were dry, with only spots of dusty green, sometimes they appeared lush, and in the evening they were almost purple against the sunset.

The remaining three walls of his office were papered with autographed pictures, news clippings, schedules, and theater bills.

His large desk faced the door that led to his secretary's office; his back was to the windows. But Konnie's red leather chair swiveled around so that whenever he pleased he could turn and look at the mountains.

The rug on the floor was red like his chair, and against one wall there was a sofa, and in front of his desk a collection of chairs. Behind a secret door in the paneling there was a well-stocked liquor cabinet that swung into view with the press of a button.

Konnie sat in his chair and slyly glanced at his watch. It was four o'clock, and outside, the sun was low over the hills. He wished for all the world to be outside, to be home by his pool talking with Miklós and sipping a cool drink. But such was not the case. As fair as the weather was outside, there was a thundercloud in his office. It stood before him in the overbearing presence of Maybeth LaFarge.

She was, he concluded, a strange woman by any standards. Today she was dressed in a multicolored full-length dress that looked as if it had been borrowed from a Middle Eastern potentate. It covered every hint of her thin body's shape, and when she raised her arms, which she had done several times since bursting into his solitude, the fullness of its sleeves made her look like a bat in full flight. But the dress was not all that distinguished her. She wore a full turban—she always did—and he had often wondered if she had any hair. Today it was a purple turban and there was a glaring and quite hideous fake jewel at its center. She had on heavy spangle earrings that swung ominously as she gesticulated her bat arms, and she was further adorned with four heavy necklaces and a row of slave bracelets that traveled up her right arm all the way to the elbow. On her feet she wore leather sandals, revealing long toes painted blood-red, the same color as her lipstick. And her eyes! Who could stand to gaze into her eyes? They were dark pools seemingly without pupils, and she wore long false eyelashes and purple eye shadow. Long ago she had shaved off her eyebrows, and in their place there were now drawn eyebrows unnaturally arched.

But Maybeth was talented. She was a costume designer who understood the camera and who knew how to dress actors for black-and-white. In her field she was considered a genius, and as one might expect, no one thought she was more of a genius than she herself.

"You aren't listening to me, Konnie!" She waved her bat arms and in the darkening light of his office she actually cast a terrifying shadow on the back wall.

"I am listening. I haven't missed one word you've said. Now, let me try one more time to explain."

"And what is there to explain! You have given some little bitch her own picture and she doesn't have one whit of experience! I am the head of the design department here! It's outrageous! It's nepotism of the worst sort! I haven't even seen a single thing she's done! I've never even heard of her!"

"She is my niece. But she is also very talented. She has been designing clothes for Liptons—"

"She's married to Sandor Lipton! The little bitch has

slept her way to the top!" The earrings clanged and the bracelets slid up and down.

"She is not a bitch," Konrad said with enormous irritation. He had ignored her the first time because she called everyone a bitch. It was her favorite word and sometimes she actually used it quite lovingly.

"Well, what else has she done? Has she done anything that didn't require her to lie down?" Her necklaces vibrated.

"Stop it, Maybeth! She was previously with a catalog and she is a graduate of the Boston School of Fine Arts."

"I really don't care if she designed all the clothes for the crowned heads of Europe! And I don't care where she went to school! You hired her without even speaking to me. You gave her her own picture! Do you know how long I worked before I got my own picture?"

Her eyebrows were up, and again the arms lifted like Dracula's cape. God, she and Béla Lugosi ought to have starred together . . . no, the public wasn't ready for anything that frightening. He inhaled and prepared himself. He tried to keep his voice strong and even. "You are the head of the costume department, I am the head of the studio. No matter what you thought, the decision to hire Renee would have been mine in the final analysis. She *is* hired. She *does* have her own picture, and I think she is quite qualified. I am sorry I did not consult you, but even if I had, it would not have made any difference. I'm sure the two of you can stay out of one another's way. It's a big lot."

Maybeth's face knit into a hateful expression. "You will regret this," she replied, lowering her penciled brows and scowling at him. "And she will regret it too!"

"I don't like being threatened, Maybeth."

"I don't like being ignored! There is more than one studio in this town, and my services are highly coveted."

"Are you planning to leave, then?" It would throw things into a terrible mess, but at this moment he really wanted her to leave, and the truth was, Renee was immensely competent. He had no doubt she could pull things together quickly if she had to.

"Bastard!" Maybeth hissed. "Yes, yes, I'm leaving. I will not work with amateurs!"

"I'm sorry you feel that way." He wasn't really. She was weird even for Hollywood, too weird, no matter how talented.

"You'll be sorry, you and your little bitch!"

She whirled around and in a multicolored flurry opened the door dramatically, sailed through it, and then slammed it so hard two of the pictures on his wall fell, sending shattered glass skittering across the floor.

Konnie leaned back in his chair and covered his eyes with his hand. "Damn," he muttered, then turned his chair around and looked out on the mountains, trying to regain control. The woman was a witch, or worse.

Gradually Konnie's nerves settled and he walked to the wall where the panel slid away to reveal his bar. He poured himself a double Scotch, closed the panel, and returned to his desk and his view of the mountains. God, he was tossing a big job into Renee's lap, no question about it. But what else was he to do? Maybeth's underlings would leave with her, and there was simply no one else available. Gilbert Adrian was employed as the chief designer at MGM and Travis Banton was designing for Zukor—they had assistants, of course, and Konnie supposed another executive would hire a person who had had experience in a studio, someone who had worked for one of the big names. But he was not inclined to follow that path. First, those who had worked for Adrian or Banton or any of the others were filled with the ideas of their mentors, and more than that, they came with what might be called "political baggage." Designing for a studio required not only artistic talent but also the patience of Job and an almost superhuman ability to placate monumental egos. But alas, one did not placate one ego without damaging another, or so it seemed in this business. Those who had been around had not always played their politics well and they had too many enemies. His was a new studio, a small studio. He had to depend on Zukor for distribution, and often his stars came from elsewhere. He didn't want to employ someone in the delicate position of head designer who already had enemies. Renee, if she survived, would make her own friends and her own enemies, but she brought nothing with her in terms of studio politics, and that, he decided, was good.

Konnie finished his drink and walked to the door of his office. His secretary had left, and so he scribbled her a note telling her to find Renee in the morning and ask her to come in right away. He imagined that he could have found her himself that evening, but he decided against it. Renee and Sandor were probably going to be out on the town, and he felt they should have the evening free. God knew that once she went to work at the studio she wouldn't have much time for anything else.

6

Renee had asked Konnie not to announce her appointment as head designer for at least two weeks. During those two weeks she had visited every set, often spending the whole day simply watching and making mental notes.

On Monday, January 5, at nine in the morning, Konnie made the announcement of her appointment. Within the hour Renee found herself propelled from audience to center stage; her time of observation had past—now she had to prove herself.

Renee walked briskly from her temporary office to Stage 5 on the far side of the lot. She glanced at her watch. It was ten-thirty and it seemed to her that Konnie's announcement had circulated faster than the famed brushfires that so often swept the Hollywood Hills.

"Congratulations!" a woman dressed for the rigors of the frontier called. Her calico dress swirled in the morning breeze and her sun bonnet partially covered her face. Renee recognized her as a young ingenue working in one of the several westerns being filmed on the back lot. Behind her, a tough little man dressed in a dark suit tipped his broad-brimmed hat at her and smiled an engaging but slightly crooked smile. She suddenly realized it was James Cagney, and she smiled back. Dressed as he was, he looked every inch the Chicago gangster he was portraying. He was, she thought, wonderfully evil in *Public Enemy*, a film that was now being made. In one cut a sneering Cagney had smashed a grapefruit into the face of gang moll Mae Clarke.

Behind Cagney a troupe of clowns walked toward Stage 2, and a man dressed as a cowboy passed her, carrying a briefcase and speaking in low tones to another man dressed as a sheik.

Morning was always like this, she thought. The studio lot was bursting with actors and extras all dressed in an array of costumes and doing and saying seemingly incongruous things. But that was Hollywood, and the delightful madness spread far beyond the studio gates. She had been sitting in her car at the corner of Sunset and Fairfax waiting for the traffic light to change when a long convertible Cadillac V-16 glided to a stop in the lane next to her. She glanced sideways and suddenly realized that the seat next to the driver was occupied by a huge lion, who, as a dog might have done, sat up, looked straight ahead, and panted. What was really interesting, however, was the nonreaction of passersby. They appeared to look on a lion in a Cadillac as quite ordinary, at least as ordinary as an entire band of Indians in full war paint boarding the public bus that would drop them in front of Paramount's gate. Yes, Renee thought, here fantasy blended with reality in such a way that one could hardly tell the difference.

"Renee!"

She turned and waited as Konnie caught up to her.

"You want me to carry that?" he asked, pointing to the large, somewhat awkward box she was carrying.

"No, it's really very light."

He pressed his lips together. "Well, the news is out. Any adverse reactions?"

She laughed lightly and shook her head. "I haven't done anything yet except look and listen. I'm on my way over with an original design for Carol."

"That should be a telling experience. She can be most difficult."

"I gathered that."

"I'd like to tag along."

"No, no one will behave normally if you're around."

Konnie smiled. "You're right. I can see without being seen and hear without being heard."

"If you can manage that, I have no objection to your being there."

"I promise no one will know I'm there, but before I disguise myself, I did want to suggest a studio dinner to celebrate your appointment officially. How does a week from Saturday sound?"

"It sounds fine, Konnie. Do you have a list of those you intend to invite?"

"Yes, mostly executives of other studios and heads of departments. Did you want me to include anyone in particular?"

Renee smiled. "I want you to invite the hairdressers."

He raised a brow questioningly. "I assume you have a reason for that?"

"I do, and you'll find out soon enough."

"Done," he replied as he turned to walk toward the building where the costumes for extras were stored. "See you later," he promised as he gave her a wave.

Renee continued on her way, thinking that Konnie should have guessed why she wanted the hairdressers. It was politic, she had decided. Very politic. The stars that she'd encountered all appeared to have tremendous egos, but they were, in reality, unsure of themselves and, as a result, unsure of others. They seemed to consult their hairdressers about everything, and they always, she had noticed, consulted them about the costumes they would wear. "Does this look right on me?" was the most frequent inquiry. If the hairdresser was critical or, worse yet, silent, the star balked.

Yes, what Konnie said about politics was all too true. The designer walked on eggs, having to please a multitude of people, most of whom knew nothing about fashion and less about art.

First there was the producer, then the director, and of course the star. But as if these three vital participants were not tough enough to please, there were also the cameraman, the dresser, the hairdresser, the star's agent, the star's boyfriend—if any—and of course the president of the studio. On the latter, Rene counted herself lucky. Konnie kept out of things, though she supposed that, uncle or not, she would hear about it if he were actually displeased. Still, after all was said and done, Renee had decided that the hairdresser was the single most important influence and she had designed a personal strategy for charming them so she could work with them more easily.

Renee stood at the back of the set and listened for a few minutes as the cast ran through their lines. When they were finished, they would all go to Makeup and Costume and return for the actual shooting of the scene, which was set at a lavish New York party.

Carol La Lane, the star of the film, had platinum-blond hair, sloe eyes, and a Cupid's bow mouth. But Renee was more interested in Carol's figure. She was full-busted, but slightly short-waisted.

Renee edged up to the cameraman, who was sitting casually on a bench watching the run-through. She smiled warmly. "Could I glance at your script?"

"It's all marked up," he said, handing over a sheaf of papers.

Renee nodded. Marked-up was just what she wanted. She glanced quickly through the scene to be shot. Virtually all of the shots were marked as waist-up shots. She had suspected this would be true. She handed back the script and thanked the cameraman.

Carol finished her temper tantrum—the scene was to culminate in her tossing a drink into the hero's face—and the director stood up and stretched. Then, lowering his heavy arms, he checked his watch. "Shooting at noon!" There was a collective groan from the assembled cast and extras, who had rather hoped the scene would be shot at two, after lunch.

Renee, carrying her box, followed Carol to another empty set, off which were the stars' private dressing rooms. This set, filled at the moment with living-room furniture, was serving as a kind of lounge area. Esmeralda, the star's dresser, Tony, the star's hairdresser, Calvin Hamilton, the star's boyfriend, and "Shifty" Sam Rosen, the star's agent, sat sprawled about in chairs and on low-slung sofas. An abundance of coffee cups cluttered a small table. Renee smiled at all of them. The scene to be shot at noon was the most important scene in the film, and she supposed that was why they were all present.

"Have you got the dress?" Carol asked, lifting a perfectly plucked brow.

"Yes. Why don't we go into your dressing room and try it on, then I'd like Tony to come in and give me his advice." She smiled warmly at Tony. "I designed this with the coif you've given Carol in mind."

Tony, a slim, well-dressed young man with expressive hands, almost gushed. "It's her, you know! Those deep silver-blond waves are just so, *so* indicative of her personality. I'm so glad you admire it! I can hardly wait to see the dress. What color is it?"

"Gray," Renee replied.

"Oh, I don't look well in gray," Carol moaned.

"You're quite right. You wouldn't look well in gray at all. With your white skin and wonderful hair you were meant to wear black, but as I know you know, absolute black absorbs too much color for a film shot in black and white. Black and pure white are never used. Now, this dark gray dress in shimmering jersey is going to photograph as black, a wonderful light-catching black. You'll radiate in it."

"She's quite right," Tony put in. "Be a dear, don't keep us in suspense. Go put the dress on."

Renee handed the box to Esmeralda. "You help her, will you? And I trust your judgment—if you don't like the little bow, take it off."

Esmeralda glowed too, and she led Carol to the dressing room.

"It's a cool designer who allows the dresser to be the first to see a new dress," Tony whispered.

Renee blushed. "I don't know how cool I am."

"Well, you're nice," Tony announced. "Maybeth wasn't nice. She was a bitch, and I for one am glad she's gone. Tell me about this dress we're going to see."

Renee glanced around. The others were listening, though Calvin looked distinctly bored with the subject. She suspected he was more interested in Carol without her clothes.

"Well, most of the shots in this scene are waist-up shots, so much detail on the bottom of a dress would be lost. That's why the little bow is at the top."

"But it is a long dress, isn't it?" Tony asked.

"Oh, yes. Have you ever seen the garments worn by the Polynesian women in Gauguin's paintings? Those South Sea girls?"

"Sarongs?"

"Yes. It's draped like a sarong, with a little bow over the left breast where a real sarong would be joined."

"How very clever!"

Renee's eyes sparkled as she watched Tony respond to her. "As I'm sure you noticed, Tony, Carol is just a bit short-waisted, with high angular hips. The camera will treat her unkindly if her waist isn't lowered. After all, designing for film is a matter of optical illusion. This dress will make her torso longer, and the soft material will emphasize her bust."

Calvin grinned wickedly. "Yeah, I like that emphasized."

"And of course," Renee added, "the bare shoulders accentuate the hairstyle you've created."

"Oh, every time she turns, those creamy blond waves will caress her bare shoulders! It's just so perfect I can't stand it!" Tony said with a wave of his hands.

Esmeralda appeared first, then Carol moved across the room, obliged by the tightness of the garment to take small steps. Renee noticed that the bow remained.

"The camera's going to eat you up, you look so wonderful!" Tony announced loudly.

Calvin whistled through his teeth and Shifty Sam Rosen only grinned as he extracted a big cigar from his inside vest pocket. He leaned over toward Renee. "Hell of a swell rag," he muttered. "If you were a man, I'd offer you a cigar."

Carol touched her hair and looked at Tony. "You really like it, don't you?"

"It's stunning!" Tony glanced at his watch. "I better get you to Make-up, darling. We have a noon call, remember?"

Renee watched as the room emptied out. Then she walked over to the table that held the coffemaker and poured herself a cup. Konnie, much to her surprise, appeared framed in a doorway behind the table.

"Where did you come from?" she asked, taking in the fact that her uncle was dressed in white overalls, like one of the technicians.

He pointed up high to the scaffolding that surrounded the room, which held lights and had a catwalk. "I watched your whole performance, and I must say it was magnificent. I shall have to watch you, Renee. You can be very manipulative."

"Working with people is easier than working against them."

"You're going to do just fine," Konnie said proudly. "Just fine."

Fifteen

1

July 1934

*R*enee wore a lightweight summer frock made of royal-blue dimity. It accentuated the shoulders, was held in tightly at the waist, and flared out only below knee level. Modestly cut in front, its neckline plunged daringly in the back. Royal blue was a color she was wearing more and more now, not only because it made her eyes seem larger but also because she felt it somehow expressed her personality. Fashions changed, but color could be used to create a continuity of personal style. Royal blue was cool, yet more passionate than sky blue because of its darker hue, a hue created by the addition of red. It was a color one could have an evening dress made up in, or a business suit. Moreover, it was a color that could be combined with other colors to create a certain flair—after all, deep green and royal blue were the colors found in a number of Scots tartans, now becoming popular as fabric for women's skirts. And to be outrageous, one might combine it with gold or even a touch of orange—perhaps in a scarf. Silver and royal blue were absolutely classic, and royal blue and black velvet echoed the mood of romantic nights and star-studded skies. And as far as claiming the color as her own was concerned, she knew she had succeeded the day the wardrobe mistress said, "Ah, I see you're wearing your color today."

And today as well, she thought as she walked down the long corridor toward her large airy office on the lot.

" 'Morning, Miss Lazar, I'll be back in a jiffy with those boards," Jason, one of her young apprentices, promised as he passed her at breakneck speed. He was a bright, good-looking young man with no small talent of his own. He had a wonderful sense of humor, and she enjoyed working with him because he made her laugh.

"Before ten!" she replied, turning her head as he passed.

She opened the door to her outer office. Kristie, her secretary, was already at her desk, phone in hand. She looked up when Renee came in and put her hand over the mouthpiece of the phone. "Your father called to confirm that he's picking you up at six-thirty, your uncle phoned to cancel your after-lunch meeting, Ruby Keeler wants to speak to you about the costume for her dance number, and there's a telegram and some flowers from your husband in the office."

Renee rolled her eyes and smiled. "Relax," she urged. Poor Kristie. She was new, and the phone, which rang constantly, was her devil. Moreover, actresses in a tizzy over their clothes had a tendency toward hysteria, which Kristie took seriously and no doubt personally.

"Everyone is always in a hurry," Kristie said, shaking her dark hair in a combination of bewilderment and disbelief at the pace of life inside the studio.

Renee smiled and went into her own office. It was stark white and on its walls hung three years of awards for her costumes. Costumes, she thought with pleasure, that had in turn sparked fashion trends. She had created new lines based on these trends for Sandy's growing number of stores. Thanks to the likes of Ginger Rogers, Ruby Keeler, and Una Merkel, the little slouch hat and the tweed suit for women had become fashion hits, and Una had been particularly responsible for popularizing the suit with the little cape, which further tended to accentuate the waist by flaring out from the shoulders. Renee was not the only success, however. At Paramount, the enormously talented Edith Head had just won an Academy Award, and doubtless she would win more.

On her large oak desk, which was otherwise clear, there was a huge bouquet of roses, and beneath it a telegram:

> Darling,
>
> I am terribly sorry that I can't make it back to L.A. for your birthday. The opening of the San Francisco store is more than I bargained for . . . half the stock has yet to be delivered, and there are still minor architectural difficulties—such as the completion of the winding staircase from the mezzanine to the ground floor. The domed ceiling with its skylight is a knockout, though. In any case, we'll celebrate together when I get back. I know "your men" will take care of you.
>
> Love,
> Sandy

Renee smiled at his term "your men." He meant Miklós, Konnie, Zoltan, and Imre, who was now acting in minor roles. She refolded the telegram and slipped it back in the envelope. She was neither surprised nor upset. If indeed he had arrived on time or been able to free himself, she would have been truly shocked. For the past three years their lives had grown steadily apart. As she became more and more involved in the world of film and fashions, he became more involved with his stores, of which there were now nine. Their life together consisted of dinner one or two times a week when they were both in town, business discussions when she was about to launch a new line, and the occasional unplanned evening when, by sheer coincidence, they were both free.

And lately, she thought, Sandy had seemed more and more remote. He'd even stopped making love to her, though in fact she didn't mind and sometimes wondered if he sensed her ambivalence toward that aspect of their married life. It hadn't always been so, of course. But it was now, and she supposed that all married couples eventually cooled toward one another.

"You can't just march in there!" Kristie's voice shouted from the outer office, and Renee turned abruptly as the door opened and a tall good-looking man strode in.

"I knew it was you! I saw your picture in the paper! I knew it was you!"

Renee stood almost frozen to the spot as Aaron Lewis advanced on her, his eyes filled with excitement and anticipation, while Kristie, her glasses slipped over her nose, followed in his wake protesting.

"I told him he couldn't just come barging in here. I told him."

"I heard you. But it's all right. This time it's all right."

"Are you sure?"

"Yes, please leave us and close the door."

Kristie looked slightly miffed, but did as she was instructed.

"Aaron . . ."

"Lazar—you used to be called Horvath, Renee."

"Lazar is my real father's name. I've always used it professionally . . . Oh, it's a long story."

Aaron walked across the room to stand closer to her. "I never thought I'd see you again," he said, looking at her steadily.

Renee stood looking back into his dark eyes, emotions flooding over her at such a rapid rate she could not define them. Her face felt warm, she trembled, and it seemed as if it had been a matter of a few uneventful days since she had last seen him.

"I knew I'd find you. I knew it! Renee, why didn't you answer my letters?"

She stared at him blankly, unbelievingly. His letters?

"What's the matter, Renee?"

She shook her head slowly. "You never wrote. You never answered my letters . . ."

He looked into her blue eyes; then slowly a frown crept over his face, as if for the first time he understood. "My father," he said then, "my father!"

"I don't understand . . ."

"My father destroyed your letters. He must have. And your mother must have destroyed mine to you."

Renee shook her head. "Mama wouldn't have done such a thing."

"She took money . . . my father gave her money to take you away. He told me that just before he died. He said he didn't mind the money, because you had talent, but he said your mother was cold and calculating . . . he told me you must have known."

The money! The mysterious money that her mother had said came from her grandmother, but didn't. The money had come from Aaron's father? "Why did he give it to her?" Renee asked, still unwilling to accept the truth.

"Because he didn't want me to marry you, and your mother promised him you wouldn't if you were going to art school. I knew about that, but I never knew he'd destroyed your letters."

Renee leaned against her desk. "Mama used your father shamelessly," she whispered. And yet at the same time she understood her mother's motives. "She wanted for me what she had never had. I know that, but I never suspected you had written to me, and I never knew about the money. For years, until I found my uncle, I thought the money had come from my grandmother. When I learned it hadn't, I was mystified until now."

Aaron reached out to her and touched her hair with his hand. "It doesn't matter—none of it matters. What matters is that I've found you."

She felt then a stabbing pain followed by near-nausea. He was holding her with his eyes, making love in his mind, touching her . . . and she was responding. In seconds she had traveled back in time, let her emotions surface, forgotten everything. But she had to tell him, and clearly he had no inkling. "I'm married," she blurted out, then trembled violently and again whispered it, "I'm married."

"But your name . . ." he protested. "You said it was your father's name."

"It is, but I'm also married. My married name is Lipton."

He was holding her shoulders tightly now and looking into her eyes. "Do you love him?"

She wanted to run, she wanted to start over, she wanted this day not to have happened at all. Her life was perfect, absolutely perfect. She had everything a woman could want. She had a successful career and a loving husband. She had money and she had those to whom she was close—her father, her uncle, her brothers. "Of course I love him," she lied. "Aaron, we're not the same people . . . years have passed. Aaron, too much has happened—we can't just pretend we're teenagers again."

"You don't love him. I can see it in your eyes."

"Of course I do!"

"Renee, don't try to lie to me. I've looked for you too long and dreamed of this day for too many nights. I know you don't love him, it's written all over you. You're a terrible liar."

"It doesn't matter," she said, breaking free of his hold. "He's a fine man, a good man. I wouldn't hurt him for anything or anybody."

"You still love me. You can deny it, but I'm not going to accept what you say this time. I did that before."

"You must."

"No. If you love him so much, there's no harm in seeing me. Have lunch with me tomorrow at Pentorri's."

"I can't."

"Why, because you know you care too much? What are you afraid of, Renee, old times? Lunch is not adultery, you know."

She blushed and avoided his eyes, which seemed to penetrate all her thoughts. Everything in her warned her not to accept his invitation, but she had to see him again and at the same time she had to get him out of her office, had to be alone to contemplate her churning feelings. "All right . . . yes, I'll have lunch with you."

He grinned triumphantly. "You know where it is? Just south of the pier in Santa Monica. One o'clock."

She nodded. "Please, you must go now."

"You promise, you promise you'll come?"

"Yes."

"If you don't, I'll come here and literally carry you away."

"I'll come."

He reached into his vest pocket and handed her an engraved card. "I can be reached here in case of an emergency."

He turned then and left her holding his card. Renee stared down at it. "Aaron Lewis, Attorney at Law," it read. She smiled faintly. They had at least both realized their dreams.

2

Again Renee dressed in royal blue, but this time her dress was of flowing crepe de chine and the blue was flecked with silver threads. The gown fell to her ankles and was skin tight to the knees, where it swirled out in a long deep ruffle. Again, the back was low, but the sleeves were long and composed of three deep ruffles that seemed to match the flare at the bottom of her skirt. She wore high-heeled velvet shoes and her long blond hair was partially covered with a low-slung net made of the same material as her dress. Her jewelry—distinctive hand-crafted earrings, serpentine necklace, and collection of seven bracelets—was white gold.

In the subdued flickering lamplight of the private dining room of the Ambassador Hotel, Renee looked and felt like a royal princess flanked by her adoring court of predominantly male admirers. Her father, Miklós Lazar, sat on her right, and Konnie, her uncle, sat on her left. Zoltan, who had driven in from Nevada, where he was working on the construction of Boulder Dam, sat next to Konnie, and Imre, her younger brother, who had now become an actor of sorts, sat next to Miklós. Katrina Kern, Imre's girlfriend of the moment, and an aspiring young starlet, sat on Imre's other side, and Zoltan's fiancée, a lovely young Mexican girl named Rita, sat next to him. Also present and filling out the table were Adolph Zukor and his wife, Pola Negri whose last film had been *A Woman Commands* and who was about to leave for Germany to make a film; Béla Lugosi, who just for fun, and in case any press were about, was dressed in his Count Dracula cape; the quite extraordinary actor Paul Lukas, who was also Hungarian and who might be termed Hollywood's "continental in residence"; and Renee's two assistants, Jason Whitman and a young bright-eyed designer named Lily Rhommer.

Dinner had begun with fresh shrimp cocktail on a bed of avocado. With that course a Chablis had been served. The shrimp was followed by mock-turtle soup, and that by a magnificent tossed salad, the likes of which could only be had in California. The main course was a finely done Hungarian schnitzel accompanied by a wonderful deep red Hungarian wine.

Now in the center of the table was a Black Forest cake, and champagne had been poured. Konnie was standing to make a speech. Good company, fine food, and assorted wines had warmed him to the task. "To good friends, to old countrymen"—he nodded toward the Hungarians—"to new countrymen"—he smiled and bowed to Lily and Jason, who were American through and through—"and to my beloved niece on her thirtieth birthday." He turned, bent down, and kissed Renee on the cheek. "Happy birthday, Renee!"

There was a chorus of "Happy Birthday!" and Renee blushed and acknowledged them.

"Speech!" Zukor shouted. "Speech!"

Renee stood up, and there was a round of laughter and applause. She looked around and smiled. "Thank you, friends," and she touched Konnie and her father, "and relatives. I can only say thank you and tell you that I love it here so much that every day is like a birthday. It has meant so much to me to work in this wonderful medium, to be able to design costumes that millions of women will take to their hearts—"

"And their husband's pocketbooks!" Zukor interrupted.

There was more laughter and Renee laughed too. "The economy is getting better," she added. "So perhaps the husbands won't mind so much. But more seriously, we have brought fashion to all American women, and it's affordable fashion, fashion that allows all women the opportunity to be as glamorous as those women they see on the screen. Every woman needs fantasy, needs the means to imagine herself a Dietrich, a Bankhead, or a Blondell. Parisian women have had a monopoly on fashion for too long. It's our turn now, and we're showing the world that you don't have to be a millionaire to look good and to have class, and an image of one's own. Movies are to the culture of the twentieth century what printing was to the Renaissance. We don't just reflect style and culture, we define it and create it. So thank you all for the opportunity to be a part of something so important."

Renee sat down and Zukor led a round of applause, and then, surprisingly, he led them in singing "Happy Birthday."

Renee sat back and sipped her champagne. When they'd finished singing, conversation resumed and Renee's eyes fell on Imre and Katrina. Katrina was undeniably attractive. She had masses of red hair and large brown eyes. Her skin was tawny and her figure was near-perfect. She had long lovely legs, a tiny waist, full breasts, and rounded buttocks. Hollywood, Renee reflected, was full of beautiful young women. They flocked to Hollywood from all over the country and, indeed, all over the world. They came in hopes that their looks would make them actresses, that they would have the opportunity to live what they saw as the glamorous life. But few succeeded. Most ended up being exploited—they ended up the mistresses of producers and directors, even of cameramen and accountants. Some ended up as call girls, hoping, praying to be discovered, selected, and given screen tests. She herself could not define exactly what kind of woman actually made it. Certainly those who could act, who had studied acting and who had been on the stage, seemed to have an advantage. Yet highly independent women, women like Bette Davis and Katharine Hepburn, seemed few and far between. Most of Hollywood's women—regardless of whether they made it or not—were victims of the studio star system, of their own ambition, of the men they worked for and with, and in a sense many were victims of their own extraordinary looks. In a way Hollywood was a wonderful place, but in another way it was a tragic place, and Renee had seen both its sides. And she knew that she saw and experienced Hollywood in a far different way from her star-struck sisters. She was respected by men for her talent, even if some did admire her looks. She was behind the camera, not in front of it; she was not among the exploited masses. As she stared at Katrina, she wondered is she would succeed or fail.

Imre was good-looking. He had played only bit parts so far, but he almost didn't need talent. And Imre was not ambitious to be another Paul Lukas. He loved Hollywood because he loved women, and since he was already a part of the business—his uncle owned the studio—women threw themselves at him. He accepted their favors but gave few of his own—indeed, was incapable of giving many, though she supposed Konnie would test someone if Imre really seemed serious, which he seldom was. Vaguely she wondered if Imre were sleeping with Katrina or whether Katrina was holding out for more, for an opportunity. Did she really care? Of course Katrina was using Imre. Imre deserved to be used, indeed courted it. But there was something about Katrina that Renee found she didn't like, and it irked her that she could not come up with anything except intuition.

She turned away from the puzzle and looked at Zoltan. She liked Rita and was glad Rita was not an aspiring star who might be using her brother to meet the "right" people. Zoltan, as usual, had chosen wisely. When the dam was completed, Zoltan intended staying on as one of the resident engineers. He liked the climate on the Arizona-Nevada border, and Rita's family lived close by in the tiny community of Boulder City. Zoltan was secure, and he and Rita, when married, would probably have a zillion children and a wonderful happy, normal life.

Happy . . . normal. What had made her begin thinking of families and children? She was happy and she had meant every word she'd said in her little speech. Yet she felt a certain jealousy when she looked at Rita and realized how soon Rita would be rocking Zoltan's child.

Perhaps it had all come to mind because Aaron had appeared today out of the blue, and no doubt his sudden appearance had confused her. It's because I'm thirty, she said to herself silently. Thirty. Where was her life going? She pushed the sudden panic from her thoughts and drank some more champagne. He's stirring up too much, she thought. Well, I won't go to lunch tomorrow. I won't meet him. I won't see him ever again. He was lost to me for thirteen years, let him stay lost. It was nothing but a silly girlish crush anyway. What she had with Sandy was more important. It was stable, it was real . . . But around the edges of her mind the panic again began to creep in. What *did* she have with Sandy?

"You don't look happy," her father said, taking her hand.

Renee looked down, and the white damask cloth on the table glared back up at her. "I'm happy," she insisted.

He squeezed her hand tight. "Renee, you are many things, but happy is not one of them."

She forced a smile, half-wanting to confide in him, half-wanting to keep her own counsel. "I have things to think about," she admitted.

"Do you want to share them?"

"Not now."

He nodded. "Renee, when you need me I'll be here. I failed your mother, I won't fail you."

"Thank you, Papa."

He leaned over and enfolded her in his arms and gave her a great bear hug. Renee forced herself not to cry even though she felt like it. Thirty, she decided, was a damnable age.

3

At seven in the morning Renee had sat before her mirror brushing her hair. And with every stroke she murmured, "I'm not going, I'm not going, I'm not going."

Nonetheless, she applied her makeup with great care and donned a dazzling white suit with royal-blue accessories consisting of a paisley printed silk scarf, a see-through blouse, and blue leather shoes and purse. In her Duesenberg SJ convertible, driving to the studio across the winding mountain on Beverly Glen Road, she decided it would be unfair not to see him at least once. "We need to talk this out," she said firmly as she began her descent into the wilderness of the valley, where the studio sprawled out like an intruding alien growth on the farm landscape. At ten in her office she turned to Kristie and said, "I'm not going. I'll have lunch in my office," and then, leaving Kristie openmouthed, she slammed the door and worked till eleven-thirty, refusing all calls. At twelve she got up, went to the mirror, repaired her makeup, and cursed. Then she flung open the door just as Kristie was wheeling in a cart with her lunch. "You eat it," she said irritably. "I'm going out!"

Back across the winding drive and finally onto Santa Monica Boulevard, she checked her watch ten times and drove a little faster because she was late. At one-fifteen she pulled into the parking lot, and at one-twenty Aaron was pulling out her chair.

"I was afraid you weren't coming."

She picked up the menu and stared at its dancing words. "I almost didn't."

"You seem angry."

She looked up. "I am angry. You waltz into my life and . . . and make me feel beholden to you because your father paid my mother to keep us apart! You come back and I . . . I . . ." Her voice trailed off and he covered her shaking hand with his.

"I don't want you to feel 'beholden,' and you know that damn well. I don't give a damn about the money. My father was a very wealthy man, he put lots of people through school, albeit not to keep me from marrying them. That's water under the bridge, Renee, and it's not why you're angry. You're angry because you didn't want to come and you couldn't stay away."

The waiter loomed over them and Renee shook off his hand and looked at the man. He was utterly poker-faced, as if he hadn't heard a word. "I'll have a double Scotch on the rocks," she said, thankful to God that Prohibition was over and she didn't have to drink out of a bottle in a paper sack under the table—though she didn't drink much and had never ordered a double Scotch in her life. It was, in fact, Sandy's drink, not hers.

"And do you want to order your meal now or wait till I've brought the drinks?"

"Now. I'll have the swordfish."

Aaron smiled. In fact he looked as if he might laugh. "A simple bourbon on the rocks for me, and the prawns."

The waiter nodded and left instantly.

"Why are you laughing?" She could hear the edge in her voice and wondered why it was there. He was right, of course, she was furious at herself, and his understanding made her even more angry.

"Dare I quote from some scriptwriter and say you're beautiful when you're mad?"

"I wish you would be serious."

"I'm dead serious. I've come back for you, Renee, and I'm not satisfied that you're the happy, contented woman you claim to be."

"I am happy."

The waiter set down their drinks and she immediately took a large swallow and then coughed. "Oh, God!" she said, leaning back.

"Why did I suspect you weren't used to Scotch?"

He shook his head and then his finger at her. "Stop thinking about yourself for a few minutes. Why don't you ask how I am and what I'm doing."

"You gave me your card. I know you're a lawyer."

"A criminal lawyer. I'm very successful and I love my work. In the thirteen years since I last saw you I've been engaged three times—all simply beautiful, wonderful women. The trouble was, I didn't love them. So I never married. You see, I always remembered this girl who lied about her age and whom I fell for so hard no one has ever been able to erase the memory."

Renee stared at him. "I suppose I should apologize for not waiting for you, for meeting a man who was—is—so good to me."

"He's years older than you, Renee. And you didn't mention children. How many are there?"

She could hardly say it, but she forced herself. "None." Then, defensively, "Not everyone has to have children, you know. I do have a career. I too am very successful."

"You could have your career and have children. Quite a lot of women in Hollywood have careers and children."

"Perhaps I didn't want any."

"You wanted them. You want them now."

"Stop telling me what I want!"

"Sh! This is a family restaurant."

"Don't sh me! Why are you doing this?"

He smiled his little-boy smile, the one that had always drawn her to him. "Because I want you to realize you still love me before it's too late. I want you to think about what's missing."

She bit her lip and covered her eyes with her hand because she was too tired and too tense to hold back the tears she felt coming. "I do think about it. I do. Oh, why did you come back now?"

"What's now?"

"My birthday was yesterday and I've been thinking too much."

"Number thirty, no doubt. It's a bad one. It's a birthday that makes you look at yourself and ask questions."

"You had to come just when I'm vulnerable, didn't you?"

"I'd like to think you would have been vulnerable to me in any case."

"Maybe I would have been."

"Does that mean you're willing to admit you still care?"

She lifted her eyes and blinked. The tears were running down her cheeks and she felt as if everyone in the restaurant must be looking at her. "Yes, I still care. I felt something when I saw you that I'd forgotten, or buried, or lied to myself about . . . but it makes no difference, don't you see? I won't do anything to hurt Sandy. I really won't."

"What did he do to deserve such loyalty?"

"I was almost raped in New York . . . by my uncle. It

was horrible. His mistress came in, and she stabbed him to death. I was hurt and frightened and alone, and Sandy was there . . ."

She watched as the expression on Aaron's face clouded. "I'm glad he was there, Renee. But you must not confuse gratitude with love."

"I love him."

"You love him like a father, not like a husband."

"Even if I admit you're right about everything, it doesn't change a thing."

The waiter came and set down their food, and they fell into a long silence. Renee picked at her lunch, unable to eat, unable to straighten out the strands of her emotions, which seemed now to hang like so many ribbons from a ribbon rack, tangled and knotted together.

"I'm not going to ask you to sleep with me or run away with me," he said slowly. "Renee, I just want to see you, be with you. I promise to keep my distance physically if you'll spend some time with me, test the waters, straighten out your own desires and your own thoughts."

"I don't know if that would be wise."

"I'm here, Renee. I've already come back. You can't erase me now. You have to work it out."

She nodded, slowly accepting his rationale.

"Where is Sandy now?"

"In San Francisco."

"When is he coming back?"

She shrugged. "Perhaps Sunday."

"And then?"

"He has to go to Cincinnati and then Kansas City. He'll probably be home only a few days. Tomorrow is Friday. We'll have dinner tomorrow." Friday the thirteenth, she thought.

Again Aaron reached across the table and touched her hand. "You'll be glad you listened to your heart."

Renee looked at her plate. She was already upset that she had agreed to see him again.

4

August 20, 1934

Miklós Lazar stood at his living-room window and watched as the rain poured down. It hadn't rained in a long while, and the ground was dry, so the water didn't really soak in; instead it formed little rivulets and rolled down the hillside.

He glanced at the clock on the marble mantel and noted that Renee was late. Doubtless delayed in traffic.

She was probably coming to discuss whatever was troubling her, and he hoped he could be of some help. "An extraordinary woman," he said aloud. He could not help thinking how much he had grown to care about this daughter he had discovered so late in life. True, she had come to Hollywood with a reputation and with experience, but costume design was different and yet she had moved into it as if she'd been doing it all of her life. And God knew it wasn't easy. The stars she dressed were temperamental, sometimes downright nasty. And Hollywood was not a thoughtful town; the pace was nothing short of hectic, and everyone wanted everything yesterday. Still, she had survived and even prospered.

Konnie, he thought with a smile, hadn't intended to hire Renee as head of the costume department at first, he'd merely given her one picture and intended to let her run with it. But the head of the costume department, Maybeth LaFarge objected and when Konnie wouldn't back down, she had left, but alas not quietly. Poor Renee had been thrust into a terrible mess left in the wake of Maybeth's abrupt departure. She'd had to pull everything together and rebuild the entire department in a matter of weeks. But she had done it, and everyone respected her abilities.

He was still thinking about her early days at the studio when he heard Renee's car slosh through the water in his driveway, and he went to open the door as she hurried inside, protected by her yellow umbrella.

"My yard is running downhill," he joked as he ushered her inside.

"You shouldn't joke about it. Two houses in the canyon are nearly to the edge of a cliff."

He shrugged. "Ah, when you live here you get used to little disasters. One year it's forest fires, and the next it's floods and landslides."

She smiled. "You forgot the earthquake last year. It destroyed half of Long Beach."

"I chose to forget it. Come in here, sit down. Can I get you a drink?"

"That would be good. Have you any brandy?"

"Brandy it is."

He walked to the little bar and poured brandy into two large snifters. It was a good choice; the rain had made it cool and the dampness was penetrating. "Here you go," he offered as she snuggled into a chair.

"I don't know where to begin."

"Wherever you want."

"I know I said I was coming to talk about myself, but before I start, I want to ask about that girl—the one Imre is seeing. I was going to ask Konnie, but perhaps you know."

"Ah, Katrina."

"Yes, that one."

"Well, she's just left our employ. She's gone to another studio."

"I suppose that might end it, then. I mean, they might not see each other as often."

"You have worries?"

"I just find her . . . well, abrasive and too wrapped up in herself."

"I'm sure its more than that."

"It is, but I can't really make judgments based on my intuition."

"Your intuition is quite good. Konnie let her go even though she tested very well indeed. She's going to succeed, but she's going to do it over other people's bodies.

She isn't too discriminating in her choice of bed partners, and she drinks a lot."

Renee frowned. "I suppose she and Imre are or have been intimate."

"That would make him part of a cast of thousands."

"I can't say anything to him. He would just resent it."

"Renee, you're thirty and Imre is twenty-six. I think you can stop playing mother to him."

"I suppose you're right."

"Now, tell me about you. You've been very distracted lately."

"Papa, it's a long story. . . . This man, a man I never thought I'd see again, has turned up . . ."

Miklós leaned back and listened as she talked. Then after a time she stopped and sat with her hands folded, staring at them. She shook her head sadly. "Aaron has come back at the very moment I'm feeling most vulnerable."

"First a question, since the matter seems to be, or you've made it seem to be, important. Why haven't you and Sandy had children?"

"I've been to the doctor, and there's nothing wrong. I guess it's Sandy. He must be sterile. But he did have two sons by his first wife. I don't know what the problem is."

"Have you ever asked or talked about it with him?"

She shook her head.

"Have you discussed children with him?"

"No. Perhaps he thinks I don't want any."

"And now the hard question. Do you love Sandy, Renee?"

"I care for him. I don't think I love him, but I would never hurt him."

"You're still a young woman, and he is much older. I can tell you that without love marriage can be lonely and empty."

"I do have my work."

"It won't help solve your problem. Look at you, you're completely distracted. Have you been seeing him, this man who has come back into your life?"

"Aaron. Yes. But only in public places, only for lunch and one dinner."

"Renee, I can't solve this problem for you, but I do think that when you can, you should talk to Sandy."

"You mean tell him?"

"Something like that. You're not the type to be sneaking around. In any case, you're too well-known to get away with it for long around here. One of the columnists will pick it up. Sandy will end up reading it rather than hearing it."

"I should stop seeing Aaron—that's the real solution."

"Maybe yes. Maybe no. If not seeing him leaves you resentful and still wondering what might have been, I'd say you should go on seeing him."

"Oh, Papa, it feels good just to have unburdened myself."

"Few of us get a second chance, Renee. Keep that in mind."

"I will." She finished her brandy and walked across the room and kissed him on the cheek. He was a gentle man. No wonder her mother had loved him.

Sixteen

1

September 1, 1934

*A*s a result of forest fires in the San Bernardino Mountains, a low haze hung over the whole Los Angeles basin, and at the far western end of the bowl-shaped city it combined with fog from the ocean. The resulting smog, more dense at low levels than in the mountains, snaked its way through the valleys of the mountain roads on the northern side of Sunset Boulevard. Through the haze the September sun blazed hot, a large orange ball of heat unrelieved by any winds or comforting breezes.

On her patio, Renee sat under the shade of a huge umbrella at a glass-topped table. Across from her, Imre, dressed in gleaming white and wearing dark glasses, relaxed comfortably, his red silk shirt open at the neck, his feet resting on a chair.

It was impossible to look at him without thinking how very good-looking he was, Renee thought. Her youngest brother was tall and slim, yet muscular. He had thick straight jet-black hair and large brooding brown eyes. When he smiled, he had perfect teeth, and even his thick dark brows were well-shaped. She thought there was something both appealing and maddening in his smile and in his expression. The smile was a little crooked, the expression a trifle pouty. It was a bad-little-boy look, a look he knew how to use to advantage. He reminded her a bit of young Tyrone Power, who had just made *Flirtation Walk.* Imre, unhappily, was not as talented as Tyrone Power. What Imre wanted was unearned success and adulation. Not that a bit player got much adulation in Hollywood, but outside Hollywood or among those with no connections with film, any firsthand knowledge of the romantic "life of the stars" could be traded on. Imre was a hanger-on. He acted enough to qualify, but basically he owed his position in Hollywood to his uncle and to her. He hardly ever missed a party and she had long suspected he made extra money feeding rumors to the columnists. She wished with all her heart that he would settle down and do something substantial, but over the years she had found it more and more difficult to communicate with him.

"More coffee?" she offered, holding the pot out.

"God, no. But I'd be glad to have something stronger."

"It's only ten. Don't you think it's a bit early for something stronger?"

"A lot of people drink brandy in the morning."

"Do you want brandy?"

"No, whiskey."

"You know where the bar is."

"Okay. I'll be right back."

She watched as he went through the French doors into the house, and she silently cursed. He returned in seconds with not only a drink but also the bottle.

"Saves getting up and down." He waved the bottle at her and sat back down, his feet up. "Konnie's made a mistake, you know," he said.

"You'll have to fill me in. I don't know what you're talking about."

"He shouldn't have let Katrina out of her contract. She's dynamite and her new studio's already got her scheduled for a lead part."

"I'm happy for her."

"I doubt that. I get the impression you don't like her much."

"I think she uses people."

"Everyone here uses everyone else. It's a way of life. Hey, didn't you use Konnie? And how about good old Sandy?"

Renee felt herself go rigid. Imre had a way of making her angry, and he knew it. Perhaps, she acknowledged, because there was more than a grain of truth in his accusation. Still, she had gone to school and studied and worked hard. To a large extent she felt she had earned her position. "I admit I used the initial contact. But I was prepared and experienced. And most important, I produced for those who gave me an opportunity."

"And what makes you think Katrina won't?"

Renee shrugged. "Perhaps she will. Actually, if she's going to succeed, she'll have to produce. People won't keep on giving her chances based on her record in their bedrooms."

"Aren't we being the bitch? And self-righteous too?"

She ignored his invective. "Imre, she used you to get her contract with Konnie. Now everyone says she's having an affair with Sam Katz."

"She's still having an affair with me. Naturally she has to be nice to people."

"Do you really care about this girl?"

"Yes. I know you probably don't believe it, but I do. In fact, she's the first girl I've felt seriously about."

"Well, she's gone to another studio, and from what you say, she's destined for stardom. I think you should prepare yourself for the fact that she may not want to continue her relationship with you."

"On the contrary, my dear sister. On the contrary. I, as a matter of fact, am also going to Katz. He's offered me a very good role—the best I've ever had—and I'm taking it."

Renee stared at Imre and tried to think what to say. Certainly Konnie would not deem Imre's departure any more of a tragedy than Katrina's. At the moment they both had an exaggerated idea of their importance. Of course, ego was the first requirement of any actor, she reminded herself. "Well, I for one wish you luck."

Imre smiled, then tilted his head. "Well, now you've

quizzed me on Katrina and I've told you my news. Tell me, how is your new romantic interest?"

Renee's fingers closed tightly on the small handle of the coffee cup and she fought to control her expression and her tone of voice. "I really don't know what you're talking about."

"Oh, Mr. X. The man you've been seeing for lunch and dinner. You know, you used to be so perfect that you could make me feel guilty, but now I see you're just like everyone else, Renee. Perhaps a little smoother than most."

Imre's dark eyes flashed and Renee suddenly felt a wave of familiar uneasiness. For a moment they were Béla's eyes and they seemed threatening. "I am not having an affair with anyone," she said firmly and evenly. "The man you refer to is an old friend and nothing more."

"Now, now. You can tell that to good old Sandy and I suppose he'd believe you. But don't tell it to me. The man is Aaron Lewis. Good old Aaron. Oh, Renee, I remember seeing you with him in New York."

"That was a long time ago, Imre. He came to my office because he's seen my picture in the paper. He's a lawyer here in Los Angeles. I've had lunch and dinner with him a few times and that's the beginning, the middle, and the end of it. Actually, I doubt we shall see each other again." It was the truth, and even as she said it, she knew she couldn't see Aaron again and that she would indeed have to tell Sandy. Not that there was a thing to tell. She hadn't done anything and yet she felt guilty, and Imre was feeding that guilt with his mean innuendo. Her father was right. For years she had mothered Imre and tried to discipline him. He resented her terribly, enough that she now feared he might try to hurt her.

"Time will tell," Imre said with maddening confidence.

Renee shook her head. "I'm sorry you dislike me so much, Imre." His expression changed slightly and she could see her words had caught him off guard.

"I don't dislike you," he protested. "I just don't want you running my life."

"But you keep coming to me for things—for money, for a car . . . Imre, I want you to be able to stand alone."

"I can . . . I will. Look, this picture with Katz is a big opportunity, you'll see."

Renee nodded. "I hope so. I hope it goes well."

He stood up and looked at her for a long moment. "I have to go now," he said slowly. "I have a fitting with Maybeth, and you know how she is."

"Oh, do I."

Imre walked across the patio toward the gate that led to the driveway, where his car was parked. "I just can't be Zoltan," he said as he left.

Renee sat back down and listened as his car backed out of the drive. It wasn't even noon and she felt emotionally drained. Her every encounter with Imre convinced her he was headed for some kind of fall, and her every instinct told her he wanted to be holding on to her skirt when it happened.

2

Rippling white clouds like a great sheepskin blanket filled the dark sky, and out over the ocean, where it was clear, a weak rainbow ring encircled the moon.

Renee and Aaron had driven out the Topanga Canyon Road, eaten at a small fish restaurant on the coast, and now walked along the deserted beach. The sand was still warm from the sun and the great rocks that separated the highway from the strand of white sand and the sea acted as a windbreak.

"It's hard to believe it's September," Renee remarked. "It's so warm and dry."

"They call it a Santa Ana. It's a desert wind and it blows through a gap in the mountains just the other side of Santa Ana. It's partly responsible for the forest fires. When it's this dry, fires start by spontaneous combustion."

"I've been here four years and you've been here two and you know more than I do about California."

Aaron laughed. "That's because you live in a cocoon

called Hollywood. Try taking a trip into my world sometime—that'll wake you up."

"Do you think I'm asleep?" she asked.

"I think a lot of Californians are asleep. We're in the middle of a pretty important election, you know."

"Oh, I know. I do read the papers. Westbrook Pegler says that Southern California needs a guardian and that the whole region should be declared incompetent."

"He's right for the wrong reasons. Mind you, I came here to practice law because it's the weirdest state in the union."

"Mushroom burgers and revolving old-age pensions." She laughed. "Well, who is *your* candidate for governor?"

"Upton Sinclair, naturally. Not that I completely support the EPIC movement, but hell, I can't support either of the other two candidates. Do you have any idea how many cases of vagrancy are prosecuted every day in Los Angeles, or how many people are unemployed?" he asked, sitting down on the sand.

Renee sat down beside him. She was enjoying their discussion. Most of the people she knew discussed only fashions, films, or business. But her mother had taken great pride in her right to vote and and she had taught Renee how important that right was. "They say that if Sinclair is elected, every bum in America will come to Los Angeles for a free handout," Renee commented.

"I'm delightfully surprised you know that much about this election."

"Why? Because I live behind the gilded portals of Hollywood? Look, a lot of the film studios have been making films of the destitute coming here, and passing them off as newsreels to frighten the voters. That was happening even before the primary in August."

"Yea, well, God knows we wouldn't want any more starving farmers from Oklahoma out here, or 'bums,' as they're called. We only let nuts come here," he said sarcastically.

"Oh, Aaron, we may have all the crackpots in America here, the religious cultists—you know, Maybeth LaFarge, the designer at the studio when I came, was a practitioner of serpent worship—the Utopians in Long Beach, the big railroad barons and their cohorts, all the political crazies, and we may have all those real problems of unemployment and bad housing, but it's nothing like Europe. Certainly nothing like what I've read about Germany."

"I can't argue with that. Say, do you know Pola Negri?"

"Yes, of course. She's Hungarian. If she comes back, she's going to have lost most of her friends, I think. You know she used to tell everyone she was a Gypsy. The publicity department had a ball giving her this 'wild romantic past,' but she wasn't a Gypsy, she was half-Jewish. Then she went off to Germany when talkies came along to make films, and told the press she wasn't—in fact, she made a lot of anti-Semitic comments." Renee shook her head in disgust.

"And now," said Aaron, "they say she's having an affair with Hitler."

"Yes, I heard that story too. I really can't understand it."

They sat for a time in silence. Then Aaron said, looking at the ringed moon, "There's a storm at sea."

She didn't respond, but instead kept her eyes on the rock formations that lay ahead. Every time she saw him she vowed it would be the last time. It was a vow she had taken often in the last two months. But now it was different. Somewhere, somehow, they had been seen. Imre knew, perhaps Katrina as well. It had to end. It had to end before it caused irreparable harm, before Sandy found out.

Yet she wanted to be with Aaron. She dreamt about him at night, thought about him at breakfast, and relived both their past and their present whenever she had time to think. In addition to her attraction to him was the fact that she loved having the kind of conversation with him that they had just had. He took her away from her work, away from the kind of people with whom she usually associated. God, how could she give him up?

She had loved him long ago, when there was a world between them, and she knew she loved him now, had perhaps always loved him in some strange suppressed way.

"My mother was forced into her marriage," her mother, Margaret, used to tell her. "And I was forced into mine. But you, Renee, can choose, you can marry anyone you wish, you are free to marry for love."

Free? What was free, really? Béla had nearly raped her and Sandy had been there. She had married for security, married because she had a myriad of responsibilities. Her mother and indeed her grandmother had been victims of a culture, victims of a way of life that made men kings and women chattels. But she had created her own chains, welded them link by link in her desire for success and for security.

"You're quiet," Aaron commented.

Renee looked at him. "Aaron, we can't go on this way."

"Of course we can't."

He turned to face her, and suddenly his arms were around her and the weight of his body pushed her backward. She looked into his eyes and felt paralyzed, not with fear, but with overwhelming desire. He lowered his face and pressed his lips hard against hers. There was no resistance in her, no thought of anything but him. She returned his kiss and her arms flew around him. He nuzzled her, then kissed her neck and ears before again returning to her lips.

And they were on the strand at Coney Island and she was sixteen and he was twenty-two. His hands excited her, his breath was warm, his presence vital. Then she had felt her surging emotions and broken away. She had run down the beach barefoot and she'd begged him to stop. Then he had.

But she did not even try to break away tonight. His hand slipped under her skirt and she felt him as he explored between her legs, even while kissing her and breathing heavily into her neck. Then both his hands slipped under her buttocks and she lifted them ever so slightly to press against him.

"You have a beautiful bottom," he said playfully.

She felt herself flushed and anxious as he moved his hands again and this time undid the top of her dress. She was wearing a net bra and she could feel her breasts pressing against the flimsy fabric. They did not have to wait long to be freed. He undid her bra and pushed it aside, kissing her nipples and caressing them till she glowed with pent-up desire for him.

Oh, why don't I have the strength to stop him? She asked the question only once to herself; then she held him closer and allowed herself to enter the ecstasy of the moment. Her hands roamed his broad back and she felt weak beneath his bulk. Yet he was gentle, gentle but at the same time passionate, wild, uncontrollable. And she yielded to his eager probing and deep caresses as they rolled on the sand, clutching one another—touching, kissing, each now taunting the other. Her clothes lay in disarray on the sand, and he too was naked in the moonlight.

Suddenly, in a fit of girlishness, she broke away from him and ran toward the cool surf, running till she had to swim. And he was there beside her, touching her in the water as her nipples hardened tight and she struggled, laughing in his arms. He pulled her back toward shore till they were standing and once again she was in his arms. He carried her to the shelter of the rocks and then fell on her, licking the salt from her skin till her flesh was again as hot as if she had been lying in the sun and until she moved in his arms and against him so wildly that neither of them could stand it. Her arms were around his neck and her legs were wrapped around him and they were both breathing hard and fast and it seemed to her that the whole world had stopped. She cried out and squeezed him when she felt the spasm of pleasure she had felt so seldom in the past years. Aaron shook against her and then rocked her in his arms and they lay there till the moon disappeared behind the growing clouds and the warm wind began to come up.

Aaron sat up and shook his head. Then he laughed and ran down the beach shouting, "Damn! Our clothes are blowing away!" And she followed, laughing, trying to find her undergarments, but succeeding only in finding her dress.

He drove home without a shirt and she sat close to him, wearing her damp dress and wrapped in a blanket. A wonderful happiness filled her completely. It chased away everything, and for the first time in her entire life, Renee felt reckless.

3

"Upstart!" Maybeth intoned. She was attired in a long skintight print dress and she wore a green turban. Her face was wrinkled, a million lines intersecting like so many streams in a great river delta. She wore outlandish long false eyelashes, purple eye shadow, rouge, and her lips were a pronounced bow painted the color of blood. Maybeth was in her sixties and her body was scrawny and brittle, though her voice was so deep it might have been male. She picked up her gold-tipped cigarette holder and inhaled dramatically, then laid the holder back down so that the cigarette hung over the rapidly filling ashtray.

"I was the most famous couturiere in Paris before she was even born! When she was in diapers I was known for my *haute couture*. Imagine making someone who is only twenty-six the head of an entire costume department! Imagine even giving her a film of her own!" Maybeth spoke with a faint French accent, but from her mouth the accent was no longer a soft romantic sound. It was purely invective.

Katrina faced the full-length mirror and watched as Maybeth draped the diaphanous fabirc, pinning here and there, stepping back now and again.

"You've got a good body," Maybeth interjected. "Good enough to lower the neckline." With that she moved in front of Katrina and pushed the fabric downward, revealing considerable cleavage. Maybeth allowed her hand to fondle Katrina's breast slightly, and when Katrina did not object, she smiled. "I can't imagine why they let you go. You're going to be a star. I feel it. Certainly I'm going to dress you like a star. I'm going to dress you as that upstart doesn't know how."

Katrina smiled. "You're a wonderful designer," she said. Maybeth was a power, and power was not to be ignored, Katrina knew.

"She's there only because her uncle owns the studio," Maybeth went on. "And her clothes are mass-produced only because her husband owns department stores. You must be angry that they let you go. Aren't you?"

"I was at first. But then I got the contract here, and of course my first big chance."

"Well, we'll show them. I hear you go out with her brother and that he's going to be working here too."

"Imre?"

"Yes, good-looking boy. If you like boys."

Katrina giggled. "They have their uses."

"But why is he here too? Because of you?"

"Partly, I suppose. But he's got a better contract too. He says his sister held him back because she didn't really want him to be an actor."

"Bitch!" Maybeth's hand slithered down Katrina's buttocks and then she tapped the actress lightly across the backside. "Turn around, darling."

Katrina did so slowly. Maybeth's tastes were well-known, and so were the gifts she lavished on those starlets who allowed the old harridan her way. Poor girls could not be choosy, she had learned, and Imre was unfortunately not rich, though she relished their relationship and enjoyed her power over him. He had gone from girl to girl until he met her. But now he was trapped, a victim of his own desires. True, he did get terribly jealous, and she would have to watch that his obsessiveness did not interfere with her many plans.

"Yes. I may win an award for this film. You're going to be stunning, simply stunning. I love redheads, and, my dear, your hair is ravishing. And it's so thick! Yes, you'll wear only golds and reds . . . of course, they won't show in black and white, but I'll use wonderful fabrics and you'll wear your costumes on publicity tours so everyone can see the color then. Yes, we'll see who's the best with this film."

"You really dislike Renee, don't you?" Katrina strained to sound innocent.

"I abhor her," Maybeth answered without bothering in the slightest to hide anything.

"I know a secret about her. Imre told me something quite juicy."

Maybeth arched her perfectly drawn-on brow even higher. "Really, you know something juicy about Miss Goody-Goody?"

"I know she's been seeing a man, her childhood sweetheart or something like that. Anyway, they've been meeting secretly. Sandor Lipton certainly doesn't know."

"My, my, just imagine Miss Perfect even having a childhood sweetheart! Well, I wonder if we can make use of that. I'll have to give it some thought."

Katrina stretched and then yawned.

"Oh, poor little dear. You must be tired of standing there. Why don't you just step down now and take all that off. Here, let me help you."

Katrina did little to undrape herself; instead she watched as Maybeth undid her pins and tucks and finally pulled away all the material, leaving Katrina in her lacy undergarments.

"Why don't you lie down for a few minutes on my couch," Maybeth suggested, as with a wave she indicated the sheepskin-covered chaise longue against one wall.

"Oh, thank you," Katrina purred. "You're so kind." She lay down, careful to lean to one side so the curves of her body were more obvious. Maybeth was leering. Indeed, she looked almost ill with desire. "I don't suppose I could impose on you for a drink?"

"Of course, darling. What would you like?"

"Oh, anything you happen to have around."

"I'll be right back."

Maybeth disappeared and Katrina's eyes fell on a painting on the wall. It was a painting of what appeared to be a Roman orgy.

"Here we are."

Maybeth set down two tall glasses filled with a deep pink liquid and crushed ice. She also set down a quite lovely hand-carved pipe.

"Singapore gin slings," she announced, handing one to Katrina. "And something special. Have you ever smoked?"

Katrina took a long sip of her drink. It was strong and she felt the effects almost immediately. "Smoked?"

Maybeth had lit the pipe, and from it a pungent, almost perfumed smell emerged. "Here, darling, just try a little. It's quite heavenly."

Katrina inhaled deeply and felt suddenly quite warm, then a kind of total relaxation, as if the sheepskin beneath her flesh had turned to a great soft white cloud. She glanced around the room and saw a profusion of colors. "Oh, my," she murmured.

At Maybeth's urging she finished her drink and smoked more. She felt dizzy, though it was not unpleasant. She was unable to focus her eyes, but somehow she felt she could see better. She looked down and seemingly for the first time noticed that Maybeth had removed her bra and was teasing her breasts. But it was as if they were someone else's, and she only sighed.

"Have you ever had a woman, darling?"

Katrina shook her head and lay back among the cushions, her eyes again seeking the picture as sensations of hands moving over her naked flesh began to arouse her.

"Such a lovely body," Maybeth was saying as a warm comfortable darkness closed in on her.

4

October 1, 1934

Renee had furnished the dining room of their home with rich, highly polished mahogany furniture and decorated in deep blues with muted gray and dusty-rose accents. It was a wonderful formal dining room, but when they were alone, Renee much preferred to have supper served in the solarium. There they could sit at a small intimate table among the flowers and talk in a relaxed way.

Tonight she had the little table covered in gleaming white, with a centerpiece of tiger lilies. The gold candles burned slowly in milk china candleholders. She had prepared a main dish of fresh Pacific salmon in fresh basil sauce.

Sandy poured a third glass of Chablis. "A wonderful dinner," he said, holding up his glass.

"I'm rather proud of it. I made it myself, you know. It's the cook's night off."

"Then it tastes even better."

She tried to laugh, but somehow couldn't manage. It was all a pretend game. She was pretending to be a good and faithful wife. And Sandy! Even the candlelight could not hide the lines under his eyes. He looked tired. More tired than she had ever seen him. "Are you feeling well, Sandy? You look terribly tired."

"All this traveling—it's nothing, really."

"I think you should go to a doctor. Can't someone else do the traveling?"

"If you don't look after your own business, no one looks after it for you. We have nine stores now."

"Well, I wish you would slow down."

"I must say you look well. Actually, you're glowing. I haven't seen you look so alive and so beautiful in a long while. Tell me, darling, what is your secret?"

Renee stared at him and fought to hold back tears. What was she to say? "My secret is that a month ago I ran naked on the beach with another man and I've been sleeping with him ever since"? Or perhaps just "I'm in love." God, she thought with a certain horror, I want to tell him! I want to confide in him as if he were just a friend and not my husband. I want to actually share my happiness with him.

"Did I say something terrible?"

He leaned across the table with concern and she forced a smile. "Of course not. I guess my mind was just wandering."

"Renee, is there something I should know? Something you want to discuss with me?"

She looked into his soft eyes intently. Was she so transparent? Even Aaron said she was a bad liar, but certainly she didn't feel competent to handle the truth either. How long could she possibly go on this way? "I don't think so," she replied. "Unless you want to discuss the new line for the store?"

"No. I don't even want to think about the store. Renee, I did have a thought—perhaps you'll think it's insane, but hear me out."

"Your thoughts are seldom insane."

"I want to go back to Hungary."

Her eyes opened wide. "To live?"

"No," he laughed. "No, just for a few weeks, a sort of vacation. I'm getting old. I want to visit the place I was born. I want you to come with me."

"Oh . . . I don't know. When?" She felt stunned by the suggestion.

"Immediately. We could take the train to New York and a ship to Germany from there. I want to stay in Europe for a while, perhaps four weeks."

"I don't think I could be away that long."

"You could come home sooner on one of the faster German ships. What do you say?"

What could she say? "I don't want to leave my lover"? But then, perhaps going away would help her sort out things in her own mind. Perhaps it would actually be a good idea. "Yes," she said. "I'm between pictures. I could go now, if I can leave after two weeks."

Sandy smiled broadly and reached across the table to pat her hand. "Wonderful," he said enthusiastically. "I'll book tomorrow!"

5

Seldom did Renee ever go to downtown Los Angeles, and it occurred to her that she had never been in the twenty-eight-story city hall that dominated the skyline, nor even known exactly where the courts were until today.

But here she was, and she was struck by the sheer bleakness of it all. Long corridors lined with uncomfortable benches and plain numbered doors. Judges in their robes scurried down the halls, followed by what seemed legions of lawyers and clerks, while on the benches varieties of people sat staring into space, waiting. As she looked around, she was struck by the absence of any hint of affluence. The people waiting were all dressed poorly; it was as if no one with money every committed a crime.

She stood at the information desk and felt markedly out-of-place. Her world was one of make-believe; the real world, she suspected, was here. On the waiting benches there seemed to be a lot of Mexicans, and it occurred to her that one hardly ever saw Mexicans in Hollywood or at the studio, unless a western were being filmed, or perhaps a movie about the Mexican Revolution.

Then she turned her head and saw Aaron coming down the hall, walking rapidly, a sheaf of papers under his arm.

"Renee," he said breathlessly, "I couldn't believe it when they called me."

"I have to talk to you, it's important."

"It must be. Christ, you look like you're in disguise with that hat and those sunglasses."

She was wearing a large broad-brimmed hat that dipped down and almost covered her face. And she was wearing dark glasses.

"It's not really a disguise, I just didn't want to be noticed."

"I'd say you were pretty hard to miss, myself. C'mon, I think I know of an empty room where we can talk. I haven't got long, though. I have to be in court in thirty minutes."

He took her arm and propelled her down the hall. It occurred to her that until now she had never really thought much about his profession or the fact that he led a busy and obviously hectic life. He was really very patient with her, she thought. So often when they met she spent all her time complaining about the rigors of her own job. "I had no idea you were so busy," she told him as he opened the door to a small room and ushered her in.

"Oh, well, there's plenty of crime here. There's definitely no shortage of people to defend. This room should do. It's a place we use to talk to our clients before going into court, or during the trial sometimes."

He closed the door, then turned and bent down and kissed her cheek, pulling off her hat at the same time. "Let's take off that damn hat," he said cheerfully. "And now, my darling, to what do I owe the pleasure of this unexpected, unplanned, and unannounced visit?"

"I had to come because there isn't much time. I'm going away for a while, Aaron."

"Away? Where?"

"Sandy and I are taking a month and going back to Hungary. He's staying for a bit, but I'll be coming back sooner."

"Hungary? A whole month? Renee, I don't know what to say."

"Please don't say anything. I have to do this, Aaron. I need to sort things out in my own mind. I've made the decision to go with him. By the time he gets back, I'll know what I have to do. Either we'll stop seeing each other, or I'll tell him and ask for a divorce. I can't go on living like this."

He watched her face and could see she was controlling herself, trying to sound logical. And he knew too she was telling the truth. She was a loyal woman and she was suffering because she loved him. "You'll decide to tell him and ask for a divorce, because you love me, and if you weren't honest with him, your whole life would be a lie."

She nodded and murmured, "Perhaps, but I still have to think, and it's better if I do it away from you." He put his hands on her shoulders and she looked up into his face. Then he bent down and kissed her on the lips.

"I love you, Renee, and I don't want to let you go, not even for a month. But I know it's hard for you, so I guess I'll have to live with it."

She leaned against him, her face buried in his chest. "I

was hoping you'd be understanding. It is hard for me, Aaron. Harder than you'll ever know."

"I'll be waiting for you," he finally said, and she pulled away then and took her hat from the table where he'd put it. "We're leaving right away."

"I thought as much, or you wouldn't have come running down here."

"I have to go now."

"Renee, remember I love you."

"I couldn't forget," she answered. And inside she knew she had already made the decision: she was going away to make Sandy happy and to make sure her decision was right.

6

Imre drove past the frog-shaped restaurant, the Temple of Divine Redemption, the Perfect Body Salon, and Whammy Sammy the Exterminator. Then for several miles Sunset was lined with houses and less-memorable storefronts, till it reached the Beverly Hills City Hall, which was partially hidden behind a grove of graceful eucalyptus trees. It looked like a gleaming white Spanish mission with a blue-and-gold tile roof. As the boulevard wound its way through Beverly Hills where Renee lived, it became a street of mansions set back behind the trees and protected by wrought-iron fences, winding drives, and expanses of green lawn with ornate gardens tenderly cared for by an army of Japanese gardeners. Then Sunset gave way to a less-developed area of dense trees, a veritable forest that was in fact the extreme northern end of the University of California campus. The long street wound on through canyons and areas of low brush and wild brown hills, past farms, and then, as it finally approached the sea, there were again houses. For the most part they were lavish sprawling bungalows that hung over the side of cliffs and were surrounded by acres and acres of undeveloped brush.

Imre turned his car off on a dirt road and presently

passed through a wide stone arch, its wrought-iron gate ajar. Down the winding drive through a grove of brush pines he eased to a stop in front of a pseudo-medieval castle in pink stucco complete with two turrets, a glass dome such as might be found on an arboretum, wrought-iron balconies, and a giant eucalyptus tree that seemed to pierce the roof as if growing in one of the rooms.

The servant who silently admitted him was a tall gaunt man with pasty white skin, sunken cheeks, and slicked-back hair as shiny as patent leather.

The first room they passed through had a huge dome and was filled with plants and furnished only with small marble tables and low lounges covered in animal skins. But the furniture paled beside the odds and ends that covered the walls and the tables. There were animal skins from a film about prehistoric times, stuffed iguanas that before the camera had been creatures from the age of dinosaurs, a huge spider, a bow and arrow from a Robin Hood film, and a large tin replica of a Roman shield.

The next room was equally large, but its ceiling was midnight blue and little lights flickered from the ceiling in imitation of the night sky. Half of one wall was paneled wood and somehow looked as if it didn't belong. A winding staircase on either end of the room led to the turrets, and a Moorish tiled archway led to a sunken sun room with a medium-size indoor pool, tables filled with fake marble statues from *The Last Days of Pompeii*, and more low-slung sofas covered in skins. This room, like the other two, was filled with movie props. On the wall there was even a deadly sharpened glass bejeweled replica of Excalibur, King Arthur's sword. Beyond the wall of glass that made up one side of the sun room, the ground fell dramatically to the coast highway, beyond which the ocean glittered a bright blue punctuated by diamonds of sunlight.

Katrina was lying on a sofa covered in black fur, her red hair wild and loose. She was wearing big gold hoop earrings, ropes of fake gold necklaces, and a gold-plated breast covering with straps of fake coins.

The same coins formed a low belt around her hips, and

from it yards of black satin fell to cover her from just below the navel to her ankles. On her ankles and arms she wore slave bracelets, and her toes were painted bright red to match her lips.

"Isn't this camp!" she said with enthusiasm. "Look at this outfit! Pola wore it in one of those naughty-slave-girl-and-the-Arabian-prince things they used to make."

Imre stared at her and felt almost instant sexual arousal. It might all have been outrageously artificial, but the effect on his imagination was real enough. "Camp," he repeated, trying to hide his lust for at least a few minutes.

"And the house. My Lord, have you ever seen anything like this? She's a theosophist, you know. Upstairs there's the most incredible library filled with books on ancient Greeks and Egyptians, and astrology, and magic . . . and every night at seven there's this music—weird music that just starts playing. You can hear it all over the house."

Imre stood there taking it all in. "Who's *she*?" he finally asked.

"Maybeth, of course. Maybeth LaFarge. This is her house, isn't it just the campiest place you've ever seen?"

"Where is she?"

"At work. She's insanely wealthy, you know. And very eccentric. She only drinks champagne and claims only to eat smoked oysters. Can you live on that?"

"I imagine," Imre said, looking at one of the statues. It was quite lewd. "Did you call me to come and take you home, Katrina? What are you doing here?"

"I live here. Maybeth invited me to live here. Isn't it wonderful! And I can wear all these costumes . . . she has trunkloads of them. Of course, she has closets of other clothes. I can wear those too."

"Live here . . . you're going to live here?" He felt somewhat bewildered.

"Yes. I moved out of my apartment yesterday. Maybeth says I'm going to be a star and so I should live like one."

"What about us?" Imre asked somewhat petulantly.

"We'll have plenty of time. Maybeth isn't a prude, you know. Anyway, she's gone a lot."

Imre digested the information and nodded. The house was huge and, in some strange way, stimulating. And the bar would be well-stocked . . . it was certainly an improvement on Katrina's small apartment. "She must like you."

"She says I'm like a daughter to her. I can even drive the cars."

"Where's the bar?" Imre asked.

"Oh, I'll get you something. Just wait here."

Imre watched her as she walked across the room. The slave anklets had little bells on them and they tinkled as she walked barefoot across the tiles, swinging her hips as the satin shimmered in the afternoon sunlight that glowed in from the big window.

She returned with drinks and two hand-carved pipes. "You must try this, Imre. It's quite wonderful . . . a feeling I can't even describe."

He nodded and drank his Scotch first. Then, as she reclined, he sat down next to her and smoked just as she did. He felt light-headed at first, but then intensely aware of the softness of the fur beneath her and of the smoothness of her skin. Gradually he removed her fake armor and slid the satin folds aside. She seemed totally aroused in a dreamy kind of way, and he fondled her for a long while before he was finally able to actually enter her. She moaned and groaned and moved about beneath him like a slithery snake, and finally he achieved satisfaction. They slept for he wasn't sure how long, but when he opened his eyes it was dark outside and the house was filled with the aroma of lilacs and the sound of eerie music. He shook his head and it ached slightly. "Katrina . . ." He shook her gently and she opened her large eyes and smiled and sighed.

"Isn't it wonderful?" she said, pulling the fur cover over her nude body.

Imre nodded and checked his watch. It was after ten P.M. "I have to go, Kat. In fact, I'm late. I was supposed to meet my agent for drinks at nine."

"I'm sure he's still in the bar."

Imre dressed quickly. "I'll call you tomorrow," he said, hurrying away. "Don't get up, I'll let myself out."

Katrina propped herself up on one elbow and watched him as he rushed off.

Quite suddenly Maybeth appeared in the archway. Her long dress shimmered and her turban was held together with a large fake jewel that glistened.

Katrina smiled at her. "I want some more," she said, reaching out to Maybeth. "Please give me some more."

Maybeth smiled. "You both did seem to enjoy yourselves."

Katrina squirmed and rolled over so that the cover fell away. "You could see everything?"

"Yes, everything."

"Can I have more now?"

Maybeth reached out and touched Katrina's throat, then lingered, looking at her white flesh lustfully. "If you're a good girl," she said. "You must learn not to smoke too much opium. We wouldn't want it to interfere with your work, would we?"

Katrina seemed oblivious of Maybeth's advances. She shook her head and whispered, "But I'm not working now."

"True, my dear. How very true."

Quickly Maybeth filled the pipe from a small packet she withdrew from her pocket. Again Katrina lit the pipe and smoked. Her eyes grew distant, glassy, and she laughed lightly. "You're so good to me. . . ."

Seventeen

1

November 1934

*L*ittle round marble tables, straight-backed cane chairs, a wooden coatrack with brass antlers, a tile floor, and above, an ornate but dim chandelier. It was, Renee knew, the congenial world of the Viennese coffeehouse. As Sandy hurriedly pushed her inside, her nostrils were greeted by the scent of rich coffee and the mouth-watering aroma of freshly made pastries. She was also greeted by silence, sound being muted by the great high ceilings and dark wood paneling. But silence was what they sought, or, more correctly, refuge from the chaos in the streets.

"Here, sit down," he urged. "We'll be fine here until the streets are cleared."

Renee slipped into the chair and took her heavy raincoat off. November in Vienna was always cold and rainy. She seemed to notice the chill more too, and thought that her blood was thin from the perpetual summer of Southern California.

She looked around, childhood memories surfacing, though she had been in Vienna only once, and that was only for a few days. Still, there was something familiar . . . The aroma perhaps. Or maybe it was the wallpaper, the deep darkness of the mahogany paneling and furniture, and the high ceilings.

Vaguely she wondered why coffee in America did not smell as it did in Vienna, or why indeed there weren't any coffeehouses. Coffeehouses and Vienna were practically synonymous. Ever since the Turks had left behind sacks of coffee beans after their siege of Vienna in 1683, the coffeehouses had been the center of cultural life in the city.

"It's fortunate that we were right in front of this place," Sandy said, joining her at the table after hanging his coat on the brass antlered coatrack.

"Its horrible out there," Renee agreed. Mobs of students and workers carrying protest signs about the banned Social Democrats had flooded the streets, and their protest had been met violently by club-swinging police and horses ridden into the crowd. Sandy had steered them away from the worst of it, and then he'd pushed her inside the coffeehouse, cursing under his breath about the Nazis and muttering, "We'd better stay here till it's over."

"There's going to be another war," Sandy said as he signaled for the waitress, who, spying their American clothes, came running. "Two coffees," he ordered abruptly.

"Do you really think so?" Renee peered through the window. Demonstrators were being hauled to waiting police wagons lined up in a row by the far curb.

"Without a doubt. The peace treaty created more trouble than existed before. Think of it, Renee. At the end of the Great War fifty million Austrian citizens suddenly acquired new nationalities—whole provinces became independent countries, and others were absorbed into Yugoslavia and Rumania."

"I'm going to one, remember?" It had been agreed that he would remain in Budapest while she went to Kassa, which was now a part of the new nation of Czechoslovakia.

"Perhaps I should go with you."

"I think it's quite safe. I made inquiries, and there have been no difficulties there. I suppose it's quite peaceful because the minority Magyars no longer rule."

"And you really want to go back there?"

"Yes, I want to go. When you first suggested this trip I thought of it as a sentimental journey for you. But I see now that it can also be important to me. I have ghosts that haunt me in Kassa. I have to put them to rest."

The waitress brought the coffees and set them down. Sandy stirred his slowly, then covered her hand with his. "Renee, you've given me seven wonderful years. Your love, your companionship, have been everything to me, everything."

Guilt flooded over her and she fought back tears. Why did he have to say such things? She wanted desperately to be honest with him . . . but what price in pain would he have to pay just so she could rid herself of guilt? No, not now, not here, maybe not ever. She pushed it all aside. "Why are you speaking in the past tense? Don't I make you happy anymore?"

"Of course you do, darling. It's just that I want to say things to you, things I might forget to say before I die."

"I know you're upset by the demonstrations and all the anti-Semitic signs, but don't be morbid." She looked at him hard. When she had married him he had been the picture of health and had looked far younger than his age. But she had to admit he didn't look well now, and he had aged terribly.

"I'm not morbid, Renee. Life is a terminal illness. I'm many years older than you, and I shall simply die sooner."

She looked into his tired eyes. "Did you go to the doctor before we left? Sandy, are you all right?"

"Yes, I had my checkup. Now, now, just because coming back here is making me a little more thoughtful about my mortality and a trifle nostalgic is no reason to think I'm at death's door. Actually I'll be glad to get to Budapest. I never did like Vienna all that much, you know."

"I thought everyone loved Vienna."

"Not really. It's a facade, almost as much of a fake as a Hollywood set. Do you know there are more suicides here than anywhere else in the world? No, I don't like Vienna. The gaiety is forced, and underneath, there is this strange, dramatic, very morbid German temperament. You know the Slavs cry a lot. They cry when it is spring, and the cry in church, and they cry when their wives have babies . . . but the Germans and the Austrians, ah, they have a talent for dramatic death scenes and they play them out in real life."

"My grandfather committed suicide."

"Yes, and the Hungarians too. We Hungarian Jews are not much better, because we are so thoroughly Magyarized, but the Hungarians are quite like the Germans, except they speak a different language. The suicide rate is high in Budapest too."

"Now that you bring it up, my mother was always talking about Mayerling and the suicide of the prince and his mistress—her grandmother thought it quite excitingly dramatic."

"What a wonderful example. Mayerling is almost a national shrine—a wonderful example of just the kind of Germanic sentimentalism I'm talking about. Two star-crossed lovers who make love and then take their lives. . . . How much better to live and go on sleeping together."

She laughed and so did he. "Well, we're leaving here in the morning for Budapest, more familiar ground."

"Are you looking forward to seeing your grandmother?"

"Oh, yes. I've wanted to see her for years, but as you well know, I couldn't convince her to leave Europe. But we've written over the years. She's a very old lady now, seventy-three, you know."

"Is she one of your ghosts?"

"No. But I suppose she can tell me things I'd like to know. No, my only ghost is Janos."

"Tell me, Renee, is Imre like Janos or Béla?"

She was surprised by his question, and a chill passed through her. For years she had avoided all comparisons, but as he grew older it was getting harder. He looked like Béla, as children so often look like their uncles. "Béla, I think. But that's mostly his looks."

"Does that make you ill-at-ease with him?"

"No. He's not calculating like Béla, he's more vulnerable because he's ambitious without the real ability to plot. I worry about him, worry that he'll get into some serious trouble. Imre is not really evil or bad, he's just lazy and, I guess, spoiled."

"You spoiled him, Renee."

"I didn't mean to."

Sandy lifted the lace curtain and peered through the window. "It's safe now. I think we should return to our hotel."

Renee drained her coffee cup and stood up. "You've given me a lot to think about," she said, her mind half on Vienna and half on Imre.

"Well, we shall have a better time in Budapest when you arrive."

"I'll be in Kassa only a few days at the most."

"I'll be waiting," he said, helping her on with her coat.

2

The train sped along through the night, and Renee laid her head back on the lace doily on the plush velvet seat. It was a far cry from the first journey she had taken from Kassa to Budapest; tonight she traveled first class, and tonight she had no fears of being followed by Janos Horvath.

The city she had just left had developed rapidly, and even its name had changed. Now Kassa proudly went by its Slovak name, Košice, and it was the capital of Vychodoslovensky in the Eastern Slovak region of Czechoslovakia. Still, the populace was nervous; they feared they would once again be occupied by Hungary and again the Magyars would rule the majority Slovak population as they had done before.

Renee had arrived in Košice yesterday morning at the same train station from which she had fled with her brothers twenty-two years ago. After looking around the town, which she hadn't remembered as being so pretty, she had hired a car and had driven down the winding dirt roads that followed the river, until she reached what had been the Horvath estate. To her surprise, the once stately mansion, in which she had been born, had been reduced to a ruin. A single wall of the house remained standing; the rest was picked-over rubble. Where once the well-cared-for garden had been, there was now a cornfield. But the woods remained, and so, she discovered, did the ruin of the old chapel where she had been conceived.

After some time, Renee found an old Slovak peasant willing to talk. He sat in front of his fire and roasted meat on a long stick, not looking at her, but staring into the flames as if in their crackling center he could see into the past.

"What happened to Count Horvath—Janos Horvath—who lived in that house?" she asked.

"Janos Horvath." The old man repeated the name and spat on the ground. "An evil person," he said finally. "Evil."

"Yes, but what happened to him?"

The old man shrugged. "He was hanged."

"But why?" Renee persisted.

"He raped so many of our women—four young girls and some older ones. After the war there was a revolt, we took him. We hanged him from that tree . . . see, the big one right over there."

Renee had stared at the tree, and in her mind she could almost see Janos hanging from it, stripped of his lands and his wealth, punished for what he was, a sadist and a rapist.

"No one came to his defense," the old man said. "Some people were killed for no reason, and many were chased away, but his death was justice."

"Yes, justice," Renee agreed. She thanked the old man and he held out his hand for money. She gave him some coins and then returned to her car and drove back to Košice to wait for the next train back to Budapest.

She opened her eyes and looked out the window of the train. It was almost daylight, and the train was running next to the river, past farms and homes, chapels and fields filled with row on row of neatly stacked hay. Ahead, a glow on the horizon announced the rising sun. Her ghost had been laid to rest. Janos Horvath was no more.

3

Countess Anna Maria Bodnar lived comfortably in a four-room suite on the fifth floor of one of Budapest's fine old hotels, the Vadászkurt on Turr Istvan Street. It was a hotel long frequented by the aristocracy and by large landowners. It was also restricted; no Jew could live there or even rent a room for the night. That fact bothered Renee, but she was quite certain her grandmother was unaware of such matters, even though she knew Renee was half-Jewish. As Sandor had so kindly put it, "If you live in a world where Jews never cross your path, you are not likely to even understand such injustices. Your grandmother is an old woman living out her life in a world that no longer exists. She couldn't change anything even if she moved out in protest, so why disturb her and ruin your visit by mentioning the fact that Jews cannot rent a room in the place where she lives?" Reluctantly Renee agreed. Certainly her grandmother knew she was half-Jewish, and she was quite certain her grandmother was not the least bit anti-Semitic. She was, like so many women of her generation, simply ignorant of such matters.

And so Renee had ventured into the world of yesteryear. Her grandmother had furnished her little suite with her own furniture and filled it with mementos of her travels with her second husband, Count József Bodnar, who had died two years ago. Her title meant nothing now, but out of respect people always called her "Countess," and certainly she was far from poor. József had left her three residences, antiques, jewelry, and considerable cash. She had sold the residences and many of the antiques; the rest she used to furnish her rooms. She lived as she did because she did not need more, and she liked the hotel because the staff cared for her and she was close to all the finer shops on Vaci Street. She was also near the museum and the theater.

All her life Anna had eaten carefully, taken care of herself, and dressed well. The result was that at seventy-three she was nothing less than elegant, the kind of woman people turned to look at and the kind with whom they enjoyed talking. Her once stunning blond hair was now snow white, but still thick. She had not cut it in fifteen years, and wore it wrapped in a huge bun pinned on top of her head. Her skin was relatively smooth, though she had not escaped the lines of age. Still, it had a delicate tissue-paper quality, and was clear and unblemished. Her startling blue eyes were still lovely, and her body was slim, in part due to the fact that she walked a few miles each day, rain or shine, in summer or in winter, and once a year she traveled to Baden Baden to take the waters, have treatments from masseurs, and to submerge herself in the therapeutic mud baths.

On this particular day she wore a stunning long-sleeved blue crepe dress that fell to her trim ankles. Around her neck she wore four strands of pearls and four gold necklaces. On her arms she wore matching bracelets, and on her fingers four individually designed rings. Her wedding ring was most unusual. It was actually two rings—one of heavy gold and the other heavy gold with a pearl-and-sapphire setting. The pearl was huge and the sapphire a full two carats. But the two rings fit one inside the other so that they appeared to be one ring with a double band. The outer ring actually formed a full frame around the ring with the settings, so that it seemed the pearl and the sapphire were prisoners in a gold triangle.

She opened the door and stared at Renee; then a smile covered her face and she held out her hands in greeting and in an invitation for a hug. "Oh! You look just like your mother! It's amazing! Truly amazing!"

Renee stepped into the room and hugged her grandmother tightly.

When they separated, they were both crying and Anna was ushering her inside, trying to find her own voice.

"I should have come much sooner," Renee said, sitting down. "I wish now I had."

"I should have come to you when you wrote so long ago and asked me. But József couldn't have made the trip then, and I wouldn't leave him."

"You could come home with me now."

Anna shook her head. "Oh, no. I couldn't leave my things. And what would I do with Franz József?"

"Franz József?"

Anna laughed lightly. "Oh, there he is. See, I'm quite all right."

Renee looked down to see a little black poodle whose tail seemed to be wagging him. "Franz József, I presume?" She leaned over and patted him and he jumped up beside her on the sofa.

"He's terribly spoiled," Anna said with an expressive wave of her hand. "Here, dear, I did make some tea." She indicated the beautiful Bavarian china tea set on the round leather-topped coffee table. Delicate little silver spoons lay next to the china cups and saucers, and on the table there was also a Slovakian crystal cigarette box filled with long gold-tipped cigarettes.

"Would you like me to pour?" Renee asked.

"Yes, that would be nice. My hands aren't as steady as they once were."

Renee poured the tea and handed her grandmother one of the cups. She took it then set it down on the table next to her chair. "We haven't said a dozen words to one another yet, but it's as if I've always known you, Renee. Of course, we've written. I've enjoyed your letters so much. Your Hungarian is still very good. I'm surprised."

"There are quite a few expatriate Hungarians in Hollywood. I get a lot of practice."

"Your mother was good with languages. She was tutored in several, but not taught to read, just to speak. Your grandfather didn't believe girls needed to know how to read. My father was the same. I learned, though. I had a tutor come three times a week for the first year after the count and I were married. I could read a little before that, but in my day hardly any women were taught to read."

"Mama read," Renee said. "She kept it a secret, but György taught her and Konnie got her books. She could read English too. She learned that from my father."

"What a surprise that was for me! Margaret had a

secret life I didn't dream she had. It makes me happy to know that. But I should have done more to stop her being married to that monster."

"He's dead," Renee told her. "I went back to Kassa and I found out he'd been hanged."

"Too good for him," Anna said, arching her brow. "Far too good. But let's discuss something pleasant. Let's discuss you. I'm so proud! To think that you're in the world of fashion! It was a dream I had and a dream your mother had—we always loved clothes. I still do. I walk on Vaci Street almost every day. Such wonderful, wonderful shoe salons! You should go to Kovacs Bertalon. And milliners! Have you been to Frank Irma?"

"No, I am going shopping tomorrow before I leave."

"Yes, yes, you must. Perhaps I could go with you."

"Of course we can meet. I'd love it," Renee answered.

"I always wanted to shop with Margaret, but your grandfather never wanted me to bring her along. Your mother knew a lot about fashion, though. She made some quite delightful dresses from material in my mother's trunk."

"Mother taught me so much. She was talented, and finally she had a very good business in Boston."

"Tell me everything, Renee. Tell me about your life, about your brothers, your husband, your lovers if you've had any . . . tell me about your father. I want to know everything."

Renee sipped her tea and tried to think where to begin. "Do you remember Irina, the upstairs maid?"

"I certainly do."

"Then I shall begin with her," Renee said with a smile. "Yes, Irina is a good place to start the story."

4

The private glassed-in terrace of Renee and Sandy's suite in the Ritz overlooked the Korzó, beyond which the Danube and the two bridges that spanned it were clearly visible. The closest of the two bridges was alive with lights that shimmered in the dark swirling waters below.

They sat at a small table facing each other and sipping dark strong coffee.

"I'm glad we had dinner brought up tonight. I was much too tired to dress for the dining room."

Renee laughed. "Oh, you just didn't want to spend another evening with those bogus Gypsy violinists stomping about while you were eating."

"You mean they're not real Gypsies?"

"You know perfectly well they aren't. Gypsies are so prejudiced against they couldn't get near a hotel this expensive."

"Jews and Gypsies. They're going to kill us all."

"It is oppressive. I'll be glad to get home."

"Are you certain you want to leave tomorrow?"

"I have to get back. How long are you going to stay?"

"No longer than you. I've decided to go to Paris in the morning when you leave for Germany. I don't want to stay here or go to Austria or Germany. My friends are either dead or moved away. I find the oppression more depressing now that I've spent so many years without it. No, I want to go to Paris, maybe Spain, then I'll come home. Two months' longer at the most."

"It seems unfair that you wanted to come here and I've been the only one to find my past."

"Perhaps I really just wanted to get you out of Los Angeles. Perhaps I didn't really want to come to Hungary at all."

He suddenly looked quite serious, and Renee was taken aback. "Is that true?" she asked, frowning.

"In a way, yes, it is. Oh, I wanted to come back to Europe one more time. And by going to Paris and Spain I'm following a path I followed long ago. When you start to get old, really old, you want to return to all the places you've been because you can't remember them. Then, when you get there they're so changed it doesn't matter. Still, I want to make the trip."

"You're not really old." She wondered if this conversation were going to take up where the one they had had in Vienna left off—he kept bringing up his age and talking about dying. It worried her.

"I am, Renee. I am old, but I'm not blind."

Renee felt the blood draining from her face, and her hands were growing cold. He did seem very serious. Did he know about Aaron? Had someone told him? She hated herself for not telling him herself.

"Renee, please don't look so stricken. Let me speak. I know women as some men do not. In my life I have been blessed with two women, both beautiful, both loving, both wonderful. And both gave me great happiness. When a woman is in love, she radiates—she has a kind of raw sexual appeal that says, 'I know I'm wanted and desirable because I love and am loved.' You, Renee, have had that glow since July. You have also had guilt, and, I'm sure, knowing you as I do, it is a terrible guilt, because you are an honest woman."

Renee covered her face with her hands. Tears were flowing, but they were silent and she trembled. "No, no, I'm not honest, and I'm a coward."

"Please, Renee, there's no need to cry. Look at me. Do I look as if I'm going to jump off the balcony?"

"I can't help it. I do love you. I do love you."

"I know that. I also know you have given me great happiness. I love you too, Renee, and that is why, in my own way, I am happy for you. You're still young, I know you want children. You may feel guilty about your 'affair,' but I too am guilty. I should have told you I couldn't have children."

"But you had two sons—"

"I said my sons were killed, I did not say my *adopted* sons. No, I knew I was sterile and I didn't tell you. At the time, I didn't think you wanted children. Now I see what a terrible thing I did."

She shook her head. "Not as terrible as what I've done."

"Renee, you gave me your love and your youth. I'll always love you. But it's time for me to give you your freedom and the opportunity to fulfill yourself."

Renee took a deep breath. Her period was two weeks

late, and while she had refused to think about it, she was quite certain she was pregnant. She let her hands drop to her lap and looked across the table into his eyes. "I didn't mean for it to happen—I didn't look for it."

"I'm certain you didn't."

"I began to tell you a hundred times, and couldn't, Sandy. I kept telling myself it would burn itself out. But I do love him and I do love you."

Sandy smiled at her and reached across the table to take her hand. "Ah, it's so painful to be young. I'm glad it's over. When I get home I'll go to a lawyer. Everything will be fine, Renee. Please, let me do this. Don't try to stop me with your misguided loyalty. I only want to know this: is he a good man? Will he always be good to you?"

"Oh, yes. I knew Aaron before you. We were both very young. He came back into my life, and I couldn't control it—I tried, I really did try."

"I know. I could see it in your eyes and feel it when I held you. I wanted you to tell me, and then I decided that I was asking too much. So I thought if I got you away, then we could talk, be ourselves. I thought I could confess my sin and you could confess yours. I love you, my darling, and I want you to be happy with a man your own age, a man who can give you what I could not."

Renee tried to smile, but his kindness made her sad. "I wish you were coming home with me," she said slowly.

"I'll always be your friend, Renee. Always."

She nodded and squeezed his hand. "And I yours," she promised.

5

December 16, 1934

Max, the hollow-cheeked servant with skin the color of flour, silently guided Imre through the house and out a side door into a virtual jungle of a patio surrounded by a wall the same color as the house. It was here that the eucalyptus tree jutted upward, giving the impression that it grew inside the mansion. In the center of the lush greenery was a small stone patio, and on it, a table laden with food. Around this inlaid stone oasis a tangle of flowering bushes, weeds, and small shrubs fought for life and sunlight.

"Ah, it is the young aristocrat," Maybeth said with a flourish. "Do come in and join us for brunch in the side garden."

Imre bowed slightly and took Maybeth's proffered hand, kissing it in the old European fashion.

On this Sunday morning in mid-December, Maybeth was attired in a flowing red silk caftan with a matching turban. Around her neck, yards of colored beads swung loosely, and, Imre noted, four large diamond rings adorned her fingers.

She beckoned him to sit down and motioned an invitation to partake of the food she had laid out. The table was laden with exotic fruits, bottles of champagne, sparkling crystal glasses, and a plate of Maybeth's traditional smoked oysters. "I imagine you've come to call on Katrina," she said, smiling.

Imre returned the smile, and then, though he didn't really mean it, told her, "I came to see both of you."

"Katrina will join us shortly."

Imre's eyes recorded the details of the garden. Its cracking pink walls were covered with creeping vines of flowering bougainvillea. In one corner there was a stone statue depicting entwined human forms grotesquely arranged so that each was penetrating the other in some sexual way. He frowned at it in fascination—no orifice of the human body seemed to have been ignored by the depraved artist.

"Ah, you like my little statue," Maybeth observed in her deep syrupy voice.

"It's quite unusual," Imre returned. It was a comment he reserved for all artwork he wasn't certain he liked, and while this one was biologically interesting, its appeal ended there.

"It's a masterpiece of erotica. From the Kama Sutra, you know. I bought it on my last trip to India."

"Really, it's extraordinary," Imre added, trying to sound sincere. Then, hoping to change the subject, "That's a stunning gown you're wearing."

"It's a caftan. They're quite popular throughout the Levant, though most are not as ornate as this one. My dear friend the late Madam Tingley of the Point Loma Theosophical Society introduced me to the freedom of the caftan. One doesn't have to wear much underneath them."

Imre smiled weakly; the thought of Maybeth's nude body beneath her flowing caftan was something less than arousing.

At that moment Katrina slipped through the side door and into the garden. Her costume was yet another tribute to early films; it was both outlandish and sexually suggestive. Her long red hair was again loose and fell to slightly below her shoulders. Her dress was skintight gold lamé with two deep side slits to mid-thigh. The gown was sleeveless, and on both Katrina's arms gold serpent bracelets wound about to just below the elbow, where their little snake heads protruded out, great green glass stones serving as eyes. She also wore a gold lamé headband, from the front of which a single peacock feather pointed upward, its eye staring outward like some sort of otherworldly periscope.

"Do open the champagne for us, Imre," Maybeth said.

Imre took the bottle and carefully began to undo the tiny wires that held the cork. He wondered vaguely if Maybeth were going to be home all day or if, as was usually the case, she was going to leave them alone.

"Tell me, Imre, when is your sister coming back? In time to do the costumes for *Heartache,* I imagine."

"She arrived yesterday," he replied, still unable to take his eyes off Katrina, who had casually sat down at the table and allowed the slit in her skirt to fall open, revealing the full length of one shapely leg.

Maybeth held out her goblet and Imre filled it nearly to the brim, then filled Katrina's and his own.

"Yesterday? Well, I suppose she'll have enough time. I've been working on our film for over six weeks, and they do come out at the same time."

"And will both be contenders for awards," Katrina put in.

"How true," Maybeth murmured. She sipped her champagne and leaned back in her chair, simultaneously taking one of the oysters.

Imre carefully opened a pomegranate and began eating it, while Katrina simply sipped her champagne. Imre watched her with growing desire. Her eyes were wide and luminous, as if she were hiding some secret, and he thought that he had never seen her look so vulnerable, so soft.

Maybeth popped several more oysters into her mouth and drained her glass. "I'm going to the studio," she announced. "I have a great deal to do this week and I need a head start."

"Must you go now?" Imre asked even though he wished her gone.

"I'm afraid so. Now, you children have a good time. Oh, and if you want to smoke, have Max bring you a pipe."

"I'd like to smoke now," Katrina said softly.

Maybeth smiled indulgently at her and clapped her hands. Max appeared almost instantly, pipes in hand.

Maybeth whirled around and followed her servant through the doors. In moments she was seated in her car, headed down the winding road. Pity to miss watching today, she thought, but there would be other days and as many opportunities as she cared to create. Dear Katrina was quite firmly now in her control—so much so that she now considered allowing Max to make love to her one night simply because it might be amusing. But enough for now, she thought, banishing all pleasant thoughts of Katrina and concentrating on her mission. So, Renee was back. Well, having been away a month, she would no doubt want to see her lover almost immediately. Opportunity was at hand. One certain way to win the award she so coveted was to eliminate her only real competition. And that, she reasoned, could be accomplished by making Renee so miserable that she couldn't work. And even if somehow she did manage to win the award, Renee's marriage would be ruined. In Maybeth's mind the little bitch upstart designer had had it too easy. Rich husbands, influential uncles, and handsome lovers were more than any one woman deserved, and Maybeth set herself to seeing that Renee could not easily continue.

6

December 17, 1934

Aaron lived in a sprawling bungalow court on Normandie and Sunset next to a restaurant built in the shape of a Viking ship with a voluptuous naked green mermaid carved on its bow. Obliged to park her car in front of the restaurant, Renee hurried down the sidewalk as torrents of rain whipped by the wind fell in sheets and dripped from the two-foot-high breasts of the mermaid above.

She ran into the court and searched the numbers, seeing number twelve toward the end of the row on one side. She darted for the shelter of the overhang on the porch and rang the chimes. It seemed no one in California had an ordinary door buzzer. Instead they all had chimes that hit three or four notes on the musical scale. Aaron's chimes ended on a high note rather than the usual low one.

He opened the door smiling. "You're soaked," he said needlessly as he pulled her inside.

Her hair was wet and fell in long ringlets, with some of the shorter strands clinging to her forehead. She collapsed her dripping umbrella and slipped off her blue raincoat. "It's coming down sideways," she said by way of explanation. "But I'm mostly dry under my coat. Just my hair and the top of my sweater are wet."

"God, it's good to see you." He held her hands and looked at her longingly. "I missed you."

"I missed you too."

He took her in his arms and kissed her, a long passionate kiss. She leaned against him. There were a thousand things to say, to tell him. But for the moment she was satisfied just to be in his arms. Then, after a few minutes, he let her go.

She smiled. "I've never been to your lair before. Are you going to invite me in, or must we stay in the hall?"

He laughed. "This way."

She followed him into his living room. It was of medium size, but cluttered with dozens of publications, hundreds of books, and not a few dirty coffee cups and overflowing ashtrays.

"My candidate lost the election," he said, pointing to a publication with Upton Sinclair's picture on it.

"The forces of evil strike again," she remarked. "Be grateful, Aaron. Here he just lost an election. In Austria he would have been put in jail."

"Are we going to discuss politics?" he asked, looking at her hungrily.

"You started it."

"I didn't want to ask the question I really want to ask. I'm afraid of the reason why you're here. Afraid you've come to tell me it's over."

She looked up at him steadily. "No, it's not over. Sandy knows. I told him everything and he was wonderful. He's agreed to give me a divorce."

Aaron let out his breath. "Oh, Renee." He sat down on the sofa and pulled her down next to him and took her in his arms. "I don't know what to say or how to say it. I really love you, always have."

She leaned against his shoulder. "I love you too."

"I know it was hard for you. I know the kind of person you are."

"He made it easy. He already seemed to know."

"And how do you feel?"

"Very sad. He'll always be my friend, Aaron."

"I know that. Look, let's go out for a quiet little dinner and then come back here. There's no need to sneak around now, no need to hide."

"That much I'm glad about."

"Aren't you glad that we can spend the rest of our lives together?"

"Yes, you know I am. It's just that all the turmoil has to settle."

"I understand. Come on, I know a great little place where we can get some really fine Italian food and a good bottle of wine."

"Can't we eat here? It's pouring out."

"I've got the wine. I suppose I could rustle up an omelet."

"I'll help you."

They walked to his small kitchen, and surprisingly, it was clean and neat, quite unlike the living room. She perched on a high stool while he mixed the eggs and tossed a salad. She set the dinette table and opened the wine while he brought the omelet and the salad.

They ate slowly, talking about their work and for the present avoiding talk of their future. Renee kept silent about the possibility of being pregnant. She was not, after all, completely certain.

"You could live in a larger place. Why do you live here?"

"I don't need a larger place. All the money my father left me is invested in other businesses or real estate. I've got a great car, but apart from that I guess I'm just not a big spender."

"A lot of your clients can't pay you, can they?"

"Most of them. I wanted to be a lawyer so I could help people take advantage of their rights. I was born rich. I don't actually have to make money in my profession."

"So you don't charge them anything?"

"I charge them. If I didn't they'd think it was charity, and most of the people I defend are pretty proud. I charge them what they can afford. Last week I had a kid from Oklahoma. He was hauled in on a pretty minor charge—stealing oranges. The family was really up against it. But his mother insisted on paying me, so I had her do all my mending."

Renee smiled at him. "You're even nicer than I thought."

"What are you going to do about your house?" he suddenly asked.

Renee shrugged. "It's Sandy's house. I'll get a small apartment for a while, or perhaps go and stay with my father. He has lots of room because Abraham is living in San Francisco now. Of course, Imre is there . . . Oh, I don't know. I'll have to think about it."

"Will you stay here tonight?"

Renee nodded. "Yes. I hate being in the house alone. Especially now."

"We could move in together right away."

"No. I'd rather wait for the divorce. It won't take long. Sandy says we can go to Nevada, it's fast there."

"Six weeks."

"How do you know?"

"I'm a lawyer, remember?"

She laughed lightly and stood up, stretching. Then she cleared the table and together they washed the dishes.

As Aaron dried the frying pan and put it away, he said, "Well, that's it. Tell me, do you still like to dance?"

"Yes, but I'm out of practice."

"Let's get back in practice." He turned off the light in the little kitchen and they returned to the living room. He put some records on the Victrola and they began dancing to the crooning of Rudy Vallee.

Renee leaned against him as they moved slowly around the room. "I'm glad I'm staying here tonight," she said softly. "Can I tell you something silly?"

"You can tell me anything you want."

"Well, now that we don't have to sneak around anymore, I keep having this feeling I'm being watched."

"I'm sure all the normal men in this city watch you."

She shook her head. "I knew you'd tease me. That's not what I meant."

"I know. I'm sorry. I think it's just a carryover from your previous feeling of guilt."

"I suppose."

"How about a brandy?"

"Yes, please."

Aaron poured them each a brandy. Renee lay on the sofa and he sat beside her on the floor.

"It's strange being with you like this," she said after a

bit. "I feel so relaxed now, as if this great weight had been taken away."

He set his glass down and kissed her cheek, then her lips, feeling her move her mouth beneath his, responding to the gentle pressure of his kiss. "Renee, you're beautiful and I love you."

She smiled at him sleepily and ran her hand through his thick hair. He kissed her hair, her neck, her ears, and she moaned softly and returned his kisses as he undid her blouse and pushed the thin straps of her silk slip away. He kissed her cleavage and undid her bra. She in turn unbuttoned his shirt and ran her hands through the hair on his chest. In a few minutes they were both naked, caressing each other and kissing passionately as they lay on the sofa. She was lying flat on her back, her head slightly turned, her eyes closed. He was on his knees straddling her body. His hands covered her breasts and he was toying with her nipples when suddenly the door burst open and blinding lights filled the room.

Renee jolted up and screamed as she caught sight of two strange men. At that moment another flash of light almost blinded her.

"Fuck!" Aaron shouted. Naked, he sprang from his position and moved toward the door, but he stopped at the threshold, suddenly seeming to remember that he was nude.

Down the path to the street the men could he heard running; then car doors slammed and a car screeched away into the night. Renee covered her face with her hands, disbelieving that what had taken seconds could so completely shatter her.

Aaron had grabbed a robe and was now outside in the rain. He returned soaked. "Damn, I couldn't get the license number," he cursed.

Renee quickly pulled on her skirt, then her blouse. "Who were they?" she asked. "Why were they doing that? What were they doing here?" She was beginning to shake. "Were those flashbulbs? My God, they have pictures!"

Aaron slumped into the chair. "Damn!" he muttered.

Then he reached for the brandy bottle and poured himself a good-size shot. "Here, you better have some too," he suggested.

"I don't understand," Renee said, leaning back. "Why?"

"They're sleazy private eyes. They specialize in getting pictures for divorce hearings . . . adultery has to be proved. They follow people around till they're pretty sure what's going on—then bang!" He shook his head in disgust. "I guess Sandy isn't going to quite *give* you a divorce, Renee."

Renee shook her head. "No. It wasn't Sandy. First of all, he wouldn't do such a terrible thing, and second, he's still in Europe and won't be back for at least six weeks."

"You're certain?"

"Oh, Aaron, I know Sandy. Believe me, he wouldn't do anything like this."

"Then, my dear, one of us, and I suspect it's you, is being set up for blackmail."

"Blackmail?"

"Either that or someone who doesn't know either you or Sandy very well thinks he's going to ruin your marriage." He smiled and shook his head. "Given the fact that Sandy already knows about us and has agreed to a divorce, I guess the 'someone' is going to be pretty disappointed."

"It's still horrible. It's the worst kind of invasion of privacy. And who knows where the pictures might turn up? God, who hates me so much?"

"Who knows about us? I mean, I suppose there might be rumors, but who actually knows about me?"

Renee stared at him as the enormity of his question sank in. "Sandy knows," she said slowly. "Miklós," and then almost inaudibly, "and Imre."

Eighteen

1

January 5, 1935

*"I*t is a black, *dark* deed you do, sir!
"It is a *black,* dark deed you do, sir!
"It is a black, dark *deed* you do, sir!"

As Imre drove along the twisted canyon road, he repeated and repeated the line, giving it a slightly different emphasis each time, until finally he settled on giving the word "dark" the greatest importance. "Yes, that's the way," he said aloud. He'd been working with his acting coach all afternoon, and then, after dinner, they had continued till quite late. Now it was, he guessed, around nine. Not too late to drop in on Katrina and at the same time relax his jagged nerves with one of Maybeth's pipes.

He reached across to the bottle on the empty seat beside him and took a long swig of whiskey, then leaned over the wheel and cursed to himself. He would no doubt have to spend the night at Maybeth's—if indeed he got there. A thick coast fog was rolling in, and it hovered low on the road and clung to the trees. Such fogs were common this time of year. One minute it was clear, the next you couldn't even see the front of the car.

With relief Imre saw the secluded drive ahead, but he cursed when he saw that the tall wrought-iron gates were closed. He brought the car to a halt and climbed out.

Shivering in the night air, he walked to the gate and gave one tug before he saw that a great heavy chain was wrapped around both, locking them closed against intruders. "What the hell," he muttered, kicking the gate, to no avail.

Hands in his pockets, Imre looked around helplessly. The fog was getting thicker. "What the hell?" he said again. Then, without further thought, he climbed back in the car and parked it neatly close to the gate where it could not be hit by a passing vehicle. First taking another good swig of whiskey, he climbed out and began to walk through the brush along the outside of the wall.

"There we are," he said brightly as he spied a eucalyptus tree with reasonably low branches. He grabbed hold of one of the branches and swung himself up into the tree, then carefully moved from the tree to the top of the wall. For a few minutes he sat there looking down on the soft earth. It was a mere ten feet, nothing but a short two-foot drop if he hung by his arms. He did so, and tumbled to the ground in momentary disarray. He stumbled to his feet and brushed himself off, staggering a little drunkenly toward the house. As he approached, he could see that the front of the house was dark but that the glassed-in solarium that hung off the back was ablaze with an eerie green light. He smiled and chuckled. Maybeth was such a character. How like her to have made the lighting green. Christ, her whole house looked like the prop room of a studio. It was quite obvious that over the years she had brought home every piece of junk that had caught her fancy. Not only were her closets bulging with sexy costumes, but Aladdin's fake lamp was in her living room, there were half a dozen stuffed snakes from *The Lady and the Serpents,* a loincloth from a Tarzan film lay across her coffee table, and then there was his absolute favorite—a glass-jewel-encrusted replica of Excalibur, King Arthur's sword. Imre reached the front door and knocked lightly. When no one answered, he turned the knob and walked in, removing his shoes in the hall as Maybeth required. The front room was in utter darkness, and he picked his way through it to the room that opened onto the solarium, but when he came to that room he stopped short and stared, his mouth open as through his own drunken haze he tried to grasp what danced before his eyes.

The panels all along the far wall had been opened. He hadn't dreamed they'd open. And what he saw, in effect, was a wall of glass that looked directly into the solarium. He shook his head as if to clear it. What he saw meant that the wall of mirrors in the solarium was in fact one-way glass!

Imre blinked and again shook his head. On the other side of the glass he could quite clearly see a naked Katrina, and above her, an equally naked Max, his blue-white skin even more bizarre in the green light. "Shit," he muttered under his breath, and then was startled by Maybeth's sudden croak of surprise. He hadn't seen her in the darkness standing to one side, but there she was, clearly watching Katrina and Max.

"What the hell is going on?" he shouted. His own voice seemed loud to him, but neither Max nor Katrina seemed to hear.

"What are you doing here?" Maybeth demanded, a sharp edge of anger in her deep voice.

Imre stared at her. She was watching. She had certainly watched him and Katrina as well. He felt himself begin to shake with rage. "You filthy old whore!" he swore. "You fucking dirty old degenerate!"

Maybeth sprang toward him, her long nails ready to scratch him. "Out of my house! Out! Out!"

Imre backed up to the wall, and as he turned, his hand folded around the handle of Excalibur, which he tugged on. It came loose instantly and he stood holding it as if he were onstage. He mimicked Doug Fairbanks, leaping toward her and shouting, "*En garde,* you old witch!"

"You're drunk! Get out!"

Drunk? Out? His face was burning with indignation and anger at the fact that Maybeth had watched him and Katrina. And he was furious at the sight before him—Katrina and Max wrapped in one another's arms. He was beginning to perspire in the hothouse atmosphere. "How dare you call me drunk, you perverted old bitch!" He charged with the sword and Maybeth screamed as it penetrated, pinning her like a butterfly to the Chinese silk screen she was standing in front of.

Imre pulled the sword out and her scrawny body crumpled to the floor. He turned and ran, sword forward, to the door of the solarium, and pausing for dramatic effect, kicked the door open. "Get off her!" he shouted as he charged toward Max. But Max rolled away, and so great was Imre's momentum that he couldn't stop. The sword penetrated Katrina, who made no sound as she stared glassy-eyed at him. For a long moment Imre stood stock-still and stared at her. In the distance Max's retreating footsteps echoed as he ran away, out of the house, and into the foggy night.

Imre stood frozen, staring at Katrina, at the blood, and at the fake jewels in Excalibur's handle as they sparkled in the eerie green light. Then tears began to flood his eyes and run down his cheeks. "It is a *black,* dark deed you do, sir," he muttered as he sank to the floor sobbing.

Imre sat for over an hour; then in the distance he heard sirens on the coast highway. He couldn't move. His head ached and he was sick to his stomach. He wanted nothing so much as for the studio lights to go off. It was time, he thought, to go to black.

2

BIZARRE MURDER ROCKS MOVIE COMMUNITY, the black headline on the *Times* read, while the industry paper, in typical fashion, reduced the events to a series of short rhyming couplets, contenting itself with, "Cad's Stabs Hex Sex," which, roughly translated, meant "a cad had stabbed a girl to stop her from having sex."

Renee sat ashen-faced in the office of Captain of Detectives William Henderson in the Beverly Hills police station. Aaron stood by the side of the chair, shifting his weight now and again from one foot to the other.

"I won't try to fool you," Henderson said matter-of-factly. "I've been here quite a while and this is, without question, one of the most lurid crimes I've ever dealt with."

"It isn't possible that the other person, that man who ran way, did it?" Renee asked.

Henderson shook his head. "Your brother is the murderer."

"Alleged murderer," Aaron corrected. "He hasn't been tried yet."

"All right, alleged, counselor. But he *will* be convicted."

"May I ask what his story is?" Aaron prodded.

"Sure. He says he doesn't remember anything. He says he was drunk, and he certainly was. He's still sleeping it off, as a matter of a fact."

Aaron nodded. "I'll be talking to him myself later this morning."

"I can tell you the girl was blotto—an opium addict. I can also tell you that house is full of weird things. Hell, in one of the rooms upstairs we found a bunch of live snakes, big fat diamond-headed things. Had to call a fella from the university to come and get them. He said they were cobras." Henderson shook his head in disgust. "In my considered opinion, the other victim, Maybeth LaFarge, was a real cuckoo clock. And she was also the supplier of the opium. We found about a pound of it in her room."

"What about the servant?"

"Scared out of his tree. He seems to have been coupling with the girl when this fellow—your brother—charged in, sword in hand."

Renee bit her lip and looked up pleadingly at Aaron. "We have to help him," she said softly.

Aaron touched her shoulder reassuringly. "I'll do everything I can, Renee."

"Frankly, I'd go for temporary insanity. Given the circumstances, I'd say none of them was what you'd call normal, though sometimes, working here, I wonder what normal is. Hell, last year we had this doctor who belonged to some witches' club, and it was reported they were making human sacrifices. Turned out to be pigs, though. Still, you can't go around building altars and sacrificing pigs by candlelight. Not in Beverly Hills, anyway."

"I think I'll take Mrs. Lipton home now," Aaron said, not wanting to hear any more stories of strange crimes.

"This is a nightmare," she whispered as he led her down the hall.

"Yeah. Belá Lugosi should be staring in it. I think I'll take you home and then go out and visit the scene of the crime before seeing Imre."

They reached the gleaming front steps of the police station, and in unison a mass of reporters climbed out of their cars and converged on them, flashbulbs popping loudly.

"Why did your brother kill Maybeth LaFarge?"

"What was he doing at Miss LaFarge's home?"

"Was he in love with the girl?"

"Is your brother an opium addict?"

"Mrs. Lipton has no comment at this time," Aaron said authoritatively. "C'mon, boys—"

Aaron was interrupted when someone shouted cheerfully, "Was your brother a member of a serpent-worshiping cult?"

Renee covered her face with her hands to shield her eyes from the flashbulbs, and Aaron helped her thread her way through the crowd of shouting onlookers and across the street to where his car was parked. He opened the door and Renee gratefully climbed inside. He shoved his way to his side of the car and then hurriedly got in and pushed the starter button. In a moment they were on the highway, though several cars full of reporters followed.

"I can lose them," Aaron said. "Then I'll take you home."

"They'll wait for me there. Why don't you take me to the Hollywood Hotel? I can send for my things."

"Good idea," he agreed. "I'll come there after I've been out to Maybeth's and after I've talked to Imre."

"Oh, God. Zoltan! I'll have to call him right away. He'll hear it on the news."

"Yes, you better get in touch with him."

"Oh, Aaron, I'm so sorry to involve you in all this. It's so awful, I can't believe it."

"I'm a lawyer. Do you still think Imre had those photos taken?"

"No. I think perhaps he told Katrina about us and she told Maybeth. Maybeth always hated me. I think she may have been trying to cause me trouble."

"Sounds logical. Tell me, Renee, did Imre take opium?"

"Not that I know of. He drank too much, though."

He suddenly turned the car, then turned again. "Hold on. I'm going to lose our friends."

For a time he made one sharp turn after another, then raced through a traffic light and pulled into a private driveway. The one car that remained on his tail stopped in front and Aaron zoomed out the back, onto a side street. "That's it," he said finally. "The jerk didn't realize that driveway went out onto this street."

"How did you know?" she asked.

"An acquaintance of mine lives there."

In a few minutes they were back in the flow of traffic and shortly he pulled up in front of the Hollywood Hotel. "What name are you going to register under?"

Renee looked at him and smiled weakly. "How about yours?"

He grinned at her and kissed her on the cheek. "Good, at least I won't forget it."

3

"The place gives me the heebie-jeebies," the police guard said as he escorted Aaron into the house. "Jesus, look at all this one-way glass. They were doing it out there—the doped-up girl and the servant—and it looks like the old lady was watching it all. In fact, she may have used this place to make some pictures. She's got a filing cabinet full of obscene photographs upstairs, stuff you wouldn't believe! I mean, hell, I haven't seen so many bodies tangled together since that movie about the volcano exploding on that island, or whatever it was. And they at least had some clothes on."

"She was a voyeur," Aaron concluded.

"Naw, I don't think she traveled much. Too busy taking pictures."

Aaron suppressed his laugh. "No, I mean she got sexual pleasure from watching others. That's 'voyeur,' not 'voyager.' "

"Oh, yeah. Well, I guess she was one of those, all right. My wife says everyone in Hollywood is weird and that I should transfer to Long Beach because everyone in Long Beach is from Iowa and they don't commit sex crimes."

"There's some truth in that," Aaron agreed. There were twenty thousand Iowans in Long Beach and to his knowledge the vast majority were over sixty-five—that alone seemed to negate the possibility of too many sexual crimes.

"Can I go upstairs?"

"Sure, just don't move anything."

"I wouldn't dream of it."

Aaron climbed the winding stairs to the left turret. He'd been warned not to go to the other, since all the snakes had not yet been removed. He went directly to the filing cabinet and hurriedly looked at some of the pictures. Five pictures down, and he whistled through his teeth. "Voyeur" hardly covered Maybeth LaFarge. He didn't waste any more time looking at assorted couples having sex; he went directly for the negatives, and right in front he found the ones of him and Renee. It certainly wasn't ethical to take the negatives, but they had nothing to do with the case, so he decided to take the chance. He quietly withdrew them and stuffed them in his front pocket. Then he backtracked through the photos till he found the ones of Katrina and Imre. He wondered if the police had found them yet; they were not in front and they hadn't been tagged as evidence. Well, they would neither help nor hinder Imre's case. He closed the cabinet and went back downstairs.

"Seen it all?" the policeman asked wearily.

"I think I have the picture," Aaron replied. Then, seriously, "Officer, try not to become corrupted by your surroundings."

The policeman looked at him and smiled a bewildered smile. "No need to worry about me," he replied. "I only go to the movies, I don't live them."

Within an hour Aaron was sitting in front of a pale, sick-looking Imre. "Do you want to tell me about it?"

"I don't remember much. I was drunk."

"Well, tell me what you remember."

"I remember she was watching through this immense glass. Just watching as Katrina and . . . Max . . ." His voice dropped away and he began to shake. "I loved Katrina," he said softly.

"You didn't know Maybeth watched?"

"Hell, no. Christ, that old witch!" He rubbed his head as if it were throbbing.

"Have you ever had opium?"

Imre nodded. "She used to give it to us. I only had it a couple of times, but Katrina loved it."

"How do you want to plead?"

Imre stared at the floor. "Guilty," he replied.

Aaron stood up and brushed the wrinkles out of his suit. "No, you will plead not guilty—this is a crime of passion, temporary insanity. You didn't mean to kill them, did you?"

"No, I loved Katrina," he sobbed, holding his head in his hands.

"I'll be back tomorrow,"Aaron told him.

Imre looked up at him with almost contrite eyes. "Tell Renee I'm sorry," he requested. "Just tell her I didn't mean to involve her . . . or . . . anything."

"Okay," Aaron replied. "Just take it easy."

"Can I see her?" Imre suddenly asked.

Aaron frowned, then nodded. "I'll see if I can arrange it."

4

Renee's room on the fifth floor of the Hollywood Hotel overlooked Hollywood Boulevard. The new hotel was a few blocks east of Grauman's Chinese Theater, and even though new, lacked the ambience of the Ambassador on Wilshire. But Renee had purposely not gone to the Ambassador because it was the first place after her home and the studio that reporters would stake out.

Nor was the room she rented at all posh. It was in fact quite ordinary and furnished only with a double bed, a dresser, a chest of drawers, and a small sofa.

On arrival she had phoned her maid, and some hours later a small suitcase arrived with her clothes. She also phoned Zoltan, who told her he would take the first train to Los Angeles and hopefully be there by morning. Then she called Konnie and Miklós to tell them where she was.

At six Aaron arrived.

"You're later than I thought you'd be," she said, letting him into the room.

"I stopped for some booze and then I went over to the studio costume department and picked up this for you." He handed her a bag.

Renee opened it and laughed. "A brunette wig!" she exclaimed. "Oh, Aaron, if I weren't so miserable and so tired, I'd laugh."

"I hoped you might."

"I can't stay in hiding forever. I'll have to come out in a few days and face it all."

"Yes, I agree. But this way you can get some rest and prepare yourself."

"It's awful. I'm glad Sandy's not here. I wired him, though. Now tell me, did you see Imre?"

"Yes. He's still hung-over. I'll talk to him tomorrow when he's a bit clearer. He wants to see you. Are you up to it?"

"Oh, yes."

"I also went out to Maybeth's. Jesus, you wouldn't believe the place. And I committed a crime."

"You committed a crime?"

He reached into his breast pocket and pulled out the envelope with the negatives. "Yeah, I snatched these when no one was looking. They have no bearing on the case."

Renee opened the envelope and held the negatives up to the light. "Oh, dear," she murmured.

"I'm afraid if there were developed pictures they're gone."

"Oh, do you think there are?"

"Yes. But who knows what she did with them? She didn't send them to the press, that's for sure."

"How do we know that?"

"They'd have used them by now, or at least alluded to them or to our relationship. But there's nothing."

Renee sat down on the edge of the bed. "What if she sent them to Sandy? Oh, I don't want him to see these. It would be so painful."

Aaron nodded. Then he opened a bag and took out a bottle of Scotch. "Have you got glasses?"

"In the bathroom."

He got up and in a few minutes returned with two glasses, each containing some Scotch. "Here, you look sort of ill."

Renee smiled weakly. The truth was that she'd been nauseated all day and assumed it was her condition. Surely she was pregnant, though in fact she had not yet gone to a doctor to confirm it. On reflection, she thought she probably would have been ill in any case—the events of the day had left her totally drained.

She took a gulp of the Scotch and then jumped off the bed and ran into the bathroom.

Aaron sat on the bed too and he could hear her being violently ill. After a moment he called, "Are you okay?"

She answered a muffled "Yes."

Then after a time she returned, deathly pale. "Oh, Renee." He held out his hands and she came to him. "You'd better lie down. Is there anything I can get you?"

"No. It's nothing really, no . . . it's not nothing, it's everything." Again she began to cry softly, and Aaron made her lie down and he covered her with the blanket on the foot of the bed. "I'm going to stay with you tonight. I'll sleep over on the sofa."

She looked up into his eyes. "Sleep with me, Aaron. Hold me, please, just hold me."

He stretched out beside her and took her in his arms. She curled up like a lost kitten, and in minutes was sound asleep.

Nineteen

1

January 7, 1935

*R*enee sat in the small private office of the head of detectives and waited patiently. Outside it was raining again, but this time it was a light rain, and looking out the window, she could see a strip of blue sky on the horizon.

Aaron came in and perched on the edge of the desk. "I've arranged for you to see him in a room down the hall. Better than in his cell or in the normal visiting room. There'll be a police guard outside and you can only have twenty minutes."

Renee frowned. "Only twenty minutes?"

"It's something special, Renee. Usually you can't see a prisoner unless it's in the regular room and an officer's present."

"How did you arrange it?"

"I hinted that after talking to you he might plead guilty and save the D.A. a lot of time, trouble, and tribulation."

"Is he going to plead guilty?"

"He wants to plead guilty but I'm trying to change his mind and use a temporary-insanity defense. Although we could go the crime-of passion route. I haven't made up my mind yet which would be best."

"I can't think about him being convicted and . . ."

"Don't think about it. Come on, I'll take you to Imre."

He guided her down the long corridor and showed her into a bare room furnished only with a long bench. There were bars on the window.

"They'll be bringing him in here. Look, I'll wait for you outside."

Renee nodded and sat down on the bench. How had it come to this? She felt horrible as she sat in this grim little room waiting for her brother. A thousand memories flooded her mind, a thousand arguments they had had. But she knew in her heart that Imre was not truly evil.

The door opened and Imre was ushered in. He looked terrible, she thought. His face was gray and there were lines under his eyes. "Oh, Imre," she said, holding out her arms.

He came to her and they held each other silently for a few minutes; then he pulled away. "I'm sorry, Renee. I really am," he said, almost choking on his own tears.

"Imre, can you tell me how this happened?"

He shook his head. "I hardly remember anything. I didn't mean to kill Katrina . . ."

"I know you didn't."

"I'm going to die for this, for killing that old witch."

"No . . . no, Imre. Aaron's a very good lawyer."

Imre sniveled and then wiped his nose on the sleeve of his jacket. He shook his head. "I deserve to die."

"No, you don't. Imre, don't talk that way."

"Renee, I've never told you the truth about anything. You don't have to feel sorry for me now."

"I don't really know what you mean, Imre." She bit her lip and stared at him; he was pitiful, robbed of his cockiness. He was like a child.

"In New York I was running booze for a bootlegger and I spent everything on myself while you and Zoltan worked to keep us going. And it was never that I didn't want to go to school. I just wasn't very smart. You and Zoltan were smart, Renee, but I fail at everything."

"Imre, I love you so, why wouldn't you let me help you? Zoltan loves you too."

He ran his hand through his thick unkempt dark hair. "Got a cigarette?" he asked.

Renee opened her bag and handed him the pack. "Keep them," she said.

Nervously Imre lit his cigarette and inhaled deeply. "I love you too," he said, even as tears again flooded his eyes. "I guess I thought there was an easy way. I guess I thought I could get by."

She was speechless and she felt totally helpless in the wake of his confessions.

"There's something . . . I don't even know how to tell you."

"The pictures," she guessed.

Imre nodded. "I didn't have anything to do with it. Katrina told Maybeth about Aaron. She told me Maybeth had pictures. When I went over the other night, I was going to try to get them back. But I got to drinking and . . . and I stumbled in on . . . on everything."

"It's all right about the pictures, Imre."

"Tell me you forgive me."

"There's nothing to forgive you for. I know you wouldn't do such a thing." She hugged him again and he put his head on her shoulder the way he had when he was a child. Renee comforted him and finally the door opened and the guard said, "Sorry, time's up."

Renee kissed Imre on the cheek. "Zoltan will be here this afternoon. Konnie's coming tomorrow. Imre, we're all going to do everything possible."

He nodded and squeezed her hand. "Good-bye, Renee." He kissed her again and she turned and fled, feeling far worse than before she had seen him.

2

January 9, 1935

Aaron drove slowly up the winding road toward the secluded mansion where Konnie and Miklós lived. Zoltan had arrived and persuaded Renee to go there instead of remaining in the hotel. At least, he thought, she was surrounded by those she loved. Still, he could not think of how to tell her the news he bore. She was so fragile now; she seemed so close to the breaking point, he could not help but wonder how much more she could possibly take.

He glanced at his watch. He had less than two hours before the news would be released. Then there would be more black headlines, more reporters, more stories on what had now been called "Hollywood's most bizarre crime." And would that it were confined to Hollywood. Not a chance. It was coast-to-coast news, the kind of crime that captured the lurid imagination of every reader in the country. Today's paper had featured a two-page spread on the inside of Maybeth's house and even an interview with the snake handler from the university who had removed the cobras.

"I'm driving slowly because I don't want to get there," he said aloud. And it was all too true.

Then, like it or not, he was turning into the drive, and in a few minutes he pulled to a stop in front of the house.

Aaron got out and smoothed out his suit, only too aware that it looked rumpled. He ran his hand through his hair, thinking absurd thoughts, such as the fact that he had never met Renee's father or uncle. And most absurd of all, he thought what a bad impression he was going to make. "What difference does it make?" he asked himself. I'm not important right now, he thought silently as he climbed the steps and rang the buzzer.

Mercifully, it was Zoltan who opened the door. He smiled broadly and held out his hand. "It's been a long time, Aaron."

"Too long. Sorry we have to meet under these circumstances."

"Come on in." Zoltan beckoned him to follow.

Aaron walked through the house and hardly noticed anything about it. Zoltan ushered him into a comfortable study. Two men were sitting in easy chairs. Both stood up when he came in.

"Aaron, I'd like you to meet my uncle Konnie Szilard and Renee's father, Miklós Lazar."

"Glad to meet you," Aaron said awkwardly as he shook hands. Both men smiled at him warmly, and he felt slightly better.

"Renee's asleep," Milkós told him. "She should be up soon. Can I offer you something? We're all drinking rum, but there's brandy and gin and Scotch . . ."

"Brandy," Aaron replied. He sat down and watched as Miklós went to a little bar hidden in a cabinet and poured him a brandy.

"I imagine you've come to see Renee," Konnie guessed.

Aaron shook his head. "I've come to see all of you." He took the proffered brandy and for a moment stared into the snifter.

Miklós returned to his chair. "All of us?" he questioned. "Shall we wake Renee?"

Aaron shook his head. "Perhaps I should talk to the three of you first, then see Renee alone."

"About Imre's defense?" Zoltan asked.

Again Aaron shook his head. He couldn't look up, he felt so lousy. "It won't be necessary to defend Imre," he said slowly. "Imre hanged himself in his cell."

Zoltan covered his eyes with his hands and Miklós and Konnie sat in stunned shock.

Aaron gulped his brandy down and without asking went to the little bar and poured himself another. Then he turned to face them. "I'm sorry to bring that kind of news. There isn't much time—it's going to be made public at six."

Zoltan pulled himself out of the chair. There were tears in his eyes, but he seemed to have good control. He walked over to Aaron and put his arm around him. "Let me tell her," he suggested. "I'm her brother and Imre was our brother. It'll be too hard for you, Aaron. I'll do it."

Aaron met Zoltan's eyes and he nodded. God knew he didn't want to see the look on her face when she heard about her brother. Something profound had happened between them yesterday; he knew that—he'd seen how moved she was when she'd left Imre.

"Be gentle," he said needlessly.

"We talked about Imre this morning," Zoltan told him. "I know what happened yesterday. It's going to be doubly hard to tell her because, in a way, she thinks she just really got to know him."

That was exactly it, Aaron thought. He pressed his lips together and watched as Zoltan left the room to go up to Renee's bedroom.

Then he sat down and swirled his brandy around in circles. For a few minutes Konnie and Miklós and he tried to talk, but it was no use. They quickly fell silent, each lost in his own thoughts. Then Aaron heard Renee scream from upstairs. It wasn't an hysterical scream; it began with the word "No" and then turned to a mournful wail. When it stopped he knew she was weeping and he knew she and her brother were crying together.

3

February 28, 1935

The living room of Miklós' house was long and narrow. It had a deep green carpet and soft gray furniture with colorful pillows. On the walls Miklós had hung Toulouse-Lautrec prints, and Konnie had contributed some theater posters.

It was raining again; it was a year for rain, Renee thought as she held the long velvet curtain back and peered out at the unusually green expanse in front of the house.

"You seem better," Miklós said from his favorite chair.

Renee turned around and looked at the dancing girls in the Toulouse-Lautrec print. "Yes, I think I'll have to go back to work soon."

"I think that would be good for you."

"I wish I'd hear from Sandy. He hasn't written for over

two weeks and he's stayed in Europe much longer than he intended."

"For a man you're planning to divorce, you worry about him a lot," Miklós commented.

"In a sisterly way. We will always be friends."

"Is there something more troubling you, Renee? Something I don't know about?"

She turned and looked at her father and smiled. "I do have a secret."

"And it's not troubling you?"

"No. It concerns me, but it's not troubling me."

"Are you being intentionally mysterious?"

"Yes, I'm not certain you should be the first to know."

He laughed softly. "Well, I *am* your father."

Renee walked over and pulled out the footstool and sat next to him. "All right. I'll tell you. I'm four months pregnant, Papa."

Miklós half-grinned and characteristically raised one brow. "Aaron's?" he asked.

"Oh, yes, Aaron's."

"It's getting a little late, Renee. Hadn't you better tell the father?"

"I intend telling him tomorrow night. I didn't tell him before because I was afraid I might lose the baby, but the doctor says I'm fine now. I had a little trouble when I was so upset."

"Ah, now I understand."

The double door to the living room opened and Konnie came in. "Phone call for you, Renee. It's some lawyer who isn't Aaron. I think he said his name was Greenberg . . . yes, Saul Greenberg."

Renee stood up. "That's Sandy's lawyer."

"Maybe Sandy has decided to stay in Europe and handle the divorce from there."

"Yes, that must be it." She turned and walked toward the phone in the hall. Then she looked back at Miklós. "You keep my secret."

"I will," he answered cheerfully.

Renee picked up the phone. "Yes, Mr. Greenberg."

The voice on the other end sounded somehow emotional. "Renee, we met once, do you remember me?"

"Yes, of course."

"Can you come right over to my office? It's of the utmost importance."

"I can come." She glanced at her watch. "I can be there by two."

"Fine. I'm on Wilshire, 1245, third floor."

"Thank you," she answered, hanging up. Surely, she thought, the divorce was not that urgent. Well, lawyers worked in mysterious ways, she told herself.

It was a long drive in the rain from Miklós' house in the hills to Saul Greenberg's office on Wilshire, but Renee parked the car at exactly five minutes to two and by two she sitting in Greenberg's office.

She had only just picked up a nearby magazine when he opened his own office door and stepped out. "Renee, I didn't want to keep you. Come in, please come in."

Renee smoothed out her skirt and followed him into his office. There was a strange man sitting in a chair in the corner. He was holding a package and he looked distinctly ill-at-ease.

"Renee, this is Jeff Collins of the U.S. Consular Service."

Collins was in his forties. He wore wire glasses and he was dressed conservatively in a dark blue suit. He held out his hand and shook hers.

Renee looked from Greenberg to Collins. There was something wrong; she sensed it in their solicitous attitude toward her. "What is it?" she asked abruptly.

"I have sad news for you," Collins said.

"Sanday . . . what's happened to Sandy?"

Collins stared at the floor. "He died in the hospital in Spain two weeks ago."

"Two weeks ago!" Renee stared at both of them. "Why wasn't I told sooner? . . . Of what? Was he in an accident?" She had begun to shake and Greenberg was helping her into a chair.

"We were following Sandy's own instructions," he told

her. "Mr. Collins has brought Sandy's personal belongings and a letter for you from him. Renee, Sandy's had terminal cancer for over a year. He didn't want you to know till it was over. He left money and instructions for Collins here to come personally. I know you're shocked. I told him you should know sooner."

She took in all that he was saying and understood why Sandy hadn't been intimate with her for so long and why he'd been glad to let her return alone. It was probably even the reason he was glad she had found Aaron.

"Are you all right?" Greenberg was asking. "Would you like something?"

Renee shook her head. "Let me have the things . . . leave me alone somewhere to read his letter."

Greenberg nodded, and Collins handed over the package.

"There's some mail here that was forwarded from his office here in L.A. He never got to open it. And there's his watch and two rings, his tie clip, and his letter to you."

Renee took the package.

"You can take them into my library if you like."

Renee shook her head. "No, on second thought, I think I'll take them home."

"Are you up to getting home on your own?"

"Yes." She wanted to be gone, to leave the sterile atmosphere, to be alone with her thoughts.

"You understand there's more to settle. He left you everything."

Renee nodded.

"Mind you, he made all the necessary arrangements. Everything is running fine. We don't need to go over the details until you're ready."

"I'll call you soon," she said, turning toward the door.

Renee walked through the rain to her car, clutching the package. The rain fell on her bare head and she didn't even think to put up her umbrella. Sandy . . . kind to the end.

She drove down Wilshire to where it crossed Santa Monica, then drove down Santa Monica till she came to

Fairfax. She went up Fairfax to Sunset and then drove along Sunset to their house, the house she hadn't been back to since Imre's death.

Inside, all her beautiful furniture was draped in white sheets, and she walked through the house, blinded by tears. The sun porch was devoid of flowers and she sat down on one of the little chairs and listened as the rain hit the glass windows. Then slowly she opened the package. She put Sandy's gold watch on the table and looked at it for a long while. Then she put his rings and tie clip next to it. Slowly she sorted out the mail, but she stopped when she came to a large manila envelope. It was the only letter without a return address and it had been forwarded to him in Spain from his office. She tore it open and out fell the pictures of her and Aaron.

Renee leaned back. He had never seen them . . . he had been spared the pain of seeing her with Aaron. Renee took the pictures and tore them in little pieces, then set them in an empty flowerpot and lit them with her cigarette lighter. The smoke curled around and she watched it.

When the fire died, she opened Sandy's letter:

My dearest Renee,

By the time you receive this, I will be dead. I know you will cry, but I wish you wouldn't. Crying makes your eyes red, and you have lovely eyes that should be clear and bright. I, my darling, have had a simply wonderful life. I had the love of two wonderful women, I made millions of dollars, I've traveled all over the world, and I've done everything I ever wanted (some things twice). There is no reason for you to mourn for me, my darling. No reason at all.

Please, Renee, marry your young man and be happy. Looking back causes sadness; looking forward to your dreams is what matters if you are to be as happy as I always was. My years with you were a great joy, but you couldn't have helped me through these last months—this was something I had to see to myself.

Love,
Sandy

Renee reread the letter. Then she repacked Sandy's things and dried her tears. There was no point waiting till tomorrow. She wanted Aaron tonight and she wanted him to know everything.

4

Between eight and nine o'clock in the evening a mild wind came up and blew the heavy cloud cover that had hung over the city all day out to sea. At ten-thirty, when Renee went to her car to drive to Aaron's on Normandie Avenue, the moon and stars shone brightly, promising a crystal-clear tomorrow.

They hadn't planned to see each other until tomorrow because Aaron had to work late, but she had called him and he'd told her he'd be home by eleven.

Renee pulled the long sleek black Auburn 851 to a stop in front of the bungalow court where Aaron lived. She climbed out and for a moment looked at the car. It was Sandy's car, the last thing he'd bought before they left for Europe. "Quite the car," he'd said proudly. "It's virtually built by hand and it's powered with a straight-8." She had confessed to him she hadn't the slightest idea what a straight-8 was and he had explained that it was an engine built by Lycoming, well-known builder of aircraft engines. "So," he had told her, "driving this car is the next best thing to flying." She touched its fender, patting it. The car lived up to all his expectations. It had a long low hood, a sort of cockpit, and chrome exhaust stacks. It was a car of considerable style too. It had a racy, powerful look. It occurred to her now that he had really bought this car for her. At the time, he had known he wasn't coming home.

It was strange. Under other circumstances, she might have wanted to get rid of the car, the furniture, and even the house. Reminders of the past could, she knew, be painful. But she didn't think she would mind being reminded of Sandy. In fact, she was quite sure she didn't want to forget him. Her feeling for him was strong, and her memories were all pleasant. And his letter to her was wonderful. He had made her understand his reasons for wanting to be alone and he had gone to great lengths to make certain she felt no guilt.

Slowly Renee turned away from the car and walked through the courtyard. Aaron's light was on—he must have arrived just before her.

She knocked on the door and he opened it, kissing her on the cheek as he ushered her inside.

"Sorry it's so late," he said. "There's nothing wrong, is there? I mean, you didn't say why you had to see me."

She smiled at his concern and shook her head. "Nothing is wrong with me, but something has happened and there are things we must talk about."

He took her coat and she went into his little living room. The clutter had been picked up and there weren't even any dirty coffee cups. "Did you hire a maid?" she asked cheerfully.

"No, I just cleaned up after the election. Can I get you a drink?"

"I don't suppose you have some tea?"

He grinned. "I know you'll be surprised, but I do."

She followed him into the kitchen and watched as he put some water on to boil and unceremoniously spooned some tea into the pot. "That's rather a lot, isn't it?"

"I'm having some too," he answered.

"Oh, I thought you'd have something stronger."

"Maybe later. Anyway, I want you to read my tea leaves."

"And what makes you think I can read tea leaves?"

"You're Hungarian. All Hungarians can read tea leaves."

She laughed. "Yes, that's right. I was just holding out on you."

The kettle boiled quickly on the gas burner and Aaron filled the pot. They waited in silence while the tea steeped, and then he poured it into two cups. He didn't ask her to begin. Renee wanted to be sitting down and settled; he could tell she had something important to say to him.

He handed her a cup and led the way back to the living

room. Renee sat in the chair and put her tea on the table next to her. He sat on the sofa facing her.

"I have something for you to read," she said, taking Sandy's letter out of her purse. She handed it to him.

Aaron unfolded the letter and slowly read it while she sipped her tea and watched his expression. When he finished it he had tears in his eyes, and he just shook his head sadly.

After a few minutes he looked up at her. "Are you all right, Renee?"

"Yes. That is, I will be all right. I know he meant every word in that letter. He was really a most unusual man."

"Hard to live up to," Aaron said.

"I love you. You're very sensitive, even though sometimes you don't seem to be."

He pressed his lips together and half-smiled. "It's something we lawyers try to hide." He drained his teacup and set it down.

Renee reached over and picked it up, turning it this way and that.

"What do you see?" he asked, trying to smile.

"I see a very nice man. A tall, dark, handsome man. Oh, I see now, it's you."

"So far, so good. Go on."

"I see you are a little conceited."

"Just a little." He laughed.

"I see you are about to acquire a new set of responsibilities—a wife and . . . yes . . . yes, I see a baby. I see you holding this baby—"

"Renee!" He cut into her predictions abruptly and the look on his face was one of sheer joy.

She smiled faintly. "If we're to be married before you become a father, I thought I should tell you tonight. I'm four months pregnant, Aaron."

"Four months! Renee, why didn't you tell me sooner?"

"I had a little trouble after Imre died. I thought I was going to lose the baby. But the doctor says I'm fine now and that it's a perfectly normal pregnancy."

Aaron got up and took a few steps till he was standing

in front of her chair; then he took her hands and pulled her up into his arms and kissed her tenderly. "I am sorry about Sandy."

"I know. But it's a finished chapter now—I feel sad, but I have to look ahead. He wanted me to look ahead."

"We can drive to Nevada tomorrow and get married, Renee. That way, Zoltan can be my best man."

"I want my uncle and brother too."

"I wouldn't leave them out."

She leaned against his chest and he ran his hands through her hair and kissed her ears, then her neck. "I am happy about the baby. Oh, Renee, I love you so much."

"And I love you," she returned, hugging him tightly.

He held her away slightly. "What was it your grandmother used to call the dying days of the empire?"

"Our glory years," Renee repeated.

Aaron shook his head. "No. Our glory years are ahead, Renee. The best is yet to come."